The Button Box

Dilly Court is a *Sunday Times* bestselling author of over thirty novels. She grew up in North East London and began her career in television, writing scripts for commercials. She is married with two grown-up children and four grand-children, and now lives in Dorset on the beautiful Jurassic Coast with her husband.

To find out more about Dilly, please visit her website and her Facebook page.

www.dillycourt.com
f /DillyCourtAuthor

Also by Dilly Court

Dilly Court

The Button Box

HARPER

HarperCollins
PUBLISHERS
— Since 1817 —

This novel is entirely a work of fiction.
The names, characters and incidents portrayed in it are
the work of the author's imagination. Any resemblance to
actual persons, living or dead, events or localities is
entirely coincidental.

Harper
An imprint of HarperCollins*Publishers*
The News Building,
1 London Bridge Street,
London SE1 9GF

www.harpercollins.co.uk

Published by HarperCollins*Publishers* 2017

1

MIX
Paper from
responsible sources
FSC www.fsc.org **FSC™ C007454**

For Xavier James Evans with love.

Chapter One

Drury Lane, London 1872

It all started with a single button. Clara Carter smiled to herself as she locked the door of Miss Silver's drapery shop in Drury Lane, and set off for home. That button was still her pride and joy, secreted away amongst the rest of her collection in the wooden button box that her grandfather had made for her tenth birthday. Grandfather Carter had understood her fascination for small things, beautifully crafted, and the button that had fired her imagination had all those qualities. She had spotted it lying in the snow outside St Mary le Strand church one Christmas Eve. Sparkling like the evening star, the whorls of tiny French paste stones imitated diamonds to perfection. Nine-year-old Clara had snatched it up and hidden it inside her fur muff, hoping that no one had seen. Surely something so lovely must be valuable and the person whose clothing it had adorned would be searching for it. Her conscience had bothered her during Midnight Mass, but not enough to make her give up her prize. At home, in the comfort of her bedroom at the top of the four-storey house in Wych Street, Clara had hidden the button beneath the feather mattress, away from the prying eyes of her younger sisters, Lizzie, Betsy and Jane.

That was ten years ago, and since then things had changed drastically for the Carter family. Clara wrapped her cloak around her as an icy blast of wind from the north brought the first flakes of snow floating down from an ink-black sky. It was dark now and the lamplighter was finishing his rounds, leaving islands of yellow light in his wake like a good fairy illuminating a wicked world – Clara had never quite grown out of her romantic childhood fantasies. Her button collection had filled Grandpa's box long ago: each one held a special memory for her and they were all precious. Now she was forced to work in the draper's shop out of necessity, but it was no hardship. The long hours and poor pay were compensated for by the pleasure she derived from handling the merchandise. The rainbow colours of the ribbons and the feel of silks and satins as she measured out lengths of fabric were a sensual delight. One day she would own such a shop, but it would not be a tiny, one-room establishment like Miss Silver's. Clara had ambition, fired by a visit to Peter Robinson's in Oxford Street, and, in the not-too-distant future, she was certain that the busy thoroughfare would be filled with large department stores and one of them would belong to her.

She quickened her pace as she headed for Wych Street. Despite the comforting glow from the gaslights, she was well aware that the darkness of the underworld lurked in the narrow alleyways and courts of Seven Dials and the area around Clare Market: St Giles Rookery to the north was a place to be avoided even in the daytime. She hurried homeward to the house her family had once owned, but due to her father's addiction to the gaming tables and the enforced sale of the property, they now occupied two rooms on the ground floor, paying an exorbitant rent for the privilege of living in damp, draughty accommodation.

'Clara.'

She stopped and turned to see Luke Foyle emerge from an alleyway. His tall, broad-shouldered figure cast a grotesque shadow on the frosty pavement. 'Oh, it's you,' she said crossly. 'You scared me.'

He was at her side in two long strides. 'A good reason for seeing you safely home.'

'Luke, I walk this way twice every day, except Sundays, and I've been doing so for the last five years.' She was tired and she walked on.

He fell into step beside her. 'That's because my name means something round here, Clara. No one takes liberties with my woman.'

'I wish you wouldn't talk like that. I'm not a piece of property to be squabbled over by rival gangs.'

He took her hand and tucked it into the crook of his arm, but it was a possessive move rather than a gallant gesture. 'I might consider making an honest woman of you, if you play your cards right.'

She shot him a sideways glance. 'You take a lot for granted.'

'Come on, Clara, don't tease me. We've been walking out together for two years, and I've had to be satisfied with the occasional kiss and cuddle. I don't know any other red-blooded man who would put up with such a state of affairs.'

Clara came to a halt, snatching her hand free. 'Then find someone else, Luke. I like you a lot, but I don't like the way you make your money. You could do so much more with your life if you finished with the Skinners' gang. They're bad news and always will be.'

'You know nothing, Clara.'

She faced him angrily. 'I know that you'll end up in prison if you carry on the way you are.'

'What I do to earn a living shouldn't concern you. When we're married I'll look after you and you'll want for nothing.'

'Married?' Clara tossed her head. 'Don't flatter

yourself, Luke.' She hurried off but he caught her up.

'I thought we had an understanding.'

'You were different when I first knew you, but then you got mixed up with the Skinner brothers and you've changed.'

'Not towards you, Clara. My feelings for you are the same.'

'Then prove it, Luke. Leave the gang and find employment somewhere they can't get to you.'

He shook his head. 'What brought this on? You were fine when we met on Sunday and now you've changed.'

'I read the newspapers,' Clara said simply. 'The police are hunting for Ned Skinner. He killed two men, Luke. He shot them because they owed him money. I don't want to be associated with people like that, and you shouldn't either.' She trudged on, wrapping her cloak around her as the snow began to fall more heavily, and she did not look back. Luke Foyle was handsome and charming, and his fair hair and wide grey eyes gave him the appearance of a romantic poet, but he was too sure of himself and she was no man's property. His allegiance to the Skinner gang puzzled her greatly, and had always been a source of contention between them. Why an educated, intelligent man like Luke would mix with the worst thugs in the East End was a total mystery. She quickened her pace, slowing down only when she entered Wych Street with its gabled sixteenth- and seventeenth-century houses, rowdy pubs, second-hand clothes shops, and booksellers whose stock in trade were indecent prints and lewd literature.

Clara's home was next to the barber's shop and she could smell the pomade and shaving soap wafting out as a customer emerged, clean-shaven and shiny-faced. He looked like a poorly paid but respectable clerk, who should have been on his way home to his wife and children, but he lurched across the road and entered the pub. Clara sighed. That would be another family who would go without because the breadwinner frittered away his wages. She had lived with that problem since her mother died nine years ago and Pa had drowned his sorrows in drink and the excitement of the gaming tables. She glanced over her shoulder to make sure that Luke had not followed her before letting herself into the building.

What had once been a happy family home was now divided into cheap rented rooms. Clara was used to hearing the tenants swearing at each other in half a dozen different languages, with children screaming and babies crying. The smell of boiled cabbage mingled with a strong odour of overflowing chamber pots and rising damp. The wallpaper was peeling off in long strips and the paintwork was scuffed. From a room on the top floor she could hear the out-of-work musician playing his trumpet; soon he would have to pawn it in order to buy food and pay the rent. At least they would get a bit of peace and quiet until he begged or borrowed enough money to redeem his instrument. A woman screamed and a door slammed, causing the windows to rattle. It was nothing out of the ordinary. Clara hurried along the narrow hallway and rapped on the kitchen door. Moments later it was opened by Betsy. 'Where have you been, Clara? Do you know what time it is?'

Out of habit, Clara glanced at the place where the clock used to stand on the mantelshelf, between a spill jar and a brass candlestick. Like everything of any value in the Carter household, it had ended up in the pawnshop.

'I know I'm late but I couldn't close up until the last customer had gone.' Clara slipped off her cloak and hung it from a peg on the wall. 'Where's Pa?'

'Where do you think?' Betsy asked crossly. 'He's gone out and taken every last penny we had.'

'He said he's on a winning streak.' Fourteen-year-old Jane raised herself with the aid of her crutches. 'There's tea in the pot, Clara. I'm afraid it'll be a bit stewed.'

'That's all right,' Clara said hastily. 'Sit down, Jane. There's no call for you to wait on me.'

'But you work such long hours, and I'm at home all day. I feel so useless.'

'Nonsense.' Clara moved swiftly to her side and gave her youngest sister a hug. 'You keep us all sane in a mad world.'

'There's nothing to eat.' Betsy returned to her seat at the table and picked up the hat she had been trimming. 'I've got to have this finished by morning. It's an order from the woman Lizzie works for. Miss Lavelle promised it would be ready in time, only she's not the one who'll have to sit up half the night working by the light of a single candle.'

Clara glanced anxiously at Jane, who had always been delicate but this evening her pallor was even more pronounced and dark shadows underlined her blue eyes. 'Have you eaten today, Jane?'

'I don't get hungry sitting down doing next to nothing.' Jane picked up the silk flower she had been making and her nimble fingers added another petal. 'You mustn't worry about me.'

'I've only had a slice of bread and dripping,' Betsy said mournfully. 'I wish I'd gone into service like Lizzie. At least she gets three square meals a day.'

Clara reached for the teapot and filled a cup with the straw-coloured liquid. She took a sip, trying hard not to pull a face. It was lukewarm and bitter, but it revived her enough to take command of the situation. She was the eldest and her younger sisters had been her responsibility since their mother's death from the illness that had left Jane crippled. Clara went to retrieve her cloak.

'Where are you going?' Betsy demanded. 'I need you to help me.'

'We'll all work better on full stomachs.' Clara opened the door leading into the room that had once been their mother's parlour and was now their bedroom. She returned with her precious button box tucked under her arm.

'Not that,' Jane murmured, her eyes filling with tears.

'I've nothing left to pawn other than the clothes I'm wearing,' Clara said sadly. 'I'll redeem it when Miss Silver pays my wages, but we can't work if we don't eat.'

'It's just a collection of odd buttons.' Betsy tossed her dark head. 'I don't know why you keep it anyway, Clara. It's not as if they're worth much.'

Ignoring her sister's last remark, Clara braved the snow to walk to the pawnbroker's in Vere Street. She arrived just as Fleet was about to shut up shop.

He peered at her from beneath shaggy grey eyebrows. 'Oh, it's you. I suppose it's the button box you've brought me, yet again?'

Clara slipped inside the shop, eager to be in the warm, if only for a few minutes. The thin soles of her boots were no protection from the cold and they leaked at the best of times. 'How much, Mr Fleet?' Her teeth were chattering so uncontrollably that she had difficulty in framing the words.

He took the box from her, opened it and plunged

his mittened hand into the colourful assortment, allowing the buttons to trickle through his dirty fingers. Clara held her breath. It made her feel physically sick to see her precious collection manhandled in such a way, but her stomach growled with hunger and she was beginning to feel light-headed. They went through this ritual every time she pawned her treasure, and each time the amount she received grew less. She left the shop with enough money to purchase two baked potatoes and a bunch of watercress, but she had to run to catch up with the man who was trudging homeward, pushing his cart.

Despite Clara's efforts Betsy remained unimpressed. 'I'd have thought you could get three taters instead of a bunch of wilted watercress. I hate that stuff.'

'Don't be ungrateful,' Jane said, frowning. 'I like watercress.'

'Then you have it and I'll have your share of the murphy.'

'Stop it,' Clara said sharply. 'You sound like two five-year-olds. We'll share and share alike. Two potatoes was all the man had left in his can, and he gave me the watercress.'

'I suppose it's better than nothing.' Betsy held out her plate. 'It's all Pa's fault anyway. He only ever thinks of himself.'

'He might win tonight.' Jane took a small portion of the potato. 'I'm not very hungry, Betsy. You can have the last piece.'

Clara took her seat at the table. 'Are you feeling unwell, Jane?'

'I'm just a bit tired, that's all. But I'll be able to finish off the silk flowers before bedtime.'

'No, you won't.' Clara laid her hand on her sister's thin shoulder. 'You'll finish your supper and go straight to bed. I'll help Betsy with the bonnet and you'll get your beauty sleep.'

'It would take more than that to make me pretty,' Jane said, chuckling.

'You are by far the best-looking of all of us.' Clara sent a warning look to Betsy. 'Isn't that so?'

'Yes,' Betsy agreed reluctantly. 'You take after Mama with your fair hair and blue eyes and so does Lizzie, only she's got a turned-up nose, which spoils her looks – in my opinion,' she added hastily.

'I'd rather have dark hair and eyes like you and Clara, and Pa. You must admit he's the most handsome man you've ever seen.'

Clara and Betsy exchanged wry smiles. 'You haven't been out much,' Betsy said, laughing. 'But I suppose Pa is good-looking in his way. The man I marry will have golden hair and hazel eyes, and he'll be very rich and never go near a gaming table.' She turned to Clara. 'What about you, sister? Will you wed Luke and join the Skinner gang?'

Shocked, Clara stared at her in dismay. 'What do you know about the Skinners?'

'Everyone knows that they're the toughest gang

in the whole of London,' Betsy said airily. 'I heard a customer in the shop talking about them this morning.'

'I love Luke.' Jane glanced anxiously at Clara. 'He's been very kind to me, and I worry about him. He shouldn't mix with those bad men.'

'I'm sure he can take care of himself,' Clara said firmly. 'Anyway, I have no intention of marrying Luke – or anyone, come to that. I intend to have a shop in Oxford Street and turn it into a department store like no other.'

'You'll need more than a button box to do that.' Betsy reached out for the last piece of potato. 'Does anyone want this? It's a shame for it to go to waste.'

'No, you have it.' Jane struggled to her feet. 'Thank you for finishing what I started, Clara. I think I will go to bed, if you don't mind.'

'Of course not.' Clara watched her sister as she made her way across the kitchen to their bedroom, leaning heavily on her crutches as she negotiated the flagstone floor. 'I wish I could do something for her, Betsy. It's no life for a girl of her age, cooped up all day with no one but Pa to talk to, and he's not always here.'

'We'd be better off without him, if you ask me.' Betsy pushed her plate away. 'I know we don't earn much, but he shouldn't use our money to gamble on the turn of a card, or whatever horse takes his fancy at the races.'

'You're right, of course, but he's our father. He can do what he likes, but not for much longer, Betsy. I swear I'll make things better for us – no matter what it takes.'

Next morning the streets were ankle-deep in snow when Clara made her way to Drury Lane. She opened up as usual, but the only people braving the weather were those who were slipping and sliding their way to their places of business. Miss Silver lived above the shop, but she rarely came down before noon these days. An ageing spinster who had cared for her invalid mother for most of her life, Rebecca Silver was not a well woman. Clara had witnessed the bouts of coughing that laid her low for days, and sometimes for weeks in winter, but the shop was Miss Silver's living and the customers were her friends. She was not going to retire gracefully, and she sometimes said, in her rare moments of levity, that she would die behind the counter and be buried in a shroud made from Spitalfields silk.

Clara busied herself sweeping the floor and dusting the shelves, and was about to rearrange bolts of muslin when the door opened and her first customer of the day rushed in, bringing with her a gust of ice-cold air and a flurry of snowflakes.

'Lizzie!' Clara stared at her sister in surprise. 'What brings you here?'

'It's not from choice, you may depend on that.' Lizzie stamped the snow from her boots, creating icy puddles on the newly swept floorboards. 'Miss Jones sent me to buy silk thread to mend Mrs Comerford's best gown, which madam intends to wear tonight.' Lizzie glanced out of the window, pulling a face. 'Although I can't see her going anywhere unless the weather improves.'

Clara pulled out the drawer containing spools of silks in rainbow hues. The sight of them always made her smile, but Lizzie was frowning ominously. 'What's the matter?' Clara asked anxiously.

'It has to be an exact match. Miss Jones doesn't know how madam managed to snag the skirt, but the tear is quite noticeable and so the thread must blend in perfectly.' Lizzie fished in her reticule and produced a tiny scrap of pink silk.

'I think that is the nearest.' Clara picked up a spool and held it against the material. 'Take it to the door and look at it in a good light.'

'Such a fuss over a tiny tear.' Lizzie examined the colours in daylight. 'You're right. It's a good match. I'll take it.'

Clara wrapped the spool and handed it to her sister. 'That will be twopence, please.'

'Put it on Mrs Comerford's account,' Lizzie said grandly. 'Wouldn't you just love to say that when you went into a shop, Clara?'

'I hadn't given it much thought.' Clara noted the

purchase in the ledger Miss Silver kept for account customers.

'Something's wrong – it's Pa, isn't it?' Lizzie gave her a searching look. 'I can tell by your face, Clara. He's up to his old tricks again, isn't he?'

'He'll never change,' Clara said, sighing. 'He went out before I got home yesterday and hadn't returned when I left this morning.'

'And your button box is in Fleet's pop shop, I suppose.' Lizzie shook her head. 'You ought to take our father in hand, Clara.'

'There's nothing I can say or do that would make any difference.'

'Then leave home, like I did. I didn't want to go into service, but now I have my sights set on becoming a lady's maid, and that will give me all sorts of advantages. Mrs Comerford's husband might be in trade, but I dare say he has more money than most of the titled toffs that she tries to imitate. It's quite pathetic the way she fawns and grovels when she entertains Lady this and Lady that to afternoon tea. I have to stand there ready to pick up a napkin if one of them drops it on the floor, and hand round the food, watching them stuff their greedy faces, all the time pretending that I'm invisible.'

'At least you're well fed and they provide your clothes. I'm sure it's worth putting up with their odd ways just for that.'

'I suppose so, but I go out of my way to help

Miss Jones. It's her job I'm after – that's if I don't land a rich husband first.'

Clara closed the ledger with a snap. 'Have you anyone in particular in mind?'

'That would be telling,' Lizzie said with an arch smile. She tucked the spool of thread into her reticule. 'I must go.'

'It's a long walk to Bedford Square in this weather,' Clara said anxiously.

'No matter. Miss Jones gave me the cab fare. She trusts me and so does Mrs Comerford.' Lizzie left the shop with a cheerful wave of her hand and a faint trace of attar of roses in her wake. Clara could only guess that her sister had been sampling Mrs Comerford's perfume while she dusted her room. Only Lizzie would be so bold. If she were discovered it would mean instant dismissal, but then Lizzie had the cheek of the devil.

Clara was about to replace the drawer when she heard a commotion upstairs. It sounded like someone choking, and she hurried through to the tiny parlour at the back of the shop, coming to a halt at the foot of the staircase. 'Miss Silver. Are you all right?'

A loud thud was followed by silence and Clara took the stairs two at a time. The door to Miss Silver's bedroom was open and she was sprawled on the floor, motionless, with her head on one side and a pool of blood soaking into the rag rug. Clara attempted to lift her, but despite her thin frame,

Miss Silver's lifeless body was too heavy for her to move without help. Trying hard not to panic, Clara raced downstairs and burst into the street, peering blindly into a veil of snow. There were only a few people braving the inclement weather and most of them hurried past despite Clara's pleas for help. Snowflakes were settling in her hair and soaking through the thin material of her plain grey cotton gown. Her feet were already wet from her walk to work that morning, but she was oblivious to any discomfort and growing desperate when she saw a familiar figure striding towards her.

'Luke,' she cried. 'Luke, come here quickly.'

He quickened his pace and hustled her into the shop. 'What the hell are you doing? You'll catch your death of cold, running about in weather like this without a coat.'

'Come upstairs. It's Miss Silver – I think she's dead.'

He snatched a woollen shawl from its stand and wrapped it around Clara's shoulders, despite her protest that it was new stock and would be ruined. 'Never mind that, you'll be joining her if you're not careful. Where is she?'

Teeth chattering, Clara led him through to the parlour and up the narrow staircase. She pointed to the inert body. 'I tried to lift her but I couldn't manage on my own.'

'Wait there.' Luke entered the room and leaned

over to place his hand in front of Miss Silver's blue lips. He straightened up, shaking his head. 'She's a goner, I'm afraid.' He lifted her with ease and laid her limp body on the bed.

Clara stood in the doorway, hardly able to believe her eyes. 'She'd been ill with her usual chest complaint, but she gets that every winter. I had no idea that it was so serious.'

'Has she any relations who ought to be told?' Luke drew the coverlet over the dead woman's body.

'She had no one. I've worked for her for five years and in that time she never mentioned any relatives. She spent all her waking hours in the shop and the only time she went out was to visit the warehouses that supplied her merchandise. Poor Miss Silver.'

He crossed the floor, stepping carefully over the blood-stained rug and placed his arm around Clara's shoulders. 'You've had a shock and you need something to keep out the cold. A glass of rum punch at the White Hart would be just the thing.'

She managed a watery smile. 'I'd prefer a cup of tea.'

'Have you eaten today?' His steel-grey eyes scanned her face and his lips hardened. 'Did you have supper last night?'

'Please, Luke, not now. I have to do something for Miss Silver. I can't just go out and leave the poor soul here.'

'She's not going anywhere and she's past feeling

lonely. It's you I'm worried about, Clara. Be sensible, come with me and let me look after you first, then we'll go and find someone to take care of the body, and register the death. At least I know how to do that.' He tweaked her cheek, smiling. 'In my line of business it happens all too often.'

'Don't joke about things like that, especially now. I should have come upstairs first thing and made sure she was all right, but I didn't want to disturb her. I could have sent for the doctor . . .'

He gave her a gentle shake. 'The poor woman was suffering from consumption. You don't have to be a doctor to see that's what caused her death. Nothing you could have done would have saved her. Now come with me and we'll get you warm and dry first. Then we can attend to the departed.'

The undertaker came downstairs, walking slowly as if in a funeral procession. 'There will be costs, of course, Miss Carter. Has the deceased any family that you know of?'

Clara shook her head. 'No, sir.' She had shut the shop out of respect for Miss Silver, and at Luke's insistence she had drunk a cup of strong, sweet coffee laced with brandy. Her stomach had rebelled at the thought of food, but the alcohol had made her feel drowsy and detached from the proceedings, as if she were in a bad dream and might wake any minute to find that everything had gone back to normal.

Mr Touchstone pursed his lips. 'Have you any idea as to her financial status? Did Miss Silver leave a will? Otherwise I'm afraid it will have to be a pauper's burial.'

'I really don't know,' Clara said dazedly. 'It's not the sort of thing she would have talked about.'

He glanced at the small escritoire where Miss Silver used to sit and do her paperwork. 'Might I suggest that you take a look and see if she has left any instructions? The poor lady must have known that her condition was serious and unlikely to improve.'

'It seems so heartless talking about money and what she was worth when she's lying upstairs, cold and lifeless.' Close to tears, Clara turned her head away.

Luke had been standing by the fire, having refused to leave until Clara was ready to go home. 'I'll take a look, Touchstone. I'm a friend of Miss Carter's and I didn't know Miss Silver, so I can approach the matter in a more practical manner.'

'It would be beneficial if we could sort something out, sir.' Mr Touchstone picked up his top hat and made a move towards the shop door. 'I'll arrange to collect the deceased. Let me know how you want me to proceed.' He nodded to Clara. 'I'll be back shortly with the hearse.' He let himself out into the street, closing the door behind him.

Clara turned to Luke, who was going through the

papers in Miss Silver's desk. 'That's private. I don't think you ought to be doing that.'

He turned to her with a satisfied grin. 'I don't need to look any further. I've found her will. It's lucky that the old girl was so good at keeping things neat and tidy.' He handed the document to Clara. 'You'd best have a look at it and see if she had enough put by for a decent burial.'

Chapter Two

A pale wintry sun had struggled through the mass of pot-bellied clouds that threatened yet more snow, and the north wind whipped at Clara's black veil as she stood beside Jane at the graveside in Brookwood Cemetery. They were the only mourners present and had travelled on the Necropolis railway from Waterloo Bridge station to give Miss Silver a proper send-off. The oak coffin with shiny brass handles had been lowered into the frozen heart of the hard earth, and the vicar had intoned the words of the interment. He acknowledged Clara with a nod and strode off with unseemly haste to the relative warmth of the chapel.

The whiteness of the fallen snow was in stark contrast to the dark green of the fir trees and the bare branches of the elms that surrounded the cemetery, and Clara shivered in spite of the thick woollen cloak she had purchased especially for the occasion. The musty smell of the second-hand shop still clung to the folds, but that was the least of her worries.

Jane squeezed her sister's hand. 'She's not suffering any more, Clara.'

'I know, but I miss her all the same. She was kind to me in her own way.'

'She must have been fond of you or she wouldn't have left you everything she had.'

'I know and I still find it hard to believe.' Clara tucked Jane's small hand into the crook of her arm. 'The least I could do was to give her the first-class funeral, although it's sad to think that we're the only ones who came to mourn her.'

Jane tugged at her arm. 'Look over there. Do you know that fellow? He seems to be waving to us.'

Clara turned to see a young man slipping and sliding on the hard-packed snow as he hurried towards them. He was clutching a bunch of wilting Christmas roses in one hand and waving frantically with the other. He skidded to a halt, sending a powdering of snow onto the coffin. 'I am too late. I was afraid I would be.' He hesitated, peering at Clara over the top of his steel-rimmed spectacles. 'I say, I'm dashed sorry to intrude. I'm not even sure if I've got the right funeral.'

Clara eyed him curiously. His clothes were well-cut, but his shirt cuffs were slightly frayed and his black jacket was unbuttoned to reveal a scarlet-and-gold brocade waistcoat, which was in stark contrast to his otherwise sober appearance. 'This is Miss Silver's grave. Who are you looking for, sir?'

'Then I am in the right place.' He doffed his top hat, revealing a wild mop of auburn curls tinted with chestnut in the feeble rays of the sun. 'I'm her nephew, Nathaniel Silver. How do you do?'

'How do you do?' Clara replied automatically. 'I'm sorry, sir. I didn't know Miss Silver had any living relatives. I really would have—'

He held up his hand, cutting her short. 'A family feud, ma'am. Aunt Rebecca and my late mother fell out long ago. A bitter quarrel over a gentleman, so I believe. I haven't seen my aunt since I was a child, but I read the announcement of her demise in *The Times*, and I don't know quite why, but I felt I had to come here today.'

'He's after the shop,' Jane whispered. 'Don't speak to him, Clara.'

Nathaniel blinked and took a step backwards. 'I don't know what you're talking about, Miss, er – I didn't catch your name.'

'That's because I didn't tell you,' Jane said sharply. 'You've left it a bit late to show concern for your aunt.'

Clara was quick to see the look of embarrassment cross Nathaniel's mobile features, followed by one of shame. 'It's none of our business, Jane.' She held her hand out to him. 'I'm Clara Carter and this is my sister Jane. I used to work in Miss Silver's drapery in Drury Lane.'

Nathaniel grasped her hand and shook it. 'I didn't know she had a shop. No one spoke of her at home.'

'It's very cold,' Clara said, glancing anxiously at Jane, whose pinched features were turning blue. 'We have to catch the train back to London.'

'There's little point remaining here now.' Nathaniel dropped the drooping flowers onto the coffin. 'I'm sorry, Aunt Rebecca. I should have tried to find you after Mama died.' He shot a sideways glance at Clara. 'I don't suppose she can hear me.'

'Who knows?' Clara managed a smile even though her lips were stiff with cold. 'Come along, Jane. Let's go before we freeze to death.'

Nathaniel proffered his arm to Jane. 'I seem to have difficulty keeping upright on the icy surface. Would you care to assist me, Miss Jane?'

Clara held her breath. Jane was acutely conscious of the leg irons she was forced to wear, and for a moment it looked as though she was going to react angrily, but then, to Clara's surprise, her sister subsided into a fit of giggles. 'Don't worry, I'll look after you, Mr Silver.' She handed him her crutch and allowed him to take her arm.

Holding on to each other in an attempt to remain upright, they negotiated the frozen paths leading to the place where carriages waited to take mourners to Brookwood station. Nathaniel suggested they share the cab and it would have been churlish to refuse, although Clara was feeling acutely uncomfortable in his company. Nathaniel Silver seemed like a nice young man, but he could challenge his aunt's will if he so chose; she could see her bright future vanishing before it had even begun.

It was a short ride to the station and Nathaniel insisted on paying the cabby, which only added to Clara's embarrassment. 'This is where we must say goodbye,' she said as the train came to a halt with a grinding of the brakes and a loud burst of steam.

'I'm going to London too.' Nathaniel opened the carriage door and helped Jane board the train in such a casual way that she did not protest her independence. He proffered his hand to Clara and waited until she was safely settled before climbing in after them. He placed his hat on the luggage rack and sat down.

Clara felt the need to make conversation. 'Do you live in London, Mr Silver?'

'I have a room in Great Queen Street.'

'And how do you make your living?' Jane asked eagerly.

'I don't think that's any of our business.' Clara turned her head, hiding her embarrassment by gazing out of the window. It was bad enough having to travel to town with Miss Silver's long-lost nephew without Jane making things more difficult by asking personal questions.

'I'm a musician,' Nathaniel said easily. 'I play the violin.'

'Are you in an orchestra?' Jane nudged her sister. 'Did you hear that, Clara? Isn't it exciting?'

Clara shot a covert glance at Nathaniel. 'Yes, very.'

'I'm a classical violinist, but at present I'm working on a composition of my own.'

'Does that mean you don't perform in public?' Jane asked. 'What a pity. I was hoping we could hear you play. How do you live if you have no work?'

'Hush, Jane,' Clara said, frowning. 'You don't ask questions like that.'

'Why not? It's nothing to be ashamed of. Pa is always looking for work.'

'I'm sure that Mr Silver is not interested in our problems.' Clara glanced at Nathaniel and was relieved to find that he seemed to be enjoying her younger sister's naïve comments.

'I have a private income, Miss Jane, and if I get short of funds I take my violin out on to the streets, and if people like what I play they put money in my hat.'

'What a good idea.' Jane clapped her hands. 'I wish I could do something like that, but I cannot play an instrument, although I do have quite a good singing voice.'

'It's not a comfortable way to earn a living in weather like this,' Nathaniel said, chuckling.

Clara was consumed with guilt. Here was a decent young man, a close relative of Miss Silver's, who should have inherited her property and yet it had all been left to her, a humble draper's assistant. She cleared her throat. 'Your aunt left the shop to me, and a small legacy. I didn't know that she had family living or I would have tried harder to trace her heirs.'

'You weren't to know of my existence, Miss Carter. The fault is mine in allowing such a state of affairs to continue. I was fond of Aunt Rebecca when I was a child.'

'You're her nephew. By rights, everything should have come to you.'

'No, not at all.' Nathaniel met her anxious gaze with a steady look. 'I did nothing for my aunt, but it's obvious that she liked and trusted you. It was her intention that you carried on after her and I would not want to go against her wishes.'

'You're a toff,' Jane said, clapping her hands. 'You see, Clara? Mr Silver agrees with his aunt.'

'I do indeed.' Nathaniel nodded vigorously. 'It was pure chance that we met today, and for that I'm very grateful. I hope we three might meet again under happier circumstances.'

'I'd like to hear you play,' Jane said without giving Clara a chance to think of a suitable answer. 'I don't go out very often because I'm a cripple, but I'd like to see your performance if you're playing somewhere near Wych Street. That's where we live – opposite the Angel Inn.'

'I think I can do better than that, Miss Jane. I'm going to audition for the orchestra at the Gaiety Theatre. It's not what I trained for, but it's a job and keeps me in practice. If they take me on I'll see to it that you and your sister have tickets.'

Jane's eyes shone. 'That's wonderful, but what about Lizzie? She's our other sister, although she's in service so she doesn't live with us now. Can she have a ticket as well? And there's Betsy too. She loves music.'

'Jane, really,' Clara said, exasperated. 'You should know better than to ask for things.'

'I'm sorry, Mr Silver.' Jane gave him a winning smile. 'But I'm sure my other sisters would like to come, too.'

He held up his hand as Clara was about to protest. 'It would be my pleasure to give you as many tickets as you need, providing, of course, that I get the job.'

'You will get it, I'm sure of that,' Jane said enthusiastically. 'What do you think, Clara?'

Nathaniel took off his spectacles and polished them on a grubby handkerchief. 'You don't have to answer that, Miss Carter.'

Clara met his quizzical gaze with a smile. His

myopic blue eyes twinkled and she found herself warming to him. 'I'm sure Jane is right, Mr Silver.'

He replaced his glasses and tucked the hanky back in his pocket. 'Thank you, Miss Carter.'

'Oh, please!' Jane looked from one to the other. 'Do we have to be so stuffy? Might we not use first names now? After all, you both have Miss Silver in common. She would have introduced you formally, had she still been with us.'

'Aunt Rebecca might approve,' Nathanial said, smiling. 'What do you think, Miss Carter?'

'I think she would be turning in her grave if we overstepped the boundaries, Mr Silver. She was a stickler for etiquette. I was only a little older than Jane when I first worked for her, and she taught me such a lot. I'll always be grateful to her.'

'Well, I am going to call you Nathaniel,' Jane said firmly, 'and you must call me Jane. If my sister wants to be stuffy, that's her business.'

'Very well, Jane. But we must allow your sister to do as she sees fit. I am, after all, a complete stranger.'

'But not for much longer,' Jane insisted. 'You must call on us, mustn't he, Clara?'

'Yes, that would be nice,' Clara said vaguely. She sat back, allowing Jane to chatter, and Nathaniel answered her sister's eager questions with good-humoured ease. Clara found herself liking him despite the problems that must inevitably arise from too close a friendship with Miss Silver's nephew, and it was good to see Jane enjoying herself. Her disability had left her a virtual prisoner in their home, making silk flowers and trimmings for the milliner. It was poorly paid work, but every penny counted, and Clara herself had spent long hours in the shop, coming home late in the evening too exhausted to be much company for her youngest sister.

They parted outside the house in Wych Street. Nathaniel had insisted on sharing a cab from Waterloo Bridge station as he was going their way, and he refused to accept payment for their part of the journey. Clara was at once grateful and mortified. She had not wanted him to see where they lived, but he seemed to have made a great hit with Jane, and she could not deny her sister the pleasure of having the full attention of such a pleasant young man. Jane was bubbling over as she made her way down the dark corridor to their tiny apartment.

Clara opened the door and was met by the sight of her father slumped over the table with Betsy and Luke standing over him.

'What happened?' Clara cried anxiously. 'Is he ill?'

'Is he dead?' Jane clapped her hands to her mouth, her eyes wide with horror.

Luke shook his head. 'He's dead drunk. I found him like this and I brought him home.'

'He's been missing for three days,' Betsy said angrily. 'His pockets are empty, as usual. We should leave him here and move into the rooms above your shop, Clara.'

'Your shop?' Luke looked from one to the other. 'What are you talking about?'

'It's all right, Betsy. I'll tell Luke all about it.' She shooed Jane towards the bedroom they shared. 'Take off your wet things, love. I'll look after Pa.'

Pale-faced and trembling, Jane hesitated in the doorway. 'He won't die, will he?'

'No, of course not. He's drunk too much rum, but he'll get over it. Now do as I say and then we'll have supper.'

Jane took one last look at her father's inert figure before going into the bedroom and closing the door. Clara stepped in between Luke and Betsy, who were glaring at each other. 'Help me get Pa into bed, Luke. And, Betsy, put the kettle on. Jane and I have had a long day and we're chilled to the bone.'

'I'm not your slave,' Betsy grumbled, but she picked up the kettle and went out into the back yard where they drew their water from a communal pump.

Luke hefted Alfred Carter over his shoulder. 'Where do you want him?'

Clara pointed to a truckle bed in the far corner of the room. 'Over there.' She crossed the floor and folded back the coverlet.

Alfred groaned when Luke dumped him unceremoniously on the wooden bed, but he did not open his eyes.

'Dead drunk,' Luke said grimly. 'He must have been pouring booze down his throat for days.'

'I don't know where he got the money.' Clara covered her father with the patchwork quilt and tucked him in.

'He'll have put it on the slate and that will have added to his debts. I did what I could, Clara, but I'm not going to cough up sums like that simply to get your old man off the hook. He's a millstone round your neck and you ought to walk away and leave him to it.'

'Oh, but I couldn't do that.' Clara stared at him, horrified. 'He can't manage on his own. He never has any money because he gambles it away, and he wouldn't eat properly.'

'Then let the old devil starve. He's a lost cause.' Luke turned away from the bed where Alfred lay slack-mouthed and snoring loudly.

Clara was prevented from answering by Betsy, who erupted into the kitchen stamping ice off her boots. 'The pump is frozen solid. I had to scoop snow off the privy roof.' She slammed the kettle down on the range. 'That's the last of the coal, Clara, and there's nothing in the larder for supper. It's all very well for you and Jane to pay for the old girl's funeral and go gallivanting off on the train, but that money should have fed us for the month.'

'It was Miss Silver's money,' Clara protested. She shot a sideways glance at Luke. 'The will has to go to probate, but she left me everything. Giving her a proper send-off was the least I could do.'

Luke took a handful of coins from his pocket and tossed them onto the table. 'This will keep you girls going, but I meant what I said. If you stay here you'll get a visit from Patches Bragg's men. It was her gaming house where I found your pa, and you don't want to owe Patches money. She takes her debts in the most painful ways imaginable, if you get my meaning.'

'I understand,' Clara said, wincing at the thought. She knew of Patches Bragg – everyone in Seven Dials and the surrounding area knew of the French woman who was a legend in the criminal underworld, and ran her gang with more brutality than any of the other gangland bosses, including the Skinner brothers. Scarred by smallpox, Amelie Bragg wore the once-fashionable patches to cover the worst of her blemishes, and it was these that had earned her the nickname. Clara had seen her on one occasion, and that was enough to convince her that Luke's warning was timely.

'You must move out of here,' Luke insisted. 'I can't protect you if you stay. Leave your father to sort out his own problems.'

'He's right,' Betsy said urgently. 'I've heard what

that woman does to people who can't pay up, and I don't want my face scarred like hers.'

'Are you sure that Pa owes her money?' Clara had to ask the question, but Luke's grim expression was answer enough.

'You've got the shop. You'll be safe there as long as Patches doesn't find out where you are, but you can't take Alfred with you.' Luke met Clara's anxious gaze with a tight-lipped smile. 'He's brought it on himself. You don't have to share his punishment.'

'You're right, Luke.' Betsy thumped the kettle down on the table. 'I'm going to pack a bag and you've got to take us to Drury Lane, Clara. I refuse to spend another night in this place.'

Clara looked from one to the other. Luke's jaw hardened and his mouth tightened into a grim line, and Betsy faced her with a determined toss of her head. But Clara was not going to be browbeaten into doing something she knew was wrong. No matter what their father did, he was still their flesh and blood. 'No,' she said firmly.

'No?' Luke stared at her, frowning. 'What do you mean by that, Clara?'

'Exactly what I said. I'm not abandoning Pa to the mercy of Patches Bragg.'

'You're crazy.' Betsy flounced into the bedroom and slammed the door.

Clara faced Luke with a defiant lift of her chin. 'I want to speak to Patches, woman to woman.'

'What?' He stared at her as if she had spoken in a foreign tongue.

'You heard me, Luke. I want to meet this woman and reason with her. I'll offer to pay back what Pa owes bit by bit.'

'She'll slit your throat as soon as look at you, or she'll set her roughs on you. Either way, you won't come out of there with your pretty face as it is now. I won't allow it.'

'You can't stop me. If you don't tell me where to find her I'll walk the length and breadth of Seven Dials until I come across someone who will.'

'You're out of your mind, girl. Be sensible, Clara. You don't know what Patches is like.'

'Maybe not, but she's a woman like me. I'll appeal to her better nature.'

'Patches Bragg isn't a woman – she's a creature from hell and you are a simpleton. Don't blame me if she cuts your throat – or worse.'

'Then you'll take me to her?'

He took a deep breath. 'In the morning, but tonight I want you to take your sisters to the shop and spend the night there.'

'No. Not good enough. By morning Pa might be lying in a pool of blood and I'll have that on my conscience for the rest of my life. I'm going now, Luke – with or without you.'

*

It had stopped snowing, but the temperature had plummeted and the filthy streets were buried beneath a blanket of crisp white snow. The moon had emerged from behind the clouds and the world around them sparkled with frosty light, but Clara was oblivious to everything other than the need to find the woman who quite literally held Alfred Carter's life in her blood-stained hands. Luke strode along with fierce intent, and she had to struggle through the deep snow in order to keep up with him, but she did not protest. If she hesitated she might lose courage.

He came to a halt in front of the narrow alleyway that led into Angel Court. 'This is where I have to leave you. But you can still change your mind and come home with me.'

She shook her head. 'No, I can't. I've come this far and I must do what I set out to do or I'd never forgive myself.'

'You are a stubborn woman, and I was a fool to bring you here.' Luke glanced up and down the street, but few people had braved the freezing temperatures, and an eerie silence made their surroundings seem dreamlike and unreal. 'There's time to change your mind. I doubt if they'll come for Carter tonight.'

'That's not what you said earlier.'

'It wasn't as cold as this then. Everyone has gone to ground, and that's where we ought to be. Come on, girl. Be sensible, or do I have to throw you over my shoulder and carry you home?'

'I'm not giving up so easily.' She turned on her heel and before he had a chance to carry out his threat she entered the gaping maw of the alley. The snow had not penetrated this far and her eyes took a while to grow accustomed to the darkness. The air was thick with the smell of rotting vegetables and night soil, and the buildings that towered above her were shuttered and silent. All her instincts told her to run away and the hairs on the back of her neck stood on end like the hackles on an angry dog, but she kept walking. The alley opened out into a small court surrounded by equally tall buildings with only a scrap of midnight-blue sky visible and a single, solitary star twinkled at her as if it were wishing her well.

A faint glimmer of candlelight flickered in a basement window, and Clara was about to knock on the door of what might once have been the home of a respectable family, when it opened suddenly and a hand shot out. She was dragged unceremoniously into the building.

'What d'you want? You ain't one of the usual girls.'

A lantern held close to her face dazzled her so that she could not see her assailant, but his voice was gruff and his breath smelled strongly of stale beer and rotten teeth.

'I don't know who you think I am, but you're

mistaken.' Clara was nauseated and terrified, but she was not going to give up now. She stood her ground. 'I want to see Patches Bragg.'

'Does you indeed? Well, you got a nerve, I'll say that for you. You must be one of them salvationists, come to rescue our souls. Patches eats girls like you for breakfast.'

'I'm here on a private matter,' Clara said hastily. 'I'd like to speak to her and then I'll leave.'

'That'll be up to her.' He leaned closer. 'Take a tip from Old Tom. Go home now and forget you ever heard of Patches Bragg.'

'Thank you, but it's really urgent. Please take me to her.'

Old Tom held the lantern higher and for the first time she could see him clearly. His snuff-stained whiskers and wispy white beard contrasted oddly with his shiny bald pate. He shook his head. 'You might live to regret this, but if you insist you'd best follow me.' He ambled off along a narrow corridor and came to a halt at the far end where he tapped out a pattern of knocks on the door. It opened, and a wave of sound and the smell of raw alcohol, tobacco smoke and other unpleasant odours enveloped Clara in a noxious cloud.

'Come this way.' Old Tom walked past the man at the door, who leered at Clara, giving her a gap-toothed grin. 'Keep yer hands to yerself, Bones. This one wants words with the boss.'

The sound of Bones' cackling laughter followed them down the steep flight of stairs to the basement, which opened out into a large room, hazy with smoke. It was heated by an enormous range, which took up most of one wall. The fug was sickening, although it did not seem to worry the male occupants and the gaudily dressed women, most of whom were the worse for drink. They lolled against the men, who seemed to be more intent on their cards than the charms of their female companions. Piles of coins lay in front of the players and no one took the slightest notice of Clara.

Old Tom led her to the bar, where a large woman perched on a stool with a glass of gin in her hand. Her low-cut gown exposed a vast expanse of bosom with the odd patch dotted here and there, and when she turned her head to look at Clara it was easy to see why she had earned her nickname. At a quick glance Clara guessed that Patches Bragg must be fifty years old or thereabouts. Her grey hair and sagging jowls might give her the appearance of a respectable matron, but her heavy-lidded grey eyes were sharp and shrewd. Her thin lips seemed to disappear beneath folds from her plump cheeks, which were heavily rouged and with patches carefully applied to conceal disfiguring scars. It was a fashion that Patches' grandmother might have adopted many years ago, and it was one that made her instantly recognisable.

As the pale eyes raked over her, Clara felt a shiver of fear run down her spine, but she held her head high.

'Who have we here, Old Tom?' Patches demanded in a gruff voice with just a hint of a French accent.

'She's come wanting to see you, boss. I never asked her name.'

'She don't look like one of them salvationists.' Patches beckoned to Clara. 'Come closer so I can get a better look at you. What's your name and what d'you want with me?'

'My name is Clara Carter. I think you know my pa.'

Patches raised the glass to her lips and drained the contents. She thumped it down on the counter where the barman was quick to add a generous tot of gin. 'I know many men. What's so special about your pa?'

'His name is Alfred Carter and I know he comes here. I think he owes you money and I want to come to an arrangement.'

Patches threw her head back and laughed. 'Well, here's a novelty. Are you saying he ain't good for what he owes?'

'I don't know how much it is, but I'll make sure you're paid every last penny. I just need time.'

'Don't that beat everything you've ever heard?' Patches downed another mouthful of her drink, but her eyes narrowed to slits in her pudgy face and the black stars and moons moved closer together. 'Suppose I don't like that arrangement? What will you do then?'

'My pa is a good man at heart, but he hasn't been the same since Ma died and my youngest sister was crippled by the same disease.'

'Stop, you're breaking my heart.' Patches leaned closer, fixing Clara with a hard stare. 'Your old man is a gambler and you'd be better off with him out of the way, which is what will happen if I don't get my money in full.'

'How much does he owe you?' The words came out in a single breath – a whisper of desperation. Clara was scared, but determined to see this through, whatever the cost.

Patches straightened up and turned to the barman. 'Alf Carter, Wych Street, Bob. How much is on the slate?'

He reached beneath the counter, produced a dog-eared notebook and flipped through the pages. 'Eight guineas, boss.'

'Eight guineas it is then, and to show you that I'm a fair woman I won't add any interest, but I want my money.'

'That's a huge sum.' Clara stifled a gasp of horror. Eight guineas was more than she earned in a whole year. A wave of anger washed over her. How could Pa have been so profligate with the money they needed to survive?

'But I ain't such a bad woman,' Patches continued cheerfully. 'I'll give you three days to find the cash.'

Clara licked her dry lips, forcing herself to remain calm. 'And if I can't raise that much?'

'Put it this way, my duck, your pa has two good legs at the moment. He might find it difficult to walk again if I don't get my money on time. My boys are experts when it comes to maiming and crippling them as get on the wrong side of Patches Bragg. Do you understand, sweetheart?'

Lost for words, Clara nodded.

'Three days, Miss Carter. Not an hour more. Now get her out of here, Old Tom. I'm sick of looking at her milkmaid complexion.'

Chapter Three

The chill outside hit Clara like a slap in the face. Quite how she arrived on the pavement outside the alley she could not remember, but taking deep breaths of ice-laden air brought her abruptly back to her senses. She looked round, half hoping to find Luke waiting for her, but he was nowhere to be seen. It was only now that the impact of what had happened in the illegal gaming club hit her with full force. Eight guineas was a small fortune and she had about as much chance of raising such a sum in three days as she had of flying to the moon. She wrapped her shawl around her slender body and set off for home, ignoring lewd suggestions from the few men who were about on such a night, and the shrill threats from the women who braved the winter weather to solicit from doorways or open windows.

She was numbed not only by the cold and the fact that Luke had abandoned her, but by the sheer impossibility of her situation. Patches Bragg was not like any other woman she had ever met and Clara felt completely out of her depth. Miss Silver might have been a martinet at times, but she was a saint by comparison.

Clara arrived home to find Betsy waiting for her in a state of considerable agitation. 'Where've you been? I thought something terrible must have happened to you. Where's Luke?'

'He abandoned me, if you must know.' Clara sank down onto a chair by the fire, which had burned down to a few desultory embers. A loud snore from the truckle bed made her glance over her shoulder. 'I don't know how he can sleep after what he's done.'

'What happened? You're scaring me, Clara.'

'Pa owes Patches Bragg eight guineas and she's given me three days to find the money.'

Betsy's eyes widened. 'That's a fortune. How are we to raise such a sum?'

'I don't know, and that's the truth.'

'What will happen if Pa doesn't pay up?'

'He'll end up a cripple or worse. Luke was right about Patches. She's a bad woman, but Pa is to blame too. His gambling has led us to this.'

A loud knock on the door made Clara jump to her feet. 'They can't have come for him already.'

'I told you we should have left Pa and gone to your shop.'

'Clara, are you there?' Luke's anxious voice was followed by another rap on the door.

She hurried to open it. 'Where were you when I needed you? I had to walk home on my own—' She broke off at the sight of his bloodied face. 'What happened to you?'

He closed the door and leaned against it. 'You might say that I had an argument with a lamppost.'

'You've been fighting again, Luke Foyle. When is all this going to stop?' Clara guided him to the chair she had just vacated and pressed him down on its seat. 'Sit still and I'll bathe your face.' She plucked a towel from the rail and handed it to him. 'There should be some warm water in the kettle.' She turned to Betsy, who was standing by the bedroom door, pale-faced and trembling. 'You look exhausted. You should get some sleep.'

'I don't want to be murdered in my bed. We've got to get out of here, Clara.'

Luke staunched his bleeding nose with the scrap of towelling. 'You're safe for tonight. I saw to that, but I can't be here to protect you girls all the time. You need to leave this place and Alfred must get as far away from here as he can, if he wants remain in one piece.'

Clara's hands trembled as she filled a bowl with tepid water. 'Pa has to leave London, and when he sobers up I'll tell him so.' She took the towel and tore off a strip, using it to bathe the gash on Luke's forehead. 'How did you get this?'

'I told you that Patches Bragg and the Skinners don't get along. They've been fighting for control of Seven Dials for years, and I decided to go back to the club to make sure you were all right when I happened to bump into Patches' son, Dagobert.'

'You bumped into his fist, by the look of you,' Clara said crossly. 'You'll have a black eye in the morning and I wouldn't be surprised if your nose is broken. Why couldn't you just walk away?'

'You don't know Bert Bragg.'

Momentarily diverted, Clara paused with the bloodied cloth in her hand. 'If he's anything like his mother I'd prefer to keep it that way.'

'You're right, he's a nasty piece of work and you must keep clear of him.'

'Maybe you should take your own advice. Just look at the state of you.'

'If you think I'll walk away from a fight, you don't really know me, Clara.' Luke snatched the damp cloth from her and held it to his bleeding nose. 'He came off worst, if you're interested. I left him lying in the snow in White Hart Court. Patches won't like that, but it will take her mind of your father's debts for a while.'

'And if this man is as bad as you say he is, you'll be the next one who has to leave London.' Clara emptied the contents of the bowl into the stone sink.

'Not me, sweetheart.' Luke rose to his feet. 'I'm going to marry you and raise a family of boys who'll keep the streets free from Bert Bragg and his mother.'

'That's not what I want for myself.' Clara pushed him away as he moved to embrace her. 'I want to be free from gamblers and gangsters altogether, and I intend to make a better life for myself and any children I might have in the future.'

Luke's eyes narrowed. 'I want a wife who'll pay attention when I give her good advice.'

'Then I am not the right woman for you, Luke Foyle.'

His expression lightened, and his lips twitched. 'You'll change your mind, sweetheart. You've had a bad time and you're tired so I'll leave and let you get some rest.' He took her hands in his. 'I might be able to find the money to get Alfred out of harm's way, so sleep easy, my darling.' He leaned over to brush her lips with a kiss and was gone before she had a chance to argue.

'There you are,' Betsy said triumphantly. 'You should be nicer to Luke. He's going to take care of us.'

'That's what worries me.' Clara set about clearing spatters of blood from the table. 'I won't have anything to do with money gained from crime. I wish I'd never met Luke Foyle.'

'You don't mean that, Clara.'

'Yes, I do. I've had enough of living like this, and I'm going to do something about it.'

'Like what?'

'Miss Silver left the shop to me. I intend to build up the business and expand when the time is right.'

'That's just a dream.'

'Maybe, but sometimes dreams come true, especially if you're prepared to work hard. If everything goes to plan I'll take you on as head of the millinery department.'

'And maybe one day we'll go to bed with a full belly. I'm starving, Clara.'

'So am I, but we have the money Luke loaned us, and first thing I'll go to the bakery and get some fresh bread, and a pot of jam from Mr Sainsbury's shop in Drury Lane.'

'Could we run to a pat of butter?'

'I'll see what I can do. Now go to bed and I'll just make sure that Pa is all right, and then I'll be in. Don't wake Jane; she needs her sleep, poor child.'

Alfred lay groaning and calling for water when Clara entered the kitchen next morning. It was still dark outside but the snow made it seem that dawn had come early. Clara lit a candle and went over to the truckle bed.

'I suppose you're feeling very ill this morning, Pa. It really does serve you right.'

He covered his eyes with his hand. 'My head hurts

and my throat is parched. A cup of tea would go down well, Clara.'

'I'm sure it would, Pa. But we have no coal, so I can't boil the kettle. You'll have to make do with melted snow because the pump is frozen solid.'

Alfred raised his head only to fall back against the pillow. 'What have we come to?'

'What indeed, Pa. And whose fault is it that we're penniless and in debt?'

'Don't go on, girl. I'm a sick man.'

'You're suffering from the effects of drink, so don't expect sympathy from any of us.'

'What have I done to have such ungrateful children?'

'You've run up gaming debts of eight guineas, Pa. That's why we're in this state.'

He sat up and this time he remained upright. 'How do you know that?'

'I went to see Patches Bragg last evening and she's given you three days to find the money, or else . . .' Clara did not need to finish the sentence. She could see by her father's expression that he understood only too well. 'You have to get away from London, Pa. I agree with Luke on that.'

'Luke? Where is the boy? He can help me.'

'No, Pa. He can't. You have to go somewhere the Braggs won't find you.'

'But I can't leave my girls. Who would look after you?' Alfred's once-handsome face creased into lines of distress, adding ten years to his age.

'We will be safer if you aren't here,' Clara said, moderating her tone. Despite his failings he was still her father and she could remember the time when he had been her hero. 'I can take care of Betsy and Jane, and Lizzie is all right where she is now. Is there anywhere you can go?'

Alfred clutched his forehead, rocking backwards and forwards. 'I can't think. I don't know what to do . . .'

'It's all right, Pa.' She patted his hand. 'I have to go out and get food and a bag of coal so that we can light the fire. We have three days to find a way out of this – three days, that's all.'

She put on her outdoor things, picked up a basket and set off for the bakery.

When she returned she found to her surprise that Betsy had cleaned the grate and laid twists of newspaper and the last of the kindling ready to light to fire. Alfred had raised himself from his bed and had attempted to shave in cold water, but had cut himself and was holding the towel to his cheek.

Clara gave the shop boy a farthing for carrying the coal and she set the basket on the table. She shot a wary glance at her father. 'I'll get the fire going and make a pot of tea. We'll talk after we've eaten, Pa. But we have to come to a decision soon.'

'I've filled the kettle with snow,' Betsy volunteered. She peered into the basket. 'Did you get butter and jam?'

'It was a choice between the two, so I bought jam.' Clara set to and lit the fire before placing the kettle on the hob.

Betsy was already slicing the loaf and Jane emerged from the bedroom, yawning and blinking as a ray of sunlight filtered through the window. 'Bread and jam – how lovely.' She shot a wary glance at her father. 'Are you quite recovered now, Pa?'

Alfred bowed his head. 'I'm so sorry, girls. You deserve a better father. I've let you all down and I'm ashamed of myself.'

'That's as may be.' Betsy slapped a slice of bread onto a plate and thrust it in front of him. 'Being sorry isn't going to help us out of this tangle.'

Clara shot her a warning glance. 'Pa knows what he's done, Betsy. Give him a chance to put things right.'

'I have a cousin who lives on the Dorset coast,' Alfred said slowly. 'Is the tea ready yet, Clara? My mouth is so dry I can hardly speak.'

'Be patient. It will take a while longer. What were you going to tell us about your cousin?'

'I haven't seen Jim since we were boys. I doubt if we would recognise each other now, but we were friends once.'

'Where is Dorset?' Betsy gave the kettle a shake as if encouraging it to come to the boil. 'I have to leave for work in a few minutes. I need a hot drink to ward off the cold.'

'Never mind that now.' Clara took a seat next to her father. 'Dorset is a long way from here. You'd be safe there, Pa.'

Alfred gazed at her, his bloodshot eyes swimming with tears. 'But what would I do there, Clara? Jim is a fisherman and he lives in a tiny thatched cottage. Can you see me in such a place?'

She laid her hand on his arm. 'I can see you alive and well, living by the sea. You know what will happen to you if you remain here.'

'You have to go, Pa,' Betsy said firmly. 'You haven't any choice in the matter.'

'I haven't got the fare, girls.'

'Then you'll just have to walk.' Betsy snatched her bonnet off the peg and rammed it on her head. 'I'll be late if I don't go now, and I haven't had my cup of tea.' She picked up her shawl and hurried from the room, muttering beneath her breath.

'What have I done?' Alfred held his head in his hands. 'What have I brought you all to?'

'It's too late to worry about that now.' Clara rose to her feet. 'Betsy's right, though. You have to leave London and the sooner the better. The week's takings have yet to be paid into the bank. I'll borrow enough to buy you a railway ticket to Dorset but you must leave today.'

'I can't have you stealing money from Miss Silver. I'm a lot of things, Clara, but I won't allow my daughter to take what doesn't belong to her.'

Clara was tempted to tell him that she had inherited the shop and its entire contents, but she knew that would be fatal. The gleam would return to her father's eyes and he would see the opportunity to double or treble his stake at the gaming table. It was a disease that was eating him away, for which there was no apparent cure. 'I'll work twice as hard to pay the money back, so you mustn't worry.'

'But, darling girl, if you have the money to send me to Dorset, wouldn't it be better to give it to Patches? Then I'd be a free man and I could find work and support my family.'

'It's no good, Pa. Patches wants the money in full. I think you know her well enough to realise that she means business.'

'All right, I'll go to Dorset, Clara. But I want you to promise me that you'll never go near Patches Bragg's place again.' Alfred reached out to grasp her hand. 'Promise.'

Clara crossed her fingers behind her back. 'All right, I promise. Now pack your things and I'll go to the shop. The sooner you're away from London the safer we'll all be.'

Clara kept the shop closed for another day, ostensibly out of respect for Miss Silver, but in reality to accompany her father to Waterloo Bridge station. Even though he had promised to leave London, she was only too well aware of his erratic tendencies.

When he was in a sorry state and riddled with guilt he would act and think rationally, but as the effects of drinking too much wore off and his optimistic spirit returned, he was likely to head for the nearest gaming club with his ticket money in his pocket.

Having made sure that he was on the train when it pulled out of the station, Clara set off to walk back to Wych Street. The sun shone palely on the snow-covered rooftops but the icy pavements were still slippery underfoot. The River Thames was swollen with snow melt on the ebb tide as it snaked its way towards the sea, swirling around the stanchions of Waterloo Bridge, playing with the vessels tied up at the wharfs so that they bobbed up and down like toy boats.

Clara made her way as quickly as possible in the icy conditions, intent on getting her sisters to the relative safety of Miss Silver's shop. A wry smile curved her cold lips and she reminded herself that it belonged to her now, but a chill ran down her spine at the thought of what Patches Bragg might do if she discovered that Alfred Carter's daughter owned such a property. She quickened her pace, calling in first at the milliner's in the Strand where Betsy was at work in the backroom.

Miss Lavelle did not welcome such intrusions, nor did she encourage visits from ladies whom she considered to be unsuitably dressed for a high-class establishment, and from the pained expression on her face when Clara entered the premises, that obviously included her. Tall and painfully thin, Miss Lavelle was able to look down her nose at someone who barely came up to her shoulder. Clara had never considered herself to be short, but Miss Lavelle made her feel small and insignificant.

'You know the rules, Miss Carter,' Miss Lavelle said icily. 'No visitors during working hours.'

'I do know, and I apologise, but this is something of an emergency. Might I have a quick word with my sister, please?'

'She is busy. We have an order for a titled lady that must be completed today.'

'Then would you be kind enough to pass on a message?' Clara said firmly. 'Betsy is not to go home tonight. Please tell her to go to the shop in Drury Lane. She'll know what I mean.'

'That sounds ominous, Miss Carter. If your family is in trouble I would like to know. I have to be very careful whom I employ. I am patronised by the carriage trade, and any taint of scandal would ruin me.'

'Your reputation is quite safe, Miss Lavelle, but I would be grateful if you would give my sister the message.' Clara swept out of the shop, head held high. She could only hope that Miss Lavelle's notorious love of tittle-tattle would lead her to pass on the information in the hope of discovering a new scandal. One thing was certain – Betsy could stand up for herself. Sometimes she was too forthright for her own good, but she would not allow Miss Lavelle or anyone to browbeat her, and she would not breathe a word of their father's fall from grace.

It was Jane who was now Clara's main concern. Jane and Betsy were complete opposites. Betsy had the face of an angel and a core of tempered steel. No one got the better of Betsy Carter, but Jane was sensitive and easily hurt, and her disability made her an easy target for mockery in Seven Dials. Clara was not looking forward to breaking the news of their father's sudden departure, and she had no intention of telling her youngest sister about Patches Bragg. There was something important she had to do before she went home.

The pawnshop in Vere Street exuded the familiar smell of sweaty old clothes, lamp oil and mildew. Fleet emerged from the back room, wearing two military overcoats with a striped woollen muffler wrapped several times around his scrawny neck. He had to climb over several piles of books and a jumble of pots and pans in order to reach the counter.

'What you got to pawn this time, miss?'

'Nothing, Mr Fleet. I've come to redeem my button box.' Clara took the money from her reticule. She had taken the week's takings from the strong box in Drury Lane, intending to use the money for her father's railway ticket, but she could not allow her treasure to remain with Fleet for another day. He would only keep it for a specified amount of time before placing it for sale, and then it might be lost to her for ever, and with it the precious memories attached to each of her tiny treasures. There was little or no loveliness in the dark and dirty streets she knew, but one day she would escape the squalor of Seven Dials and create a place where colour and beauty could be shared by all. It was a dream, but to her the button box represented hope over despair, and success over failure. She placed the coins on the counter and Fleet reached up to retrieve the box from the top shelf.

'Here you are, but I expect you'll be back with it before the month is out.'

She shook her head. 'I hope not, Mr Fleet. I sincerely hope not.'

Jane was seated at the kitchen table, finishing off a spray of silk flowers for Betsy. She looked up and a slow smile transformed her pale face. 'Things must be looking up, Clara. You've got it back.'

'Yes, I called in at the pawnshop on my way home. I couldn't leave it there another moment.'

'And we have jam,' Jane said happily. 'I had some on my bread, although I only took one slice. I didn't want to be greedy.'

'Having enough to eat isn't being greedy.' Clara felt the teapot and it was still warm. She filled a cup with the weak, straw-coloured liquid. 'Jane, I have something to tell you. Pa has had to go away for a while. He's gone to stay with his cousin in the country.'

'Are those people after him for money, Clara?'

'Yes, I'm afraid so, but he'll be safe in Dorset with his cousin Jim.'

'But you look sad, Clara. That's not all, is it?'

'No, dear. We have to move out of here today. I need you to help me pack our things, such as they are. We're going to live above the shop in Drury Lane.'

'But that's a good thing, isn't it, Clara?' Jane said, smiling. 'I mean this isn't what we are used to. I can remember when we owned the whole house and we had a cook and a maid, and Pa was a different person when Mama was alive. He used to kiss me goodbye every morning before he left for the City, and he dressed smartly and smelled of cologne.'

Clara put her cup down with a sigh. 'You're right, Jane. Things were better then but we have a chance to make a new life for ourselves, and you can play your part.'

'What can I do? I'm a cripple and always will be.'

'Don't say things like that. You might not be able to walk very far, but you're a bright girl and you have a good head for figures. You can help me in the shop.'

'Can I really?' Jane's eyes shone with excitement. 'I'd love that.'

'But first we have to move our things to Drury Lane. Let's make a start. The sooner we leave here, the better.'

It was not far from Wych Street to the shop in Drury Lane, but the snow on the pavements was rapidly turning to slush. Clara had hoped that Luke might turn up and offer to help, but there was no sign of him and she had no intention of going to his lodgings to beg for assistance.

As soon as they had sorted out what to take and what might be left until another day, Clara took Jane to the shop. It was slow going, but Jane was determined to walk and the distance hardly merited spending precious funds on a cab. Clara lit the fire in the back parlour and left Jane to settle in while she went home to collect as much as she could carry. She lost count of how many trips she made, but darkness was falling as she left the house in Wych Street for the last time, and under a cloudless sky the temperature plummeted.

Slipping and sliding on the frozen slush, she was close to exhaustion and every muscle in her body ached. Her fingers were clawed around the handles of a valise and a carpet bag, and she had lost all feeling in her toes. A man, walking head down against the bitter wind, almost collided with her and she lost her footing, saving herself from falling by clutching a lamppost.

'Clara, is that you?' The young man she had met at Miss Silver's funeral hurried to her side.

'Mr Silver?' Clara managed to regain her balance and salvage her dignity.

He bent down to retrieve the carpet bag and valise. 'Did you hurt yourself? I saw that fellow barge into you. He didn't even stop to see if you were all right.'

'My feet went from under me.' She leaned against the lamppost, rubbing her hands together in an attempt to bring back the feeling in them. 'I'm not hurt.'

'Where are you going? May I help you? These bags are very heavy.'

'I'm going to the shop in Drury Lane.' Clara eyed him warily. He was hatless and his wildly curling auburn hair reached almost to the shoulders of his jacket, which was little protection on such a cold night. He pushed his spectacles up the bridge of his nose, an unconscious gesture she recognised from the time they met at Miss Silver's graveside. She had a sudden desire to laugh. 'We do seem to meet in the oddest places, Mr Silver.'

'Nathaniel, please.' He smiled shyly. 'Did you say you were going to the shop?'

'Yes, I'm afraid I have no choice but to move in. Do you mind?'

'No, of course not. I told you before that I have no moral claim on my aunt's estate. Let me prove my good intentions by helping you with your luggage.'

Clara was too tired to argue, but she realised that he had his violin case slung over one shoulder. 'May I carry that? You have your hands full.'

He unhooked it and handed it to her. 'I've just come from the audition I told you and Jane about at the Gaiety Theatre.'

'Did you get the job?' She started walking in the direction of Drury Lane.

'Yes, it will do until something better turns up.'

She came to a halt, turning her head to give him a questioning look. 'I don't understand. If you have to take any work that comes along, why are you allowing me to take your inheritance? You could challenge the will, if you chose, and I don't want to think of the shop as my own and then have it taken away from me.'

'That won't happen, I promise you.'

'But you might need the money.'

'I can assure you that is not the case.'

'You told me that you play on street corners in order to buy food or to pay your rent. That doesn't sound like the action of a man of means.'

'Might we continue this conversation somewhere out of the cold? My hands are turning blue and I've lost the feeling in my feet.'

Clara nodded. 'Me, too. Let's get to the shop and sort this out once and for all.'

Chapter Four

The shop was in darkness but a flicker of light beneath the parlour door was a welcome sight. Clara unlocked the door and Nathaniel staggered in with the heavy bags, which he dumped on the floor with a sigh of relief.

'I don't know how you managed to carry these any distance.'

The parlour door opened and Jane peered anxiously into the dark shop. 'Is that you, Clara?

'Yes, and I met Nathaniel in the street. He was kind enough to help me with the last of our bags.'

'Nathaniel! How lovely to see you again,' Jane cried excitedly. 'Would you like a cup of tea? I've had the kettle on the hob for an hour or more, and I found some tea in one of the cupboards in the scullery.'

'That would be nice,' Clara said hastily. She laid a restraining hand on Nathaniel's arm as he made to follow her sister into the back room. 'Tell me why I should trust you not to make trouble for us in the future. I really need to know.'

'I am not a poor musician. Well, that's not quite true. I am poor at the moment, but in a few months' time, when I reach the age of twenty-five, I'll come into the fortune left to me by my late father. He was of the opinion that if I was young when I inherited the money he had worked so hard to make I would run riot and squander it. So you see, Clara, you have no need to worry. Now, shall we join your sister for a cup of tea?'

'In a minute,' Clara said warily. 'If what you say is true, your family must have property somewhere. Why then do you live in London, playing for pennies on street corners?'

'You're right. There is a town house and a country estate, but one of the conditions of my father's will was that should I ignore his wishes and follow my dream to become a serious musician and composer, I had to leave home. I have to prove that I can earn my living and to survive without any financial help.'

'That seems extremely hard,' Clara said, frowning.

'My uncle is executor of Father's will, and he sees to it that I don't put a foot over the threshold until I'm of age. I have a suspicion that he hopes I might die of some terrible disease or starve on the streets in the meantime, or should I give up and prove myself a failure, I forfeit my claim and he gets everything. You see, my father was of a whimsical turn of mind.'

'I wouldn't call it that,' Clara said hotly. 'He sounds a very spiteful man.'

'You know all there is to know about me now, Clara. You can trust me.'

'Yes, but it's a strange state of affairs.'

'Not in my family. If you knew the rest of the Silvers you wouldn't be surprised.'

'And yet Miss Silver lived very frugally and never took a day off work,' Clara said, frowning. 'That does seem odd when her brother was so well-off.'

'I didn't know, or I would have tried to help her.' Nathanial pushed a stray lock of hair back from his forehead. 'I really would.'

Jane emerged from the parlour, leaning heavily on one crutch. 'Are you going to stay there chatting all evening?' Her eyes widened and her lips formed a circle of surprise. 'Who is that outside? I saw a shadow in the glass.'

Clara had barely turned to look when the person outside in the street hammered on the door. 'Clara, open up. I can see you.' Betsy's angry voice made Clara hurry to let her in.

'Why was I locked out? I need a key of my own, Clara.' Betsy came to a halt, staring at Nathaniel. 'Who is this?'

'Please come through to the parlour,' Jane said plaintively. 'You're letting in the cold air, and the room has only just warmed up.'

Betsy eyed the cases. 'Where are my things? You haven't left them in Wych Street, have you, Clara? Miss Lavelle passed on your message – or part of it, anyway. She just said I was to come straight here after work.'

Clara turned to Betsy with a sigh. 'If you would just give someone else a chance to speak, I'd introduce you to Nathaniel Silver, Miss Silver's nephew.'

Nathaniel bowed over Betsy's hand. 'How do you do, Miss Betsy?'

Betsy smiled coyly. 'How do you do, sir?'

'As to your things,' Clara continued, 'Jane and I packed everything we could and I've been going to and fro all day bringing whatever I could carry, so I don't want to hear any grumbling from you, Betsy. If it hadn't been for Nathaniel, I might still be clutching a lamppost in Wych Street after someone almost knocked me flying.'

Betsy cast a sideways glance at Nathaniel. 'I'm sorry, but I've had a busy day and I wanted to go home to my own bed.'

'This is home for the present.' Clara ushered her sister into the parlour. 'I saw Pa off on the train this morning, so he should be with his cousin by now, and we'll be safe here unless the Bragg gang discover our whereabouts.'

Nathaniel followed them into the small room. 'I've heard of them. They're a bad lot.'

'You mustn't worry,' Jane said confidently. 'Clara's gentleman friend, Luke, is with the Skinners. He had a fight with Bert Bragg and I think Luke's nose was broken, but I'm sure that Bert came off the worst.'

'Thank you, Jane.' Clara sent her a warning look. 'The kettle is boiling, so why don't you make the tea? I'm sure Nathaniel would like something hot to drink before he braves the cold.'

Betsy tossed her bonnet onto the sofa and shed her mantle with a dramatic flourish. 'I'm starving. I haven't eaten all day because Miss Lavelle made us work until the wretched hat was finished.'

'We're all hungry, Betsy.' Jane struggled to lift the kettle off the trivet. 'I filled it too full.'

'Allow me.' Nathaniel moved to her side, retrieved the kettle and placed it safely on the hearth. 'I must admit to being famished too. There's a coffee stall not far from here. The fellow sells hot pies, and baked potatoes, as well as boiled eggs and ham sandwiches. If you all agree I'll go out now and purchase our supper.'

'Oh, yes, please,' Jane said eagerly. 'I'd like a pie and an egg, if it's not too much to ask.'

'I'd like a baked potato and a ham sandwich.' Betsy settled herself on the chair nearest the fire. 'Thank you, Nathaniel. You are a true gentleman.'

Clara reached for her reticule, acutely aware that

their funds were running low. 'I'll give you the money, Nathaniel. It is very kind of you to offer to go out on such a night. I should come with you to help carry everything.'

'There's no need for you to brave the weather yet again, Clara.' Nathaniel made a move towards the door. 'You haven't said what you would like.'

'A pie would be just the thing.' Clara followed him into the shop. 'You must let me pay for our supper.'

He shook his head. 'I wouldn't hear of it. I wasn't looking forward to eating alone in my room, yet again. I'll enjoy your company and that of your sisters. It will make me feel part of a family.'

Clara was about to unlock the shop door when a male figure loomed outside, making her leap back in fear. Her encounter with Patches had left her feeling nervous, and Luke's fight with Bert was not going to make things easier. The person rapped on the door.

'Who's there?' Clara demanded, hoping that she sounded braver than she was feeling.

'It's me, Luke. Let me in.'

Clara unlocked the door and Luke stepped in on a gust of ice-cold air. His smile of greeting faded when he saw Nathaniel standing in the shadows. 'Who are you?'

Clara stepped in between them. 'This is Miss Silver's nephew, Nathaniel.'

'What's he doing here?' Luke demanded.

'Nathaniel, this is my friend, Luke Foyle,' Clara said hastily.

'How do you do?' Nathaniel held out his hand, but Luke ignored the gesture.

'We're more than just friends.' Luke placed his arm around Clara's shoulders. 'So I'll say it again. What are you doing here?'

Clara twisted free from his grasp. 'Really, Luke. Is this necessary? Nathaniel saw me struggling with two heavy cases and he offered to help.'

Before Luke could respond Betsy appeared in the doorway. 'What's going on? I'm faint with hunger and all you can do is argue. Anyway, you're upsetting Jane. You know how she hates the sound of raised voices.'

'I'm sorry,' Nathaniel murmured. 'Perhaps I should go.'

'That's the first sensible thing you've said.' Luke opened the shop door. 'Thanks for helping Clara, but we don't need your services now.'

Clara grabbed the door and slammed it. 'I won't stand for this behaviour, Luke. That was very rude and extremely ungrateful. You don't know how much I am indebted to Nathaniel, and he was trying to help us.'

'Even so, you don't know a thing about this fellow.'

'I'll go, Clara.' Nathaniel rammed his top hat on

his head. 'You've got the wrong end of the stick, Foyle. I think you should apologise to Clara.'

'I can see how the land lies. Maybe I should be the one to leave.'

'Yes, you should go, Luke,' Clara said angrily. 'Come back when you've calmed down and remembered your manners.'

Luke slammed out of the shop.

'I'm sorry,' Nathaniel said hastily. 'I seem to have placed you in an awkward situation.'

'Don't apologise, it was Luke who was in the wrong. He doesn't own me, and he shouldn't jump to conclusions.'

'Perhaps I should leave anyway.'

'If you go now I will be forced to venture out into the snow to buy our supper,' Clara said, smiling. 'And you would face another evening eating on your own.'

'If you put it like that, how can I refuse? I'll be as quick as I can.'

Clara let him out of the shop, taking care to lock the door after him. She did not want Luke to come barging in and create another scene. He could be arrogant sometimes, and jealous; two qualities she disliked in anyone, especially the man she might marry, although that possibility was becoming more and more remote. Better to be an old maid than to be shackled to a man who wanted to dominate her and take control of her innermost thoughts. That was not for her. She returned to the parlour to comfort Jane and reassure Betsy.

Despite the circumstances, Clara felt relaxed and surprisingly happy as they sat round the fire eating the food that Nathaniel had bought for them. The parlour was small and shabbily furnished; the seats on the chairs were threadbare and the delicate floral wallpaper was stained and peeling, but a fire blazed up the chimney and the room was warm and cosy. While they ate, Nathaniel entertained them with accounts of his experiences busking on the city streets. When the remains of the meal were tidied away he took his violin from its case and, with a little persuasion, played a merry jig that had their feet tapping and their hands clapping.

Clara joined in the applause. 'That was lovely, Nathaniel, but I would like to hear one of your own compositions.'

'Mine?' He ran his hand through his unruly hair, causing it to curl around his brow in wild profusion. 'Are you sure?'

Betsy leaned forward, eyes shining. 'Oh, yes. Let us hear something you've composed.'

'Is it sad?' Jane asked wistfully. 'Sad music makes me cry.'

'Let him play and then we'll find out.' Clara settled back in Miss Silver's favourite chair, resting her feet on the brass fender, as Nathaniel launched into a hauntingly sweet melody. In his skilful hands the violin seemed to sing and the music filled Clara's head and made her heart swell with joy and sadness. It was as if all the emotions she had ever felt had been transposed into sound and she closed her eyes, floating away on the tide of Nathaniel's lyrical creation. She was still enraptured when the piece came to an end, and as she opened her eyes she realised that Jane was crying and Betsy sat with her hands clutched to her bosom, gazing at Nathaniel with moist eyes and a wistful smile.

He dropped his hands to his sides and bowed.

'That was so beautiful,' Clara said in a whisper. 'It melted my heart.'

'Yes, it was lovely.' Betsy jumped to her feet. 'You are so clever, Nathaniel.'

Jane sniffed and wiped her eyes on her sleeve. 'Your music made me cry, and I've lost my hanky.'

'You are all too kind.' Nathaniel placed the instrument in its case, treating it as tenderly as a mother would a newborn infant. 'It still needs some work.'

'What is it called?' Clara asked. 'I'd love to hear it again some time.'

'I haven't given it a title; perhaps you can help me there.' Nathaniel glanced at the mantel clock. 'I didn't realise it was so late. It's time I returned to my lodgings.'

'Don't go yet,' Jane cried. 'Please stay a little longer.'

Clara rose to her feet. 'Thank you for our supper and for allowing us to hear your composition. It was wonderful.'

'It was my pleasure, but now I really must leave you.' Nathaniel made his way through to the shop, pausing to wrap his muffler round his neck. 'I'm sure that Luke will come round, Clara. He obviously cares a great deal for you.'

She tossed her head. 'He can do as he pleases. I choose my own friends.'

'Does that include me?'

'I'm proud to know you, Nathaniel Silver, and very much indebted to you.'

'Nonsense. You were my aunt's choice and I respect her wishes.' He stood aside as Clara unlocked the street door. 'I haven't forgotten the tickets for the Gaiety. As soon as I'm in a position to get some I'll bring them round.'

She held the door as he stepped outside into the bitter winter night. 'You're welcome to call at any time.'

'Thank you, I will.' Nathaniel backed away, smiling, and disappeared into the darkness beyond the pool of yellow light that surrounded the gas lamp.

Clara was about to close the door when she saw the dark shape of a man lingering in a doorway on the far side of the street. She could not be certain but it looked very much like Luke. It would be typical of Luke to spy on her; he had done it before and she had found it oddly touching, but now it had become irritating and downright insulting. Nathaniel was just a friend, and he had been magnanimous enough to allow her to keep her inheritance without challenging his aunt's will. The mere fact that they had a roof over their heads tonight was because of the generosity of the Silver family. Clara locked the door, snatched her button box off the counter and went into the parlour.

Betsy was in the process of helping Jane to negotiate the narrow staircase. 'We're going to bed. Will you be up soon?'

'Yes, don't worry about me.'

'I said I'd share the back room with Jane. You'll have to sleep on your own for the first time,' Betsy said, smiling.

'At least I won't be kept awake by you snoring.' Clara blew them a kiss. 'Night-night.'

'Don't let the bed bugs bite,' Jane called over her shoulder.

Clara had intended to put the fireguard in place before making sure the back door was locked, but she needed first to check the contents of her button box. She trusted Fleet, but she knew she would not sleep unless she was certain that her collection was intact, and she sat cross-legged on the floor, close enough to the dying embers of the fire to take advantage of the last vestiges of warmth. She opened the box and scooped up a handful of the small buttons, allowing them to slip through her fingers in a kaleidoscope of colour. Her most valued items were a set of tiny mother-of-pearl buttons from the bodice of her mother's wedding dress. The gown had been cut up to make clothes for herself and Lizzie when they were children, but she had persuaded Ma to let her snip off six of the twelve buttons. Then there were the much larger millefiori buttons that she had found lying in the mud on the Thames foreshore while out walking one Sunday afternoon with Pa. He had bought her a penny lick from the hokey-pokey man and she could still remember the taste and the sweet icy sensation on her tongue. A brass military button winked at her as if to divert her attention from its fellows, and she held it between her fingers, wondering as to the identity of the gallant soldier who had gone into battle with this button on his uniform. Then, last but not least, there was her favourite, her special button, it was still there glittering in the firelight as it had done when it lay lost and forgotten in the snow.

The fire crackled and a blue flame licked around an ember and was immediately extinguished by a draught of cold air. It was time to close the memory box and go to bed. Clara snapped the lid shut, turned the tiny brass key in the lock, and rose to her feet. Tomorrow would be her first day as shopkeeper. She must get some sleep, although her stomach was churning with excitement at the prospect of being in sole charge. She could do it, of that she was certain. This was the start of a new and better life for her and her family. There was just one problem – Patches Bragg.

Trade was slow next day, but the freezing conditions did not encourage housewives and maidservants to venture out unless absolutely necessary. Clara spent the time rearranging the shelves to her satisfaction, but while she worked her mind was wrestling with the problem of how to raise the eight guineas she needed to pay her father's debt to Patches. She was deep in thought when the shop door opened and Lizzie burst in, pink-cheeked and flustered.

'Clara, you're here. I wasn't sure if you would be opening so soon after Miss Silver's funeral. I mean, it doesn't seem very respectful to carry on as if nothing has happened.'

'Miss Silver only closed the shop on Sundays and on Christmas Day. She would come back to haunt me if I let her down.'

'It's not funny, Clara. I don't know how you can treat the woman's death as a joke.'

'Far from it. I was very fond of Miss Silver, and I owe it to her to look after her legacy.' Clara stared at her sister, frowning. 'What's the matter? You're all of a twitter.'

'I should think I am. Miss Jones sent me out to

purchase blonde lace, only I don't know how much she needs. It was all said in a bit of a panic.'

'Does she want it in black or white?'

'I'm not sure. Madam is going out to an important function this evening and the lace on her gown is torn. Miss Jones was very particular that it had to match.'

'I've got Chantilly lace as well.'

'I'd better take both. You have to come with me, Clara. I'll be in trouble with Miss Jones if I bring the wrong material.'

'I can't shut up the shop simply because Miss Jones is fussy.'

'Please come with me. You'll need to bring the unwanted lace back to the shop because I won't be allowed out again.'

Clara had never seen her sister in such an agitated state. 'All right. I'll close the shop for an hour. There aren't many customers about this morning.'

'Thank you. I can't afford to lose my job.'

'I'll have to warn Jane not to open the door to anyone but me, and I'll fetch my bonnet and cloak.'

'Why is Jane here?'

'We had to leave Wych Street. I was going to tell you when I had a chance. I'll explain on the way to Bedford Square.'

'This is ridiculous,' Clara said, shivering as they came to a halt outside the four-storey terraced house in Bedford Square. 'Miss Silver never made house calls.'

Lizzie opened the gate which led down to the tradesmen's entrance. 'Maybe she would have made more money if she had. I don't know, Clara, I'm not a businesswoman, but Mrs Comerford is very rich, and if Miss Jones is satisfied she'll tell her so, and then who knows? Maybe Mrs Comerford will recommend your shop to her friends.'

'I'm only doing this as a favour to you.' Clara followed her sister down the steep, ice-coated steps to the tradesmen's entrance.

Lizzie knocked on the door and it was opened by a tiny scullery maid who could not have been more than ten years of age. The child scuttled off in the direction of the kitchen and Lizzie led the way through a maze of narrow corridors and up the back stairs. On the other side of the green baize door was another world. A marble-tiled passage opened out into a wide hallway with large, gilt-framed mirrors reflecting the ornate candle sconces. The scent of beeswax and lavender mingled with the spicy aroma of crimson and gold chrysanthemums, arranged in large urns. A liveried footman cast a sidelong glance at Lizzie, and Clara was quick to see a blush staining her sister's cheeks.

'Miss Jones sent me for material to mend madam's ball gown, James,' Lizzie said hastily.

'And who is this young lady?' He looked Clara

up and down with an appreciative grin. 'I'm afraid I can't allow you to wander round the house uninvited.'

'This is my sister Clara.' Lizzie hesitated, eyeing James warily. 'I'll have to find Miss Jones. Stay here, Clara.'

'Don't worry, I'll look after her,' James said, winking at Clara. 'I always enjoy the company of a pretty girl.'

Clara put her head on one side, looking him up and down. He was a handsome fellow, tall and broad-shouldered, and he obviously traded on his good looks. She was not impressed.

'I don't need looking after,' she said coldly.

Lizzie cast her a sidelong glance, shaking her head. 'Be nice to him,' she said in a low voice. 'But not too nice, if you know what I mean.' She snatched the basket of lace from Clara and hurried off towards the staircase.

'Why don't you make yourself comfortable, miss?' With a sweep of his hand, James indicated a dainty hall chair. 'You're likely to have a long wait. You know how ladies like to chat.'

'I'm in trade,' Clara said stonily. 'I don't have time to *chat*, as you call it.'

James bridled visibly. It was obvious that he was not used to his clumsy advances being spurned. 'I can see the family likeness. Lizzie is as prickly as a briar rose.'

Clara was saved from replying by the sudden appearance on the staircase of a young man dressed for outdoors. He was plain to the point of homeliness except for a head of golden curls, which would have been the envy of any woman. He strolled down the stairs, coming to a halt in front of Clara. 'Are you waiting for someone?'

She rose to her feet. This person was obviously a member of the family and by rights she ought to have been waiting for Lizzie below stairs. 'My sister, sir. Lizzie Carter – she ran an errand for Mrs Comerford's maid. I have to wait to take the unwanted lace back to the shop, but I'll be gone as soon as she returns.'

A slow smile spread across his even features. 'My mother always demands the best. Only she would send a servant out in such inclement weather.'

James stood to attention, staring straight ahead, although Clara thought she saw the muscle at the corner of his mouth quiver, as if he were suppressing the desire to laugh. She thought it wiser to remain silent, hoping that Mrs Comerford's son would go about his business, but he seemed reluctant to leave. He held out his hand. 'I'm Joss Comerford. How do you do, Miss Carter?'

Remembering her place, she bobbed a curtsey. 'How do you do, sir?'

'It's very cold outside and the pavements are treacherous. May I escort you home, Miss Carter?'

'That's very kind of you, but as I said, I have to wait for the unwanted lace.'

'Have you a connection with the textile trade?'

She looked him in the eye and realised that he was teasing her. 'You make it sound as though I'm dealing in smuggled goods, Mr Comerford.'

'Now that would be exciting. Are you a smuggler, or a river pirate?'

'Nothing so interesting, sir.'

'So your connection with lace is . . . ?'

Clara could see that he was not going to be satisfied with anything other than a full explanation. 'I am a shopkeeper, Mr Comerford. I own a drapery in Drury Lane.'

His blue eyes widened and he stared at her with renewed interest. 'You're a shopkeeper?'

'I am, sir.'

'How intriguing. I must visit your emporium one day.' He held his hand out to take his top hat and cane from a young maidservant who appeared seemingly from nowhere. 'I'm going your way, Miss Carter. I have a luncheon appointment in the Strand, so it's no trouble to see you safely home.'

Clara was about to refuse politely when Lizzie came hurrying down the wide staircase, the basket in her hand. 'Madam has taken all the lace, Clara.' She came to a halt, gazing anxiously at Joss. 'I'm sorry, sir. I didn't mean to interrupt.'

'That's all right, Lizzie. I'm glad that Mama is

supporting local shopkeepers.' He turned to Clara with a disarming smile. 'My father is also in trade. He has a warehouse on the docks filled with exotic imports from foreign lands. I used to think it was like Aladdin's cave when I was a child.'

Clara shifted from one foot to the other. At any other time, and in a different place, it would have been a pleasure to talk to someone like Joss Comerford, but James was listening to every word and Lizzie was staring at her open-mouthed. Their reaction was typical of most people. The sons of wealthy families, whether their fortune had been made in the Caribbean sugar plantations or from privateering centuries ago, or in trade, did not mix socially with girls from the lower classes. That was the way things were and Clara could feel disapproval radiating from both her sister and James. If Joss Comerford had taken a liking to her, it was a recipe for disaster.

'Isn't it time you were going, Clara?' Lizzie said in a low voice. 'Jane will be wondering what's happened to you.'

'Yes, of course.' Clara took the empty basket from her. 'Madam is keeping all the lace?'

'Put it on her account,' Lizzie said grandly. 'Goodbye, Clara. I'll come and see you on my afternoon off.' She turned on her heel and headed towards the servants' quarters.

'I must go.' Clara glanced at James, who leaped to attention and opened the front door.

Joss proffered his arm. 'Allow me. It's a long walk so I suggest we take a cab.'

There was nothing Clara could do without appearing rude and she laid her hand on the sleeve of his cashmere coat. James kept his gaze fixed on a distant point as he held the door for them.

'Go and find a cab, James, there's a good fellow.' Joss hesitated on the top step. 'Dashed inclement weather. I was in two minds as to whether to venture out or not.' He glanced down at Clara and smiled. 'But I'm very glad I did or I would not have had the pleasure of your company, Clara. I hope you don't mind my using your Christian name?'

She shook her head. 'No, sir.'

'It would please me greatly if you would call me Joss. I'm uncomfortable with formality.'

'I doubt if your mama would agree with that – Joss.'

He threw back his head and laughed. 'I was right. I took you for a spirited woman, Clara. I'm a very good judge of character.' He leaned forward to get a better view of James, who was slipping and sliding on the snowy street as he attempted to hail a cab. 'I'd laugh if he took a tumble. James is so stiff-necked he'll make an excellent butler one day. I sometimes think he must have been born middle-aged, and I doubt if he is a year my senior.'

Clara was just about to tell him she would prefer to walk when James succeeded in attracting the attention of a cabby who had just dropped a gentleman off at a house further along the street. Joss handed her into the hansom cab and climbed in after her. Sitting side by side with a relative stranger was a nerve-racking experience for Clara and she stared ahead, wishing she had risked offending him by refusing his offer. Joss Comerford might not be this friendly if he knew of her involvement with one of the most vicious gangs in London. It was a relief when the cab drew to a halt outside her shop, but the feeling was short-lived.

A man wearing a battered top hat and a greasy woollen muffler was leaning against the pub wall. She recognised him at once and her heart sank.

Chapter Five

'Thank you, sir.' Clara gathered her skirts around her and climbed down from the cab before Joss had a chance to assist her. Standing on the icy pavement, she flashed him a smile. 'I'm very grateful for the cab ride, Mr Comerford.'

'Don't mention it, Clara. I hope we meet again soon . . .' His voice trailed off as the cabby flicked his whip above the horse's ears and the cab lurched on its way.

Clara waited until it was out of sight before turning to Bones, Patches' right-hand man. The mere sight of him was enough to make her flesh creep, but she put on a brave face.

'I have another day to find the money, Mr Bones.'

'Not by Patches' reckoning you ain't. You're to come with me and no argument.'

'All right, I'll come, but first I must make sure that my little sister is all right. I left her alone in the shop.'

'You should have thought of that afore you got mixed up with Patches Bragg, my duck.' He grabbed her by the arm and propelled her along the street with surprising strength for a small man.

Clara gave him a shove, catching him off guard. 'There's no need for force. I want to see Patches anyway.'

'I hope you got the readies.'

'That's something I want to discuss with Patches.'

His cackle of laughter made people stop and stare at the odd couple, but Clara held her head high. Patches Bragg might be the leader of one of the roughest gangs in London, but she was still a woman. There must be some common ground for negotiation. Clara's heart was pounding, but she fought down the instinct to run way and allowed Bones to lead her to Angel Court.

It was daylight above ground, but in the underworld of the illegal gaming club it was permanent night. The smell of oil lamps and the fumes of alcohol mingled with tobacco smoke and the stench of unwashed bodies, and Clara had to fight down a feeling of nausea. Her empty stomach rebelled against the noxious odours and the sight of unkempt, unshaven men lolling in their seats at the gaming table, some of them head down and snoring, while their fellow gamesters played on, staring at their cards with bloodshot eyes.

Patches was in a small cubbyhole, counting her takings.

'I don't like to be kept waiting,' she said gruffly. 'What kept you, Bones?'

'She weren't at home, boss. Had to wait in the freezing cold and then she turns up large as life in a cab with a toff I ain't never seen afore.'

'So you got a fancy man, have you?' Patches leaned forward, her large breasts bubbling over the top of her low-cut gown. 'He should be good for a bob or two. Where's me money?'

Clara drew herself up to her full height. 'I've never met the gentleman before today. He's nothing to me, and I haven't got the money. You said three days and it's only been two.'

'I was counting from the day you turned up here, so don't play games with me, and that was before your feller blacked my Bertie's eye. I got a score to settle with Luke Foyle, but that's another matter. Have you got the cash or not?'

'I can't raise that much so quickly. I must have more time.'

'*Must have*?' Patches spat the words as if they were a bitter taste in her mouth. 'I don't think you've got much choice, not if you want your young sister to walk again. One gammy leg is bad luck, two is a tragedy that you can prevent, and it'll cost ten guineas. The price has gone up now.'

'That's not fair.' Clara was too angry to feel intimidated. 'Leave my family out of this. I've taken on responsibility for my father's debts; it has nothing to do with my sisters.'

'Then you got to pay up, or . . .' Patches narrowed her eyes so that they disappeared into slits. 'There is one way you could make things square.'

'Go on.' Clara knew she was not going to like the alternative, but she had little option.

'I got a score to settle with the Skinner brothers, and I ain't too pleased with Luke Foyle, neither. He's supposed to work for me, and keep an eye on the other gangs, but I fear he's let me down, and that ain't acceptable.'

Clara's heart was beating so fast that she could hardly breathe. 'That has nothing to do with me.'

'Hoity-toity, ain't you? But you should be more respectful. I could wring your pretty neck with one hand tied behind me back, and Bones is an expert in other methods of making people co-operate. Do I make meself clear?'

'Yes,' Clara said, nodding. 'Crystal clear.'

'I knew you was a clever girl.' Patches lowered her voice. 'Your feller is small beer and I'll deal with him, but it's Ned and Sid Skinner I want put out of the way – permanent like.'

'I don't know how I can help you with that. I have nothing to do with the gang.'

'But your feller does. I want information and it's worth ten guineas.' Patches reached for the gin bottle and half-filled her glass. She took a mouthful, swallowed and breathed gin fumes into Clara's face. 'The Skinners have gone to ground. I want to know where they're hiding out. It's as simple as that.'

'But surely your men could get that information much quicker than I would?'

'Not necessarily.' Patches took another swig of her drink. 'It ain't much to ask. Don't tell me you can't wrap your man round your little finger if you so wish. Get me what I want within the next twenty-four hours and your pa's slate is wiped clean.'

'And if I fail?'

'You won't if you knows what's good for you and your sisters. Don't think you can play fast and loose with me, because you can't.'

Clara faced Patches with what she hoped was an outward appearance of calm, but she could see no way out other than to agree to her terms. 'All right,' she said reluctantly. 'I'll do my best.'

'I think you'll do better than that. I want those sewer rats put away for good.' Patches turned to Bones. 'Get her out of here. I'm sick of looking at her pretty face.'

'Why were you so long, Clara?' Jane asked tearfully. 'People have been banging on the shop door and I didn't know what to do.'

'What sort of people?' Clara glanced over her shoulder, hoping that Bones was now out of sight. He had marched her back to Drury Lane in grim silence, and, although he had left her at the door and walked away she was afraid he might return later to spy on her.

'There was an old man in a top hat who kept peering in the window, but that was not long after you left. He knocked several times, but I ignored him. The others were women and they didn't look too pleased when they realised that the shop was shut.'

'They'll come back if they really want something. I'll open up now. Anyone else?'

'Luke came and I did open the door to him, Clara. I didn't know what else to do and he looked so angry I didn't want to make things worse.'

'It's all right, Jane. What did he want?'

'To see you, of course. He brought me some sugared almonds. He knows they're my favourites. I hope you make it up with him, Clara. I know he's in with a bad lot – Pa told me so – but I think deep down Luke is a good person.'

'Yes, I'm sure he is.' Clara tried to sound positive, but she was not so sure. The gangs had not affected them directly – until now. 'What did Luke say? Is he coming back?'

'I'm still here.' Luke emerged from the parlour. 'Where have you been, Clara?'

She was tempted to tell him everything, but

Patches' threats were fresh in her mind and she had no doubt that they would be carried out. 'I had to deliver some lace to Lizzie's employer.'

'On a day like this?' He stared at her in disbelief.

'Yes, you know what rich people are like. They don't think about anyone else, least of all shop-keepers and servants. I had to do it for Lizzie's sake.'

He glanced at the sodden hem of her skirt. 'Come and sit by the fire. Jane has just made a pot of tea. You look as though you could do with a hot drink, and something to eat.'

'I should have stopped to buy some bread,' Clara said, sighing. 'I haven't stocked the larder yet.'

He shook his head. 'You girls would starve if it weren't for me.'

'Where are you going?' Clara asked as he picked up the empty basket.

'To buy food, of course. If you get any thinner I'll be able to see through you, Clara Carter.' Luke winked at Jane. 'And you can't live on sugared almonds alone.'

She giggled. 'I'd like to try.'

'Look after your sister, Jane,' he said firmly. 'I'll be back in five minutes or so.'

The door closed on him as he left the shop, and Jane's smile faded. 'Where did you go? You lied to him. I was in the shop, and I saw you getting out of a cab. Then you went off with that nasty-looking old man.'

'I didn't tell him the whole truth, which isn't the same as lying.' Clara took off her bonnet and shawl. 'I would love a cup of tea, and maybe you could spare me a sugared almond?' She hurried into the parlour.

'I'm not a baby, Clara.' Jane followed her into the room. 'You can trust me to keep a secret. Where did you go?'

'I had to sort out Pa's gambling debt, Jane. It's nothing for you to worry about.'

'How can you pay? Did Miss Silver leave you a lot of money?'

Clara thought of the empty strong box and sighed. 'There was a little, but I used that to pay for her funeral and to buy Pa's railway ticket. I should have kept it to buy new stock, but you mustn't worry. We'll manage somehow. We always do.' Clara filled two cups with tea and handed one to Jane.

'You shouldn't go off with people like that. Luke wouldn't like it.'

'Then we won't tell him. I know what I'm doing, Jane.'

'We never seem to be free from trouble.'

'This is our new start. Just you wait and see.' Clara spoke with more conviction than she was feeling. Getting out of debt meant betraying Luke – it was a terrible choice to have to make. 'I'll take my tea into the shop, just in case the customers come back.'

Jane popped a sugared almond into her mouth and nodded.

Luke returned with a basketful of groceries. Clara shook her head. 'You can't keep doing this. We're not your responsibility.' She emptied the contents onto the table in the parlour. 'Bread, cake, ham, cheese, butter. This must have cost a small fortune.'

He shrugged. 'You can repay me by letting me take you to a chop house for dinner this evening. There's plenty here to feed Jane and Betsy, with some over for tomorrow.'

At any other time Clara might have refused his invitation to dine, but she was desperate to find out where the Skinner brothers were hiding. 'Thank you. That would be lovely.'

'Really?' He stared at her, eyebrows raised. 'I was expecting an argument.'

'Things have changed,' Clara said, forcing her lips into a smile. 'With Pa safely in the country we can start afresh, as I was just telling Jane.'

Jane eyed the food, licking her lips. 'Is all this for us, Luke?'

'It is, and I don't want to see any waste.' Luke tweaked a stray golden curl that had escaped from the ribbons in Jane's hair.

'There won't be. I promise.'

*

Clara was just about to close the shop that evening when Luke arrived.

'I'm ready,' she said, tipping the day's meagre takings into the strong box. The weather had kept customers away and sales had been poor even when the shop was open, but that was to be expected in the middle of winter. Things would look up with the first hint of spring. She glanced at Luke, who was staring at her, a frown creasing his brow. 'What's the matter?' she asked suspiciously.

'Is that all you have to wear?'

She glanced down at her serviceable, but plain grey dress. 'Yes, as a matter of fact it is. You know how things were with us, Luke. We had to pawn or sell everything we owned, or starve.'

'I knew things were bad, but I didn't realise that you only had that rag.'

'It's not a rag. This material is best-quality cotton.'

'It's dull grey and makes you look like a drab.' Luke fingered the bolts of brightly coloured fabrics. 'I want you to have a gown made in this.' He pulled out a length of emerald-green silk.

It was all Clara could do not to laugh at his choice, but even so, his words had hurt. She tossed her head. 'That would make a wonderful afternoon gown for a lady, but not for a shop girl.'

His winged eyebrows drew together in a scowl. 'Marry me and forget all this, Clara. I don't want my woman serving in a shop all day.'

She met his gaze with a straight look, but this was not the right time to assert her independence. It was an argument they had had on numerous occasions, always ending in a stalemate. Tonight must be about gaining the information that Patches wanted, and personal feelings would have to be put aside. 'I'm sorry, Luke, but this is my only gown. If you're ashamed to be seen out with me . . .'

He reached out to grasp her hand. 'Of course not. I just want to show you off. Is that so wrong?' He lifted the bolt of silk and placed it on the counter. 'I'm a customer now, Clara. I want enough material to make a dress. You know more about that sort of thing than I do.'

'And what then? Are you going to take sewing lessons?' She could not resist the temptation to tease him. He meant it kindly, she was sure, but such a gown would be far too grand for her purposes.

'You can laugh, girl, but I'm serious. I leave it to you to choose the style and find a good dressmaker.' He put his hand in his pocket and took out a leather pouch. 'How much would that cost?'

'I'd have to work it out, but it's an unnecessary extravagance and I'm not sure that it's proper to receive such a gift from you.'

He threw back his head and laughed. 'You're such a little prude at heart, my love.' He tossed a handful of coins onto the counter. 'Put that in the strongbox and fetch your cloak. It's bitterly cold outside.'

'I'll just make sure that Jane and Betsy have everything they need.'

'They're quite capable of looking after themselves for a couple of hours,' Luke said impatiently. 'We'll walk to the Gaiety; it's not very far.'

'All right. Just give me a minute to get my cloak and bonnet.' Clara went through to the parlour where Jane was putting the finishing touches to the supper she was to share with Betsy. 'That looks good,' Clara said, smiling. 'I wish I was staying at home, but Luke is taking me to the Gaiety.'

'You might see Nathanial,' Jane said eagerly.

Clara shook her head. 'I hope not. Luke didn't take too kindly to him when they met. It would be embarrassing.'

Betsy rested her stockinged feet on the brass fender. 'I'd love to be taken out to supper, but I'm really too tired. Miss Lavelle was at her worst today. I'm sure she must be troubled with chilblains or something; she's so crotchety these days.'

'Perhaps she's crossed in love,' Jane said, sighing.

'You read too many penny dreadfuls.' Betsy stretched and yawned. 'Pass me my plate, Jane. I'm dying of hunger.'

Clara put on her bonnet. 'Don't squabble while I'm out, and don't open the door to anyone but me. Make sure you lock up after we've gone, Betsy.'

'Stop fussing,' Betsy said with a careless wave of her hand. 'We can look after ourselves. Go out and enjoy your evening. I just wish it was me going to a nice restaurant and not you.'

'I'm sure your turn will come, and yours too, Jane.' Clara turned to see Luke standing in the doorway. He might have taken to a life on the wrong side of the law, but with his fair hair waved back from a high forehead, clean-cut features and wide-set grey eyes he had an air of distinction and could easily pass as a gentleman. Just when she thought she knew every facet of his character, Clara discovered something new about Luke Foyle. She hated his way of life, but there was something about him that was both intriguing and fascinating.

Betsy shot him a sideways glance. 'Ta for the grub, Luke.'

He bowed from the waist. 'You're most welcome.'

'You look very smart,' Betsy added, looking him up and down. 'Look at those buttons on his waist-coat, Clara. I bet they're real silver.'

'I wouldn't wear anything less,' Luke said, chuckling. 'You have an eye for fashion, Betsy. I paid a handsome price for them.'

'You're a shameless peacock.' Clara hustled him into the shop. 'We won't be late, girls.'

The ice-cold air took Clara's breath away as they trod carefully on the frozen surface of the snow. Above them the indigo sky was studded with twinkling stars and wisps of cloud danced across the silver face of the moon. It would have been a night for romance, had it not been for the grim task ahead. Luke tucked her hand in the crook of his arm, and the scent of bay rum and Macassar oil filled her nostrils. It seemed that the noxious smells of the city had been frozen out of existence, for the time being at least, and when they reached the Strand, lights blazed from the theatres and eating houses, creating a magical snow scene. Ice seemed to fill Clara's lungs as the cold grew more intense and it was a relief to step inside the Gaiety restaurant where they were enveloped in the aroma of good food and the heady scent of wine, gentlemen's cologne and expensive perfume.

The cloakroom assistant checked in their outer garments and the maître d'hôtel seemed to know Luke and led them to one of the best tables. A waiter hurried up to present them with menus and took their order. Luke made a selection from the wine list. 'You've very quiet, Clara,' he said when the waiter had filled their glasses and moved away. 'Is there something on your mind?'

She covered her confusion by taking a sip of the ruby-red claret. 'No, of course not.'

'I don't believe you.' He eyed her over the rim of his glass. 'I know you too well. What is it?'

She met his intense gaze and realised suddenly that a lie was out of the question. 'I went to see Patches again.'

'You did what?' His raised voice attracted the attention of the diners at the next table.

'She had given me three days to pay off Pa's debts, but she sent for me today.'

'Why didn't you tell me this before?'

'I didn't know what to do. She wants certain information and she's threatened to take it out on Jane if I don't do as she asked. She plans to get even with you for fighting with her son.'

'I can stand up for myself, but that's not all, is it? What is it she wants you to do? Come on, Clara, you know that you can't keep anything from me.'

She could see the tell-tale pulse throbbing in his temple and his knuckles were white as he grasped the stem of his wineglass. 'She said she would cancel Pa's debt if I found out where the Skinners have their hideout. She wants them dead.' Clara's voice broke on a sob.

'Why didn't you tell me all this in the first place? How much did Alfred owe?'

'Eight guineas, but she's increased it to ten because I can't raise that much money, at least not quickly. I suppose I could if I sold the shop, but that's my livelihood now.'

'Your father has a lot to answer for. He's taken the coward's way out and left you to take the consequences.' Luke drained his glass and reached for the bottle. 'You won't have to do what Patches wants and you won't have to find the money. I'll sort that old bitch out once and for all, and that idiot son of hers.'

'How? What are you going to do?'

'It's not your problem now. This has become personal.' Luke sat back as the waiter appeared with their food. 'Enjoy your dinner, and then I'm taking you home.'

'You don't know Patches. She's evil.'

'I know Patches only too well, and it would take more than a pock-marked old woman to frighten me.'

'You won't do anything stupid, will you?'

His eyes twinkled and he raised his glass to her. 'So you do love me?'

'I don't want your death on my conscience,' she said with a reluctant smile.

'I suppose that's a start.' He raised his glass. 'Let's enjoy the evening.'

Clara hardly slept that night for worrying about Luke. He had seen her home, but had left immediately, having laughed off her fears and promised to return next day to let her know that matters had been settled satisfactorily. He had seemed supremely confident in his own ability but she had her doubts. The whole sad affair could end up in one of the gang wars that were the scourge of the East End.

She rose early and went about the chore of lighting the fire and filling the kettle with snow as the pump in the back yard was still frozen. The grey-white world outside felt cold and alien, adding to her feeling of foreboding.

Betsy appeared just as the kettle came to the boil, and after snatching a cup of tea and a slice of bread and jam, she rammed her bonnet on her head and wrapped her shawl around her shoulders. 'If Miss Lavelle isn't in a better mood today I'm giving in my notice. I don't care if I never find another job, but I won't be treated like a skivvy.'

Clara was used to listening to her sister's grumbles before she set off each day and she ignored this last remark. 'I've made a sandwich for you.'

Betsy eyed the brown paper package with distaste. 'She won't allow us to eat in the workroom in case we get grease on the material.'

'Never mind. Take it anyway and eat it on the way home.'

'I wish you'd stop being so cheerful. We're stuck here, in this tiny shop with hardly a rag to our backs and we have to rely on Luke for our food. It's all Pa's fault and I hope he's suffering too, wherever he is now.' Betsy tucked the sandwich into her reticule and flounced out of the parlour.

Clara sighed and shook her head. Betsy was right, of course, but there was no point in dwelling on the past. What happened now was more important. She followed her sister through the shop and out into the street. She was about to lock the door when

Betsy uttered a gasp and bent down to pluck something from the snowy pavement.

'Look what I found.' She held out her mittened hand and a tiny silver button winked in the light of the gas lamp. 'I'll swear this is from Luke's waistcoat.'

Clara took it from her. 'Yes, I'm sure it is. It must have come off when he saw me home. I'm certain he would have noticed if it was missing in the restaurant.'

Betsy pointed to a dark stain on the churned-up snow. 'That looks like blood.'

'It's your imagination,' Clara said sharply. 'You'd better hurry or you'll be late for work.'

'Maybe he slipped and fell,' Betsy insisted. 'You should go round to his lodgings and make sure he's all right.'

'Luke can take care of himself.' Clara stepped back into the shop and closed the door, but her knees were trembling and the button seemed to burn into the palm of her hand. She hesitated for a moment and then reached under the counter for the button box. It would be safe there, and buttons came off easily enough. She would make sure it was sewn on more securely when she returned it to Luke.

'Clara, are you there?' Jane's voice brought her down to earth with a bump. It was silly to worry about a lost button, and the stain on the snow might be anything. Even if it were blood that didn't mean to say it was Luke's. Betsy was over-imaginative at the best of times. Clara hurried into the parlour.

'I'm here. I just saw Betsy off to work.'

'She's forgotten to take the hat I finished off,' Jane said anxiously. 'She'll be in trouble again.'

Clara thought quickly. It was still only half-past seven, and there was no point in opening the shop before nine. 'I'll take it to her, if you don't mind being left alone again.'

'Of course not. I feel quite safe here, and thanks to Luke I can make some toast for my breakfast. There's butter and jam – it feels like Christmas.'

'I'll open up when I get back. There probably won't be any customers until later this morning. It's still freezing outside.' Clara took her cloak from the peg and slipped it on. 'I'll be as quick as I can.' She picked up the bandbox containing the hat, blew Jane a kiss and set off after Betsy.

Knowing her sister only too well, Clara had guessed correctly. Betsy did not know the meaning of the word 'hurry'. She caught her up as she meandered along the Strand in the direction of Miss Lavelle's shop.

'You left this behind,' Clara said breathlessly. 'And you're going to be late as it is.'

Betsy glared at the hat box as if it were to blame for her employer's faults. 'Thank you.'

'Hurry up, slowcoach.'

'I will if you promise to go and see Luke. I'm worried about him.'

'Anyone would think he was your beau, Betsy. I'm going there now, if you must know. Now please, run the last few yards so that at least it looks as if you've tried to get to work on time.'

Betsy rolled her eyes and turned away, but she did walk a little faster than usual, and Clara waited until she saw her enter the premises. She could sympathise with her sister, but they needed the money, little though it might be. One day Betsy would be a fully qualified milliner and able to command a high price for her creations – until then she would have to put up with Miss Lavelle's idiosyncrasies and foul moods. There was no escape for working girls, other than a suitable marriage, and even then that was not necessarily a recipe for a happy ending. Life was not a fairy tale. Clara set off for Luke's lodging house in Hanging Sword Alley. It was a long way down Fleet Street, she had only been this way once before and that was in Luke's company. She put her head down, ignoring the comments from passing draymen and carters, all of whom offered to give her a lift in return for favours not expressed in words, but their meaning was obvious.

She reached the lodging house in the narrow alleyway off Whitefriars Street, and knocked on the door. A feral cat shot past with a dead rat in its mouth and a mangy dog in hot pursuit. She knocked again and this time the door was opened just a crack.

'What d'yer want?' The woman's voice was gruff and the words were slurred with drink although it was still early morning. The smell of gin fumes curled upwards in a plume of bad breath as it evaporated into the cold atmosphere.

'I want to speak to Mr Foyle.'

'He ain't here. Never come home last night, according to the slut I pay to empty the slops. Best try the brothels, love. That's where they usually end up.' She slammed the door in Clara's face.

Chapter Six

As the hours went by and still no word from Luke, Clara's fears intensified. Until now she had had supreme confidence in Luke's ability to take care of himself, but that was before she had met Patches Bragg, when the world of the gambling dens and the criminal gangs had seemed unreal. It had not occurred to her that Pa was so deeply involved with the criminal fraternity, but now she realised just how far he had sunk. For the rest of the day her thoughts kept returning to the silver button nestling amongst its brothers, and the patch of blood in the snow. It had all but disappeared into a mushy grey slush, but the memory of it was still fresh in her mind.

Clara closed up early, making the excuse of going out to purchase hot pies for their evening meal, but instead she made her way to the club in Angel Court.

There was no hope of finding the money that Patches had demanded, but that paled into insignificance in the light of Luke's disappearance. There was only one way to find out if Patches and her gang were involved. She rapped on the door and waited, but no one came. She knocked again, and when there was no reply she turned the knob and found to her surprise that the door was not locked. With her heart hammering against her tightly laced stays, she stepped inside.

'Is anyone there?' Her voice echoed throughout the building. There was no sign of Bones or Old Tom, and the only sound was her own ragged breathing. Her first instinct was to turn and run, but perhaps Luke was there in that dank cellar, bound and gagged and unable to communicate.

She made her way through the dark corridors and down the flight of narrow stairs to the basement, and there was no sign of life or sound of anything other than the creaking of old timbers. She opened the door to the gaming room. Light filtered hazily through the grimy window; it was dim but even so she could see that the place was deserted. The tables were bare, as were the shelves behind the bar. Patches and her punters might never have existed other than in her imagination. Clara bent down to pick up a round gaming token that had been overlooked. Even in the semi-darkness she could see that it was similar to the ones that Pa sometimes brought home in his pocket. But for this tiny object she might have been led to believe that she was in the wrong place, or that she had dreamed the whole sorry business.

The sound of footsteps on the stairs made her spin round. She held her breath, poised and ready to run. She had expected to see one of Patches' men, but it was an elderly woman who stood in the doorway and she looked as scared as Clara was feeling.

'Who are you?' the woman demanded tremulously. 'What are you doing here?'

Clara was shaking from head to foot, but it was with relief and not fear. 'I might ask the same of you. Where is Patches?'

'Are you one of her gang? I don't want no trouble. I'm just the cleaning woman.'

'No, I'm not one of the gang,' Clara said angrily. 'Where have they gone?'

'I dunno, and I don't ask questions. Nor will you if you've got any sense. I've got work to do, and you'd better go about your business, whatever that might be.'

'I need to know what happened here last night. Please tell me anything you know.'

'Go away and let me get on. I got a family to feed and I don't know nothing.' The woman glanced over her shoulder. 'He's coming.' She scuttled into the room and pushed past Clara, brandishing a broom.

Clara attempted to leave but found her way barred by a swarthy man wearing a billycock hat and a heavy overcoat with its collar pulled up to his unshaven chin. 'Who are you?' he demanded, squinting at her from beneath bushy black eyebrows.

'I'm looking for Luke Foyle,' Clara said, hoping she sounded more confident than she was feeling. This man had an air of menace about him that made her feel distinctly threatened, but to her surprise his frown was replaced by a broad grin, exposing a row of uneven, yellowed teeth.

'What's your name, lovely?'

'I'm Clara Carter.'

'So you're the one,' he said, chuckling. 'Luke has an eye for a looker, and that's the truth.'

'Where is he?' Clara demanded breathlessly.

'You might say he's had to go on a trip for the sake of his health, miss. You won't be seeing him for quite a while.'

'I don't understand.'

'Haven't you heard? There was a fight between the Skinners' gang and the Braggs' last night. Very bloody it was too. Those what are left have scarpered.'

'Who are you?' Clara demanded furiously. 'How do I know you're not lying?'

'It don't matter who I am, my duck. I'll be off soon meself, but it's a pity about Foyle. You'll get over him in time.'

Clara felt a bubble of hysteria welling up inside her, but she mustered every scrap of self-control in an attempt to sound calm and collected. 'What happened to him?'

'I told you, girl. He left the country and he won't be coming back for a long while. If he does he faces the hangman's noose. D'you understand me now?'

'Did he kill someone?' Clara's breath caught on a sob. 'Was it Patches? Is that why this place is deserted?'

'I ain't prepared to say no more. The less you know, the better. Go home, girl.' He was about to walk past her but she caught him by the sleeve.

'Why won't you tell me where Luke has gone?'

He shook her hand off as if it were an annoying bug. 'Oh, didn't I say? How very remiss of me. He's taking in the delights of Paris, so I believe.' He sauntered off to inspect the bar, or what was left of it, giving Clara the opportunity to escape.

It was not until she was outside that the full force of events overtook her and she leaned against the wall, gasping for breath. It had all begun with a gambling debt, but everything had spiralled out of control, and now Luke had left the country, if that man was to be believed. There must have been a scuffle outside the shop, which would account for the bloodstain on the snow and the loss of a waist-coat button, but what happened after that would remain a mystery.

She walked home slowly, stopping to buy three hot mutton pies from the pieman, and three baked potatoes from the stall a little further along Drury Lane. Her movements were automatic and she was still in a state of shock. She had done her best to persuade Luke to get away from the gangs, and he had managed to keep that part of his life separate, treating it almost as a joke. Now the reality of gang warfare had struck home – Luke must have killed someone, maybe Patches herself, and he had fled for his life. He was a marked man and if he returned to England he would face the full force of the law.

The sound of footsteps made Clara glance over her shoulder. Home and safety were just a few yards away, but to her relief she recognised a familiar figure. With his muffler flying and his hair tousled by the wind, Nathaniel came hurrying towards her with his violin case slung over his shoulder. As he came to a breathless halt she noticed that he had done his coat up on the wrong button and his stiff white collar was coming undone as if he had lost a stud in his hurry to get dressed.

'Clara, I thought it was you.' He sniffed the air, like a hungry hound. 'Mutton pie, my favourite.'

'You're welcome to join us, Nathaniel. There's plenty to go round.'

'I wish I could, but I'm already late. I should have been at work ten minutes ago. I just hope the conductor hasn't noticed that I'm not in my place.'

'Another time then,' Clara said, smiling, 'but perhaps you ought to stop off for a moment and fix your collar. You do look a bit untidy, if you don't mind me saying so.'

'I was so busy composing that I forgot the time.'

'You seem to have lost a collar stud.'

'Devil take the wretched things.' Nathaniel ran his hand through his windblown hair. 'I'm always losing them, but I can't stop now. May I call on you soon, Clara? I don't want to intrude.'

'That would be very nice.' Clara had to suppress the sudden desire to laugh. In the midst of murder and mayhem Nathaniel represented a different world that was infinitely more appealing.

'Splendid.' He backed away, smiling. 'And I haven't forgotten about the tickets for the show . . .' His voice trailed off as he broke into a run, heading in the direction of the Strand.

Clara walked on slowly, making a huge effort to compose herself before she arrived at the shop. What had happened last night was something she wanted to keep to herself for as long as possible.

Jane answered Clara's knock on the door and she entered the shop with a smile on her face. 'Look what I've got for supper. We'll eat well tonight.'

'Did you find Luke? Is he all right?'

Betsy stuck her head round the parlour door. 'Do I smell hot pies?'

'Yes to both questions. Luke has gone away for

a while, Jane, but he'll be back before you know it. Betsy, get the plates out, please. The pies are getting cold.'

When her sisters had gone to bed, Clara stayed downstairs on the pretext of locking up, but although she was physically exhausted, she knew that sleep would elude her. She sat by the dying embers of the fire with the box containing her treasures on her lap and she held Luke's silver button between her fingers. It was beautifully crafted, and the whole set must have been very expensive, but that was typical of Luke – only the best would do. She sighed, wondering what had happened to him. Luke had left the country, or so the man had said, but he could have been lying. Perhaps Luke had simply left London. As far as she knew he had no family living. He had told her that his mother was dead, but he had always been reluctant to talk about his past, and she had respected his right to keep silent about matters that were obviously distressing. She wished now that she had questioned him further as it might have given her a clue as to his whereabouts.

Clara closed the box and rose to her feet, but as she replaced it beneath the counter she remembered that Luke had wanted her to have an elegant gown made from the emerald-green silk. Generosity had been one of his more endearing qualities, and, despite her reservations as to his character, she realised with a sense of shock that she would miss him more than she would have thought possible. She had managed to keep her emotions in check all evening, but now she was alone she could give vent to her feelings and tears trickled down her cheeks. If she were being honest she had to admit that she cared deeply for Luke, despite his many failings, or maybe because of them, but it was his involvement with the criminal world that had made her wary of falling in love. The gangs were constantly at war, but last night Luke had acted on her behalf, and it was her father's inability to repay his debt to Patches that had brought matters to a head. If she had kept her worries to herself none of this would have happened. She bowed her head and sobbed as if her heart would break.

Lizzie breezed into the shop next morning, smiling triumphantly. 'Madam was delighted with the lace.' Her smile faded. 'What's the matter with you, Clara? You look dreadful.'

'I didn't sleep very well, but I'm fine.'

'Don't fib. You can't fool me. What's happened?'

There seemed little point in lying. Lizzie would not be fooled easily and Clara knew that she was not looking her best. When she had eventually fallen asleep she had suffered terrifying nightmares that had made her fearful of dozing off again in case they returned. She glanced over her shoulder to make sure the parlour door was closed. Jane was working on a creation that Betsy had brought home to finish off, and Clara did not want her to hear what she had to say.

'I'll tell you, but you must keep it between us. No one else must know.'

Lizzie's eyes brightened and she pulled up the stool that was reserved for privileged customers. 'Do tell, but make it quick. I'm sure Miss Jones times my absences so that she can report me to the house-keeper. She knows I'm a threat because madam likes me, and I know how to keep on her good side.'

Clara launched into a brief summary of the events leading to Luke's disappearance. 'I only have a stranger's word for it that Luke has left the country. He wouldn't tell me what really happened, but when I went to Angel Court yesterday there was no sign of Patches or any of her men.'

'How awful, but very exciting, even though I don't approve of you taking matters into your own hands.'

'I still don't know what happened to Luke.'

Lizzie put her head on one side, eyeing her sister with a wry smile. 'You said you didn't care for him.'

'I don't, not in a romantic way, but I am fond of him. I wouldn't want any harm to come to him, especially when he was trying to help us. Patches threatened to hurt Jane, and I believed her.'

'You didn't tell me that.'

'I thought I could handle it on my own, and I

certainly don't want Jane to find out. The poor child suffers enough as it is.'

'So what happened to Patches? She can't have disappeared in a puff of smoke.'

'I don't know, Lizzie. I wish I did, but I'm not going back there.'

'Then you must try to put it out of your head.' Lizzie rose to her feet. 'Heavens! I'd almost forgotten why I came here today.'

'You needed to buy needles and thread? More lace?'

'Yes, that's it. Miss Jones needs more blonde lace. Madam has taken a liking to it and she wants another gown trimmed with it, but she needs at least ten yards. It's a very grand gown and I think she wants to show off in front of her husband's business colleagues and their stuffy wives. Have you got that much in stock?'

Clara shook her head. 'No, there might be three yards but that's all, and it means I'd have to go to the warehouse to order more, which would take time.'

'She wants it by tomorrow. What will we do?'

'You could probably get some in Oxford Street.'

'I wouldn't know where to start.' Lizzie reached across the counter to grasp her sister's hands. 'But you would, Clara. You have an eye for these things.'

'I have to look after the shop, Lizzie. I can't just close up on a whim. I'll lose customers.'

'Mrs Comerford is a very influential woman. If she's satisfied with your service she'll recommend you to her wealthy friends. Please, Clara.'

Lizzie's pleading expression made it almost impossible to refuse, and the temptation of a shopping trip to Oxford Street outweighed all other considerations. The lure of the big department stores was too strong to refuse. 'I suppose I could shut for an hour at midday. It's quite a long walk but I could do it.'

'Miss Jones gave me the money for a cab. I don't mind walking back to Bedford Square. If you could bring the lace to the house you'd be saving my life.'

'I don't think Miss Jones would stoop to murder,' Clara said, chuckling, 'but I'll do it for you, Lizzie. Just remember you owe me a favour.'

'I'll be in your debt for ever.' Lizzie delved into her reticule and took out a purse. She pressed some coins into her sister's hand. 'That should be enough for the lace and the cab fare.' She moved to the door and paused to blow a kiss. 'Thank you. I won't forget this, Clara.'

Oxford Street was thronged with carriages, cabs and horse-drawn omnibuses. People had braved the snow, and the shop windows were filled with displays designed to tempt customers to come in and look around. Clara alighted from the cab outside Peter Robinson's department store. She headed for the drapery department and stopped for a moment to take in the sheer size and the vast quantity of stock compared to her own small establishment. She took off one glove and fingered the silks, satins and crisp cottons on display. Filmy muslin and delicate lace hung like cobwebs from tall stands, and black-uniformed shop assistants offered their services with a smile. Bolts of linen and other materials had their own fresh smell that acted like wine on Clara's heightened senses, and she drifted towards the counter, drinking in the atmosphere until she was dizzy with delight. This was what she wanted for herself. An emporium to satisfy the senses and provide beauty and luxury at prices that almost everyone could afford.

'Can I help you, madam?' A small, pretty assistant was suddenly at her side. 'What would madam like to see?'

'Blonde lace,' Clara said firmly. 'I need ten yards.'

'I'm afraid we don't stock it any more. It's fallen out of fashion, but we have some very fine Valenciennes lace, which is very popular at the moment.'

Clara thought quickly. 'I'd like to see it and also if you have any Chantilly lace, perhaps I could compare the two?'

A flicker of respect lit the girl's dark eyes and she inclined her head. 'Certainly, madam. If you would like to take a seat for a moment I'll fetch them for you.'

Half an hour later Clara had her purchase of Chantilly lace tucked under her arm and she had taken time to walk through the store and inspect the merchandise. She stood outside, and was about to hail a hansom cab when she spotted a 'To Let' sign a little further along the street. She could not resist the temptation to have a look at what was on offer.

The four-storey building had once been a town house but the ground floor had been turned into a shop. Peering through the grimy window she could see very little, apart from an upturned chair and the floor strewn with rubbish. The dilapidated exterior, with peeling paintwork and faded lettering on the fascia indicating that it had once been the premises of a bespoke tailor, gave the impression that the shop had been empty for quite some time. In her mind she began refurbishing the interior and filling the shelves with irresistible items that would tempt women of all classes to come and buy. She sighed and turned away. It was just a dream after all. She hailed a cab.

The thaw had set in and the trees in Bedford Square seemed to be weeping as the snow on the branches melted and fell in icy tears to the ground. Spikes of grass had begun to poke through the white blanket and the pavements were slippery with slush. Clara made her way carefully towards the steps leading down to the area, but as she was about to open the gate a waft of warm air made her look up to see Joss Comerford emerge from the house and head down the steps. She was about to continue but he had spotted her and smiled.

'Miss Carter, this is a pleasant surprise. Has my mama been putting more business your way?'

'In a manner of speaking, sir.'

'There's no need to use the servants' entrance.' Despite her protests, he ushered her into the house. James stood to attention, gazing into the distance, but Clara could feel disapproval emanating from him in waves. She walked past him with her head held high.

'I have a package for Miss Jones,' she said firmly.

Joss took off his top hat and tucked it under his arm. 'James will see that she gets it.' Joss curved his lips into a lazy smile as he slowly peeled off his kid gloves.

Clara tightened her grip on the package. 'Thank you, sir, but I really need to speak to Miss Jones in person.'

'Oh, all right, if you insist. James, I want you to find Miss Jones and ask her to come to the morning parlour.'

'Yes, sir.' Holding himself stiffly erect, James headed for the back stairs.

'Come, Miss Carter. I'll show you to the morning parlour. It's much warmer in there and you'll be more comfortable.'

'Thank you, but I really can't stay long. I had to close the shop.'

'Really? An inconvenience, I'm sure.' Joss led the way across the wide entrance hall and ushered her into an elegant reception room where a fire burned in the grate. He laid his hat on a rosewood side table together with his gloves. 'Do take a seat and make yourself comfortable. Would you like some refreshment?'

Clara remained standing. 'No, sir. Thank you, but as I explained I have to get back to the shop.'

'Ah, yes. The shop – it's rather small, isn't it? I mean it can't provide much of an income.'

'It's a living, sir. I'm only just starting out in the drapery business, but I have ambition to go much further.' She glanced around, taking in her surroundings with a feeling of envy. The morning parlour had been decorated and furnished with a feminine touch, and no expense had been spared. The delicate blues and greys of the silk upholstery and the elegant furniture seemed dwarfed by Joss Comerford's presence.

He unbuttoned his greatcoat and perched on a chair that seemed too fragile to bear his weight. 'Have you indeed? I'd like to hear more about that.' He stretched his legs out to the fire.

'There's not much to tell. It's a dream really, but when I've made enough money I'd like to rent premises in Oxford Street. I'd start quite small and I'd build up gradually until I had a treasure house filled with beautiful things at a price that most people could afford.'

'That sounds wonderful, but aren't there already several department stores in Oxford Street?'

'The more, the better. It would bring people in from the country, and with the railways spreading ever further it's not beyond the bounds of possibility that people could come to London just for the day. Imagine Christmas with lights and decorations all along the street and shop windows filled with luxury items.'

'By golly, you've sold the idea to me already. When will you start this odyssey?'

Clara folded her hands tightly around the parcel of lace. 'As I said, sir, it's just a dream at present, but one day—' She broke off at the sound of a faint tap on the door.

'Enter,' Joss said grandly.

The door opened and Miss Jones sidled into the room. 'You wanted to see me, sir?'

'Miss Carter has something for you, Jones.' Joss rose to his feet. 'I'll wait for you in the hall, Miss Carter.'

Clara shot him a questioning look. 'Why, sir? I explained that I have to hurry home.'

'I'm going your way. Another luncheon at Simpson's. A bit of a bore, but I have to keep in touch with friends.' He left the room, allowing the door to swing shut.

'What is this, Miss Carter?' Miss Jones looked down her pointed nose, glaring at Clara as if she had done something unforgivable.

'I had to go to Oxford Street to get the lace, Miss Jones.' Clara handed her the neatly wrapped package. 'They didn't have any blonde lace and the assistant told me that it went out of fashion some time ago.'

'I don't know about that. I always thought it was a favourite with royalty,' Miss Jones said stiffly. 'You provided us with such lace from your little shop.' The emphasis she put on the last two words made them sound like an insult.

'It must have been old stock,' Clara admitted reluctantly. 'I've only just inherited the business, and I'm still learning.'

Miss Jones tore away the wrapping paper. 'So what have we here?'

'It's the finest Chantilly lace. Very fashionable, so I'm told.'

'I suppose it will have to do.' Miss Jones headed for the door. 'Next time I'll go to Oxford Street myself. I doubt if you'll be receiving any further orders from this establishment. Good day, Miss Carter.' She swept out of the room, leaving Clara open-mouthed and angry. After all the trouble she had taken, that was all the thanks she was to receive. She pitied Lizzie, who had to put up with Miss Jones and her whims every day.

The door opened again and Joss filled the gap

with his presence. 'I left my hat and gloves here.' He picked them up, turning to Clara with an engaging smile. 'I thought you were in a hurry.'

'I am.' She brushed past him and marched across the hall, ignoring the smirk on James's face as he held the front door for her.

'Hold on, there.' Joss hurried after her. 'What's wrong, Miss Carter? Wasn't old Jones satisfied with the goods?'

'It's not important, Mr Comerford.' Clara made her way down the front steps and was about to walk off when Joss caught up with her.

'Something has upset you.' He stepped in front of her, barring her way.

'My dream will take a bit longer, that's all, sir. It doesn't concern you.'

He raised his hand to hail a cab. 'Maybe, maybe not. I have an idea, Miss Carter. If you will just give me a few minutes to explain . . . ?' He stepped back from the kerb as the cab pulled to a halt. 'Silver's Drapery, Drury Lane, cabby.'

Her curiosity aroused, Clara climbed in. 'What could you possibly have to say that would interest me, Mr Comerford?'

He sat down beside her. 'I might consider investing in your venture, Miss Carter.'

'Really?' She turned her head to stare at him in surprise. 'Why would you want to do that, sir?'

'Please call me Joss. After all, we might end up

as partners.' He puffed out his chest. 'I've led an idle life until now, but I've been thinking of going into business, if only to show my father what I'm made of. He has a pretty poor opinion of me, although that is between you and me.'

The confidential tone of his voice and the wink that accompanied his words made Clara feel uncomfortable. She hardly knew this young man and yet he was suggesting that they go into business together. It sounded too good to be true and she suspected that he was simply trying to impress her.

'I'm not looking for a partner, Mr Comerford.' She sat as far away from him as was possible in the confines of the hansom cab. 'But thank you for the thought. It is much appreciated.'

He stared at her, frowning. 'You are a contradictory little minx, Clara. I suspect that you are playing a clever game.'

'Indeed I am not,' Clara said angrily. 'Please stop the cab and I'll walk from here. It's not too far to Drury Lane.'

'Certainly not. I'll see you to your door, but I will not be put off so easily.' He leaned back against the worn leather squabs, regarding her with a knowing smile. 'My father is a successful businessman, Clara, and I want to prove to him that I am a suitable candidate to take over from him when he decides to retire. I can't think of a better way than to be heavily involved in a successful venture of my own.'

'Then you had better start looking for something you can do yourself. I appreciate the offer, but if I went into a partnership with anyone it would be my sister Betsy.'

'I think you might change your mind when you discover that there is only one way to succeed.'

'And what is that?'

'Capital, my dear Clara. You'll get nowhere without the necessary funds to back you. Your Miss Silver should have taught you that from the start.'

Annoyed by his patronising attitude and his casual dismissal of Miss Silver as a businesswoman, Clara tapped on the cab roof. 'Stop, please, cabby. I'll walk from here.' She waited for the cab to come to a halt, ignoring Joss's protests. 'Thank you for the lift, Mr Comerford. I'll say good day to you, sir.' She gathered up her skirts and stepped down to the pavement with as much dignity as she could muster, despite his pleas for her to allow him to see her home.

Chapter Seven

Clara arrived back at the shop to find a man, who had the appearance of a bank clerk or someone who worked in a counting house, pacing the pavement. He came to a halt beside her as she rapped on the door.

'Are you the proprietor of this emporium, miss?'

'I am.' Clara knocked, hoping that Jane would come quickly. She shot a sideways glance at the man, who did not look happy. His nose was red and his eyes were watering as if the intense cold was making him weep. 'How may I help you?' she asked, moderating her tone.

'We can talk better inside, miss. I've been waiting for a good half an hour and I'm frozen to the marrow.'

Clara peered through the misted glass and could

see Jane making her way across the shop floor. The door opened but Clara barred the man's way as he tried to push past her. 'Might I ask your business before I let you in?'

'I am here on behalf of the lessor.'

'Come inside.' Clara stood aside and ushered him into the comparative warmth of the shop. She gave Jane an encouraging smile. 'It's all right. Nothing to worry about.'

Jane shot a wary glance at the intruder. 'Shall I stay?'

'No, dear. I don't suppose this will take long.' Clara shut the street door and put the counter between herself and the stranger. He did not look menacing, but in this part of town it was better to be safe than sorry. 'Now then, Mr . . . ? I didn't catch your name.'

'Wilkes, miss. I'm a clerk in the law firm of Boswell and Boswell, Lincoln's Inn. I'm here to represent the landowner.'

Clara stared at him, frowning. 'I am Clara Carter. I thought Miss Silver was the owner, Mr Wilkes. She left the premises to me in her will. It's gone to probate, but I've taken over running the shop in the meantime.'

'Miss Silver was the lessee. She owned the premises, but the lease is held by my client and it is due to expire at the end of February. I'm surprised that she did not inform you of this.'

'Miss Silver died suddenly. I had no knowledge of the lease.'

He took off his bowler hat, shaking his head and tut-tutting. 'You should have looked into the matter before you decided to move in, Miss Carter.'

'I suppose I should, but I had very little choice. What exactly does this mean?'

'Simply that you have the chance to extend the lease for a fee, which must be paid before the end of the month.' He took a folded sheet of paper from his inside pocket and laid it on the counter. 'You will see the amount specified. It must be settled in full.'

Clara stared at it aghast. 'But that's a small fortune. I can't find that sort of money.'

'The alternative is to allow the lessor to purchase the property.' He turned the paper over, pointing to the amount written on the back. 'That is the sum offered by the landowner. It is a fair offer.'

The figures danced up and down before Clara's eyes, making very little sense. 'There must be another way. I might be able to raise the money to renew the lease in a month or two.'

'Or you could try to sell the property privately,' Wilkes said stiffly. 'I should add that it would take time, and the fact that the lease has all but expired would be likely to put off many prospective buyers.'

'I need to think about this,' Clara said evasively. 'I should speak to my lawyer before I sign away my livelihood.'

Wilkes blinked as if taken my surprise. 'You could, of course, but as I said before, this is a very fair offer in the circumstances.' He glanced around at the half-empty shelves. 'It's not exactly a thriving business.'

'It does well enough.' Clara moved quickly to open the door. 'I need time to try to raise the necessary, Mr Wilkes. I assume that the landowner will allow me that?'

'I'll be back at the end of the week, but take a tip from me and accept the money. You'll not get a better offer.' He stepped outside, bending almost double against the buffeting of the wind.

Clara shivered as a gust of cold air blew in from the street, chilling her to the bone. Another disaster looming out of nowhere! Not only were they in danger of losing their livelihood, they would also be homeless.

'Who was that?' Jane demanded anxiously. 'What did he want?'

Clara turned to give her sister a tremulous smile. 'Nothing for you to worry about, love.'

'I'm not stupid, Clara. I know there's something wrong. I can tell by the look on your face.'

'It's a legal matter. Something to do with the lease on the shop, but it's not a problem.' Clara took off her bonnet and unbuttoned her mantle. 'I'd better open up.'

'I've had the kettle on the trivet for ages so it

should be boiling now. Would you like a cup of tea and something to eat?'

'Yes, that would be lovely.'

Jane hesitated in the doorway. 'This is quite a nice place, but I do miss the kitchen range. How did Miss Silver manage to cook her food?'

'I never gave it much thought until now.'

'We'll manage somehow,' Jane said cheerfully. 'I might be able to make some soup if I start it off really early in the morning.'

'That would be very nice.' Clara looked up as the doorbell jangled and a woman bustled into the shop. 'Good morning, madam. How may I help you?'

'I want a reel of white cotton.' The customer took a coin from her purse, dropped it on the counter and waited in silence while Clara served her. 'Thank you. Good day.' The woman dropped her purchase into her shopping basket and hurried from the shop.

Clara sighed as she placed the halfpenny in the empty tin. It would be impossible to raise the necessary sum of money to extend the lease based on such meagre takings. Mrs Comerford and others like her had monthly accounts, which would be paid eventually, but as Miss Silver had often pointed out, the wealthier the patron, the less importance they placed on settling their debts. The shop had supported a single lady in reasonable comfort, and it might have been possible for Clara and her small family to scrape along reasonably well had it not been for the renewal of the lease. She was deep in thought when Jane brought her lunch and placed it on the counter. Clara met her sister's worried look with an attempt at a smile. 'I have to go out again this afternoon. It's started to rain and there are so few people about that I doubt if we'll do much trade.'

'It's about that man, isn't it?'

'Not exactly. I have to go to Oxford Street. There's something I need to do and it won't wait.'

'I wish you'd tell me what's going on. I'm not a baby.'

'There's nothing to tell at the moment.' Clara took a bite of the ham sandwich. 'This is delicious.' She gave her sister a hug. 'I can't tell you what's going to happen because I don't know yet, but whatever transpires it will be for the better. That's a promise.'

Oxford Street was a sea of umbrellas, glistening like black mushrooms in the rainstorm. It was early afternoon, but the lowering clouds had brought an early dusk and gaslights flickered in shop windows, creating rainbow pools on the wet pavements. The sound of wagon wheels whooshing through deep puddles warned pedestrians to leap aside as horse-drawn vehicles ploughed their tortuous way along the crowded thoroughfare.

Clara made straight for the empty premises she had noticed that morning and took note of the agent's name and address. Luckily it was in Bond Street, which was only a short walk away. She quickened her pace, threading her way through the throng of shoppers, street vendors and businessmen in their black city suits. Her clothes were wet and her bonnet was sodden by the time she reached the agent's office, but she was too intent on her purpose to bother about physical discomfort.

She presented herself at the desk and informed the clerk that she was interested in renting the property in Oxford Street. His reaction was one of guarded scepticism and rigid politeness.

'It is a very expensive area, miss. The owner of the premises has given us a set of particulars as to the next tenant, and I really don't think—'

'Excuse me for speaking plainly, sir, but it doesn't matter what you think. Allow me to see the owner and I'll be very happy to put myself forward.'

The clerk, bald and with a nervous tic, blinked and swallowed hard. 'The owner leaves the business side of matters to us.'

'Nevertheless I would like to see him. Who is he and where will I find him?' She had unintentionally raised her voice and a door at the back of the office opened to reveal a portly, red-faced man wearing a mustard-coloured waistcoat and a checked suit. He looked as though he would be more at home on the tote at a race course than in a Bond Street office.

'Is there a problem, Shoesmith?'

'Not really, sir. This young person wishes to see the owner of the premises in Oxford Street.'

'I most certainly do,' Clara said boldly.

The sharply suited gentleman regarded her with a patronising smile. 'My name is Ambrose Plumley and I am the agent for the person in question, Miss . . . ?'

'Clara Carter, sir. Might I have a few minutes of your time?'

Shoesmith cleared his throat and stood up. 'Mr Plumley is very busy, Miss Carter.'

'It's all right, Shoesmith. I can always spare a few seconds to speak to a pretty woman. Come this way, Miss Carter.' He ushered her into his office.

'Thank you, sir.' Clara marched into the large, oak-panelled room, which was more like a comfortable sitting room than a place of business. A coal fire blazed up the chimney and gaslights fizzed and popped in the wall sconces and the brass gasolier. The kneehole desk, buttoned leather chairs and red Turkey carpet could have come straight from a gentleman's study, but the large oil painting above the mantelshelf depicting a voluptuous, scantily clad woman brought a blush to Clara's cheeks, and she averted her gaze.

'Take a seat, Miss Carter.' Plumley pulled up a chair. 'What is so urgent that you must speak to me in person?' He went to sit behind his desk, eyeing her curiously.

'I want to rent the shop in Oxford Street.' The words tumbled from Clara's lips before she had time to think of a more subtle approach.

He sat back in his chair and stared at her, his heavy jowls resting on a stiff white collar and his sandy eyebrows lowered over shrewd blue eyes. 'I like a direct answer, but the question is why do you want to take on such a burden? You are young and pretty, and if you were my daughter I would want you to be sitting at home waiting for a suitable man to come and claim your hand in marriage.'

'That, if you don't mind me saying so, is very old-fashioned, Mr Plumley. I am a working woman and my ambition is to own a store to rival Peter Robinson and Debenham and Freebody, and there's a famous store in Paris, the name of which I've forgotten.'

'You've been to Paris?'

'No, sir, but that's one of my ambitions. I've read about it and I would dearly love to bring something like that to London. A department store should be a place of wonder and provide an exciting experience. It should smell of expensive perfume, and there must be colour and beauty for everyone to enjoy.'

Plumley's expression was unreadable. 'How would you propose to finance such a venture? Are you a wealthy woman?'

Clara shook her head. 'If I were I doubt if I would be here now. I would use my fortune to further my ambitions, or else I might simply sit at home and enjoy being waited upon by women who have no alternative other than to satisfy the whims of rich people.'

'Aha, you are a little revolutionary.'

'Not at all, sir. I just want to bring luxuries within the reach of ordinary men and women. I have to work to support my family, so I understand the hopes and dreams of us lesser folk.'

'Would you like to explain that further?'

'I don't think my personal situation has anything to do with my desire to rent the premises. As far as I've seen, the shop is run down and badly in need of renovation and restoration. It will take hard work and won't happen overnight, but in my hands it will become a London landmark.'

'You are very confident.'

'Yes, sir. I am. I know I can do it – I just need the opportunity to prove myself. How much is the rent, and when can I move in?'

He folded his hands over his corpulent belly, eyeing her thoughtfully. 'I am the agent for the person who owns the property and many others in the street. I think you two should meet.'

'That suits me. May I see him today?'

'As it happens I have an appointment to see *her* this afternoon. I was about to leave when you arrived.'

'Her?' Clara stared at him in amazement. 'It's a woman?'

'A lady, no less.' Plumley rose to his feet. 'Come with me. This should be very interesting.'

The cab drew up outside an elegant mansion in Berkeley Square and Plumley climbed down to the pavement, puffing with the exertion. Clara was certain she heard the creak of whalebone, suggesting that he was wearing a corset, and she stifled a giggle as she stepped onto the pavement. He tossed a coin to the cabby and marched up the steps to knock on the door. They were admitted by a liveried footman and shown into a reception room on the ground floor. Plumley paced up and down, but Clara perched on the edge of a chair, taking in the details of the hand-painted wallpaper and the richly patterned carpet, the colours of which were duplicated in the upholstery of the French-style furnishings. Despite the bleak February weather there were vases spilling over with hothouse flowers and the heady perfume of white lilies lingered in the air. Clara could have spent a whole day just sitting and appreciating her surroundings, from the dainty ormolu clock and garniture on the mantelshelf, to the gilt-framed oil paintings on the walls, but her reverie was interrupted by the appearance of the butler.

'Lady Quinn will see you now.'

Plumley leaped to attention, smoothing his bushy hair into place with a flick of his plump fingers. He motioned Clara to follow him as he hurried after the butler. Clara could not wait to see more of the house, and she felt extremely privileged as they were led up the grand staircase instead of the back stairs used by the underlings. Her clothes were still damp from the soaking she had received that morning, and the hem of her skirt was muddied, but she held her head high as she entered the drawing room.

The curtains were drawn together, and the room was lit by dozens of expensive wax candles adding to the heat from the fire blazing up the chimney. The cloying scent of patchouli, orris root and bergamot added to the fug.

'Mr Plumley, my lady, and a young person.' The butler bowed and backed out of the room, closing the double doors behind him.

'Come closer, Plumley. I can't see you.' The voice from the wingback chair set close to the fire was high-pitched and querulous. 'Who have you brought to see me?'

Plumley scuttled across the room, bowing obsequiously. 'I took the liberty of bringing a prospective tenant for the premises in Oxford Street, my lady.'

A hand shot out from the deep velvet upholstery of the chair, and a bony finger wagged at Plumley. 'Stop fawning, man. I can't stand toadies. Who is this fellow, anyway?'

Plumley was purple in the face by this time and Clara would not have been surprised to see him foaming at the mouth. Her curiosity aroused, she moved quickly to stand by his side.

'I am your prospective tenant, my lady. My name is Clara Carter and I am at present the proprietor of a drapery in Drury Lane.'

Bird-like brown eyes glared at her from a thin face with skin drawn sharply over high cheekbones and an aquiline nose. It was an arresting face. Lady Quinn was handsome rather than beautiful and she could have been any age between forty and sixty. 'A girl? You've brought me a chit of a girl, Plumley? What were you thinking of? Have you lost what little mind you have?'

'No, my lady. I mean, I was impressed by Miss Carter's attitude and ambition for . . .'

The hand was raised in a gesture that made him falter to a halt. 'I'm not interested in your opinion. Let the girl speak for herself.'

Clara drew herself up to her full height. 'I intend to begin in a small way, my lady. If the rent is reasonable I am willing to pay two months in advance, and for that I would want complete freedom to run the business as I see fit.'

The knowing brown eyes seemed to bore into her soul during the silence that followed. Lady Quinn tapped her thin lips with her forefinger. 'And what would you consider to be a reasonable rent, young woman?'

'What had you in mind?' Clara refused to be

cowed by age and the trappings of wealth and privilege.

'I don't deal in vulgar commerce. I leave that to my agent.' Lady Quinn glared at Plumley, who had loosened his tie and was sweating visibly. 'What are we asking, Plumley?'

'I – I haven't got the figures with me, my lady.'

'You are an idiot,' Lady Quinn snapped. 'I've a good mind to dispense with your services and hire a man with a brain.' She leaned back against the cushions in her chair. 'Tell me what you intend to do with the premises, Miss Carter. That is, after your modest beginning. You seem to have ambition, so I'd like to hear more. Pull up a stool and talk to me.'

Plumley shifted from one foot to the other. 'Might I explain, my lady? I think I have a better grasp of—'

'Be quiet, Plumley. I don't want to listen to you prattling away. Go downstairs and wait there for Miss Carter. And tell Baxter to send tea and cake to the drawing room, and a glass of Madeira.' She dismissed him with an imperious wave of her hand and he backed away, bowing as if he were in the presence of royalty.

Clara felt quite sorry for him as he left the room, his head drooping and all his bluster blown away by Lady Quinn's biting comments. Clara pulled up a stool and sat down.

'What do you want to know, my lady?'

*

An hour later, after being treated to a thorough cross-examination, interspersed with sips of tea and bites of delicious seed cake, Clara left the drawing room with Lady Quinn's permission to take over the tenancy in Oxford Street. But there were certain conditions to which Clara had agreed, the main one being that Lady Quinn was to be kept informed of the progress of The Button Box, as Clara had insisted it should be called, and that Lady Quinn would have the final say in any schemes that Clara might want to instigate. It was a small price to pay for a new beginning.

'What did she say?' Plumley demanded angrily when Clara joined him in the entrance hall.

'She said she wants to speak to you, Mr Plumley.'

'So she's turned you down?' he said smugly.

'On the contrary, she's agreed to everything I suggested. She wants to see you now so that you can draw up a rental agreement with the terms she dictates. I'll wait for you here, shall I? We can share a cab as far as Bond Street.'

'Where are you going to find the money for the rent?' Plumley demanded suspiciously. 'You don't look very prosperous.'

'I've had an offer to buy the shop,' Clara said airily, 'and I intend to accept it, but first I want to see what I'm getting for my money.'

'You want to look round the premises?'

'Of course. It will be our home as well as a place

of business. My sisters have a right to see what we're taking on.'

He smacked his hand on his forehead. 'Don't tell me that there are more of you.'

'Three more to be exact, although Lizzie has a living-in position with the Comerfords in Bedford Square.'

'You are acquainted with the Comerford family?' His expression changed subtly.

Clara could see that he was impressed. 'As a matter of fact Joss Comerford offered to go into business with me.'

'That's very interesting.' He made for the stairs. 'I must see what Lady Quinn has to say. Wait for me here.'

First thing next morning, accompanied by Jane and Betsy, Clara stood outside the shop in Oxford Street. Her hand shook as she inserted the key in the lock. So much depended upon what they would find when they entered the building.

Betsy nudged her in the ribs. 'Hurry up. I've got to be at work in an hour.'

'I can't wait to see inside,' Jane said excitedly. 'It must be huge compared to Miss Silver's shop. Do you think there's a proper kitchen with a range and a sink?'

Clara turned the key and opened the door. 'We're about to find out.' She covered her nose and mouth with her hand as a waft of stale air enveloped them. The bare floorboards were littered with yellowed flyers and rat droppings. Cockroaches scuttled for cover as the girls entered the building and a rat disappeared into a hole in the skirting board. Despite the litter everywhere it was obvious that the premises were of a reasonable size. A wide staircase led to the upper floors and an archway led to what seemed to have been a large storeroom. Beyond that, and to Jane's obvious delight, was a large kitchen with a rusty cast-iron range, a chipped stone sink and a deal table surrounded by oddly assorted wooden chairs. The various cupboards had seen better days and some of the doors hung limply from broken hinges.

'It's a mess,' Betsy said, wrinkling her nose in disgust.

'But it could be cleaned up.' Jane fingered the range lovingly. 'A wire brush and some elbow grease and the application of black lead – this could be working within hours.' She limped over to the sink. 'And there's a cold water tap. No going out into the yard to collect snow when the pump is frozen.'

Clara went to open the back door. The yard was half hidden beneath crates, boxes and all manner of rubbish. 'I don't know how whoever was here last managed to get to the privy,' she said, chuckling. 'But it could be cleared and I think there's a service alley at the back. It's still too dark to see the gate, but there must be one. There's no shortage of fire-wood.'

'Let's look upstairs,' Betsy said urgently. 'I really must go soon, Clara. Miss Lavelle will sack me if I'm late.'

'Let her.' Clara tossed her head. 'I want you here with me, Betsy, and you too, Jane. The Carter sisters' store will be the best in Oxford Street. We'll have our own millinery department, of which you will be the head, Betsy.'

'I'll believe it when it happens.' Betsy headed for the door. 'Come on. I want to see everything before I go.'

The first and second floors were in an equal state of chaos, but the rooms were large and Clara could imagine a palace of delights, filled with exciting merchandise. They would start off with haberdashery, household linen and fabrics, but she had her heart set on a perfumery, too, and a department selling gloves and hats. Later on, if things went to plan, they would stock ready-made garments, bringing Paris fashion to London at prices that ordinary women could afford.

'Where will we live?' Betsy demanded, bringing Clara out of her dream so rapidly that she stood for a moment, blinking at the mess that surrounded them.

'We haven't seen the top floor yet,' Clara said dazedly. 'Let's go and have a look.' She glanced anxiously at her youngest sister. 'Are you all right, Jane? All these stairs must be very hard for you.'

Pale, but determined, Jane managed a smile. 'I'm fine. Lead on.'

The staircase to the top floor was at the back of the building, reminiscent of the servants' stairs in big houses. It was narrow and dark, opening out into a long corridor with rooms on either side. These spaces seemed to have been used for storage and there was an assortment of empty boxes, broken chairs, several iron bedsteads and some stained flock-filled mattresses, with a few dusty chamber pots for good measure and a rusty birdcage. Light filtered through dormer windows and cobwebs hung from the ceilings.

The last room was locked. Clara rattled the handle. 'That's funny. It seems to be locked from the inside.'

'Maybe it's just stuck.' Betsy put her shoulder to the door and almost fell inside as it opened suddenly and a wild-eyed creature, dressed entirely in black, flew out of the room and collapsed onto the dusty floor.

Chapter Eight

Jane's scream echoed throughout the building, and Betsy swore in a most unladylike way as she leaped aside. Clara's heart was thudding wildly as she stared at the shivering heap at her feet. At first she had thought it was a phantom, but the whimpering sounds and the smell of an unwashed body were enough to convince her that the sobbing mass was human. She bent down to lay her hand on the woman's shoulder.

'It's all right,' she said gently. 'We won't hurt you.'

'What is it?' Jane whispered. 'Is it a ghost?'

'She's real enough, and she smells awful.' Betsy took a step backwards. 'Maybe she got left behind when the last people moved out.'

Clara had to brace herself in order to lift the woman to her feet. 'You're not in any trouble,' she said firmly. 'What's your name?'

The woman raised her head, peering at Clara with eyes the colour of melted chocolate, which looked even more startling in a pale but filthy face. Her dark hair was mattered and hung lankly to her shoulders. 'Gertrude,' she muttered, her cracked lips bleeding with the effort to frame the words.

'What's she doing here?' Betsy demanded. 'Ask her, Clara.'

'I think we'd best get her downstairs where it's a bit warmer,' Clara said, making an effort to sound calm and in control of the situation. 'She looks ill and half starved.' She reached out to take the terrified creature by the hand. 'Come with me.'

Gertrude struggled feebly, but she had little more strength than a kitten, and when they reached the kitchen she collapsed onto a wooden chair, burying her head in her hands.

'She's a wild woman,' Jane said in a whisper.

Clara shook her head. 'She's just scared.' She turned to Betsy, who was hovering by the door. 'She needs something to eat and a hot drink. I saw a coffee stall in one of the side streets. Will you go?'

'I can't, Clara. I've got to go to work. You know what Miss Lavelle's like.'

'I'll go,' Jane volunteered. 'I'm hungry, too.'

Clara opened her reticule, and found to her dismay that her small supply of money was almost exhausted. She had hoped there would be enough for the cab fare back to Drury Lane, but she could not abandon the poor creature, who was now sobbing loudly. 'I'll go if you two will stay here with Gertrude.'

Betsy and Jane exchanged horrified glances.

'I'll go,' Betsy said reluctantly. 'Give me the money and I'll be as quick as I can. Miss Lavelle will have to wait.'

'But she might give you the sack,' Jane protested. 'Let me go. I'll manage somehow.'

'Miss Lavelle needs me to finish off a hat for an important customer, so she won't be pleased, but she can't do without me.' Betsy took the coins from Clara and made for the shop door. 'I'll be as quick as I can.'

'What are we going to do with her?' Jane shot a wary glance at Gertrude, who was rocking to and fro on the hard wooden seat, her sobs interspersed with hiccups.

'I don't know, but the first thing is to find out who she is and why she's here. Perhaps she'll be more talkative after she's had something to eat. We'll wait until Betsy returns with the food.'

Jane sank down on an upturned crate, resting her crutch against the kitchen table. 'I hope she brings enough for us as well. My tummy is rumbling.'

'Mine, too,' Clara said, smiling. She moved cautiously to stand beside Gertrude and touched her gently on the shoulder. 'You'll feel much better when you've eaten, and perhaps you can tell us something about yourself?'

Gertrude huddled into a ball with her arms wrapped around her knees and her sobs grew louder. Clara leaned against the table, her arms folded. The shop had seemed ideal for her needs, but finding this strange woman in residence posed a problem. She waited anxiously for Betsy's return, taking the time to explore the kitchen cupboards, where she found oddments of china. There were cups, some of them without handles, and a few chipped glass tumblers half-hidden beneath a mesh of spiders' webs. She washed the cups in cold water and left them to dry on the wooden draining board.

After what felt like an eternity, with Gertrude rocking and moaning and Jane growing ever more agitated, Betsy arrived with two mugs of coffee and a couple of ham rolls. 'I didn't have enough money to get one each,' she explained. 'I had to put a half-penny deposit on the mugs but we'll get that back.'

'That's all right.' Clara poured some of the coffee into one of the clean cups and offered it to Gertrude. 'Drink this; it will make you feel better.'

Gertrude snatched the cup from her and drained the rapidly cooling coffee in two thirsty gulps. She peered up at Clara through a tangle of matted dark hair. 'Hungry.'

Clara divided one of the rolls in half and handed it to her. 'There you are, Gertrude.'

'She's a savage,' Betsy said, frowning.

'She's hungry.' Clara watched Gertrude devour the

food as if she had not eaten for days. 'Who are you?' she asked. 'Why are you living like this, Gertrude?'

'Who wants to know?' Gertrude glared at her, licking her dirty fingers one by one. 'Why are you here?'

'My name is Clara Carter and I'm the new proprietor, and these are my sisters, Betsy and Jane.'

'I'm off. I can't stay any longer.' Betsy picked up the empty mugs. 'I'll return these. It's on my way.' She wrapped her shawl around her shoulders and, with a final despairing glance in Gertrude's direction, she hurried from the room.

'I had a sister once.' Gertrude cackled with laughter. 'A fine sister she was.'

'Have you any other family?' Clara asked anxiously. 'I don't want to sound harsh, but you can't remain here.'

Gertrude seemed to shrink into the chair. 'I haven't got anywhere else to go. You wouldn't turn a sick woman out onto the street, would you?'

'Does Mr Plumley know you're here?'

'Who's he?'

'He's Lady Quinn's agent.'

Gertrude tumbled off the chair and scuttled into a corner on all fours. 'Don't tell her I'm here. For God's sake, don't tell her.'

'Do you know Lady Quinn?'

'I'm Gertrude Batt. She mustn't know I'm here.'

Clara walked slowly towards her, holding out her hand. 'Don't be scared.' She lifted Gertrude to her feet. 'Why don't you want Lady Quinn to know you're here?'

'She turned me out, the heartless bitch. She doesn't care if I live or die.'

'All right, don't upset yourself, Gertrude. We're leaving now, but we'll be back again soon. You can stay here in the meantime.'

Gertrude clutched Clara's arm, digging her fingers into the soft flesh. 'Promise you won't tell her.'

'I promise.' Clara helped her back to the chair. 'I'll bring more food tomorrow. Jane and I are going now.'

Jane raised herself with the aid of her crutch. 'I'm ready. I don't think I like this place.'

'It will be fine, with a bit of hard work.' Clara made her way through the litter on the shop floor. It would take more than a little effort to get the place into shape, but anything was possible.

As she stepped out onto the pavement she took a deep breath of cold air. The street might reek of horse dung and blocked drains, but it was country fresh in comparison to the smell of Gertrude's unwashed body and tattered garments. 'That woman needs a bath and some clean clothes,' Clara said thoughtfully.

'What are you going to do?' Jane demanded. 'If you're serious about taking the shop we'll have to get her out. Can you imagine what customers would think if they saw her?'

'I'm going to see Mr Plumley. Gertrude says she doesn't know him, but perhaps he can give me an idea of who she is and how we can find someone to take care of her.' She linked her hand through her sister's arm. 'Come on, we'll go to Bond Street. At least Mr Plumley's office is warm and clean.'

Ambrose Plumley painted a smile on his face, but his eyes were wary. 'So what have you decided, Miss Carter? Are you going to take up the challenge?'

Clara leaned forward, facing him squarely over the tooled-leather top of his desk. 'I am, although we'll have to agree on the rent, and there is another thing. Have you heard of a woman called Gertrude Batt?'

Plumley's florid cheeks deepened in colour. 'What do you know of Gertie?'

'Who is she?'

'She's dead, or so I was led to believe.'

'Was she employed by Lady Quinn?'

'Employed by her?' Plumley threw his head back and laughed. 'That's a good one.'

Clara glanced at Jane, who was warming herself by the fire, and Jane shrugged in response.

'Won't you let us in on the joke?' Clara asked.

'Before she got her hooks into Sir Freddie, Lady Quinn was Miss Garland Batt, the elder daughter of a wealthy mill owner, and a noted beauty.'

Clara stared at him in amazement. 'Gertrude Batt is her sister?'

'That's right. Gertie was her father's favourite and he spoiled her. She was the child of his second marriage and there was fifteen years' difference in the girls' ages. Gertie was only ten when their father died and it was left to Garland to bring her up.'

'Good heavens,' Clara said slowly. 'That must have been difficult.'

Plumley nodded. 'Garland married a baronet and packed Gertie off to school in Paris. I think she wanted to get her out of the way, and when she was fifteen Gertie ran off with a libertine twice her age. Gertie's mother had left her money in trust with a generous income until she could inherit at the age of twenty-one, but when that dried up the fellow abandoned her. She took to the streets, but was spotted by a man who procured young and beautiful women for immoral purposes. I won't offend your sensibilities by going into detail, but Gertie attracted a series of wealthy, titled gentlemen who showered her with jewels and gifts of all kinds. She became a courtesan of some note.'

Clara shook her head. 'That doesn't sound like the person I'm thinking of, Mr Plumley.'

He rested his elbow on the desk, fixing her with a penetrating stare. 'How do you know Gertie Batt?'

'I'm not at all certain, but I think she's living in one of the attics above the shop in Oxford Street.

Although it's almost impossible to think that the woman we found could have led such a life.'

'What is she like?'

'She's crazy,' Jane said firmly. 'She's completely mad, sir.'

Clara shook her head. 'She was half-starved, cold and frightened. She was also filthy and must have been hiding in the attics for some time. But in answer to your question, I could see a definite likeness to Lady Quinn.'

The furrows on Plumley's brow deepened and his fingers tapped out a tattoo on the desk. 'I doubt if Lady Quinn will be too pleased if she finds out that her sister is back in town.'

'That's awful,' Clara said angrily. 'Gertrude is in a terrible state, Mr Plumley. She does appear to be out of her mind, but it's hardly surprising. The poor thing is all skin and bone, and in desperate need of a bath and clean clothes.'

'It's not my problem, Miss Carter, nor is it yours. I suppose her sister ought to be informed, but I'm not going to be the messenger.'

Clara stared at him in dismay. 'So if I take on the tenancy, knowing that Gertrude is in residence, she becomes my responsibility.'

'I wouldn't put it in those terms, but I suppose so.' Plumley leaned back in his chair, folding his hands on his corpulent belly. 'I need to have your decision quickly. There are others interested in the shop.'

'It seems to have been empty for a very long time,' Clara said calmly. She had no intention of allowing Ambrose Plumley to bully her into making a rash decision. 'And it's in a terrible mess. If you've been in there recently you would know how filthy it is, and there's rubbish everywhere. It will take a lot of work, and with the additional problem of Miss Batt, I'm not sure that the rent you're asking is quite fair.'

His eyes narrowed. 'Are you trying to bargain with me, Miss Carter?'

'Yes,' she said simply. 'I'm prepared to work hard and bring the premises up to a high standard, and I'll even take care of Miss Batt until she's well enough to find somewhere else to live, but I want a reduction in the rent, and then we have a deal.'

Walking home, with the signed rental agreement in her reticule, Clara felt as if her feet were barely touching the slushy surface of the paving stones. She had a ridiculous urge to throw back her head and sing, or perhaps do a little dance of sheer joy and relief. It had been an exhausting and nerve-racking time, but she had won through, and now it was up to her to make a success of the store.

Jane gave her hand a squeeze. 'I can't believe you beat him down like that, Clara.'

'I surprised myself,' Clara said, chuckling. 'But every farthing counts, and each one saved means that I have a little more money to purchase new stock. Now all I have to do is to accept the offer from Boswell and Boswell when I see Mr Wilkes tomorrow. I might even be able to persuade them to increase it.'

'You are so clever,' Jane said admiringly. 'I wish I were more like you.'

'You are perfect as you are. I'll need all your skill to help me run the millinery department when it opens. I might even be able to afford to take Betsy on as well. It would be wonderful to make The Button Box a family business.'

'The Button Box,' Jane said, savouring the words. 'Is that what you're going to call the shop?'

'Yes, and I can see the window display for the grand opening. I'll make my button box the centre-piece, with its contents spilling out onto a river of turquoise-blue satin, and I'll have sparkling buttons hanging from bare branches, with silk flowers seeming to grow from a field of green velvet.'

'It all sounds wonderful, but what are we going to do with Gertrude?'

'What, indeed? That is a problem. I'll have to think of something.' Clara wrapped her cloak around her as a cold wind whipped at her clothes and tugged mischievously at her bonnet. Gertrude was a problem, and one she could do without, but the poor, mistreated woman had had no one to help and care for her – until now. Clara tucked Jane's hand in the crook of her arm. 'We're lucky, we have each other. I think we can make room for one more, don't you?'

The next day Clara left the bank feeling like a wealthy woman. Selling Miss Silver's shop had caused her some heart-searching, but she knew that first and foremost Miss Silver had been a business-woman. She might not have been very successful, but the shop had been her life, and Clara's plans for moving the business to Oxford Street would undoubtedly have met with her approval. With money in her purse – an advance on the cheque from a reputable firm of solicitors agreed by the bank manager – Clara was set to start her new life, but first she must see what she could do for Miss Gertrude Batt.

Jane had remained at home, packing up some of their belongings in readiness for the move, leaving Clara free to start work on the new shop premises. Her first priority would be to clean the kitchen and get the range going. Hot water was an absolute necessity and when the kitchen was habitable she would turn her attention to the attic rooms, so that they could move in as soon as possible. Wilkes had given them three days to vacate the premises in Drury Lane, and that would entail working late into the evenings, and possibly all night if they were not to camp on a cockroach-infested floor.

Clara let herself into the shop and went straight

to the kitchen. It remained exactly as she had left it the previous day and there was no sign of Gertrude, not even a crust or a crumb to show that she had eaten anything other than the food they had given her. Clara took off her bonnet and cloak and made her way up to the top floor. As she had suspected, Gertrude was in the same room as before, huddled in a corner, looking terrified.

'It's me, Gertrude,' Clara said softly. 'Clara, the new owner. We met yesterday.'

Gertrude shuffled closer to the wall, burying her head between her knees. The smell in the dingy room was overpowering and Clara had to control the desire to back away, but she moved slowly across the floor, holding out her hand. 'Come with me. I've brought food for you and something hot to drink.' She had stopped at the same coffee stall that Betsy had patronised and bought rolls and coffee; she suspected that they would come to know the stall-holder very well before the kitchen was in full working order.

Gertrude lifted her head. 'Hungry.'

'I'm sure you are. Come along, there's a good girl.' Clara spoke to her as if she were a difficult child, and it seemed to have the desired effect.

Gertrude scrambled to her feet and took hold of Clara's hand. 'Is there coffee downstairs and a ham roll?'

'Yes, and we don't want the rats to get there first,

do we?' Clara led her along the narrow corridor and down the stairs, keeping up a one-sided conversation in an attempt to put Gertrude at her ease.

In the kitchen, Gertrude fell on the food and had snatched and consumed a roll before Clara had time to put it on a plate. She drank the hot coffee in several gulps before collapsing onto the nearest chair.

'I'm going to start in here,' Clara said, rolling up her sleeves. She reached for the apron she had brought with her and tied it around her slender waist. 'I'm going to get the fire going in the range.'

Gertrude's answer was to grab the roll that Clara had intended for herself. She bit into it like a ravenous hound, washing down each mouthful with Clara's coffee. Clara sighed and turned away to concentrate on clearing the ash from the firebasket. Her main priority was heating water, and her first task would be to insist that Gertrude had a wash.

A foray into the back yard produced a sack of coal and plenty of wooden crates that could be smashed up for kindling. Clara was just wondering how she was going to accomplish the task without an axe when she heard someone call her name. She looked up and was surprised to see Nathaniel, who was waving to her from the alleyway.

'You look as though you could do with some help,' he said cheerfully.

Clara picked her way through the piles of rubbish

that littered the yard and unbolted the gate. 'How did you know where to find me?'

'I called in at the shop and Jane told me you'd sold up and moved here.'

'I'm so sorry, Nathaniel. I suppose I should have consulted you first, but everything happened so quickly.'

'Silver's Drapery was yours to do with as you saw fit, but Jane was worried about you. She said there's a mad woman living in the attic and you might be in danger.'

Clara closed the gate after him. 'And you came to my rescue. How gallant, and how kind. I really am pleased to see you.'

He glanced round the cluttered yard, a frown creasing his brow. 'You've taken on a huge task. Is it as bad inside?'

'Come in and I'll show you round.' Clara hesitated. 'But first I'd be grateful if you'd smash up some tea chests. I'm in desperate need of kindling.'

He handed her his violin case. 'I think I can manage that. I'll imagine I'm stamping on the conductor's toes. He is the most unpleasant fellow I've ever met, but playing in his orchestra pays the rent.' He began demolishing a crate and in no time at all there was enough wood to light the fire.

Clara took his violin into the kitchen, leaving Nathaniel to bring the coal and kindling.

'There's someone I'd like you to meet,' Clara said,

opening the kitchen door – but the room was empty. 'She was here, but I suppose she heard your voice and panicked. She must have gone upstairs to the attic where we found her yesterday.'

Nathaniel wrinkled his nose. 'What is that awful smell?'

'I'm afraid it's Gertrude. I'll get the fire going and when I've got enough hot water I'll go and find her.'

'Who is Gertrude?'

'She's the mad woman that Jane mentioned, only she isn't mad at all. Take a seat and I'll tell you, although you might find it hard to believe.'

'I've got a better idea. Why don't you sit down for a while and I'll light the fire. It's one of my minor talents, and one I had to learn very quickly when I found myself living on my own.'

Clara gave him a grateful smile. 'If you're sure. I suppose I'd better start with when I saw the "To Let" sign in the window . . .'

It took several minutes to give him the full story, and Nathaniel set to work getting the fire blazing up the chimney while she talked.

'So you see,' Clara concluded, 'I don't know what to do about Gertrude. As her sister owns the property it would seem that Gertrude has more right to be here than I do.'

Nathaniel washed his hands at the sink, drying them on a scrap of towelling. 'I don't know about that. You say that Lady Quinn thinks her sister is dead.'

'That's what Mr Plumley told me. The sisters didn't get on well, so I doubt if her ladyship would be interested in the poor creature now. Lady Quinn struck me as a very hard woman.'

'You are the legal tenant, Clara. You have every right to evict Gertrude.'

'You haven't seen her, Nathaniel. She's a pathetic wreck of a person.'

'I'd like to meet her.'

'She's terrified of me. I don't know what she'd do if she saw a man in the kitchen.'

He picked up his violin case and opened it. 'You know what Congreve said about music having the charm to soothe a savage breast. Maybe if I play something, it will calm your wild woman.'

'You may try, but don't blame me if she shrieks and runs away.' Clara left him as he struck up a rendition of a hauntingly beautiful violin concerto.

She climbed the stairs yet again, and went to find Gertrude. The faint strains of the melody could still be heard as she opened the door to the attic room, and Gertrude lifted her head. Her expression changed subtly and she rose to her feet, moving across the floor like a sleepwalker. Clara stepped aside as Gertrude followed the sound. There was no need to persuade her to go downstairs; the music lured her like the siren's song, and she made her way slowly towards it, holding out her hands.

Nathaniel kept on playing as she approached him and, if he was shocked by her appearance, he did not betray his feelings. Clara came to a halt, watching in amazement as the music tamed the wild woman and Gertrude sank down on a chair, listening with a rapt expression on her face. She remained transfixed after the last note died away, and she sat, staring at him as if she could not take her eyes off his face. He bowed, and smiled.

'That was beautiful,' Clara said softly. 'What was it?'

'One of my favourite pieces; Mendelssohn's Violin Concerto in E minor.'

Gertrude began to clap her hands, slowly at first and then harder. 'More,' she shouted. 'Encore.'

Nathaniel crossed the floor to stand before her. 'Thank you, Miss Batt. You are a music lover.'

Gertrude appeared to shrink inside her voluminous black robe. She peered up at him. 'Who are you?'

'My name is Nathaniel Silver. I'm very pleased to meet you, Miss Batt.'

'Play something else,' Gertrude said sharply. 'Play something happy.'

He struck up a lively jig and Gertrude relaxed again, tapping her toes in time to the tune, but when the music came to an end she huddled into her shapeless garment, with a closed expression on her face. Clara placed a bowl of hot water on the table. 'It's time for your wash, Gertrude.'

'No. Get away from me.' Gertrude held her hands in front of her face, shaking her head. 'Leave me alone.'

'Perhaps you ought to go, Nathaniel,' Clara said in a whisper. 'Maybe she's shy.'

'Let me try.' Nathaniel picked up the scrap of towelling that Clara had intended to use as a flannel. 'Look at me, Gertie,' he said gently.

She raised her face and tears trickled down her cheeks, leaving pale streaks on her grimy skin.

'That's a good girl.' Nathaniel soaped the cloth and, with the utmost gentleness, began to wash Gertie's face. Clara watched in amazement; she had expected Gertrude to protest and push him away, but she sat like a well-behaved child, allowing him to wipe her face clean.

'There now,' Nathaniel said gently. 'That feels better, doesn't it, Gertie?'

She nodded wordlessly.

He rinsed the cloth and soaped it again. 'Now give me your hands, one at a time, please.'

She obeyed instantly.

'I don't know how you do it,' Clara said in a low voice, 'but you're certainly working your magic on her.'

'I was accustomed to caring for dogs and horses when I lived at home, and most creatures respond to kindness. Gertie has been ill-used, anyone can see that.'

Gertrude grabbed his hand and held it to her cheek. 'Nathaniel,' she murmured, smiling. 'I like you, boy.'

He wiped her hands on a dry cloth. 'And I like you, Gertie.' He leaned closer. 'I'm afraid I have to leave you now, but I will be back. In the meantime, I want you to behave well for Clara. She only wants to help you.'

Clara could see that Gertrude was not convinced by this. 'Must you go so soon, Nathaniel? Won't you stay a little while longer?'

'I have an urgent appointment at Silver House, otherwise I would be only too happy to stay and help.'

'Silver House?' Clara repeated. 'Where is that?'

'It's my London home. Pretentious-sounding, I know, but my forebears were in trade and they wanted everyone to know of their success.' Nathaniel stared at her thoughtfully. 'Would you like to come with me?'

Chapter Nine

'I'd love to,' Clara said eagerly, but a muffled groan from Gertrude brought her back to reality. 'But, of course, I can't. I have to stay here and work if I'm to get the shop ready for opening, and I can't abandon Gertrude.'

Nathaniel laid his hand on Gertrude's shoulder. 'This lady is quite capable of looking after herself for a few hours, aren't you, Gertie?'

Gertrude's cracked lips stretched into a smile. 'If you say so, Nathaniel.'

'I do, and I suggest you finish off what I've just started. Clara has been kind enough to give you a second chance. You must wash yourself properly. There is hot water in the kettle and soap and a towel. You can do that for me, can't you?'

'Of course,' Gertrude said sharply. 'I am not a simpleton.'

'You most certainly are not. I would like to see you at your best.' Nathaniel handed her the hairbrush that Clara had laid out, more in hope than certainty of its being used.

'It's very kind of you, Nathaniel,' Clara said reluctantly, 'but I have far too much work to do here.'

'Don't worry about that. You need a day off and I would value your company. My uncle sent for me. We didn't part on the best of terms, but I think I know why he wants to see me, and you can help.'

'Me? How could I possibly be of help to you, Nathaniel?'

'I'll explain when we're on the way.'

'But I can't come like this.' Clara glanced down at her faded linsey-woolsey skirt, and the scuffed toes of her boots peeking out beneath the muddy hem. 'I have my work dress at home, which is clean and more presentable.'

'You're perfect, just as you are.' Nathaniel caught her by the hand. 'Please come. You'll be doing me an enormous favour.'

The hackney drew to a halt outside one of the elegant five-storey terraced houses in Eaton Square. Nathaniel leaped to the ground and held his hand out to help Clara alight.

'I don't know what I'm doing here,' she said anxiously. 'These houses are so grand. I wish I'd insisted on going home to change.'

He flicked a coin to the cabby and Clara's last hope of a quick escape faded as the cab drove off. 'You mustn't allow minor details to worry you, Clara,' Nathaniel said, eyeing her with an appreciative smile. 'You look beautiful no matter what you're wearing. My uncle can't fail to be impressed. Come and meet him.' He was about to mount the steps beneath a columned portico when she caught him by the sleeve.

'Wait a minute, Nathaniel. I want to know why you've brought me here. Was it simply to impress me and demonstrate how rich you'll be when you come into your inheritance?'

'No, of course not. But you're right, I should have been more open as to my motives. I was afraid if I told you the truth you might refuse to come.'

'I think you'd better explain before we go any further.'

'When you meet Uncle Septimus I think you'll understand why I've had to resort to subterfuge. He would go to any lengths to cheat me out of my inheritance. He's already contested my father's will, but that failed. I don't know why he wants to see me, although I can guess.' Nathaniel hesitated, meeting her questioning glance with a wry smile. 'As I told you, I cannot inherit until I'm twenty-five, but there is another condition.'

'What is it? Don't keep me in suspense. This is like one of the penny dreadfuls that Jane loves to read.'

'Worse than that, I should imagine. My father's will states that I must be married and prepared to settle down.'

'That seems rather unfair, but I still don't see how I can help.'

'I'll be twenty-five in October, Clara. My uncle has had my movements watched for the past six months and he knows my situation even better than I do myself. If I fail to comply with the smallest detail in the will I forfeit my right to inherit my father's estate.'

'Are you asking me to pretend to be your fiancée?'

Colour flooded Nathaniel's pale cheeks and he met Clara's enquiring gaze with an apologetic grin. 'I know I've made a mess of things, but his unexpected summons took me by surprise, and you were the first person who came into my thoughts. I'm sorry, Clara. I'll understand if you want to leave now. I shouldn't have imposed on your good nature.'

'Wait a minute,' Clara said, frowning. 'Why do you think your uncle would believe such a tale? I look like a drab and he'll think I'm an adventuress, out for what I can get. He would see through your story in an instant.'

'He would see you for what you are, Clara. Brave and beautiful and honest to a fault. Aunt Rebecca trusted you and left you everything she had in the world. You are a businesswoman in your own right, and one day you'll be a huge success – I have no doubt about that whatsoever – but I'm a struggling musician and, if anything, I'm unworthy of you.'

'That was quite a speech, Nathaniel.' There was no doubting his sincerity but it was disconcerting, and Clara covered her embarrassment with a chuckle. 'How could I refuse after such a commendation?' She stood on tiptoe to kiss him on the cheek. 'Ring the bell and let's face your uncle together.'

'You'd do this for me?'

'I think your aunt would want me to stand by you. It's the least I can do for the Silver family.'

'Thank you, Clara.' Nathaniel rang the bell.

'Just a minute,' Clara said hastily. 'Your uncle won't believe that we're engaged if I don't have a ring. What will you say to him?'

'I didn't think of that.' Nathaniel took a signet ring off the small finger of his right hand. 'Will this do?' He dropped it into her outstretched hand.

The tiny, gypsy-set diamond winked at her. 'It's very pretty.'

'It belonged to my mother,' he said softly. 'See if it fits.'

The ring slipped onto her finger as if it were made for her, but she panicked and was about to take it off when the door was opened by a liveried footman.

'Good morning, Franklin. Is the master at home?'
'I'll tell him you're here, sir.'

Nathaniel ushered Clara over the threshold. 'We'll wait in the morning room, Franklin.' He crossed the hallway and opened the door to a large room where the furniture was swathed in holland covers. Dust motes danced in the sunbeams that filtered through tall windows and there was an icy chill in the air.

'My uncle is only interested in country sports,' Nathaniel said apologetically. 'As you can see, he doesn't spend much time in London.'

'I can't understand why you aren't allowed to live here.' Clara gazed in awe at the ornate plasterwork on the cornices and the marble mantelpiece supported by carved caryatids. The thick carpets and softly hued curtains spoke of money and good taste, and yet Nathaniel's uncle was behaving like the worst sort of miser, keeping everything for himself.

'My father and his brother were always at loggerheads,' Nathaniel said sadly. 'They were complete opposites in every sense. My father was artistic and loved music and the theatre, while Uncle Septimus lived for hunting and attending shoots. When the season ended he would travel to India to kill tigers or to France to hunt wild boar—' He broke off as the door opened and a tall, broad-shouldered man strode into the room.

'So you came, Nathaniel. I doubted you would.' Septimus Silver's voice matched his physique and it echoed round the room. He stared at Clara, looking her up and down with a calculating expression in his pale grey eyes. 'So you bribed a maidservant to accept the hand of a penniless musician. Well done, boy.'

Nathaniel slipped a protective arm around Clara's shoulders. 'Insult me, if you like, Uncle, but Clara is above reproach, and she most certainly isn't in service. She's a businesswoman.'

'Not a very successful one, judging by her appearance.' Septimus dragged a cover off the nearest chair and sat down, sprawling his legs out in front of him. 'Aren't you going to introduce us properly, boy?'

Clara stepped forward. 'I know who you are, sir. Your reputation goes before you.'

Septimus treated her to a wolfish grin. 'I like a woman of spirit.'

'Despite your lack of manners, Uncle, I would like to introduce my fiancée, Miss Clara Carter, the former owner of Silver's Drapery in Drury Lane. She is moving her business to a much larger shop in Oxford Street.'

'A shopkeeper, indeed. If this is a genuine match you aren't doing very well for yourself, boy. A young woman of birth and breeding would be more appropriate.'

'I'll wed whom I please, Uncle. I love Clara, and I intend to marry her as soon as possible.'

'In an interesting condition, is she? As my dear mother would have said.'

'No, sir. Shame on you.' Nathaniel's colour deepened and a small vein throbbed visibly in his temple.

'You, sir, are no gentleman,' Clara said angrily.

'And you are certainly no lady.' Septimus leaped to his feet. 'Look at yourself in the mirror, miss. I've seen better dressed dollymops. This is patently a pack of lies, Nathaniel. I've had you followed for months and I know that your acquaintanceship with this person began after my sister's death.'

'You didn't attend the funeral,' Nathaniel said angrily. 'You allowed Aunt Rebecca to ekc out a living in that shop. She was brought up to be a lady.'

'Trade is in the blood, though thank God it's well diluted in mine. Your aunt chose the way in which she wanted to live. Your father and I tried to dissuade her, and that's about the only thing upon which we agreed.'

'I don't know the whole story,' Nathaniel said bitterly. 'But she deserved better.'

'She turned her back on the family when she went to live with a married man, who abandoned her and went back to his wife. I wouldn't have given her a penny piece, but your father was always an easy mark. He set her up in the shop, so by rights it should have come to you. You're weak like your father, Nathaniel. This little minx has got you where she wants you and you'll end up with nothing, just like your aunt.'

Nathaniel gave his uncle a mighty shove, catching him off guard, and Septimus staggered backwards and fell into the chair, tipping it over so that he landed with his legs in the air. For a few moments he remained on his back, flailing about like an upturned beetle, until he managed to right himself. He staggered to his feet, red in the face and seething with anger. 'A lucky punch, Nathaniel. I could thrash you like the puppy you are if I so chose, but I have other ways of punishing a recalcitrant boy.'

'I'm not scared of you, Uncle.' Nathaniel reached out to take Clara by the hand. 'We're leaving now. I have nothing further to say to you.'

'Your sham engagement doesn't fool me, so you'd better think again. Time is running out for you, my boy.'

Clara could feel the tension in Nathaniel's fingers as they tightened around her hand. 'Let's get out of here,' she said hastily. 'This isn't getting you anywhere.'

Nathaniel did not speak until they were outside on the pavement. He gave her an apologetic smile. 'I'm so sorry to put you through that, Clara. I should have known how it would turn out.'

'It's all right. I understand better now I've met your uncle. You mustn't give up, Nathaniel.'

He stared at her, eyebrows raised. 'You think not?'

'Most definitely,' she said firmly. 'If that is your town house, I can't imagine what the one in the country must be like, and your father wanted you to have everything. What I don't understand is why he made so many conditions.'

'He didn't approve of my ambition to be a professional musician. He thought that being a composer was only one step up from being a poet and living a dissolute life like Lord Byron and his friends.'

'But you said he loved music and the theatre.'

'He did, but he expected me to take over the family business, even though he hated the world of commerce.'

'It must be a very successful undertaking if it bought your family a house like this.'

'It started a long time ago, Clara. My great-great-grandfather Henri da Silva was a silk weaver who fled from France with many other Huguenots and settled in Spitalfields, where he found work. Eventually he bought his own loom and built up a successful business.'

Clara shivered as an icy wind hurtled round the square like a band of rowdy hooligans, tossing bits of straw into the air and tugging at her bonnet. 'But how did they come to own a country estate?'

'My great-grandfather was a handsome fellow, by all accounts. He was delivering a bolt of silk to a grand house in Grosvenor Square when he met and fell in love with the rich man's daughter.'

'It sounds like a fairy tale.'

Nathaniel stepped to the edge of the kerb to hail a passing hansom cab. He helped Clara to take a seat and climbed in beside her. 'It was a love match, but my great-grandmother's father was against the marriage and the couple eloped to Gretna Green. It was only when my grandfather was born that Sir Henry Martingale acknowledged their union and finally gave it his blessing. He gave them a large house in the country with several acres of parkland.'

'Did your great-grandfather live the life of a gentleman?'

Nathaniel shook his head. 'He was a born businessman and he could see that the silk industry was on the wane due to cheap imports, so he bought a couple of ships and became an importer. He changed the family name to Silver and concentrated on making his fortune. It was he who purchased the town house in Eaton Square.'

'And did your father inherit his forebears' talent for commerce?'

'Ah, there you have it, Clara. My father was a dreamer with no head for business, and Uncle Septimus had no interest in trade. He wanted to live like a country gentleman.'

'So what happened to the family fortune?'

'My grandfather could see the way things were going. He sold off most of his assets and invested the money in the stock market, but he kept a couple of warehouses in Wapping and continued to import goods, but on a much smaller scale. Uncle Septimus put a manager in charge after my father died, but to the best of my knowledge he's allowed the fellow to do as he pleases. I suspect that he's lining his own pockets at our expense.'

'And is there nothing you can do until you come of age?'

'My hands are tied. I have no authority to change things, and I doubt if I would be any good in the commercial world.'

'You don't know until you try, Nathaniel.'

'Music is my life, but I'll do my best to salvage what I can of the business. Whatever happens I'll continue to compose, and I never had ambitions to perform before an audience. That was thrust upon me by circumstances.'

'Gertrude loves to hear you play,' Clara said, smiling.

'Yes, that was quite a revelation. I feel sorry for the poor woman.'

'Who knows what she's been up to since we left her? I shouldn't have left her on her own.'

'I am so sorry I put you through the unpleasant scene this morning. I didn't imagine that my uncle would react so rudely.'

Clara patted his hand as it rested on his knee. 'You mustn't worry about me, Nathaniel. As a matter of fact it's been a welcome change from worrying about how I'm going to cope with the shop, and Gertrude, not to mention my sisters.'

'I am free during the day. I could help you with some of the heavy work.'

'I couldn't ask you to do that.'

'Why not? I've just coerced you into pretending to be my fiancée. I think it's the least I can do to make up for my uncle's rudeness, not to mention my violent reaction.' He shot her a sideways glance. 'I'm not normally a rough fellow.'

She squeezed his fingers. 'I know that, Nathaniel. You were provoked, and if I'd been a man in your position I'd have done the same thing.' She took the ring from her finger. 'You must have this back.'

'You are an amazing girl, Clara. I'd like you to keep it, and I know my mother would have approved.'

'But it means a lot to you. It wouldn't be right.'

'It looks better on you than it does on me, and I might be tempted to pawn it again if things get tough. Keep it for me until better times.'

She replaced it, but this time it was on her right hand. 'I'll look after it until you're in a position to take it back.'

'Thank you, Clara. It's a pity I'm not in a position to offer you my worldly goods, but at the moment they consist of a few clothes and my violin.'

'Friendship is the most valuable commodity,' Clara said gently. 'I need a good friend.'

'What has happened to Luke Foyle? I thought you two were close.'

The question was so sudden that Clara's breath hitched in her throat. She had tried to put Luke out of her mind. He had been a part of her life for a long time, and his sudden departure had left a gap in her life and an ache in her heart. She stared straight ahead as if the horse's head and ears were the most interesting sight in London. 'He had to go away,' she said after a brief pause, 'and I haven't heard from him since.'

'But you miss him?' It was more a statement than a question, but the words hung in the cold air, separating them like a brick wall.

'He's an old friend. I've known him for several years, but I can't condone his involvement with the gangs.'

'I'm glad,' Nathaniel said simply.

'We're here.' Clara made a move to climb down first as the cab pulled up outside the shop, but Nathaniel was too quick for her and he alighted, proffering his hand as she stepped down to the pavement. He paid the cabby and followed Clara to the door.

'I can spare an hour or two, if you'd like some help.'

She turned the key in the lock and went inside. 'You don't have to, Nathaniel. I can manage.'

'I'm sure you're more than capable, but I'm at a

loose end and it's started to rain. I can't risk ruining my violin in such weather. I left it here, anyway.'

'Of course I'd be glad of another pair of hands. Are you any good with a broom?'

'I'm an expert,' he said, chuckling. 'And I'm sorry if I spoke out of turn. It was none of my business.'

Clara headed for the kitchen. 'I wonder what Gertrude is doing. I might need you to play for her again if she gets upset.'

'It would be my pleasure. At least she doesn't heckle, like some of my audience on the street.'

Clara entered the kitchen to find the fire burning brightly in the range and a kettle singing on the hob. Jane was at the sink washing crockery and she turned her head, greeting them with a smile. 'That strange woman let me in.'

'But I've got the key,' Clara protested.

'She must have a duplicate,' Jane said cheerfully. 'Otherwise I would have had to go home. She said you'd gone off with the man who plays wonderful music, so I knew it had to be Nathaniel. Where have you been?'

'Where is Gertrude now?' Clara asked anxiously.

'She's gone back to her room. I told her we'd make it more comfortable for her.' Jane wiped her hands on her pinafore. 'Sit down and I'll make some tea. You both look as though you need a hot drink. It's a pity I didn't have any money for food, but tea is quite filling.'

Nathaniel picked up his violin case and opened it. 'It's all right,' he said, closing it with a sigh of relief. 'Thank goodness. I was afraid that Gertie might have meddled with it.'

'She's quite sensible today.' Jane warmed the teapot and tipped the water into the sink. 'She looked a bit cleaner too, although she could do with a proper bath. I'm afraid she still smells awful.'

'Just don't ask me to play an accompaniment while she's being bathed.' Nathaniel made a move towards the door. 'I'll go out and get us something to eat.' He held up his hand as Clara opened her mouth to protest. 'It's the least I can do after the morning you've had. I won't be long.' His footsteps faded as he reached the shop and the bell jangled on its spring as he opened the door, and closed it again with a thud.

'What was that all about?' Jane demanded, her hand poised above the tea caddy.

'Make the tea and I'll tell you.' Clara took off her bonnet and shawl. 'It's not every day that a girl gets engaged and then breaks it off within the hour.'

'No!' Jane's blue eyes widened. 'He proposed to you?'

'Not exactly.' Clara pulled up a chair and sat down. 'Is there any sugar? I've had such a morning, I feel I deserve a small treat.'

Nathaniel returned just as Clara finished giving Jane the bare details of their trip to Eaton Square.

The aroma of hot meat pies filled the kitchen and Nathaniel placed the paper package on the table. 'I brought one for Gertie. Shall I take it up to her?'

'No need,' Clara said, jerking her head in the direction of the doorway.

Gertrude was leaning against the jamb, her wild hair tumbling over her shoulders and half-obscuring her face, but a slow smile transformed her features as she sniffed the air like a hungry hound. 'I haven't had a hot pie for so long I've quite forgotten how they taste.'

Nathaniel picked up one of the chipped plates that Jane had put out for their use and placed a pie on it. 'Come and join us, Gertie.'

She grabbed the food and backed into the store-room, as if afraid that he might change his mind and take it off her.

Clara made a move to follow her. 'I ought to make sure she's all right.'

Nathaniel shrugged. 'She'll be fine. Let's eat. I'm starving.'

'We must save a pie for Betsy.' Jane eased herself onto a chair at the table. 'As soon as the oven is clean we can start cooking our own food.'

Clara sat down opposite her, putting Gertrude out of her mind, and helped herself to a pie. 'I have a plan in mind. We'll clear the shop floor today and clean it up as much as possible. Nathaniel has offered to help, and that will leave me free to start on the top floor. If we can move our beds over tomorrow we'll be able to move in, and then the work will begin in earnest.'

Jane clapped her hands, her eyes sparkling with excitement. 'I can't wait to have a room of my own.'

'You can't have mine. You won't get rid of me so easily.' Gertrude reappeared, wiping her lips on her sleeve. 'That was a good pie. I haven't eaten so well for a long time.'

Clara gave her a calculating look. 'You could help us, if you were so minded, Gertrude. We're going to live here and you are welcome to stay, but you'd have to earn your bread and butter.'

Gertrude uttered a hoot of laughter. 'Haven't I always? You don't know what I've had to do in order to survive.'

Nathaniel pulled up a chair. 'Why don't you sit down, Gertie?'

'Yes,' Clara said. 'Have a cup of tea and tell us about yourself. I know you're Lady Quinn's sister.'

Gertrude took a step backwards, her eyes narrowed to slits. 'Does she know I'm here?'

'I haven't told her anything. In fact I've only met her once and your name didn't come up in conversation.' Clara patted the wooden seat of the chair next to her. 'Take a seat and join us, and I'll tell you what I have in mind for the shop.'

Gertrude sidled closer. 'Have I your word that you won't tell Garland that I'm here?'

'Of course,' Clara said, nodding.

'What about you, young man?' Gertrude turned her attention to Nathaniel.

He nodded. 'I've never met the lady, and I doubt if I ever will.'

Gertrude seemed to accept this and she fixed her gaze on Jane. 'Will you keep my secret, girl?'

Jane's cheek flamed with colour. 'My name is Jane, and I will keep your secret, but you have to behave yourself and, even more important, you must have a bath. I'm sorry to say so, Gertrude, but you smell terrible.'

Clara held her breath. For a moment it looked as though Gertrude had taken offence, but then she threw back her head and laughed. 'You are a saucy minx, but I could do with a dip in a nice hot bath, and a change of clothes. I've been hiding out for so long that I've almost forgotten how to live with other people.'

'Perhaps that ought to be our first task,' Clara said hastily. 'We can heat several pans of water at a time, and I saw a zinc tub hanging on the wall in the back yard.'

Gertrude sipped tea from the cup that Jane had poured for her. 'I'll have a bath, but only if he will play for me.' She shot a sideways glance at Nathaniel. 'Would you do that for me, boy?'

He nodded. 'I will, but only if you promise to stop calling me "boy". My name, as you know, is Nathaniel.'

'I'll call you Nat,' Gertrude said firmly. 'You've been calling me Gertie, so that makes us equal. I've had vast experience of men, young and old, so don't try to hoodwink me.'

'I wouldn't dream of it, Gertie.'

Clara finished her pie and rose to her feet. 'Now we understand each other I'm going to fetch the water. Perhaps you'd be kind enough to bring the bath into the kitchen, Nathaniel?'

'You also may call me Nat if you wish.'

'I'll think about it,' Clara said, smiling. 'But you've made a conquest as far as Gertie is concerned.'

'She's not the one I want to impress.'

Clara met his shy gaze with a steady look. 'We're not really engaged, Nathaniel. It's just a show for your uncle's sake. You do understand that, don't you?'

Chapter Ten

'I'm sorry I put you in such an awkward position, Clara,' Nathaniel said hastily. 'I suppose I panicked at the thought of losing everything to my uncle.'

'Let's forget it ever happened,' Clara said firmly. At least they had got one thing straight – there was nothing romantic in their arrangement. Her feelings for Luke were confused enough as it was. His apparent desertion, after he had professed to love her, was hard to bear without adding any extra complications. She met Nathanial's anxious gaze with an attempt at a smile. 'We've got more important things to think about, and the first one is to get Gertie bathed. I'm going to leave Jane to watch over her while I go back to Drury Lane.'

'Why are you abandoning us?'

'I'm not,' she said, laughing at his alarmed

expression. 'I didn't have the heart to dispose of Miss Silver's personal possessions, but she was about the same size as Gertrude. I'm going to fetch some clean clothes.'

'Let me go instead. I don't relish the thought of being left with a naked woman who might at any moment turn feral again. Jane couldn't cope on her own and you'd know how to handle Gertrude. Just give me the key and I'll be back in two ticks.'

'You are such a coward, but you're right. There's a small trunk on the landing. It would be best if you could bring the whole thing, and I can select what's needed.'

'Good idea. I'm not an expert in ladies' clothing. I'll carry it on my shoulders, if necessary.'

Clara opened the door and stepped outside into the yard. 'There's the bath. If you'd lift it down and take it into the kitchen I'll start filling pans with water.'

Nathaniel made his way between crates and piles of rubbish to lift the tub from its hook. He held it high above his head as he retraced his steps. 'I'm glad my uncle can't see me now,' he said with a rueful smile.

Clara had hoped that Gertrude might be willing to lend a hand clearing away the rubbish on the shop floor, or would help clean the rooms in which they would sleep, but the moment Gertrude was bathed and dressed in one of Miss Silver's best gowns she seemed to think she was a lady of leisure. With her hair washed and tamed into a neat chignon it was possible to see traces of her former beauty and she looked ten years younger. Her large brown eyes were framed with thick lashes, and, in common with her sister, high cheekbones and a patrician nose gave her a distinguished look far removed from that of the wild woman who had been hiding in the attic.

Nathaniel stayed for a while, wielding a sweeping brush and shifting most of the detritus that had been left in the shop and the storeroom, but in the end he had to return to his lodgings to get ready for the evening performance at the Gaiety Theatre.

His departure coincided with the arrival of Lizzie, accompanied by Joss Comerford. Of all the people in London, he was the last person Clara had expected to walk into the shop.

'I simply don't know why the master's son decided to come with me, Clara,' Lizzie said, treating Joss to an arch smile. 'I told Mr Comerford that the shop isn't open yet, but he would have his way.'

Joss hesitated, staring at Nathaniel with a hostile expression. 'I don't believe we've met, sir.'

Nathaniel held out his hand. 'Nathaniel Silver. How do you do?'

'Joss Comerford.' He shook Nathaniel's hand. 'How do you do? I see you are about to leave, so don't let me detain you, Silver.'

Clara did not like the way Joss spoke to Nathaniel, and she was angry with Lizzie, who seemed to be enjoying the sight of two young men squaring up to each other. 'Thank you for everything, Nat.' Clara kissed him on the cheek. 'You've been a tremendous help today.'

Joss bridled visibly. 'Are you going to invite me to stay, Miss Carter? I've come out of my way to view your new premises.'

'I have to go.' Nathaniel raised Clara's hand to his lips. 'I'll see you tomorrow, and I haven't forgotten the theatre tickets. I hope to get some this evening.' He doffed his hat to Joss and Lizzie, and stepped outside.

'There really isn't much to see, Mr Comerford,' Clara said as she closed the door. 'We have quite a lot of work to do before opening the shop to the public.'

'We came in a hansom cab,' Lizzie said importantly. 'It's my afternoon off.'

'I knew that,' Clara agreed affably, 'and I thought you might have offered to help.'

'I try to avoid manual work. I have to keep my hands nice and smooth in case I'm required to do Mrs Comerford's hair.' Lizzie strolled around the shop floor, trailing her gloved fingers along a shelf and inspecting them for traces of dust. 'A lady's maid has to be very careful about her appearance.'

Clara was tempted to remind her sister that she

was still a chambermaid, but she happened to glance at Joss and found to her annoyance that he was staring at her. She could feel the blood rushing to her cheeks and she turned away. 'I could offer you both a cup of tea, but I'm afraid that's all we have at the moment.'

'I wouldn't want to rob you,' Lizzie said with a careless shrug. 'I know that you girls have to be very frugal, but we live very well in the servants' hall. Mrs Comerford is a very generous employer.' She wandered off to continue her investigation in the storeroom.

Clara waited until Lizzie was out of earshot. 'Why are you here, Mr Comerford?' she asked in a low voice. 'What possible interest can you have in an empty shop?'

Joss took off his top hat and placed it on the windowsill. 'My dear Miss Carter, is it not possible that I have more of an interest in the shopkeeper than the place itself?' He smiled as if bestowing a wonderful gift upon her.

'I would not have thought so,' Clara said flatly. 'You have wealth and position, and I think you are simply amusing yourself with us. You're not being fair to my sister. She is a servant in your house, and she would be dismissed without a character if your mother knew that you were showing her undue attention.'

'But it's not Lizzie who interests me, Miss Carter. May I call you Clara?'

'No, you may not. If I've given you cause to think that I wish to attract your attention, then I'm very sorry.'

'It's always the way with pretty women. They make sheep's eyes at a fellow and then they make out that he has the wrong idea.'

'I think you should go now, sir. Lizzie will find her own way back to the servants' quarters.'

'You are even prettier when you're angry. Your eyes darken to the colour of smoky topaz and your cheeks are soft and pink, like rose petals. I must make sure I annoy you very often.' Joss moved a little closer, but Clara backed away, turned and hurried into the storeroom.

'Mr Comerford is just going, Lizzie. Say goodbye.'

Lizzie came to a sudden halt. 'What?'

'I said he's leaving, but if you've got any sense you'll let him go. He's not interested in you, Lizzie.'

'I suppose you're the one he came to see, are you?' Lizzie faced her angrily. 'You think you're so clever, but you're wrong. Joss pays particular attention to me.'

'Oh, Lizzie,' Clara said, sighing. 'You know he's toying with you, as he is with me. It amuses him to make us think he cares, but when all is said and done we don't move in the same social circle as the Comerfords.'

'We're just as good as they are,' Lizzie protested.

'Of course we are, but they don't see it like that.'

'He's coming this way.' Lizzie's expression lightened. 'Don't you dare say anything that will embarrass me, Clara Carter,' she added in an undertone.

'You have plenty of room here,' Joss said with a patronising smile. 'It's obvious that this space has not been used to its full advantage, but you could easily extend the shop floor.'

'Yes, I've thought of that, Mr Comerford.' Clara kept her voice even out of politeness, but she was irritated by his presumption. She had not sought his opinion, neither had she asked his advice. Worse still, he was lingering when it should have been obvious to him that he was not welcome.

'All you need is a decent amount of capital and good-quality stock, and I think you would do well here.'

'Thank you,' Clara said stiffly.

Lizzie moved in between them. 'Perhaps we ought to be on our way, sir?'

He took a couple of silver coins from his pocket and pressed them into her hand. 'Take a cab, Lizzie. I'm not going home yet.'

Her mouth dropped open and she stared at him with a look of surprise and shock. 'But, sir . . .'

'Is there anything further you wish to say, Carter?' His eyes had a steely look and his tone was icy.

Clara shuddered inwardly. Lizzie had been deluding herself, but it grieved her to see her sister put down in such a harsh manner. She slipped her hand through Lizzie's arm. 'Mr Comerford is just leaving, dear. Come and see what we've done upstairs. There's always a room for you, should you decide that being in service is no longer what you want.'

It was Joss's turn to stare. For a brief moment his self-confidence appeared to falter. 'But I have a business proposition to put to you, Clara.'

'Another time, perhaps, Mr Comerford. I don't see my sister very often, so you must understand that family comes first. Good day to you, sir.' She propelled Lizzie into the kitchen and closed the door. 'I'm not gloating, but I told you what he was like, Lizzie. Now do you believe me?'

Jane looked up from the sink where she was washing the crockery from their midday meal. 'So you've dropped in to see us, Lizzie? That was very gracious of you.'

'Don't.' Lizzie held up her hand as if to ward off a blow. 'I've been a fool, I admit it, but I thought he was interested in me.'

'What's she talking about?' With her head on one side like an inquisitive sparrow, Jane stared at her sister. 'What's happened, Clara?'

'It's nothing that a hug won't cure, and perhaps a nice hot cup of tea. Would you be an angel and make some, Jane?' Clara wrapped her arms around Lizzie, who was red-eyed and sniffling. 'He's not worth it. Don't upset yourself.'

'His horrid mother will find out and dismiss me,' Lizzie wailed. 'I had a good job and now I've ruined things for myself.'

'Nonsense,' Clara said firmly. 'You weren't to know that he was simply amusing himself. He's a handsome fellow, and I've no doubt he can be very charming when it suits his purpose. Sit down and have a nice cup of tea.' She released Lizzie with a last hug.

Lizzie slumped down at the table, holding her head in her hands. 'I'll get the sack, I know I will.'

Clara went to the door and opened it just far enough to allow her to peer into the storeroom. 'He hasn't gone yet. I can hear him pacing about. Don't worry, Lizzie, I'll settle matters with Mr Comerford. You won't lose your job.' Clara flung the door wide open and marched into the storeroom. 'I thought I asked you to leave, sir?'

'Surely you weren't serious?'

'I believe I was.'

'I apologise if I've given your sister the wrong impression,' Joss said with a disarming smile. 'She's a very pretty girl, it runs in the family, and I suppose I was flirting, just a little.'

'I'm sure she will appreciate your apology, but it would be better if you made it in person.'

'I'll agree to that, but only if you will allow me to explain my real reason for coming here today.'

'All right,' Clara said evenly. 'I'm listening.'

'Might we go into the shop? It's more pleasant in there and we can speak freely.'

Clara followed him reluctantly. The scrubbed oak floorboards in the shop exuded a faint smell of carbolic soap, and the pungent aroma of vinegar still clung to the recently cleaned windowpanes.

'Well?' Clara eyed him warily. 'Please say what you have to say and then go.'

'My father disapproves of my way of life. I told you that when we first met. He is a self-made man and he wants me to follow him into trade, but I've always resisted, until now.' He paused, meeting her sceptical glance with a hint of a smile. 'We are, as you know, in the importing business, and my father recently bought up a sizeable warehouse containing all manner of exotic silks and brocades from India, Siam, China and Japan.'

'I'm sorry, but I don't see how this applies to me. I haven't enough money to purchase vast quantities of cloth, however beautiful and rare. I can only start with what I already have.'

'But if you had a business partner who could put up the money and supply the goods, you would be assured of success.'

She gave him a straight look. 'Are you suggesting that you and I should go into business together?'

'Precisely that. I need to have an interest and I have to show Papa that I am serious, and not the wastrel he thinks I am.'

Clara did not answer immediately. Her first instinct was to send him away with a flea in his ear, but the offer was too tempting to dismiss out of hand. 'I need time to think it over,' she said slowly.

'Of course. I understand completely, and I wouldn't have it any other way.' Joss puffed out his chest and for a moment Clara thought he might crow like a cockerel, but he sighed and inclined his head. 'Thank you. I apologise if I've offended you and your sister. It's my way to be open when I admire a pretty woman, but I realise now that I might have placed Lizzie in an awkward position, and for that I am genuinely sorry.'

'I'm sure she'll get over it,' Clara said more sharply than she had intended.

'I will escort her back to Bedford Square, if she will agree to accompany me.'

'I think she would rather stay a while, but I thank you on her behalf. I hope this won't affect her position in your parents' household.'

'It won't, I promise.' Joss picked up his hat and put it on at a jaunty angle. 'Good day, Miss Carter.' He swaggered out of the shop and the bell jangled on its spring as Clara shut the door, turning the key in the lock.

'That's enough surprise visitors for today,' she muttered as she made her way through to the kitchen.

Lizzie turned her head to give her sister an

enquiring look. 'Has he gone? I don't think I can face him again.'

'He offered to take you home, but I said you wanted to stay on for a while. I don't think you'll have any problems when you return to Bedford Square.'

Jane filled the last of three cups with tea. 'You ought to give your notice in, Lizzie. We could all live here quite happily. Betsy loves having a room to herself and when she's not helping here she takes me to spy on the other stores. We go round and see what's selling best. It's great fun.'

'I don't know,' Lizzie said, shaking her head. 'I like living in the big house, even if I am only a servant. If I could get Miss Jones's job I'd be more than happy. There are advantages to being a lady's maid.'

'If you change your mind there's plenty of work for all of us,' Clara said, sipping her tea. 'Be careful of Joss Comerford, that's all. He's not to be trusted.'

'You would say that. You're just jealous, Clara.' Lizzie picked up the chipped china cup, staring at it with her nose wrinkled in distaste. 'I have just as good manners as the toffs, and I've watched how they behave.'

'Have it your own way,' Clara said, shrugging, 'but don't blame me if it goes horribly wrong.' She replaced her cup on a saucer that did not match. 'I'd love to have a china department one day.

Wouldn't it be wonderful to see shelves stacked with best-quality tea sets and dinner services?'

'Being in trade is so vulgar,' Lizzie sighed.

'It's better than being part of the Skinner gang, or admitting that Pa frittered his money away at the gaming tables.' Clara rose to her feet. 'I'm going to start on the storeroom. If you're not going to help with the cleaning perhaps you'd like to go upstairs and start unpacking our bags, Lizzie. Another couple of trips to Drury Lane and we'll have all our belongings here, and then it's just a question of transferring the stock. I'm going to see if I can borrow a handcart from one of the traders in Covent Garden so that I can bring it in one trip.'

'Better you than me. That's all I can say.' Lizzie stood up, shaking out the creases in her black cotton skirt. 'I think I'll have a look round Peter Robinson's store and then I'll walk back to Bedford Square.'

'Mr Comerford gave you money for a cab.' Clara shook her head. 'I suppose you intend to spend it on yourself.'

'As you said, he gave it to me, so I can do what I like with it, and I mean to spend it on something frivolous. You are such a killjoy, Clara.'

'Don't be mean,' Jane protested. 'Clara is doing everything she can to make life better for us. Can't you at least try to help, Lizzie?'

'I'll come to the opening of your shop, and if I have any money left I'll spend it here, but don't ask me to work behind the counter, because it's simply not my style. One day I'm going to be a real lady with a rich husband, just you wait and see.' Lizzie went to give Jane a peck on the cheek. 'Don't let Clara work you too hard, dear. You know you're not very strong.'

'I'm fine,' Jane protested. 'Just because my legs don't work properly doesn't mean that I'm an invalid.'

Clara followed Lizzie through the storeroom to the shop. 'You know how sensitive Jane is about her disability. She hates wearing calipers.'

'She'll simply have to get over it. I've no patience with people who moan all the time.'

Clara's patience was at snapping point. 'You are so hard, Lizzie. Just wait until something happens to you that you can't control and see how you like it.'

'I don't have to stay and listen to you telling me what I ought to do.' Lizzie flounced over to unlock the door. 'Goodbye, and good luck with your shop. You'll need it.' She let herself out into the street, slamming the door behind her.

Clara hurried to lock it again but she was too late to prevent a well-dressed woman barging in. 'I'm sorry, madam. We aren't open yet.'

The woman glanced round the empty shop. 'There's no sign outside to say that you are closed, and why wasn't the door locked?'

'I was about to do so, but you forestalled me, madam. I do apologise.'

'When will you be open for business? What sort of premises is it to be?'

'I hope to start trading in two weeks, maybe sooner, and to begin with we'll stock haberdashery, but I plan to expand later in the year.'

'I usually take my custom to Debenham and Freebody, but I might consider giving you a fair trial.' She took one last look round, pursing her lips. 'You'll have to work hard to make these premises look appealing. Good day.'

Clara shut the door and locked it. She could see that there were some people who were very hard to please, but it was a lesson well learned. The first thing she must do was to brighten up the dark interior and make it attractive to the customers. It was going to be a challenge, but one that she felt she could take on and win.

Next day Clara was in the shop, directing the carter and his mate as they hefted the furniture off the van. The men were not too pleased when they discovered they had to carry the beds and chests of drawers up to the top floor, but a cup of tea and a bun purchased from the bakery in Vere Street brought smiles to their faces.

Finally, the stock from the shop in Drury Lane arrived, packed in tea chests and clean sacks. Clara was just supervising the unloading when a carriage drawn by a pair of matched bays and driven by a uniformed coachman drew to a halt outside. A footman leaped from the box to open the door and assist a woman to alight. Half-hidden beneath the folds of a voluminous scarlet velvet cloak, she crossed the pavement, shooing passers-by out of the way as if they were irritating insects.

'Open the shop door, you stupid fellow.'

Clara's heart sank as she recognised Lady Quinn's strident tones, and the confused footman rushed to do as she directed. Lady Quinn sailed into the shop as if she owned it, and came to a halt, looking round with an expression of distaste.

'What a dreadfully poky establishment. I wouldn't shop here if it were the only emporium in London,' she said in a loud voice.

Clara remembered only too well her first encounter with Lady Quinn, and she approached her with a degree of caution. 'Good afternoon, my lady.'

Lady Quinn poked one of the bolts of silk with a bony finger. 'I suppose this is your stock in trade. Not the finest quality, it would seem. Do you really think you'll be able to afford the rent selling this inferior material?'

'It sold well in Drury Lane.'

'My point exactly.' Lady Quinn fixed Clara with a hard stare. 'You might have been able to fool the common people from the slums of St Giles, but you will be dealing with a different class of patron in Oxford Street.'

'I will adapt,' Clara said sharply. 'You need not worry about money. The rent will be paid on time.'

'Don't be impertinent, girl. Money matters are not my concern; I leave that to Plumley.'

'Then I don't understand why you are here, Lady Quinn. Unless, of course, you wish to purchase some inferior silk.'

Lady Quinn's dark eyes flashed with anger. 'How dare you speak to me like that? Who do you think you are?'

'I'm the proprietor of this shop, and if you are not here as a customer or to wish me luck in my new venture, then I would ask you to leave.'

'You are a rude young woman and I was mistaken in allowing Plumley to take you on as a tenant.' Lady Quinn rapped on the window, beckoning to her footman. 'I would cancel the agreement, but unfortunately it is not in my power to do so.'

'Might I ask why?'

'I have no wish to continue this discourse. However, I will say that this property was bequeathed to my sister, but it will shortly come to me and I fully intend to sell.'

'But I have an agreement.'

'Which is not worth the paper on which it is written.' Lady Quinn moved majestically towards the door.

'Wait a moment,' Clara said angrily. 'You can't treat me like this.'

'That is where you're wrong. I can do as I please because I am extremely wealthy and you are poor. That is the way of the world.'

'I don't care how rich you are,' Clara protested. 'A real lady wouldn't go back on her word. You are no lady.'

'Every word you utter shortens your tenure. I could tell Plumley to destroy the documents and have you thrown out on the streets this afternoon.'

'I don't think you'll do that, Garland.'

Chapter Eleven

Lady Quinn's face paled to ashen. 'Gertrude?'

Dressed in one of Miss Silver's outmoded gowns, Gertrude advanced on her sister with her head held high and her jaw set in an uncompromising line. 'Yes, Garland. It is I, your long-lost sister – risen from the dead – or at least you hoped I was dead.'

Lady Quinn collapsed into the arms of her astonished footman. 'I'm going to faint,' she moaned.

Gertrude moved swiftly across the floor and slapped her sister's face. It was not a hard blow, but it brought Lady Quinn to her feet and she grabbed her sister around the neck.

'Stop it, both of you.' Clara leaped forward and seized Gertrude by the shoulders. 'Don't just stand there,' she told the footman, 'do something.'

Gertrude twisted round to face Clara. 'Leave us alone. I've got a score to settle.'

The footman backed away, his pale eyes bulging and his lips trembling. 'I'll fetch a constable, miss.'

'We don't need to involve the police,' Clara said hastily. 'Help her ladyship to her carriage.'

'Touch me and you're dismissed,' Lady Quinn snarled, terrifying the footman, who retreated to the safety of the pavement. With a mighty shove Lady Quinn pushed Gertrude away. 'You allowed me to think you were dead, you wicked woman.'

'You wanted me out of the way, Garland. Freddie had his eye on me and you knew it. Anyway, I was always prettier than you.'

'Well, look at you now. You're a positive fright.'

'And you look like mutton dressed as lamb.'

Clara stepped in between them. 'Ladies, please. You're attracting a crowd of onlookers. Do you really want to make a show of yourselves?'

'She started it,' Gertrude muttered. 'Look at the silly old fool. Dressed like a debutante and her not a day younger than—'

'Silence!' With a defiant toss of her head, Lady Quinn wrapped her scarlet cloak around her thin body. 'I'm leaving now. In future we'll deal through Plumley, my man of business, or my solicitor, Giles Makepeace, if you want to go that way. Don't imagine you'll get the better of me, Gertrude Batt.' She beckoned imperiously to the unfortunate footman and he hurried to escort her through the crowd of curious onlookers to her waiting carriage.

'Good riddance,' Gertrude shouted as she slammed the door. 'So the shop is really mine. She kept that a secret, the crafty bitch.'

'What will happen now?' Clara asked. Her knees were shaking, but she felt oddly calm. It was as if she were in a bad dream and would wake up at any moment to find that everything had gone back to normal. She turned her head at the sound of Jane's crutches tip-tapping on the storeroom floor.

'Who was shouting?' Jane asked tremulously. 'What's happening, Clara?'

Before Clara had a chance to respond, Gertrude struck a pose. 'You just missed a show, little one. It was me versus my sister, and I think I won, but you never know with Garland. She was always a difficult person, even as a child, or so I was told, because she's years older than me. Anyway, it's obvious that my sister hasn't improved with age.'

Jane sent an enquiring glance in Clara's direction. 'I don't understand.'

'I'll explain later,' Clara said hastily. 'The carter has just arrived with the rest of our things. We'll talk about it over supper.'

That evening, when the carter and his mate had finally left, the beds had been made and the shop left reasonably tidy, Clara set the table for supper while Jane stood by the range, singing to herself as she stirred a pan of pea soup. Gertrude breezed into the kitchen and took her place at table. 'That smells good, Jane.'

'You're joining us?' Clara asked, trying not to sound too surprised. It was hard to believe that just a short time ago this woman had been a wild thing, terrified of her own shadow. Now she was Miss Gertrude Batt, owner of the premises and heir to part of her late father's estate. She seemed to have changed out of all recognition.

'I feel more like my old self, thanks to you and Jane, not to mention your young man and his wonderful music.'

'He's not my young man,' Clara said hastily. 'Nathaniel is just a friend.'

'He's a talented musician and it was his playing that brought me back to the world I had been trying so hard to shut out, and the person who had hurt me and left me destitute.' Gertrude reached for a slice of bread and butter. 'I'm hungry.'

'But you must have known you would inherit some property from your father?'

'I never gave it a thought.' Gertrude sniffed the air. 'That soup smells good, Jane. You are an excellent cook.'

'Thank you,' Jane said, blushing prettily. 'No one has said that before.'

'Maybe it's because I've been living on next to nothing for so long that I'd forgotten what good food tasted like.'

'Oh . . .' Jane's smile faded. 'I expect that's it.'

Clara frowned at Gertrude, who was munching the bread, seemingly oblivious to the fact that she had hurt Jane's feelings. 'Nonsense. You cook wonderful meals, Jane. Don't be so modest.'

At that moment, before Gertrude had a chance to rectify her blunder, Betsy flounced into the kitchen. 'I'm exhausted. I've had to rearrange all the furniture in my room.'

'We had a lot to do and you were at work, so we couldn't ask you where you wanted to put things,' Clara said mildly.

'It's all right now, but I'm not sure I like sleeping on the top floor. What happens if there's a fire?'

Clara sighed. 'Oh, Betsy, this building has been here for a very long time and it hasn't burned to the ground, so I don't think it's going to any day soon.'

Betsy flopped down on the chair next to Gertrude. 'What's she doing here?'

'Gertie owns the whole building,' Jane said eagerly. 'You should have been here when she was shouting at her sister. I think the whole of Oxford Street could hear them.'

'But she's poor. Gertie is wearing Miss Silver's old cast-off.' Betsy stared at Gertrude, shaking her head.

'You behaved like a wild woman when we found you – now look at you.'

Gertrude shrugged. 'You would be a little odd if you'd suffered as I have.'

'Tell us.' Jane handed her a bowl of soup. 'I want to hear it all.'

'Maybe later.' Gertrude spooned soup into her mouth as if it were her last meal on earth.

'So you must be very rich?' Jane sat down opposite Gertrude, fixing her with an intense stare. 'Are you rich, Gertrude?'

'You don't ask questions like that,' Clara remonstrated.

Gertrude swallowed a mouthful of soup. 'Haven't got a penny piece to my name, child. I am as poor as the proverbial church mouse.'

'But you own this shop,' Jane insisted. 'So you aren't really poor.'

Gertrude frowned thoughtfully. 'I suppose you paid rent in advance, Clara?'

'Yes, I did.'

'It would have come in handy, but Garland has it. I can see I'll have a fight on my hands if I want to claim my inheritance.'

Betsy went to sit beside Gertrude. 'But of course you must. Why would you allow yourself to be cheated out of what's due to you?'

'My dear girl, solicitors cost money, which I haven't got.'

'Then we must help you.' Betsy turned to Clara with an eager smile. 'You have money from the sale of the shop.'

Clara shook her head. 'The cost of the move and the purchase of new stock has left me with very little. Then I have to pay the carpenter who is putting up more shelves and another counter. Money is very tight, and we have to start trading as soon as possible.'

'Oh!' Betsy's rosy cheeks paled visibly. 'That's not good.'

'What's the matter?' Jane asked anxiously. 'Are you sick, Betsy?'

'Not exactly.' Betsy shot a wary glance at Clara. 'I told Miss Lavelle what I thought of her this afternoon.'

'You didn't!' Clara gazed at her in dismay. 'Have you lost your job?'

'I thought we were all right now, and I could work on the perfume counter or sell kid gloves and silk scarves.'

'But we haven't got a perfumery, Betsy. It's my ambition to have one, of course, but for the moment we only have haberdashery.'

'It seems that we are in Queer Street,' Gertrude said casually. 'I know my sister and she'd rather cut off an arm and a leg than help me financially.'

Clara pulled up a chair and sat down. 'If you can prove that you own the shop, you could sell up and live comfortably off the income, Gertrude. You don't owe us anything.'

'That's where you're wrong, my dear. I was a wreck until you found me. You could have turned me out on the street, but you didn't. You treated me like a human being and I'll never forget that. If you are all in agreement I'll stay and see this through with you.' Gertrude licked her lips. 'Is there any more of that delicious pea soup, Jane?'

A week later, after everyone had worked late into the evenings, the shop was open for business and the button box had pride of place in the window, just as Clara had imagined. Nathaniel was one of the first customers to come through the door, even though they had been open for three hours. He took off his hat with a flourish and bowed.

'I salute you, Clara Carter. You've worked miracles.'

She smiled. 'I can't take all the credit. We've all done our bit.'

'The window display is splendid and it's attracting a lot of attention from passers-by.'

'That was what I'd hoped for, but trade is slow. What we really need are some customers with money to spend.'

'I'm sure they'll come.' Nathaniel's smile faded. 'Can we talk privately, Clara? I've something I have to tell you.'

She could tell by his expression that it was not good news, and she beckoned to Betsy, who was unpacking a fresh consignment of ribbons in the storeroom. 'Watch the shop, please. I won't be long.'

Betsy abandoned her task and glided across the floor to take her position behind the counter. 'I was hoping you'd give me a chance to prove myself,' she said smugly. 'I'm very good at persuading ladies to part with their money.'

Clara hurried into the kitchen, safe in the knowledge that Jane and Gertrude had gone to market. She leaned against the table, watching Nathaniel closely. 'You have something to tell me?'

He laid his hat on the table, avoiding meeting her curious gaze. 'The Paris Conservatoire Orchestra have asked me to perform with them for a whole season. It's a great honour, and I'm not sure how it came about, but it's too good an offer to turn down.'

'But that's wonderful, Nat,' Clara cried enthusiastically. 'I'm so pleased for you.'

He raised his head to give her a steady look. 'You are?'

'Of course I am. You are far too talented to waste your time busking on street corners. It will be a wonderful experience and you can spend your free moments composing. I'm sure that Paris is a beautiful city and will inspire you to even greater things.'

'So you don't mind that I'll be deserting you at your time of need?'

'Nat, don't be silly. You and your aunt are the reason that I have all this.' She encompassed the store with a wave of her hands. 'Well, it's not much at the moment, but it will be. I have such plans for the shop. Miss Silver would be proud to have been a part of it all.'

'My uncle believes that we're to be married.'

'But that was a ruse. You have no ties here that I know of.' She gave him a quizzical look. 'Unless you have a wife and children hidden away somewhere?'

His tense expression melted into a broad grin. 'No, that's not the case.'

'I'm very glad to hear it.'

'You are?'

'For your sake, Nathaniel. You don't need anything or anyone to get in the way of a brilliant career. I know that one day you'll be a famous musician and composer, and I'll be proud to have known you.'

He reached out to grasp both her hands. 'This isn't goodbye, Clara. I'll be back at the end of the season. You won't forget me, will you?'

'Of course not. You've been a good friend to me, and I wish you every success. When will you be leaving?'

'That's the trouble. It was such short notice – I have to leave tonight.'

'It is rather sudden, but it must mean that they are very keen to have you.'

His brow puckered in a frown and his eyes darkened. 'I have a feeling that there is more to this than is obvious. I think my uncle has pulled some strings in order to get me out of the country.'

'Surely not? What would he gain from your success in Paris?'

'He thinks my music is awful. If he had any hand in the matter it would be because he thinks I'll be a miserable failure.'

She reached up to kiss him on the cheek. 'Then prove him wrong. I know you can do it.'

'I hate to leave you when you are just starting out in your big adventure, Clara. I never did get the tickets for the Gaiety Theatre.'

'We'll go there when you return. Perhaps we'll both have something to celebrate.'

He tightened his grip on her hands, holding them to his lips. 'I wish I could take you with me.'

'Clara, I've got a customer who—' Betsy broke off, blushing furiously. 'Oh lawks! Have I come in at the wrong moment? You weren't going to propose to my sister, were you, Nathaniel?'

He released Clara's hands, his face flushing almost as pink as Betsy's. 'I was just saying goodbye. Well, I suppose it's *au revoir*, as the French say. Until we meet again.'

Clara clasped her hands together. They were still warm from his touch and she knew that she would miss him more than she had thought possible. 'Nat has the opportunity to play with a famous orchestra in Paris. He's leaving tonight.'

'So soon?' Betsy's eyes filled with tears and she rushed over to hug Nathaniel. 'We'll miss you.'

'Shop!'

The sound of an irate female voice made Clara turn with a start. 'I'll go.' She hurried into the shop. Nathaniel's news had come as a shock. She was pleased for his sake, but the future had become even more uncertain, bereft of his friendship and support.

'Good morning, madam,' Clara said automatically. 'How may I help you?'

The overfed, overdressed matron glared at her. 'I don't deal with shop girls. Fetch the proprietor.'

The woman's abrupt tone brought Clara back to the present. She drew herself up to her full height. 'I am the proprietor, madam.'

'You? A slip of a girl? What is the world coming to?'

'How might I be of assistance to you, madam?' With great difficult Clara managed to keep her tone even, and a smile painted on her face.

'I want to see the button box you have in the window.'

'That one is simply window dressing,' Clara said quickly. 'I have another in stock.'

'But I want the one in the window.'

'It isn't for sale, madam. Besides which, it's not

new. I'm sure you wouldn't wish to purchase a second-hand box.'

'That's my business. How much is the one in the window including the buttons? I have a mind to purchase it for my daughter. She becomes bored very quickly, but it might amuse her for a while.'

The thought of her most treasured possession being ill used by a spoiled child made Clara furious, but she maintained an outward appearance of calm by taking a quilted button box from the shelf behind the counter. 'This might suit your purpose better, madam.'

'But it's empty. The whole point of purchasing the one in the window is that it's full.'

'I'll throw in a dozen assorted buttons, if that's what you want. Your daughter could then add to her collection.'

'If I can't have what I want I'll take my custom elsewhere, and I'll tell my friends not to patronise your establishment.' The woman tossed her head so that the ostrich feathers on her bonnet waved frantically, as if they were trying to fly away. 'Good day to you.' She marched out of the shop and slammed the door.

The sound of clapping made Clara glance over her shoulder. Betsy and Nathaniel were standing in the doorway applauding loudly.

'Well handled,' Nathaniel said, chuckling. 'What a dreadful woman, I pity the daughter.'

'So do I, although she's probably as bad as her mother.' Clara replaced the box on the shelf. 'But I can't afford to lose customers, Nat. Maybe I ought to have given in to her.'

He shook his head. 'You don't need her trade, nor that of her friends, if they're anything like her.'

'I hope you're right,' Clara said fervently.

'We need more merchandise.' Betsy pointed to the empty shelves at the back of the shop. 'We could do so much better if we had a perfumery and stocked gloves and silk scarves and the like.'

'I'm sure it will come,' Nathaniel said, smiling. 'Your sister will make it work, Betsy.' He slipped his arm around Clara's shoulders and kissed her cheek. 'I have to go now, but I'll write to you from Paris.'

Somehow it was impossible to return his smile. Clara turned her head away, afraid he might see the tears that filled her eyes. 'Yes, you must. We'll be waiting to hear all your news.'

'I'll miss you,' Nathaniel said earnestly. 'All of you.' He made a grab for his hat and put it on. 'Goodbye, Betsy. Take care of your sisters and Gertrude.'

Moments later he was gone, leaving Clara staring after him as he hurried along the street.

'Why are you crying?' Betsy demanded. 'He'll be back.'

Clara dashed her hand across her eyes. 'I'm not

crying – it was a bit of fluff from the counter, or a speck of dust in my eye.'

'If you say so.' Betsy strolled around the shop examining the contents of the shelves. 'As I keep telling you, we really haven't got enough stock, Clara. It might have looked a lot in Drury Lane, but we need more if we're to attract customers.'

'I was hoping to purchase more as the money came in, but trade is painfully slow. I've only sold six yards of cotton print this morning, and I don't think we'll see that last customer again.'

'Perhaps things will look up,' Betsy said hopefully. 'We haven't been open for long. When word gets round I'm sure we'll do better.'

But matters did not improve, and after several weeks of slow trading Clara was beginning to think she had made a terrible mistake, and that she had allowed ambition to cloud her judgement. If they could not raise the money for the rent she was certain that Lady Quinn would take great pleasure in closing them down. The premises might belong to Gertrude, but she had yet to prove her claim, and her sister's lawyer was not making things easy for her.

'We'll all be homeless,' Gertrude said gloomily as she spooned porridge into her mouth one morning. 'Garland has instructed Giles Makepeace to act for her. I don't stand a chance unless I can find a solicitor to take my case on the understanding that he only gets his fee if I win.'

Clara pushed her empty plate away. The pile of unopened correspondence on the table in front of her almost certainly contained bills from tradesmen who had been persuaded to give them credit, and a demand for the next quarter's rent from Plumley – none of which she could pay. The shelves in the storeroom were empty and she could not afford to replace the items that had been sold. It was her worst nightmare, and Jane and Betsy's trusting faces made her dilemma even harder to bear. She had led them to this parlous state and now they were facing ruin. In the dark depths of night, when sleep evaded her, she had even considered paying a visit to a moneylender, asking for a loan to tide them over, but she knew from experience that the interest he charged would be crippling, and failure to pay could prove painful. She had seen her father limping home with a cut lip and a black eye given as a warning when he failed to repay a gambling debt. Pa was safe now, away from London, but for herself and her sisters there was nowhere to run. She missed Nathanial's cheerful optimism, even though it was often misplaced, and most of all she missed Luke's hard-headed, pragmatic way of dealing with problems. But she was on her own now – she was in charge and she was not going to let her family down.

She broke the seal on the most official-looking

document and for a moment her vision blurred. The copperplate writing danced around the paper like tiny tadpoles, and none of it made sense.

'What's the matter, Clara?' Jane asked anxiously.

'Is it bad news?' Betsy looked over Clara's shoulder in an attempt to read the document. 'What does it say? Your hand is shaking so much I can't read it.'

'Are you all right?' Gertrude leaned across the table, frowning. 'It must be something shocking. You look as if you're going to faint.'

Chapter Twelve

Clara took a deep breath. 'It's addressed to me, although it was sent to the shop in Drury Lane and then forwarded here. Who could have sent it?' She handed the paper to Betsy. 'Tell me what it says. It can't be right.'

Betsy studied the document for a moment and then she leaped to her feet with a shriek of delight. 'It's a banker's draft for fifty pounds.'

'It can't be for us,' Jane said slowly. 'It must be a mistake.'

Gertrude snatched the paper from Betsy, examining it closely. 'It's made out to Clara Carter, but the donor is anonymous. Who is your wealthy benefactor, Clara?'

'I have no idea,' Clara said weakly. 'Perhaps there is another Clara Carter and it's come to me in error.'

Gertrude pursed her lips. 'Don't be silly, girl. It's got your name on it so it's meant for you.'

'I can't accept it,' Clara said slowly. 'At least not until I know where it came from.'

'Come now, don't be hasty.' Gertrude rose to her feet. 'Think about it carefully, Clara. That money could save us all from disaster. What does it matter who sent it? Someone has your best interests at heart.'

'Yes,' Betsy said, nodding emphatically. 'Gertie is right. You might be prepared to go to the workhouse because you're too proud to accept the money, but think of us. Think of Miss Silver – you can't let her down.'

Clara stared at the figures written in Indian ink. Such a sum would enable her to pay the rent and to restock the shelves, and they could use what was left to live on until sales improved. She looked up and smiled. 'You're right, of course. I don't know who our benefactor is, but I would like that thank him with all my heart. I'll go straight to the bank and deposit this.'

'Maybe we could have lamb collops for dinner,' Jane suggested tentatively, 'and greens, too.'

'And mashed potatoes with lots of butter,' Betsy added, licking her lips.

'I don't see why not,' Clara said, nodding. 'It was worthwhile black-leading the range, after all, Jane. I was getting rather tired of porridge and pea soup.'

Gertie took a seat at the table, eyeing Clara

thoughtfully. 'Come on, girl. You must have some idea who sent you the money. One thing is for certain, it wouldn't have been my dear sister. She always was a miser.'

'The only person I can think of who might be able to lay his hands on such a sum is Joss Comerford,' Clara said slowly. 'But why would he do such a thing?'

'And why would you think it's him?' Betsy demanded. 'Have you been flirting with Lizzie's gentleman friend?'

'He's her employer's son,' Clara said flatly. 'Lizzie might have ideas above her station, but Joss Comerford is only interested in making money.'

'That doesn't make sense.' Jane pushed her plate away, leaning her elbows on the table. 'Why would he give away such a big sum?'

'He wants to invest in the shop.' Clara dropped the sheet of paper as if it had suddenly burst into flames, and it floated down onto the table. 'He wants to go into business with me.'

Gertie snorted with laughter. 'That's one way of putting it. He's got his eye on you, my girl.'

'No, you're wrong.' Clara felt the blood rush to her cheeks and she covered her confusion by retrieving the banker's draft and tucking it into her reticule. 'I've never given him any encouragement. He's just trying to impress his father.'

'So you think he's the one?' Betsy leaned back in

her chair. 'Maybe Gertie is right, Clara. Perhaps he's going make you an offer you can't refuse.'

'He can think again if that's the case. I'm not interested in Joss Comerford, and I certainly don't want to be beholden to him. In fact, I'm going to Bedford Square right now to tell him so.'

Gertie sprang to her feet. 'Wait a minute. Do you think that's wise? You said yourself that there are bills to pay and the rent is due. Until I can prove that I'm the legal owner it's Garland who holds the future of this shop in her bony hands.'

'I know all that,' Clara said slowly, 'but it doesn't change a thing. I'll find the money to carry on somehow, but I won't be beholden to Joss Comerford.' She reached for her cape and bonnet and put them on.

She was about to step outside when a carriage drew up at the kerb and, to her astonishment, it was Joss Comerford who alighted.

'My dear Miss Carter, it seems that you are going out.'

'I was coming to see you, as it happens,' she said coldly.

'Really?' His face lit up with a broad smile. 'How delightful. Have you changed your mind about going into business with me?'

Clara realised that their conversation was attracting the interest of several passers-by and she retreated into the shop. 'Come in, Mr Comerford. We can discuss this in private.'

'Joss, please.' He entered the shop, taking off his top hat with a flourish. 'You must have read my thoughts, Clara, if I might be so familiar.'

'I'd rather we kept it more formal, Mr Comerford.' Clara opened her reticule and took out the document, waving it under his nose. 'Can you explain this, sir?'

He took it from her and studied it with a genuine look of surprise. 'That's a considerable sum, Miss Carter.'

'Which I cannot accept.'

He stared at her for a moment and then a slow smile spread across his face. 'You think I am your benefactor?'

'Are you?'

'Sadly no, not this time, although I could match this easily if you would allow me to.'

Clara snatched it back from him. 'You didn't send this to me?'

'Not I. You obviously have another admirer, although I can't say I'm surprised. A handsome woman like yourself, with a property such as this, and an assured income for life, must be a lure for any unattached gentleman.'

'But I thought . . .' Clara stared at him in astonishment. She had been so certain that he was behind the generous gift, but he was obviously telling the truth.

'You were quite right in assuming that I am still interested in a partnership, purely on business grounds, of course.'

'I haven't changed my mind.'

'And that generous donation will not help my cause. But we could work very well together, Clara. My father has business contacts all over the world, and I was planning a trip to Paris myself.'

'To Paris?'

'That interests you, doesn't it?'

'Of course. I intend to go there at the first opportunity—' Clara broke off, realising that she had said the wrong thing. 'But not yet. I am not ready to expand so quickly.'

Joss glanced round at the half-empty shelves. 'This is precisely the right time to think of expanding your range. How do you think you will survive in the business world if you are not one step ahead of your competitors?'

'I know that's true, but I have to start somewhere.'

'If you are to succeed here, in Oxford Street, you will have to offer your customers something they cannot buy in the other stores or you will find yourself out of business.'

Clara knew that he was speaking the truth, but she did not want to encourage him. 'I'll think about it, sir. Now I must bid you good day as I have to open up the shop.'

Joss hesitated. 'As it happens I am going to Paris tomorrow, and I was hoping that you would accompany me.' He held up a gloved hand as Clara opened her mouth to speak. 'Hear me out, please.'

She nodded. 'Very well, but the answer is still no.'

'I was going to suggest that you allow me to act as your escort. I understand that you do not wish to accept my money, and you have no need of it now, but, as I said, I have contacts to whom I could introduce you.'

'Why would you do this for me? I'm just a shop-keeper and my sister is a servant in your parents' home. What have you to gain by helping me to succeed in business?'

'The warehouse filled with exotic linens is at my disposal. My father has given the stock to me as a test to see if I can emulate his skill in commerce. You and I might do business together yet.'

'Why don't you try the established stores? Why me?'

'I'll be frank with you, Clara. My father's repre-sentative has failed to impress the buyers with the merchandise. There's nothing wrong with it, I can assure you of that, but the answer each time was that the materials are too exotic and therefore diffi-cult to sell. I think the buyers are being very short-sighted, but you have vision and you can spot a trend.'

'I can't afford to make mistakes, Mr Comerford. If the large stores are of that opinion then who am I to gainsay them?'

'Come with me to Paris. I'd be more than happy to pay all expenses because I hate travelling alone. You would be doing me a favour and you'd see a bit of the world away from foggy London, and you might change your mind.'

'I'm sorry, it's not possible. I can't go to Paris with you. There's far too much to do here.'

'Is that the only reason?'

'Not entirely. It would ruin my reputation if I travelled unaccompanied with a gentleman to whom I am not related.'

'For goodness' sake, Clara, what are you thinking?' Gertie stepped out of the storeroom, arms akimbo. 'If he's paying your fare, say yes.'

'You've been listening,' Clara said angrily. 'This has nothing to do with you, Gertie.'

'But it does, my dear. The future of The Button Box is my future also. We have to make it a success or we'll all face ruin.'

Joss stared at Gertie, his mouth dropping open. 'I say, who is this? I don't think I've had the pleasure of making your acquaintance, ma'am.'

'I know you only by reputation, sir,' Gertie said haughtily.

Clara stepped in between them. 'Miss Batt, I would like to introduce Mr Joss Comerford.' She turned to Joss. 'Miss Batt is the legal owner of this property.'

'Gertrude – Gertie to my friends.' Gertie extended her hand to Joss. 'How do you do?'

He hesitated for a brief moment and then he bowed over her hand. 'How do you do, ma'am?'

'As you can see, I am at present in reduced

circumstances, but it wasn't always so.' Gertie fluttered her eyelashes, simpering like a girl just out of the schoolroom.

'I can tell that you are a woman of the world,' Joss said gallantly, 'and for that reason I would suggest that you accompany Miss Carter and myself to Paris. With such a chaperone there could be no question of scandal attached to our venture.'

Clara stared at him, momentarily dumbstruck, but Gertie was obviously taken with the suggestion. 'What a good idea. I used to live in Paris and am well acquainted with that beautiful city. It would be like going home.'

'Just a minute,' Clara said hastily. 'I haven't agreed to this yet.'

'But you will, of course.' Gertie fixed her with a hard stare. 'It is a wonderful opportunity, Clara. You will see a different world and find inspiration for our venture here in London.'

'I have responsibilities,' Clara said stubbornly. 'I can't leave my sisters to manage the shop on their own, but if I did agree to this wild plan I would insist on paying my way.'

Joss picked up his top hat and cane. 'I'll take my leave, Miss Carter, but I'll return later today when you've had time to consider my plan and talk it over with your sisters.'

*

'I'm sure I can cope with the shop,' Betsy said firmly. 'After all, I was often left in charge when Miss Lavelle went to visit clients in their homes.'

'You won't be away for long, will you?' Jane clasped her hands together and her knuckles whitened. 'I mean, it's going to be difficult to manage without you.'

'What are you going to say to Comerford?' Gertie demanded abruptly. 'He'll be back in an hour or so and he'll want an answer. Are we going or aren't we?'

'Why are you so keen to return to Paris?' Clara countered angrily. 'This isn't your problem, you know. You could make up with your sister and live a life of luxury, or you could sell the shop and live off the proceeds. What is there in Paris for you?'

Gertie slumped down on the chair at the head of the kitchen table. 'It's a man, of course. Isn't it always?'

Jane's pretty mouth puckered in surprise and her eyes widened. 'But you're too . . .' she broke off, blushing. 'I mean . . .'

'You think I'm too old to have a beau?' Gertie glared at her and then she laughed. 'Poor sweet child. A woman is never too old to enjoy having an admirer, and for your information, I'm only thirty, and I hope to have many more lovers before I succumb to senility.'

Jane's cheeks flamed and she covered her mouth with her hands.

Clara wanted to laugh but she could see that Jane was shocked and embarrassed by Gertie's frankness, and she frowned, shaking her head. 'Gertie is teasing you, Jane.' She sent a meaningful glance in Gertie's direction, raising a warning finger at Betsy, who was giggling.

'Perhaps I exaggerated a little,' Gertie said carelessly, 'but there is a gentleman with whom I was once agreeably engaged. He left me for a young soubrette, and I was broken-hearted.'

'Is that why you were hiding in the attic?' Jane asked eagerly.

'Was he very handsome?' Betsy added.

'He was an Adonis,' Gertie said, sighing. 'He was also wealthy and rather wild. Of all my lovers he was the best.'

Clara cleared her throat. 'Ahem, I'd love to know more about him, but we're getting too far from the subject.'

Gertie leaned towards Jane, prodding her arm with the tip of her forefinger. 'I hid away like a wounded animal. I'm ashamed to admit that I allowed a mere man to bring me to such a low point. He was and is a philanderer and I will have my revenge.'

'If that's why you want to return to Paris it might be better to forget the whole thing,' Clara said warily. 'If I choose to accompany Joss Comerford it is for business purposes only. I want to explore the new department stores in the centre of Paris and I need you to chaperone me. I don't want to return home to find my reputation in tatters.'

'I can do both,' Gertie said confidently. 'Don't worry about me, child. I am a woman of the world and this is the chance I've been waiting for.'

'In that case I'll accept your offer to accompany me, and I'll pay your fare out of the money I've just put in the bank. I refuse to be beholden to Joss, even though he offered to fund the whole trip.'

'But what about the shop?' Betsy asked anxiously. 'How long will you be gone for, Clara?'

'I've given it a lot of thought and I feel it would be best to put a sign in the window saying that we are closed for refurbishment and announce a grand reopening at a date that I've yet to decide. I hope to learn a great deal in Paris.'

Jane heaved a sigh of relief. 'Thank goodness for that. I don't think Betsy and I could have managed without you, Clara.'

'Speak for yourself,' Betsy said, tossing her dark curls. 'I'm sure I could do very well on my own.'

'I'm certain you could.' Clara smiled sympathetically. 'But I have something very important for you to do while I'm away, and Jane can help.'

'Oh, yes?' Betsy did not look convinced.

'I'd like you to go round the department stores and make a note of what appear to be their bestselling lines. We need new ideas to make our shop different from all the rest.'

'How long do you plan to stay in Paris?' Betsy asked suspiciously.

'Not long. It will cost a lot of money and I have to put the time to good use.'

'Where will you stay?' Jane's eyes brightened.

'I don't know. Perhaps Mr Comerford has some ideas as to that.'

Betsy chuckled mischievously. 'Lizzie will be green with envy when she finds out. She won't like it one little bit.'

Clara pulled a face. 'I know, but I have no option. Our success in business depends upon this, girls. We're all in it together.'

At that moment the shop bell tinkled and everyone froze.

Clara was the first to make a move towards the door. 'This might be him now.'

'What will you say?' Gertie demanded eagerly.

'I'll say yes, of course.' Clara hurried into the storeroom, making her way to the front of the shop.

The journey to France was not without a certain amount of discomfort, namely the Channel crossing, which proved to be long and uncomfortable, although neither Clara nor Gertie suffered from seasickness. Joss, on the other hand, was taken ill the moment he set foot on the boat and they saw nothing of him until they docked in Calais, where he joined them looking very sorry for himself and was unusually quiet on the journey by rail. He had recovered by the time they changed trains at Lille, and when they eventually reached Paris he was his ebullient self. He tipped a porter to find a fiacre and they were driven through the dark streets, arriving at the hotel just after midnight.

Clara was tired, but she could hardly fail to be impressed by the magnificent foyer illuminated by brass gasoliers with ruby glass shades. The gilt-framed mirrors reflected the warm glow and the central love seat, upholstered in crimson velvet, added to the feeling of luxury. Outside the night air might be chilly, but the interior of the hotel offered a welcome to weary travellers and a promise of luxury to come. Bell boys spirited their luggage away and they were shown to their respective rooms. Having said good night to Joss and Gertie, Clara was relieved to find herself alone in the elegantly furnished bedchamber. At the back of her mind there had been a nagging suspicion that Joss had an ulterior motive for bringing them to Paris, but he had behaved like a perfect gentleman, and her opinion of him was gradually changing. She climbed into bed and sank into the depths of a feather mattress.

Next morning, after a breakfast of coffee and croissants in the hotel dining room, Clara could not wait to go out and explore. Joss was a genial host and he promised to escort them to the various department stores in the most fashionable streets.

'I won't be joining you,' Gertie said as they rose from their table.

'Why not?' Clara demanded. 'I thought that was the whole point of you being here.'

'You don't need a chaperone to go shopping.' Gertie edged her way through the crowded dining room.

Clara and Joss caught up with her in the foyer. 'Where are you going?'

'I have some unfinished business, but I'll join you for dinner this evening. Don't worry about me. I know my way round Paris.'

'Surely we should keep together?' Joss said, frowning. 'Even if you are familiar with this city, you should not walk the streets unescorted.'

Gertie tossed her head. 'Don't tell me what I can and cannot do. I know my way around.' She headed for the grand staircase. 'I'll see you later.'

'I hope she'll be all right,' Clara said worriedly.

'I think Miss Batt can take care of herself.' Joss proffered his arm. 'I suggest we get an early start if we're to make the most of our time here.'

'Yes,' Clara said absently. 'Of course we must, but I'm not entirely happy about Gertie going off on her own. We don't know where she might end up.'

'Let's not worry about her.' Joss tucked Clara's

hand in the crook of his arm. 'We have more important things to do.'

After an exhausting morning, Clara felt drunk with excitement and overcome with the delights she had seen in the department stores. Her own small establishment in Oxford Street seemed dull and commonplace in comparison, but that only fired her enthusiasm to bring something more sophisticated to London. Joss had business to discuss at Bazar de d'Hôtel de Ville in the rue de Rivoli, where Clara suspected he was trying to establish himself as a businessman in his own right, and escape the shadow of his successful father.

She still did not know what to make of Joss Comerford. Sometimes she found herself liking him, but she was still suspicious of his motives in bringing her to Paris, and she was glad that she had insisted on paying her way. The only problem with being independent was financial, and she had realised the moment they entered their hotel that she could only stay for a few days at the most. There was so much to learn and so little time in which to absorb everything that was foreign to her. It was a relief to be able to wander around the store on her own, but all too soon Joss found her and whisked her off in a fiacre to visit Automne in the boulevard Haussmann.

'You have brought me luck, Clara,' he said, leaning back against the padded squabs. 'I've made a good contact at Bazar and I might have found a buyer for some of Father's unwanted stock. I knew I was a good salesman, and if it weren't for you I might not have ventured to Paris.'

'I'm glad.' Clara smiled as she stared out of the window at the unfamiliar streets. 'It's a very exciting city and I've got so many ideas for my store that I feel as though my head will burst.'

'It will take a great deal of money,' Joss said seriously. 'You will need a partner other than dear Gertie. She might own the premises but she isn't a rich woman.'

'She might not be, but her sister is extremely wealthy. Maybe she can be persuaded to share some of her wealth with Gertie. I know that I would do so if my sisters were in need.'

'Lady Quinn is renowned for being parsimonious. Gertie will have a fight on her hands if she wants a share of their father's fortune.'

'How do you know so much about them?' Clara asked suspiciously.

'I don't go into business with people unless I look into their background. I asked the person who knows more about society scandals than anyone in London.'

'Who would that be, Joss?'

'My mama, of course. She has spent a lifetime gossiping and listening to tittle-tattle. What do you think the ladies talk about over their tea and cucumber sandwiches in the afternoon?'

'I don't know. I'm a working woman so I've never been invited to such an occasion.'

'All that will change now you're with me.'

Clara turned her head to look him in the eye. 'But I'm not with you. I thought I'd made that perfectly clear before we embarked on this trip.'

'You did, of course, but I can still hope, can't I?'

Clara was about to put him firmly in his place when the fiacre drew up outside the department store in the boulevard Haussmann. Joss handed her out of the vehicle. 'Come now, Clara. We won't argue a point and there is still much to see. Can we at least be friends?'

She gazed up at the impressive frontage of the store, and nodded. 'Of course,' she said vaguely. 'Let's go inside. I can't wait to see what this one has to offer.'

That evening Clara dressed for dinner in the one and only decent gown she possessed. The pale-grey tussore with a high frilled collar and ruffled bodice was more suitable for afternoon tea than dinner in a fashionable restaurant. She knew it was dowdy and old-fashioned compared to the garments worn by the other female guests in the hotel, but she would have to ignore their condescending looks. Her hand shook slightly as she fastened a silk rose into her hair – she had done her best, although a more elaborate coiffure would have given her more confidence – she took a deep breath and went to knock on Gertie's door. They had not seen each other since they parted that morning and she was eager to discover where her friend had been during the day. She knocked and waited, but there was no reply. She knocked again, thinking that perhaps Gertie was taking a nap, and she tried the door but it was locked.

'Gertie, are you there?' There was still no response and Clara was beginning to worry. She beckoned to a chambermaid who was carrying a pile of clean towels, and using sign language she managed to persuade her to unlock the door, but the room was in darkness.

Close to panicking, Clara went to seek Joss's help. He opened his door in answer to her frantic knocking.

'Whatever is the matter, Clara?'

'It's Gertie – she isn't in her room! I don't know where she can be. I'm afraid something terrible must have happened to her.'

Chapter Thirteen

'I'm sure there's some perfectly logical reason for her absence,' Joss said as they made their way to the stairs. 'She has friends in Paris and I dare say she's safe with them, and has simply forgotten the time.'

'But she didn't say where she was going. She could be anywhere in the city.'

'All the more reason for us to continue as we would if she were here. Let's go down to dinner.'

'What will we do if she doesn't return this evening?'

'We'll give her credit for being old enough to look after herself. No doubt she speaks French like a native, and she'll return when she wants to. Come along, Clara. I'm starving, I don't know about you.'

The moment they walked into the dining room

they were surrounded by attentive waiters. Despite the delicious food and the wine that Joss ordered with the confidence of a connoisseur, Clara was too anxious to enjoy the delicacies that were put before her. Anything could have happened to Gertie and she might be in desperate need of help. The image of Gertie looking wild and dishevelled, as she had been at their first meeting, haunted Clara's thoughts throughout the meal, and although Joss tried to engage her in conversation it was obvious that her brief responses irritated him.

'Just put that stupid woman out of your mind, Clara. You're spoiling our first evening in this excellent hotel.'

'How can I? She might be in trouble of some kind.'

Joss leaned across the table, fixing her with a hard stare. 'Do you know what sort of reputation that woman has? She was the talk of the gentlemen's clubs not so long ago, and I would not like to repeat what was said about her.'

'I didn't think you were the sort of man who would listen to tittle-tattle,' Clara said angrily. 'Anyway, her past doesn't interest me. It's the future that counts and Gertie is a part of it.'

Joss held up his hand, a dull flush staining his cheeks as he glanced round at the other diners. 'Keep your voice down. We don't want the whole of Paris to know our business.'

'This is my concern, not yours.' Clara rose to her feet. 'I should have known better than to accept your offer to let us accompany you.' She walked out of the dining room, head held high, hoping that he would not follow her, but the sound of his quick footsteps made her stop and turn to face him. 'This wasn't a good idea, Joss.'

He drew her behind a giant potted palm, out of view of the guests who were making their way to the dining room. 'Don't play the innocent with me, Clara. You knew what you were doing when you agreed to come to Paris with me.'

'I came here to study the way they run their department stores,' Clara said in a low voice. 'What other reason could I have had?'

'When a young woman travels under the protection of a gentleman he has a right to expect certain privileges.' Joss grabbed her by the wrist, closing his fingers on her soft flesh. 'Don't pretend to be naïve, Clara. You knew what you were agreeing to.'

'Let me go,' she hissed. 'I may be naïve but I'm not stupid. I made it clear that this was a business trip. You are behaving like a libertine, Mr Comerford.' She wrenched free from his grasp. 'Consider our association at an end.'

'See how you get on without me,' he called after her as she made her way across the foyer. 'You are on your own now, miss.'

Clara did not dignify this with an answer and she

ascended the grand staircase slowly, with her head held high. She would not let him see that she was close to tears of anger and embarrassment. To admit her naivety had been painful, and she knew that she had allowed ambition to cloud her judgement. It should have been obvious to her from the start that Joss Comerford had an ulterior motive, and that bringing her to Paris had been a ruse. A jumble of wild thoughts filled her head as she hesitated outside her room. Perhaps he was responsible for Gertie's absence. The quiet dinner for two might have ended quite differently had she been susceptible to his charms, but even though he had badly misjudged the situation it was humiliating to think that she had given him cause to believe she was such easy prey.

Clara took the key from her reticule, but before she unlocked her door she went to Gertie's room. She knocked and waited, but there was still no answer. The clock in the foyer had just struck ten, and now she was really worried for Gertie's safety. Surely, if she had met old friends and decided to stay the night, she would have sent a message to the hotel? Gertie might be eccentric and unpredictable, but she must know that her absence would be of great concern. Clara returned to her room and locked the door behind her.

She awakened early next morning and it took her a few moments to remember that she was in a strange bed in a foreign city. The events of the previous evening came flooding back, bringing a blush to her cheeks. She was ashamed to think that Joss Comerford could have thought she was a woman of easy virtue, and annoyed with herself for giving him cause, but the problem uppermost in her mind was Gertie's disappearance. Clara washed in cold water and dressed as quickly as she could when her fingers trembled as she tried to do up the tiny buttons on her bodice. Having tamed her hair into a neat chignon at the nape of her neck, she unlocked her door and went to check Gertie's room. She knocked and waited and knocked again without any response. After a moment's pause she hurried down to the reception desk and was relieved to find the clerk who had booked them in the previous day. Joss had addressed him in English and the man had replied, albeit with a strong French accent. Clara approached him, adopting the confident stance she had noted in guests who were accustomed to having their demands met.

'Good morning,' she said politely. 'Maybe you can help.'

'Certainly, Mademoiselle. How may I be of service?' The small man with a neatly trimmed beard and moustache beamed at her.

Encouraged, she tried to explain that Gertie had gone missing. Perhaps his grasp of English was not as good as she had hoped, or maybe it was the mention of the police that made him recoil as if stung by a hornet.

'No, Mademoiselle. It should not be necessary.' He shook his head so violently that his moustache quivered. 'Not the police. It does not look good for the hotel. You understand?'

Clara did understand, only too well. She had a feeling that it would have been the same had she been staying at a hotel in London. 'I do, but my friend is missing. Where is the nearest police station?'

He explained with much hand-waving and kept lapsing into French, which only served to confuse Clara, but, after a great deal of repetition, she had a rough idea and there was only one way to find out if his directions were accurate. She wrapped her shawl around her shoulders and went outside to brave the streets of Paris on a chilly April morning. After walking for what seemed like hours she was beginning to realise that she had gone full circle, and just as she was about to give up she found herself standing outside the police station. She marched in and began once again to explain the reason for her visit. Eventually they found a more senior officer who spoke English, and although he listened patiently, smiling all the time, he was dismissive of her worries.

'This is Paris, Mademoiselle,' he said shrugging. 'The lady knows the city well, according to what you have just said. I suspect she is with a good friend, if you understand my meaning. Why else would such a person return to the place she had once called her home?'

The logic of his argument was faultless, and Clara was beginning to think that both the police sergeant and the desk clerk were right. Gertie had spoken of a man who had broken her heart – finding him was the reason for her desire to return to France. Maybe they had made up their differences, although bearing in mind Gertie's desire for revenge, it seemed unlikely. Clara left the police station and started back for the hotel. She had planned to visit the most famous of the Parisian stores that morning, but now everything was overshadowed by Gertie's disappearance. One thing was certain: she would have to face Joss and that was not going to be easy. She quickened her pace and arrived back at the hotel to find the foyer filled with guests who had just arrived and others who were on the point of departure. She had not eaten breakfast, but when she looked into the dining room she saw that the tables were being cleared and set for luncheon. She was about to mount the stairs when the clerk she had spoken to earlier hurried up to her.

'Might I have a moment, please, Mademoiselle?'

She stopped at the foot of the grand staircase. 'Of course. Have you any news of Miss Batt?'

'No, Mademoiselle. I am sorry, but I must ask you to settle your bill.'

Clara stared at him, frowning. 'But we are staying for two more nights.'

'The gentleman has already left, Mademoiselle. He said that you would be responsible for the account.'

'When did this happen?'

'About half an hour ago, Mademoiselle.' The clerk dropped his gaze and shuffled his feet. He looked so uncomfortable that Clara felt sorry for him.

'But I need to stay until Miss Batt returns,' she said urgently. 'I've reported her missing.'

'The management does not want to be involved in scandal, Mademoiselle. I am sure you will understand.' He thrust a piece of paper into her hand. 'Your luggage is with the concierge.'

'You are turning me out on to the street?'

'Your room was overbooked, Mademoiselle. There was an error.'

'But I have nowhere to go. Surely there must be another room.'

He shook his head. 'The management would be grateful if you could settle in full, Mademoiselle.'

Clara opened the folded sheet of paper. 'There must be a mistake,' she gasped. 'This is for Mr Comerford's room as well as dinner last night and breakfast this morning.'

'The gentleman said you would pay, Mademoiselle. Will you come with me, please?'

Shock and anger roiled in Clara's belly as she

followed him to the desk. Joss Comerford had bolted and left her to pay the whole bill, which would take almost all the money she had in her reticule. Moreover, he had their return train tickets and those for the ferry crossing. She had never hated anyone in her whole life, but at this moment she loathed Joss Comerford with every inch of her being.

There was nothing for it but to settle the bill and leave the hotel. She stepped outside into the pale spring sunshine. No one seemed to notice her – she might as well be invisible as she walked through the crowded streets carrying her valise. Her brain seemed to have stopped working and her thoughts were fogged and random. How happy the passers-by looked as women, young and old, leaned on the arms of their male escorts, chattering and laughing. It might be spring in Paris but it was winter in her heart, and her mind was fogged with worry. Where she was going, Clara had no idea. She was lost and alone in a foreign city with just enough money to buy a cup of coffee and perhaps a croissant. Somehow, without thinking where she was going, she found herself standing outside Automne, one of the department stores that Joss had included in their brief tour of Paris. The imposing architecture and the smartly dressed clientele made her feel inconsequential and shabby as she watched the comings and goings with a growing feeling of desperation. Her hopes of finding Gertie had already faded and there seemed no point in remaining in Paris, but without money she was in a truly desperate situation. Then, just as she was about to give way to despair, she spotted a tall young man who reminded her of Nathaniel.

She was about to rush towards him when she realised that it was not Nat, and she had almost flung her arms around a complete stranger. She turned away on the pretence of studying something in the shop window, but her eyes were misted with tears and she had to bite her bottom lip to stop herself from crying.

'What's the matter?'

A girlish voice close to her ear made Clara turn with a start. She turned her head to find herself looking into the pansy-brown eyes of a pretty young woman who looked vaguely familiar. Dressed in the severe black of a shop assistant, with her chestnut hair smoothed into a bun, she had a fresh complexion and an impish smile.

'I – it's nothing,' Clara said, sniffing. 'You speak English?'

'A little. My mother was English, but she is dead now.'

'I'm so sorry.'

'Thank you, but it was a long time ago.' The girl put her head on one side, giving Clara a searching look. 'You are in trouble? Yes?'

'I find myself in a difficult situation,' Clara said guardedly. 'I mean yes, but it's not easy to explain,' she added, realising that the girl was looking puzzled.

Even as she spoke, the sun vanished behind a bank of stormy clouds and large spots of rain began to fall, causing people to scurry for shelter.

'My name is Sabine Chastain.' Sabine grasped Clara's hand. 'Come inside, please.'

'I can't,' Clara said anxiously. 'I have no money.'

'It costs nothing to look.' Sabine's lips curved in a smile as she hustled Clara into the department store. 'There, you see. Many people are walking round, but not all are buying.'

A wave of dizziness caused Clara to sway on her feet. Perhaps it was hunger or the sudden warmth, but she staggered against the counter and might have fallen had Sabine not supported her. 'I'm sorry,' she murmured.

Sabine pulled up a chair and pressed Clara onto the seat. 'You are very pale. Are you ill?'

'No, I'm quite all right, thank you.' Clara tried to stand but her legs seemed to have turned to jelly and she sank back onto the chair.

'What is your name?'

'Clara Carter. I came here yesterday with a gentleman.'

'I remember seeing you together. He was a handsome man and I thought you made a lovely couple, but where is he now?'

'It doesn't matter, Sabine. Thank you, but I really should go.'

'You say you have no money, and you must be far from home. Where are you staying?'

'Mademoiselle Chastain.' A tall, thin woman bore down on them, glaring at Sabine. She rattled off a sentence in French and Sabine answered meekly with her head bowed.

'What did she say?' Clara whispered as the woman marched off to speak to the doorman.

'Mademoiselle Boucher is the head of this department. She doesn't approve of us girls becoming familiar with the customers.'

'I must go. I'm getting you into trouble by being here.'

'You will not get far without money in Paris.'

'I have a friend who is a musician with the Paris Conservatoire Orchestra. If I could find him I know he would help me.'

'Is that the man you were with yesterday?'

Clara shook her head. 'No. Nathaniel would never treat a woman in the way that Joss treated me.' Despite her best efforts to control her emotions, Clara's voice broke on a sob.

'You cannot go while you are so upset. Come with me. There is a room where we have our meals. Mademoiselle Boucher won't go there until it is time to eat. You can rest and have a cup of coffee.' Sabine helped Clara to her feet and, keeping a wary eye on the manager, she steered Clara through the crowded aisles to a room in the basement.

The smell of freshly ground coffee and something savoury bubbling away on the range made Clara's mouth water. 'You're very kind, Sabine.'

'We English have to stick together,' Sabine said, chuckling. 'Sit down and I'll fetch you something to eat and drink.' She hurried off, leaving Clara to gaze round the large dining hall. Long trestle tables with benches on either side took up most of the floor space, and at the far end a woman presided over a counter where piles of dishes awaited the influx of hungry diners. The scent of freshly baked bread wafted under Clara's nose and her stomach growled with hunger.

Sabine returned moments later with a cup of coffee and a plate containing a large hunk of bread and two pats of butter. 'There you are, eat up. I can't stay, but if you wait here I'll see you in half an hour when it's my break for luncheon.'

'Won't I be in the way?' Clara asked, eyeing the big woman behind the counter who was watching them from a distance, with her beefy arms folded and a stern expression on her florid face.

'Agathe is all right when you get to know her. I told her you don't speak French so she'll leave you alone. Just sit there and smile if anyone approaches you. I'll be back as quickly as I can. It's so nice to speak English again. I'm enjoying myself very much.' Sabine walked away, her movements as graceful as those of a ballet dancer.

Clara sipped the strong black coffee and ate the bread, spread thickly with butter. Food had never tasted so good and she felt her energy returning, and with it a feeling of optimism. Just talking to Sabine had given her spirits the lift she so badly needed, and finding someone who understood English had given her confidence, but she kept a wary eye on Agathe. The woman looked tough and the twin lines between her brows gave her a permanent frown. Clara was alarmed when, as she finished the last crumb on her plate, she saw Agathe marching down the aisle between the tables, heading in her direction.

Clara half rose to her feet, preparing to leave, but Agathe placed a bowl of delicious-smelling stew on the table in front of her.

'*Mangez!*' she commanded abruptly, and without another word she turned and stomped back to her position behind the counter.

'Thank you,' Clara called, but Agathe did not look back.

The food was as savoury as its aroma had promised, and Clara ate ravenously. She had just finished the last spoonful when the doors burst open and a flock of female staff, chattering like starlings, crowded into the dining hall. They lined up in more or less orderly fashion to have their bowls filled before drifting off to sit on the benches and consume their food. Clara was aware of the curious glances they gave her, and she was relieved when Sabine joined her.

'I see that Agathe has taken you under her wing,' Sabine said, eyeing Clara's empty plate. 'She is kind-hearted as long as you don't get on the wrong side of her.'

'She is an excellent cook,' Clara said sincerely. 'I love her food.'

'I'll tell her that. She'll be your friend for ever.'

It was Clara's turn to laugh. 'I don't think I'll be around that long.'

'Tell me how you came to be in this pickle.' Sabine broke her bread and dipped it in the stew. 'We only have a short break, so I'll eat and you talk.'

Clara found herself telling Sabine everything from the moment they moved into the shop in Drury Lane until this morning when Joss had left her virtually penniless and alone in a foreign country.

Sabine's eyes were round with shock. 'My goodness, what a cad. No wonder you were in tears. I'm sure I would be in such circumstances.'

'I need to discover what's happened to Gertie, but I thought if I could find Nathaniel he would help me.'

Sabine stared at her, frowning thoughtfully. 'I don't know how you would go about finding Gertie, but it shouldn't be too difficult to discover where the Conservatoire Orchestra is playing.'

'Can you tell me how to get there? I really should leave now and try to find Nathaniel.'

'The Conservatoire is not too far from here, but he might not be there. What will you do if you cannot contact him?'

'I will find him,' Clara said confidently.

'If all else fails you must return here. The store is open until late evening and I share a dormitory on the top floor with two other girls, so I am always on the premises.'

'Thank you, Sabine. It's good to know that I have one friend in Paris.'

Sabine clasped Clara's hand. 'Yes, you do, and you must let me know if you find your musician and if you have any luck in tracing Gertie. I won't be able to rest until I hear that all is well.'

With a map that Sabine had sketched on the back of a discarded receipt, Clara set off to find the Conservatoire in the 9th arrondissement. It was raining steadily by the time she reached the grey stone building but her enquiries ended with disappointment and frustration. When at last she found someone who spoke enough English to understand her predicament, the white-haired gentleman disappeared into the office, returning moments later with the news that the orchestra in which Nathaniel was now first violin was on tour, and not expected back in Paris for several days. Clara's hopes were dashed and she left the building, pausing in the street to count the last of her money. She doubted if there was enough to pay for a night's accommodation in a doss house, let alone in a respectable hotel. She found herself walking blindly, retracing her footsteps towards boulevard Haussmann, and the only friend she had in Paris.

Sabine came hurrying to meet Clara, but her expectant smile faded. 'No luck, then?'

Clara shook her head. 'The orchestra is on tour. I don't know where Nathaniel is at present.'

'What will you do, Clara? You should go home.'

'I haven't got the money for the fare, and in any case I can't leave Paris until I know what's happened to Gertie. She could be in all kinds of trouble.'

Sabine pursed her lips, eyeing Clara doubtfully. 'From what you told me earlier, that lady can take care of herself.'

'That's exactly what Joss said, but it's not true. If you had seen the state she was in when my sisters and I found her living in the attic, you would not say such a thing.'

'Mademoiselle Boucher is glaring at us,' Sabine whispered. 'I can't talk now, but I have a ten-minute break in half an hour. We'll speak then, and I have an idea that might solve at least part of your problem.' Sabine dodged back behind the counter to serve a woman who had seized a silk scarf and was waving it like a flag.

Clara caught sight of Mademoiselle Boucher

edging through the crowd and she moved away, heading towards the ladies' fashion department. Despite her worries she could not help but be impressed, yet again, by the style and magnificence of the layout, as well as the quality and variety of the merchandise. She knew that she could not aspire to anything like this in Oxford Street, but nothing was impossible, she told herself as she fingered a silk ball gown so elegantly displayed on the mannequin. Clara had seen shop dummies in London, although they were constructed of wirework, but this Parisian model was of a new material, which was smooth and more lifelike. She was tempted to touch, but a shop assistant hovering at her elbow was frowning in a discouraging manner, and Clara moved on to examine a velvet evening jacket trimmed with fur. How Betsy and Jane would love to see these garments.

The thought of her sisters and home brought a lump to her throat. They would be alarmed when she did not return on the expected date, and even more worried when Lizzie discovered that Joss had come home on his own. She wondered what story he would fabricate in order to make himself appear to be the injured party.

The shop assistant was following her at a discreet distance and Clara could not blame her for being suspicious. She must look a perfect fright. Her worries were confirmed when she caught sight of herself in a cheval mirror outside the changing room. Her skirts were creased and muddied from walking in the rain and her bonnet was ruined. She hurried through to the millinery department and her breath caught at the sight of such an array. Miss Lavelle would surely be impressed by such stylish hats in a rainbow of coloured silks, satins and dyed straw, decorated with ostrich feathers, flowers and fruit. It was easy to imagine how Betsy's nimble fingers would be itching to emulate such design, and Jane could learn from such artistry.

Another assistant glided up to her, questioning her in French; her meaning was clear even if Clara could not understand a word of what she said. Clara smiled and shook her head, moving on yet again. She had a sudden vision of herself wandering the departments in ever-decreasing circles until Mademoiselle Boucher and the floorwalkers pounced on her and threw her out onto the street. Her situation could not be more desperate.

Chapter Fourteen

Clara wandered from one department to another, but weariness was beginning to take its toll and the heat from the hissing gas jets was making her feel nauseous. Outside darkness was gobbling up the city and the lamplighters were making their rounds, creating golden pools of light against an indigo sky. Several times Clara walked past Sabine's counter, but a mere glance from Mademoiselle Boucher was enough to make her hurry on.

Eventually, after what seemed like hours and when Clara was close to exhaustion, the last customer was ushered out of the store and the great double doors were closed and locked.

Sabine beckoned to Clara, glancing anxiously in Mademoiselle Boucher's direction. 'You must not be seen to be loitering after closing time. I'll come for you as soon as the tills are emptied and I've left everything ready for the morning. Wait for me at the foot of the stairs.'

'What then?' Clara asked in a whisper. 'I can't stay here all night.'

'Don't worry. I've thought of that – just go quickly – before she sees you.' Sabine jerked her head in the direction of the glass doors leading to the stairwell, and Clara slipped away unnoticed by the tired staff who were intent on clearing up. Setting down her valise, and taking off her ruined bonnet, she draped her shawl over her arm and waited for Sabine. A sudden blast of warm air and a wave of sound enveloped her as the doors opened and the women made a rush for the stairs. They flowed past her as if she were a rock in the middle of a stream, to be avoided but otherwise unremarkable. Sabine was the last one to emerge and she took Clara by the arm.

'Come with me. We'll catch Monsieur Loussier before he leaves for home.'

'Who is he, Sabine?'

'He is second only to Monsieur Marchand, who owns Automne. If he agrees to my idea then you will have a job here for as long as it takes to find your friend.'

Clara stared at her in disbelief. 'But I can't speak a word of French. What could I do?'

'There is plenty of work in the sewing room or

the packing department. I'm sure that Monsieur Loussier will find something for you.' Sabine took the stairs, dragging a reluctant Clara in her wake.

'I'm not sure about this,' Clara said breathlessly as they came to a halt on the third floor.

'Be practical. You need a bed for the night and something to eat. Have you any better ideas?'

Clara shook her head.

'I thought not. Let me do the talking, although I'm quite certain that Monsieur Loussier speaks English.' Sabine led the way along a narrow, wood-panelled corridor, coming to a halt at the far end. She raised her hand and rapped on the door.

'*Entrez.*'

Sabine opened the door and stepped inside, clutching Clara's hand as if afraid she might break loose and run away.

Henri Loussier stood by a large knee-hole desk with his hat in his hand. He was wearing an expensive-looking overcoat with an astrakhan collar, and was obviously preparing to leave. He gave Sabine an appraising look, raising an eyebrow. 'Mademoiselle Chastain?'

Sabine spoke in rapid French, all of which was lost on Clara, apart from a mention of her name. Monsieur Loussier listened attentively, his dark eyes taking in Clara's dishevelled appearance with a hint of a twinkle.

'I see,' he said at length. 'It seems that you are in

need of assistance, Miss Carter.' His English was perfect and his French accent was pure music to Clara's ears. She did not know what she had expected of him, but she liked what she saw.

'I do find myself in a compromising position, Monsieur,' she said carefully, 'but it is only temporary.'

'Miss Chastain tells me that you own a department store in London.'

'I am just starting up in business. That was my reason for visiting Paris. I wanted to see how it was done here.'

'We pride ourselves on being the leaders of fashion.' Henri's smile faded and was replaced by a look of concern. 'But I am sorry to see you in reduced circumstances. How may I be of assistance?'

Clara opened her mouth to reply but Sabine silenced her with a frown. 'It was my idea, Monsieur Loussier. I thought perhaps you might employ Clara until she finds the friend who has vanished into the night.'

'It's possible, but it wouldn't be what you are used to, Mademoiselle.'

'I am used to working hard,' Clara said firmly. 'I would appreciate the chance to study the way you run your store, and to learn from the experience.'

Sabine stepped forward. 'There is the packing department, Monsieur Loussier. It would not matter so much that Clara doesn't speak our language if she worked there.'

'That is so.' Henri pulled on his gloves, stretching the soft leather with slow movements of his long fingers. 'You may have a month's trial, Miss Carter. If you do not discover the whereabouts of your friend in that time, I would think she does not want to be found.'

'Thank you, Monsieur. I'm very grateful.'

'Will you tell Mademoiselle Boucher, please?' Sabine asked tentatively. 'She will need to know.'

'Of course. I will speak to her in the morning, but now I am going home. I leave Miss Carter in your care, Mademoiselle Chastain.'

'Thank you, Monsieur.' Sabine stood aside, waiting until her superior had left the office before turning to Clara with a whoop of glee. 'He is such a nice man, quite different from Monsieur Marchand, who owns the store.'

'You don't like your employer?'

'It isn't against the rules,' Sabine said, chuckling. 'In fact, he is quite fair and well-liked, but he is not a man to suffer fools gladly and you don't want to get on his wrong side, as my mother used to say.'

'Thank you for warning me, although I doubt if I will meet him. I will be out of the way in the packing department, and I'm grateful for the opportunity to earn some money while I try to find Gertie.'

Sabine ushered her out of the office and closed the door. 'Perhaps Monsieur Loussier is right. Maybe she doesn't want to be discovered.'

'I don't believe that for a single moment. Something has happened to her, I'm sure of it.'

'We must hurry to the dining room, or we'll find that the food has been gobbled up.'

'How will you explain my presence?'

'I will tell the girls the truth, and luckily Mademoiselle Boucher has her dinner in her room, so she won't know about you until Monsieur Loussier speaks to her in the morning. You would think that she owns the store and not Monsieur Marchand, but she has been here for ever, and she never lets us forget it.' Sabine headed for the staircase with Clara following close behind.

'I still have to find somewhere to sleep tonight,' Clara said worriedly.

'You can share my bed. Tomorrow we will make better arrangements.' Sabine paused at the top of the stairs. 'Unless you have any objections, Clara?'

'No, of course not. I'm truly grateful to you, Sabine. I used share a bed with my little sister, and she talks in her sleep.'

'I don't think I do that.' Sabine's laughter echoed up the deep stairwell. 'Come on, I'm starving. Let's see what Agathe has put on for supper.'

Clara hurried after her. 'There's one other thing – I must write a letter to my sisters and tell them what's happened. They'll be worried sick.'

'Of course,' Sabine said breathlessly. 'I have paper and ink upstairs. You can write to them tonight and if you speak nicely to Gaston, who is in charge of the post, he will see that it is sent.'

'I don't know how to thank you, Sabine.'

'Maybe one day I'll come to London and see your store. My mother was born in a place called Barking, which always made me laugh when she translated it into French. I imagined a town filled with noisy dogs.'

'If you come to London you will be my honoured guest,' Clara said sincerely.

Sabine came to a halt outside the dining room. 'Just do as I do,' she said softly. 'I'll introduce you to the other girls, but none of them speaks English, so just smile and nod.'

A nervous tremor ran down Clara's spine as they entered the room and the aroma of garlic and wine enveloped them on a waft of hot air laced with the smell of sweating humanity. Sabine strolled over to the counter and picked up a bowl. Agathe was standing behind a huge pan with a ladle in her hand and she doled out a generous helping of meat and vegetables swimming in rich gravy. At the far end were a basket of rolls and trays of cutlery. Clara followed suit, avoiding meeting Agathe's fierce gaze.

'*Merci,*' she murmured, copying Clara in the hope that it was the French for 'thank you' and that her friend was not begging for mercy. Life was very complicated in a foreign country. It was even more confusing when she took a seat beside Sabine at one of the refectory tables, amid curious glances from the other girls and a torrent of questions, none of which she could understand.

Sabine handled them with supreme confidence and Clara simply smiled and nodded and then concentrated on her food, which was delicious.

They finished their meal with coffee, and when it was time to leave the staff room the two young women who had shown the most interest in Clara accompanied them upstairs. They chattered away in French, with Sabine throwing in the odd remark, but Clara could not understand a word, and it was a relief when they reached the room on the top floor.

Sabine lit the gas mantles and the shadows were pushed to the far corners beneath the eaves. There were three beds, and beside each one there was a small chest of drawers and a wooden chair. The bare boards were scrubbed to a silvery whiteness and the only concession to comfort was a strip of coarse red drugget in the centre of the floor.

'You've already met Hortense and Nina,' Sabine said casually. 'They know why you're here.'

Clara met Hortense's chilly gaze with an attempt at a smile. 'I'm very pleased to meet you.'

Sabine translated her remark into French but Hortense simply shrugged and went to sit on her bed, leaving Nina to smile shyly and hold out her hand.

'Welcome,' she said, enunciating carefully.

'Thank you – I mean – *merci*.' Clara smiled and shook her hand.

'Very good,' Sabine said heartily. 'We will soon be friends and you will pick up the language, Clara.' She opened one of the drawers in the chest next to her bed. 'Here is pen and ink. You can write to your sisters and tell them what a lovely time you are having.'

'Thank you so much, Sabine. I am truly grateful for everything you've done for me.'

'You would do the same for me if our situations were reversed.' Sabine handed her a sheet of writing paper. 'Gaston will seal it for you in the morning. That's something I can't do up here.' She threw herself down on the bed and stretched her long legs. 'I'll try not to kick you, and tomorrow we will ask the storeman if he can find a bed for you. There's plenty of room.' She lay back and closed her eyes, despite being fully dressed.

Clara pulled up the chair and sat down, resting the paper on top of the chest as she composed a letter to Betsy and Jane with a note to Lizzie, warning her to be wary of Joss because he was not what he seemed. The sounds of soft breathing, punctuated by the odd snore, confirmed that the girls had fallen asleep as soon as their heads touched their pillows. Clara got up and went to look out of the dormer window. Stars twinkled in the heavens like raindrops caught in a shaft of moonlight, and the boulevard below was still thronged with Parisians strolling along, arm in arm. Street lights created pools of brightness amongst the deep shadows, and revellers clustered around tables outside the cafes. The gaily coloured outfits of the ladies were in sharp contrast to the more sombre clothes worn by their escorts as they wined and dined into the night. Clara wondered if the city every slept, but her eyelids grew heavy and she knew she must get some sleep.

Next day, after being interviewed by Christine Boucher, with Sabine acting as interpreter, Clara was taken to the packing department and left in the charge of Paquet, whose wrinkled face and scraggy neck put Clara in mind of an aged tortoise. He peered at her over the top of steel-rimmed spectacles and communicated by speaking very slowly and gesticulating. If it had not been for Gaston, the post boy, who knew a few words of English, Clara would have been at a total loss. After a while, it became clear that her main task was to wrap swatches of material in brown paper and address them to the names on lists given to her by Paquet. It was Gaston's job to stick on the stamps and take them to the post office. She gave him the letter addressed to Betsy and Jane and he winked, tapping the side of his nose, as he included it with the rest of the post. Clara was satisfied that she had made at least one friend in the packing department.

She would have worked all day without stopping for a break if Sabine had not come to find her at lunchtime. Clara tried to ignore the curious glances she received when she walked into the dining room, but she could not blame the women for being suspicious of a foreigner who had suddenly appeared in their midst. Hortense turned her head away, refusing to acknowledge her, but Nina smiled and made room for Clara to sit beside her. Both Nina and Sabine made a point of talking to Clara as if they were old friends, and gradually the chilly atmosphere in the dining room began to thaw.

During the lunch break and when she returned to the packing department Clara made an effort to learn a few words of French, and Gaston was only too pleased to act as her tutor. He made excuses to stop at her desk more often than was strictly necessary, but their attempts to make conversation attracted Paquet's attention, and a stern lecture. Clara did not understand the rapid stream of words that flowed from his lips, but it was clear that he was displeased, and she could not afford to lose this job. By late afternoon her fingers were ink-stained and sore from knotting the coarse twine to secure the parcels, but she continued working diligently. When she had completed all the tasks she had been given, she offered to help the man who was struggling to pack a large order of glassware. It was done by means of sign language and at first he stared at her as if she had lost her senses, but Gaston happened to be passing and between them they managed to make the suspicious fellow understand. His baffled expression was replaced by a toothless grin.

Clara discovered that the older man's name was Hercule, and he might be strong enough to lift heavy crates and boxes, but he was very clumsy. The shards of broken glass on the floor around him bore witness to the fact that he had fingers like sausages and fists like hams. Clara wrapped the fragile glassware and laid each item carefully in the wooden boxes provided, leaving Hercule to secure them with strong cord and take them to the wagons ready for delivery. When Paquet strode up to them she thought she was in trouble again, but he muttered something to Hercule and walked on.

Hercule shrugged and hefted a box onto his shoulder. Clara watched him as he carried the heavy weight effortlessly to the waiting wagon. It was dark outside and despite the heat from the gaslights she could feel a chill wind whipping in from the street. A quick look at the large white-faced clock on the wall revealed that it was closing time, and she was more than ready to end her long day. She went to her desk and tidied away the pens and ink ready for an early start next morning. This was not the sort of work she was accustomed to, but even down here in the depths of the building, she was discovering how a large department store organised its delivery service. All this would help her when she returned home, but in order to leave Paris she must think of a way to find Gertie. It seemed like a hopeless task, although she tried to convince herself that people did not simply disappear.

Paquet strolled past her, acknowledging her with a curt nod, which was as good as receiving a pat on the back. She followed him as far as his glass-fronted office and she paused, looking through the window at the shelves piled high with ledgers and files. In a sudden flash of inspiration she wondered if Gertie had once been a customer at Automne. If she had, and if she had been registered under her own name, there would be a record of her transactions with her billing address in one of those ledgers. Clara's heart missed a beat and her hand flew to cover her mouth as she stifled a gasp of triumph. Joss had said that everyone who visited Paris came to Automne, and Gertie had lived in this city for many years. She might not be at the same address now, but it would be a start. There must be many people who had known the infamous Gertrude Batt in her heyday.

That night, as she lay in the truckle bed that had been found in the corner of the furthest attic room, her mind was racing as sleep evaded her. The soft breathing of the other women was punctuated by the odd sigh and the creak of a bedstead, but all Clara could think about was finding a way to search the ledgers without rousing Paquet's suspicion. She had seen him lock the office door when he left the packing department for whatever reason, and the staff entered the hallowed precincts only when summoned to appear before him. Eventually, overcome with exhaustion, Clara drifted off to sleep.

Inspiration came in the morning soon after she had started work. Paquet had given her a long list of customers who had requested swatches, and she had begun to write a label when the pen nib twisted, causing a large blot to spread in a dark starburst. Clara glanced round to make sure that no one was looking and, with a quick flick of the pen, she obliterated the entire address.

'Oh dear,' she said loudly.

'What's the matter, Miss Carter?'

She turned with a start to see Monsieur Marchand's deputy standing behind her. 'Monsieur Loussier.'

'You seem to have had a mishap.' His generous lips twitched as if he were trying to suppress a chuckle. 'You really should change that nib.'

'Yes, how silly of me not to notice that it's twisted.' Clara rose to her feet, hardly daring to look him in the eye. 'I'm afraid I've lost the customer's details.'

He picked up the sheet and studied it closely. 'That is one of our very good clients. I should know the address, but it eludes me.'

'Perhaps there is a record of it somewhere?' Clara said innocently.

'Of course. Paquet keeps all the information in his ledgers,' Henri said, smiling. 'Come with me, Miss Carter. I have to speak to him about another matter. We will put your case before him.'

'Am I to be dismissed for my clumsiness, Monsieur?'

'It was clearly an accident, so we'll say no more about it.'

'Thank you, Monsieur.' Clara rose from her seat and followed him to Paquet's office. She had a sneaking feeling that Henri Loussier had seen what she had done, but for some reason he had chosen to ignore her act of vandalism. He rapped on Paquet's door, opened it and ushered Clara into the office.

Paquet leaped to his feet. 'Monsieur Loussier.'

Henri spoke too rapidly for Clara to understand what he was saying, but Paquet nodded and made a vague motion with his hand to indicate a set of ledgers. Henri turned to Clara with a hint of a smile. 'You have permission to look for the address you need.'

'Thank you, Monsieur.' Clara shot an anxious glance at Paquet, but his attention was fixed on his superior and after a brief exchange of words they left the office together. Clara could hardly believe her luck, although she could not rid herself of the nagging suspicion that Henri Loussier had seen through her ruse. It was obvious that he was a man with vast experience of handling staff, and had a knowledge of human nature that was almost frightening. Her admiration for him grew by the minute, but she must concentrate on the task in hand, and it had to be completed before Paquet returned and started asking questions. Clara lifted down the first ledger and began to go through it, page by page.

She found the customer's address with little trouble, but Gertie's name did not appear in the first, or the second. She was just about to embark on the third heavy tome when she spotted Paquet walking briskly towards the office. It would be hard to explain why she had gone back two years in time when the client's name and address were in a much more recent edition. She held her breath, but then Hercule rushed up to Paquet, tapped him on the shoulder and, after a brief conversation, they hurried off in the direction of the loading bay and Clara sighed with relief as she recommenced her search.

She had almost given up when she spotted an entry dated June 1869, when it seemed that Gertie was residing at an address in the fashionable rue de Rivoli. Clara made a quick note of it on a scrap of paper and tucked it into the top of her stays. Despite the fact that three years had passed, it was her only clue as to Gertie's whereabouts, and at the first possible opportunity she would go there and make enquiries. Clara returned to her desk but she found it hard to concentrate on the mundane task in hand.

At midday she was on her way to the dining room when she met Henri on the stairs. He stopped, meeting her startled gaze with a wry smile.

'Did you find what you were looking for, Miss Carter?'

Clara felt the blood rush to her cheeks. 'I found the customer's address, Monsieur.'

'That's not what I meant.'

'You knew?'

'It wasn't difficult. You told us that your main reason for staying in Paris is to find your friend, and if I were looking for the person you describe I would do exactly as you did. Anyone who is anyone will have shopped at Automne at some time during their stay in Paris.'

'I'm sorry,' Clara said hastily. 'I should have asked your permission.'

'You are not sorry at all, Miss Carter.' Henri's laughter echoed up the stairwell, causing heads to pop over the balustrade as staff craned their necks to see what had amused Monsieur Loussier. 'You had an idea and you went ahead with it, which is what I admire about you. It's the same spirit that made you start up your business in London with very little experience in the trade, and with no apparent capital.'

'It was a risk I was prepared to take,' Clara said stonily. 'I don't see that it's funny.'

His smile faded. 'You are a brave woman, Clara Carter. If I had your courage and foresight I might be running my own business now, instead of being second in command here.'

'But you love this store. Anyone can see that it means a lot to you.'

'It does,' he said seriously, 'but perhaps I could have done better.'

Clara realised that she had touched a nerve and she laid her hand on his arm. 'Don't say that, Monsieur. I haven't been here very long, but it's obvious that the staff depend upon you. You are the heart of Automne – without you it would stop beating and die.'

'You really mean that, don't you?'

'Yes, I do. I may be inexperienced in business matters, but I've known hard times and I've seen how ordinary people have to struggle simply to survive. The streets where I grew up are bathed in blood.'

'But you survived. That must have taken great courage.'

'I never gave it a thought,' Clara said simply. 'It was just the way things were.'

Henri stepped aside to allow several of the girls from the fashion department to pass. 'I mustn't detain you, Miss Carter,' he said brusquely, and walked on.

The sudden change in his tone sent a chill down

Clara's spine. For a brief moment he had treated her like an equal, but now she had been put firmly in her place. She nodded and followed the others downstairs to the dining room. It was obvious from their covert glances and whispered comments that they were talking about her. Clara held her head high as she walked into the dining room. If they wanted to make more out of an innocent conversation, that was their business.

Despite the severity of their black silk uniform, Miss Boucher's girls always managed to look immaculate from their coiffured hair to the tips of their highly polished boots. Clara was uncomfortably aware of her shabby appearance. It was dusty in the packing department and despite the large apron provided, it was difficult to keep her dress from becoming soiled. She collected her meal and went to join Sabine, who had saved a seat for her.

'You have a smudge of ink on the tip of your nose,' Sabine said, chuckling.

Clara took a hanky from her pocket and rubbed her nose until she could see it shining. 'There isn't a mirror in the packing department. Is it gone now?'

Sabine glanced at Hortense, who was giggling with the rest of the girls. 'Yes, it is. Don't take any notice of them. They're just jealous.'

'Jealous? Of me?'

'You're far prettier than Hortense – or any of them, come to that – and you've caught dear Henri's eye. That's enough to make them green with envy.'

'Don't say things like that, Sabine. It's not true.'

'Then why are you blushing? Henri Loussier is quite a catch. There isn't an unmarried woman under fifty who wouldn't give anything to be favoured by him.'

'Hush,' Clara said urgently. 'Keep your voice down.'

'All right, but I might feel the same if I didn't have a gentleman friend who is likely to propose to me any day now.'

Clara paused with a spoonful of cauliflower soup halfway to her lips. 'Really? Who is he?'

'His name is Paul Bonnet and he is a reporter for *La Presse*.' Sabine lowered her voice. 'I don't tell the girls everything. They can be very spiteful at times.'

'I won't say a word,' Clara said, smiling. 'I'd like to meet him.'

'He might be able to help you to find your friend. Paul knows a lot of influential people.'

'I think I've found a clue,' Clara whispered, glancing round anxiously in case anyone was listening, but the others were either concentrating on their food or chattering amongst themselves. 'I know where she was living three years ago. It's an address in rue de Rivoli, and I intend to go there and make enquiries.'

'Tomorrow is my half-day off. If you ask old Paquet nicely he might let you take yours then, too.

We could go together, and I'll ask Paul to come with us. He has a knack of getting people to tell him things.' Sabine's hazel eyes shone. 'It's so exciting.'

'I'll ask Paquet when he comes back after luncheon.'

Sabine's cheeks dimpled prettily. 'He likes a drop or two of wine with his meal. He should be in a good mood. Good luck, Clara.'

Chapter Fifteen

The address in the fashionable rue de Rivoli was an apartment in one of the elegant terraces that lined the street. The suitably imposing vestibule was guarded by a ferocious-looking concierge who put Clara in mind of an aggressive bulldog. Clara had never been in such a grand building, and, in such opulent surroundings, she was even more conscious of her outdated and shabby clothing. The concierge was clearly unimpressed and denied all knowledge of a person called Gertrude Batt, and when Clara and Sabine tried to question her as to the identity of the current occupant she threatened to have them thrown out. It was only when Paul Bonnet rushed into the building, full of apologies for being late, that the concierge became more amenable.

Paul impressed Clara favourably from the first moment she set eyes on him. He was tall and lanky, with mousy hair and a pleasant, open face. His features were unremarkable but his hazel eyes gleamed with intelligence and good humour, and his lips curled up at the corners as if he were about to burst into laughter at any given moment. He doffed his top hat with a flourish, treating the grumpy concierge to a flashing smile. '*Bon après-midi, Madame Tasse.*'

'Monsieur Bonnet.' Madame Tasse fluttered her sandy eyelashes and smiled, revealing great gaps where several of her teeth were missing.

Clara was dumbfounded by the sudden change in the concierge's demeanour, but Sabine smiled proudly as she slipped her hand through the crook of Paul's arm. 'You haven't met my friend, Clara Carter.'

Paul turned to Clara with a genuine smile. 'I am very pleased to make your acquaintance, Miss Carter.'

'And I yours,' Clara said eagerly. 'You speak excellent English, Monsieur.'

'Paul,' he corrected, taking her by the hand. 'Sabine has told me all about you.'

Sabine blushed. 'All good, Clara. I hope you don't mind.'

Madame Tasse cleared her throat and rattled off a sentence in French, and Paul answered her with a nod and a smile. 'Apartment thirteen on the fourth floor,' he said, taking Sabine by the hand. '*Merci, Madame Tasse.*'

The concierge grunted and turned her back on them.

The wide marble staircase seemed to grow steeper as they made their way to the fourth floor, and they were all breathing heavily by the time they reached apartment thirteen. Paul rapped on the door and Clara waited anxiously, crossing her fingers and hoping that whoever lived here might know something of Gertie's whereabouts. Her heartbeat quickened at the sound of footsteps and the door was opened by a young maidservant.

Paul did the talking and the girl answered in monosyllables, shaking her head as she backed into the narrow hallway, preparing to close the door, but Paul put his foot over the threshold.

'Don't scare her, Paul,' Sabine said urgently. 'It's obvious she knows nothing.'

He turned to her, frowning. 'I think she's hiding something. She won't give me the name of her employer.'

'What's all the noise about, Marie?' A loud voice from inside made the girl turn with a start and she babbled incoherently as she attempted to close the door.

Clara did not stop to think. There was no mistaking the identity of the speaker and she pushed past the startled maid.

He had his back to the light but she would have known him anywhere. 'Luke.'

'Clara! What the hell are you doing in Paris?' Luke seemed for once to be taken off guard. He seized her by the shoulders and gave her a shake. 'How did you know I was here?'

'Let her go.' Paul hurried to Clara's side. 'Who are you, Monsieur?'

'More to the point, who are you?' Luke demanded angrily. 'This is a private apartment and I don't recall inviting you in.' He glanced at Sabine. 'Or her, come to that. Who are these people, Clara?'

She twisted free from his grasp. 'Never mind them – they're my friends – but what are you doing here? Why didn't you let me know you were safe? You disappeared without a word.'

He dropped his hands to his sides. 'Come into the drawing room.' He signalled to the frightened maid-servant, barking words at her in French.

'You speak their language?' Clara gazed at him, stunned by what she had just witnessed. Luke had changed subtly and it was not just the well-tailored frock coat and pin-stripe trousers, or the velvet waist-coat studded with gold buttons that made him look different. He had an air of command and the super-cilious look of a man who was used to getting his own way. 'What's happened to you?' she said slowly. 'I don't understand.'

'Who is he?' Sabine clutched her arm.

Clara shook her head sadly. 'He's someone I thought I knew.'

'Don't be ridiculous, Clara. Of course you know me.' Luke ushered them into a spacious drawing room, furnished in the style of Louis Quinze. Spindly gilded chairs and sofas upholstered in pale-blue damask were arranged around small tables set on a richly coloured Aubusson carpet. Bowls spilling over with pink and white hyacinths sent out a heady perfume in the warm and sunny room. Hanging from ornate plaster ceiling roses, three crystal chandeliers reflected the sunlight that streamed through tall windows creating rainbow patterns on the walls. Clara gazed round in awe. She had seen illustrations of such interiors in the magazines that Betsy brought home from work, but they were the stuff of dreams, and not for people who lived and died in Seven Dials. Luke had fled the country, but this palatial apartment was hardly the place in which she would have expected to find a fugitive from the law.

'What are you doing here, Luke?' Clara demanded. 'This can't be your place.'

'Take a seat.' Luke encompassed them all with a wave of his hand. 'The maid will bring refreshments.'

'That's all very well,' Paul protested, 'but you two obviously know each other well and Clara deserves an answer.'

Sabine slipped her arm around Clara's shoulders. 'Are you all right?'

'I am, thank you.' Clara sank down on the nearest sofa and Sabine sat beside her. 'I'm waiting, Luke. I think you owe me an explanation.'

'You must know why I left London, Clara. It wasn't a question of choice.' Luke stood with his back to the ornate rococo fireplace. A fire burned in the grate, sending tongues of flame curling around pine-scented logs. 'And what about you, my girl? What are you doing here in Paris? I sent you money to keep you safe in London until such time as I chose to return.'

She stared at him blankly. '*You* sent that money?'

'Who else do you think would be so generous? You're still my girl, and I intend to look after you.'

'I'm nobody's property,' Clara said angrily. 'I had no idea where the money came from, and I didn't come to Paris because of you, Luke Foyle.'

Sabine squeezed Clara's fingers. 'I think you two need to be alone to talk this over.'

'Exactly, well said, but I think we're getting away from the subject. You should tell him why we came here today, Clara.' Paul eased himself gingerly onto a chair that looked almost too fragile to bear the weight of a grown man.

'I've seen you before, sir,' Luke said, frowning. 'You're a damned newspaper man.'

'I've been called worse.' Paul stretched out his long legs, grinning up at Luke. 'Be careful what you say in front of me, sir.'

'You can leave now. You're not welcome here.' Luke made a move towards him but Clara leaped to her feet.

'Stop it, Luke. Paul and Sabine are trying to help me. We didn't come looking for you, and I had no idea that I'd find you here, or that you could speak French like a native.'

'It seems an unlikely coincidence,' Luke said doubtfully. 'Why did you come to Paris, if not to find me?'

'I'm as surprised to see you as you are to see me, but it's Gertrude I'm looking for. She's gone missing, and I'm worried about her.'

'Who the hell is Gertrude?'

'So much has happened since you went away,' Clara said slowly. 'I hardly know where to begin, but I sold the shop and moved everything to premises in Oxford Street. You know I always wanted to own a department store.'

Luke stared at her, glowering. 'I remember you talking some such nonsense, but I didn't take it seriously.'

'Luke, you're not listening to me. In fact, I don't think you ever took me seriously.'

'It seems that I didn't know you as well as I thought I did. Go on, Clara, explain why you are here with these people, and who is Gertrude?'

'I've been trying to tell you, if you'll just give me a moment. Gertrude Batt is the owner of the new store. She lived in Paris for many years but she fell on hard times and returned home to find that her sister had taken her inheritance. She accompanied me to Paris and then she disappeared. This is the only address I can find for her, and that's why we came here today.'

'It sounds like an unlikely tale, and you haven't told me why you decided to come to Paris in the first place. If it wasn't to find me, then why are you here?'

'I needed to put the money I received to good use, and I had someone who offered to become a business partner. He had connections with the department stores in Paris and he offered to introduce me to their managers and buyers so that I might learn how they operate.'

'And you believed him?' Luke's lip curled and his tone was scathing. 'Whoever it was must have thought you were easy prey. You're so naïve, Clara.'

'That's not fair,' Sabine protested.

'Hear her out, sir,' Paul added, frowning. 'You owe her that at least.'

Luke turned on him. 'Thank you, but I think I know Clara better than you do, Monsieur.'

'Stop it, Luke,' Clara leaped to her feet. 'Listen to what I have to say, or I'll leave now and you'll never see me again.'

'All right. Although I think I can imagine the rest of the story.'

'No, you can't,' she said angrily. 'You can't imagine how frightening it was to find that I was alone in Paris. Gertie had disappeared and Joss had left suddenly without settling the hotel bill; worse still, he had taken our railway tickets with him, and those for the sea crossing as well. After paying what we owed I was left stranded and virtually penniless. If it hadn't been for a chance meeting with Sabine I would have been quite destitute.' She sank down on her chair, momentarily overcome by the enormity of what had occurred as she relived recent events. 'There you have it. I didn't come looking for you because I had no idea where you were. You could have been anywhere on the Continent, for all I knew.'

'I can't believe you've done all this, Clara,' Luke said slowly. 'What does your father say?'

'Pa had to go to his brother in Dorset, away from Patches and her awful son. Pa doesn't know about any of this, and I don't want him to.'

'I can't take it all in.' Luke stared at her, his brow puckered in a frown. 'Why are you dressed like a drab? I wanted you to buy nice clothes and a decent pair of shoes with some of the money I sent.' He seized her right hand, staring at the ink stains with a puzzled frown. 'What's this?' He fingered the signet ring. 'Who gave you this? It certainly wasn't me.'

'It's none of your business,' Clara said angrily. 'I

had to find work and Sabine made it possible for me to get employment at Automne. It's a poorly paid position, but at least I get three meals a day and a roof over my head.'

'In that case I'm grateful to you, Sabine,' Luke said stiffly.

'That's the first sensible thing you've said since we arrived.' Paul leaned forward, fixing Luke with a penetrating stare. 'Now perhaps you can answer Clara's questions about her friend, which is why we came here today.'

'It's on record at the store,' Clara said simply. 'Gertrude Batt was living at this address three years ago.'

'I know nothing of that.' Luke glanced towards the door as it opened to admit a familiar figure. 'But this lady is the current tenant; she might be able to help you.'

Clara could hardly believe her eyes. 'Patches Bragg.'

'So it is you – the little shop girl – come to visit Patches in her own home.' Patches waddled across the floor, her garish crimson gown cut low across her large bosom, the skirts drawn back and draped over a half crinoline, the steels of which clanked as she moved. Her badly scarred face was, as usual, decorated with black patches, and her grey hair was arranged in an elaborate coiffure.

Paul stood up, gazing at Patches with a mixture

of surprise and awe. She stopped in front of him. 'And who may you be, young man?'

He bowed over her extended hand. 'Paul Bonnet of *La Presse*, Madame.'

She slapped him hard across the face, causing him to recoil in surprise. 'That was a warning, Monsieur. Write anything about me in your journal and you will suffer worse than a sore cheek.'

Sabine stifled a giggle, subsiding into her chair beneath a withering glance from Patches. 'I'm sorry, Madame. I didn't mean to offend you.'

'Very wise.' Patches moved on to stand beside Luke. 'What are these people doing in my apartment?'

Recovering a little from the shock of seeing the woman who had contributed to Pa's downfall, Clara found her voice. 'We came looking for a friend of mine who once lived here. I had no idea that I would find Luke, and I certainly didn't expect to see you here, Mrs Bragg.'

'It's Miss Bragg, or Madame Duclos if you want to be formal, but Patches will suffice.' Patches looked her up and down. 'I see you've fallen on hard times.' She held her hand up to silence Luke, who had opened his mouth as if to protest. 'Shut up, Foyle. Speak when you're spoken to.'

'What are you doing here, Luke?' Clara demanded angrily. 'I was told you had to leave London because you'd had a fight with Bert Bragg, and you'd left him badly hurt.'

'It was a ruse,' Patches said calmly. 'Luke has been my man from the start. He came to France because he had settled an old feud between the Skinner brothers and myself. They won't be troubling anyone ever again.'

'But you were with the Skinner gang,' Clara said dazedly. 'Were you spying on them for this woman?'

He nodded. 'That's just about it. They were a bad bunch, Clara. The streets of Seven Dials are safer now they're gone to their Maker.'

'You murdered them?' Her voice broke on a sob. 'I don't want anything to do with a killer.'

'Poor little shop girl.' Patches' laughter echoed round the room, causing the crystal drops on the chandeliers to tinkle in protest. 'You knew what Luke was, but you weren't so squeamish when you were living hand to mouth because your pa gambled away the family fortune.' She turned to Paul, pointing a fat finger at him. 'Are you noting this down, Mr Reporter? It will make a good story for your rag, but print it and you're a dead man.'

Paul held his hand out to Sabine. 'I think it's time we left. Are you coming with us, Clara?'

'Yes, but first I must ask Patches something.'

'Go ahead, love.' Patches eased her large body onto a chair. 'Don't worry about me. I'm broad-minded.'

'Do you know Gertrude Batt? This is the address she gave three years ago when she purchased something from one of the department stores.'

'I knew her.' Patches' eyes gleamed with malice. 'She was the creature who led my poor Bertie astray. Besotted with her, he was, poor boy. She'd been thrown out by her lover and she latched on to my son. She recognised a soft heart and a generous nature. He brought her here and set her up under my roof – that is, until I found out what he'd done. I came to Paris and sent her packing. That was the last I heard of her, but she broke my poor boy's heart.'

Clara stared at her in amazement. 'That can't be right. Your son isn't the sort of man that Gertie would fall for.'

'You don't know my son, so you can't say that.'

'I know his reputation, and Gertie is a lady.'

'That's a matter of opinion, love. The slut was using him. She knew she could wrap him round her little finger. Gertrude and that sister of hers are a pair of toffers. She's probably floating face-down in the Seine as we speak, and serve her right.'

Clara was shocked to the core. She did not believe a word that Patches had said, but if Gertie had formed a relationship with Bert Bragg it might explain her presence in the apartment three years ago. Clara glanced at Luke, gauging his reaction, but his stony expression gave away nothing. 'Gertie isn't like that,' she said faintly. 'She was wronged by the man she loved.'

'She ran away with her best friend's fiancé when

she was just fifteen,' Patches said through clenched teeth. 'He was a Frenchman, twenty years her senior, but he had a title and he was wealthy. She knew what she was doing.'

'Might I ask how you know all this, Madame?' Paul asked innocently. 'It seems that Miss Batt moved in somewhat higher circles than you might be familiar with.'

'You're right. But what you don't know is that my pa was French, and I grew up in Paris. I was born Amelie Fournier. Bragg was my mother's maiden name – she was English.'

'But you said your name was Madame Duclos,' Clara said slowly.

'That is my married name. I am a widow.' Patches' eyes narrowed. 'But I come from a good family. My papa was a prosperous merchant and much re-spected.'

Luke uttered a contemptuous snort. 'Be honest, Patches. Your grandfather was a free-trader and so was your father, who continued smuggling goods into England even after the Government lowered tax on luxuries. Your pa was a villain, just like you and your son, and you're here because you're wanted by the police in London.'

'That is true, my dear Luke, and you've been pleased to share our ill-gained profits, so don't look down your nose at me.' Patches punched him on the arm. 'Keep a civil tongue in your head or you might take a midnight swim in the river. The Seine or the Thames, take your pick.'

'I think I've heard enough,' Clara made a move to leave the room, but she stopped in the doorway. 'I suppose neither of you knows where I might start looking for Gertie?'

'I wouldn't tell you if I did.' Patches turned her back on Clara, and Luke shook his head.

Sabine moved to Clara's side. 'Come along. There's no point wasting any more time here.'

'Wait a minute,' Luke said angrily. 'You can't just walk away like this, Clara.'

She turned to face him. 'That's exactly what I'm doing. If I'd known the money came from you I would have returned it straight away.'

'But why? We have an understanding, Clara. It's always been you and me.'

'I was young and foolish when I first met you, and I thought you were brave and clever. I admired the way you stood up for my pa, and I was prepared to believe that you wanted to get away from the gangs. I was wrong.' Ignoring Luke's protests, she went to join Sabine and Paul, who were waiting for her outside on the landing.

'Are you all right?' Sabine asked anxiously.

'I think so,' Clara said slowly. 'It's been a shock, but I'll get over it in time.'

'You're a brave woman, Clara.' Paul brushed her cheek with a kiss.

'You won't put this in your newspaper, will you?' Clara clutched his hand. 'I know it's a lot to ask, but I think Gertie is in danger and I must find her before Patches does.'

He nodded. 'You have my word. More than that, I'll do my best to help you.'

'And I will, too,' Sabine added, giving Clara a hug. 'Let's get away from here in case that awful woman decides to throw us down the stairs, or something equally violent.'

'There's a café in rue Saint-Roch,' Paul said hastily. 'Let's go there. I'll feel safer away from this place.'

In the steamy atmosphere of the small café they sat and drank strong coffee laced with brandy, which Paul advocated for shock. Whether it was true or not, the alcohol sent a warm glow through Clara's veins and she took comfort from being with friends. The pungent smell of French tobacco mingled with the aroma of garlic, wine and ground coffee, and the windows were clouded with condensation, giving Clara a sense of security. She could think more clearly now she was away from Luke's overpowering presence, and she could see him for what he really was – a ruthless thug, prepared to kill. She was not over-concerned as to the fate of the Skinner brothers – they in turn were just as bad as Patches and her gang – but she was afraid for Gertie.

'Perhaps your friend is with that man Patches

spoke about,' Sabine said softly. 'What was his name?'

'Dagobert Duclos, or Bert Bragg, as he's known in London – her son.' Clara glanced at the people seated at the next table, but they were chatting and laughing and patently oblivious to what was going on around them. 'I never met him, but if he's anything like his mother he must be hateful. I can't imagine Gertie being involved with anyone like him.'

Paul shook his head. 'You'd be surprised. The stories I've covered in the past have often revealed the strangest liaisons imaginable. Anything is possible in affairs of the heart.'

'Then I must discover his whereabouts,' Clara said thoughtfully. 'I shouldn't involve you two. This is something I have to do on my own.'

'Never.' Sabine raised her cup in a toast. 'We're in this together. It will be difficult to get away from the store, but Paul will help us, won't you, my love?'

He took her hand and raised it to his lips. 'Of course, and when Gertie is found I will expose Patches and her gang. I'm sure the police on both sides of la Manche will be interested to know her whereabouts.'

Clara had no alternative but to return to Automne and carry on as if nothing had happened, even though the discovery that Luke was involved with Patches Bragg had shocked her to the core. She had allowed herself to be duped by his charm and good looks, but she should have realised that he was unlikely to reform. Luke had sworn that his feelings for her were genuine, but she knew now that his desire to own and possess her did not constitute true love. She was angry with him and humiliated by her own naivety. He was best forgotten, and the only way forward was to find Gertrude and return home. It was hard to imagine a worldly woman like Gertie giving herself to a man who was a well-known criminal, and she could be in mortal danger, especially if Patches decided to intervene.

Clara tossed and turned in the narrow bed, tormented by worry, not least about her sisters left on their own in London. The girls were never far from her mind and she could only hope that her letter had reached them. She had left them with enough money to keep them going, but it would not last for very long. If she could not find Gertie soon she would have to return home, and to that end she would save as much of her wages as possible.

Clara fell asleep just as dawn was breaking, but was jolted back to consciousness by someone shaking her.

'Wake up, Clara. You'd best hurry or we'll be late for breakfast.' Sabine pulled back the coverlet and padded across the floor to the washstand.

'What time is it?' Clara sat up in bed, rubbing

her eyes. The other girls' beds were neatly made and there was no sign of either Hortense or Nina.

'It's time we were on our way downstairs or there'll be nothing left other than cold coffee and breadcrumbs.'

Clara raised herself from the warmth of her bed and threw on her clothes. 'I didn't sleep very well,' she said, picking up her hairbrush and dragging it through her long hair. 'I kept thinking of Gertie with that dreadful woman's son. I must find her, Sabine, but I don't know where to start.'

'Leave it to Paul. He has contacts all over Paris, and if Bert is still in France they'll discover where he is.'

'If he's anything like his mother, heaven help Gertie.' Clara tucked her dark locks into a snood and secured it with hairpins. 'There, I only have to put on my boots and I'm ready.'

'Well done,' Sabine said, smiling. 'Maybe Paul will have some news for you by this evening.'

After closing time, Clara and Sabine walked to the café in rue Saint-Roch where they found Paul seated at a table with a glass of wine in front of him. His broad grin gave Clara hope as she went to join him. 'Have you any news for me?'

Sabine followed more slowly and Paul rose to his feet, pulling out a chair for each of them. He waited until they were settled. 'What would you like to drink, ladies?'

Clara reached across the table to grasp his hand. 'Never mind that for a moment. I can tell by your expression that you know something. Tell me, please.'

Chapter Sixteen

Paul caught the attention of a waiter and ordered more wine. 'The *vin ordinaire* is passable,' he said when the man was out of earshot.

Sabine nudged him in the ribs. 'Don't tease us, Paul. What have you discovered?'

He leaned across the table, lowering his voice. 'The son of that person we met yesterday is on the run from the police.'

'That's no surprise.' Clara could have cried with disappointment. 'He's part of his mother's gang.'

'It might surprise you to know that they confined their criminal activities to London. Neither of them was wanted here until a couple of days ago, when Dagobert Duclos, or Bert Bragg, as you know him better, lost his temper and half killed a man. Apparently he'd been hiding out in an *atelier* in

Montmartre, and someone tipped off the police, but he'd left by the time they got there.'

'How does that help us?' Sabine asked anxiously. 'It's not fair to raise Clara's hopes only to dash them again.'

'The landlord told me that Monsieur Duclos had left in a hurry, owing him money, and he had a woman with him. The man remembered her particularly because she had seemed to be ill, and had to be helped into the fiacre. He hadn't seen her before, and neither had the people in the rooms below, nor in the shop on the ground floor.'

'Do you think it was Gertie?' Clara could hardly form the words. 'Did he give you a description?'

'Was she dark or fair, Paul?' Sabine added eagerly. 'Was she young or old?'

'He couldn't tell me what she looked like because she was wrapped in a cloak and her face was covered, but Duclos has a reputation with women, so the landlord said, and he was well known in the local bars.'

Clara stared at him in dismay. 'I'm sorry, Paul, but I don't see how this helps. It might not have been Gertie.'

'There is one way to find out. We need to go there and take a look at the room. I'm well in with the landlord, so there won't be a problem.' Paul drank the last of his wine and set the glass down on the table. 'What do you say?'

'Yes, of course. We must do that,' Clara said eagerly.

'But we have to be back in our room at Automne by half-past ten.' Sabine glanced at the clock behind the bar. 'That doesn't give us long, Paul.'

He rose to his feet. 'Long enough, I'd say. I'll go and find a fiacre. We'll be there in no time at all.'

Clara downed her wine in one gulp. 'It's worth a try.'

The narrow streets of Montmartre were crowded with people out for a good time, as well as those who used the darkness to cover their less respectable professions. Gaslight created a theatrical atmosphere where anything and everything seemed possible. Revellers sat at tables outside bars and cafés, enjoying their free time, while pickpockets and prostitutes lurked in the shadows.

Oblivious to all this, Clara stood on the cobblestones outside the bar where the cab had dropped them. It was the first time she had been to this part of Paris, and had the circumstances been different she would have been enchanted by the exotic ambience, but growing up in Seven Dials had made her wary of the night people, and she moved a little closer to Paul, who was talking to the owner of the street café.

Sabine reached out to hold her hand. 'It's not the sort of place I would come to on my own, at least not at night.'

'Nor I,' Clara glanced at the crowded tables. Some

of the clientele were obviously wealthy Parisians, enjoying themselves, while others less prosperous might be artists or artisans eager to forget the hardships of daily life. Smoke from pipes and cigars rose in fragrant clouds to dissipate in the darkness above the rooftops, and a ragged girl was singing to the accompaniment of a youth playing a fiddle. Clara felt a lump in her throat as she remembered how Nathaniel had once had to supplement his income by busking on the chilly streets of London. The gold signet ring was a constant reminder of their friendship, and although she intended to return it to him one day, she knew that parting with it would make her sad. At least she had helped him to fulfil one of the conditions set down in his father's will, even if their engagement had been a sham. In a few months' time he would reach the age when he could legally inherit his late father's estate, and then she would return the ring. She jumped at the sound of Sabine's voice.

'Paul is beckoning to us,' Sabine said, tugging at Clara's sleeve. 'We can go in. Let's hope we find something.'

'Lead on. I'm right behind you.' Clara and Sabine entered the dimly lit café. The air was filled with the aroma of cooking, and steam from the kitchen enveloped them in a damp cloud. They edged their way between the packed tables, following the light of Paul's candle as it seemed to float up the narrow staircase like a will-o'-the-wisp.

The *atelier* was little more than a large attic with one dormer window overlooking the street, and a smaller window in the roof. In the flickering candle-light it was quite obvious that the last tenant had made a hasty departure. Clothes and shoes had been strewn about on the unmade bed, and the remains of a meal had been abandoned on the table. Wine had dripped from a bottle that lay on its side, pooling on the dusty floorboards that were already stained with paint. The smell of linseed oil and turpentine lingered in the musty air, as if the artist's spirit remained in the studio where he had once lived and worked.

Clara began sifting through the discarded garments. 'Bring the candle over here, Paul,' she cried excitedly. 'I think I recognise this scarf.' She examined the delicate silk. 'I'm certain this was from the stock I had in Drury Lane. I remember giving it to Gertie saying that it suited her colouring.' She turned to Sabine, who was peering over Paul's shoulder. 'Gertie is dark-haired like you and me, and she has the most beautiful brown eyes.'

'It's just a scarf,' Paul said dismissively. 'There must be many more like this.'

Sabine began sifting through the items. 'Ugh,' she said, tossing a woollen sock onto the floor. 'Whoever wore this had smelly feet.'

Paul picked up a shoe. 'What about this, Clara? Does this look familiar?'

Clara examined it carefully. 'It could be Gertie's, but I'm not sure.'

'Keep looking,' Paul said, dropping the shoe. 'I'll see if I can find another candle. We need more light.'

'I need to take another look at the shoe, or if I can find the other one it might help.' She went down on her hands and knees and was feeling about under the bed when her fingers touched something small, round and familiar. Clutching it, she scrambled to her feet. 'Just a minute, Paul. Bring the light here.' She opened her hand and lying on her palm was a fabric-covered button. 'This came off Gertie's bodice.'

'It's just a button,' Sabine said doubtfully. 'It could have come off any dress that colour.'

'That's true, but it's the thread that makes me so sure. I couldn't match the colour exactly, and there's a scrap of the cotton still attached. I'd swear that this came from the gown that Gertie was wearing.'

'Here's the other shoe.' Paul bent down to retrieve the battered item of footwear. 'Badly worn, just like its partner.'

'They were too small for her.' Clara tucked the button into her reticule. 'We couldn't afford to buy a new pair. Now I'm certain she was here and that means she's with Bert Bragg, or whatever he likes to call himself.'

Paul nodded. 'The landlord said that a Monsieur Duclos rented the room, but he didn't know anything more about him.'

Clara's hopes were dashed. 'We've missed them. I can't believe it.'

'What do we do now?' Sabine slipped her arm around Clara's shoulders. 'We were so close, but that's a good thing, isn't it? They can't have gone far.' She turned an eager face to Paul. 'If this was a case you were reporting, what would you do now?'

'I'd go back to the office and have a strong cup of coffee.'

'I'm serious, Paul.' Sabine gave Clara an encouraging hug. 'Don't take any notice of him. He thinks he's being funny.'

'There isn't much we can do,' Clara said sadly. 'He isn't likely to have taken Gertie to his mother's house. I don't think Patches would be interested, unless there was a large ransom to be had for Gertie's return.' She clapped her hand over her mouth.

'What is it?' Paul demanded. 'Why are you looking like that, Clara?'

'You're shaking,' Sabine added. 'Are you feeling faint? You'd best sit down.' She pressed Clara down onto the bed. 'This is all your fault, Paul. You shouldn't have made a joke of it.'

'No, it's all right,' Clara said dazedly. 'I think I know why Bert has been keeping Gertie a prisoner.'

'You don't know that she was held against her will.' Paul eyed her warily. 'She has quite a reputation here in Paris.'

'That's probably true, but Bert would know that Gertie's sister is a wealthy woman. I have a feeling that he *is* going to demand a ransom.'

'That's supposition.' Paul did not look convinced.

'Clara could be right,' Sabine said thoughtfully. 'This isn't the sort of place a man would bring someone he wanted to seduce.' She glanced round, shuddering. 'It's not exactly romantic.'

Clara sprang to her feet. 'This might be suitable for the sort of women that Bert normally consorts with, but it wouldn't impress someone like Gertie. For all her wild ways, she was brought up to be a lady.'

'I'm not sure that helps,' Sabine said wistfully. 'London is a long way from here. How will you know if her sister has received a ransom note?'

'It will take days for a letter to reach Lady Quinn.' Clara sat down again, suddenly deflated. 'I think Gertie is in real danger.'

'You're forgetting the electrical telegraph system,' Paul said cheerfully. 'We can send a telegram to Gertie's sister and receive a reply within hours.'

'I'm not sure that Lady Quinn will help.' Clara had a sudden vision of the eccentric person commanding her small empire from the comfort of her mansion, and she was not convinced. 'The sisters aren't on speaking terms, and her ladyship is a difficult woman.'

Paul opened the door. 'Maybe the threat of a scandal will change all that.'

'Maybe,' Clara said doubtfully. 'But we don't know for certain that Gertie was taken by force. We only have what the landlord said, and there could be all manner of explanations for the state of the woman who was with Bert.'

Sabine nodded. 'I agree with Clara. We should be careful not to jump to conclusions, Paul.'

Clara sighed, shaking her head. 'But that still leaves me not knowing what's happened to Gertie.'

'You'll find her.' Sabine patted Clara on the shoulder. 'I'm sure of it.'

'But I can't stay in Paris much longer, Sabine. I have to get home as soon as I've saved enough money for my fare. My sisters will be struggling without me there to help them.'

'I'll ask my colleagues if they know anything about Duclos,' Paul said firmly. 'His name appears regularly in the society columns.'

'I'd be so grateful.' Clara managed a smile as she left the room. The darkness of the narrow staircase wrapped itself around her, blotting out everything but the need to escape into the fresh air. She reached the ground floor and stumbled out into the cool of the night, and suddenly everything became clear. This was her problem and she could not ask any more favours from Paul and Sabine. There was only one person who could help her now.

*

It had been easy to convince Paquet that she was too ill to work, even though it meant losing several hours' pay. Clara knew she was not looking her best as she made her way on foot to rue de Rivoli, but she was desperate.

Madame Tasse grunted something unintelligible and turned her back on Clara, leaving her to make her way to the apartment, and the maid was less than enthusiastic when she answered Clara's knock on the door.

'Monsieur Foyle,' Clara said loudly. She glanced over the girl's shoulder, and raised her voice. 'Luke, are you there?'

He emerged from the drawing room, barking a command to the maid, who stood aside holding the door open. Clara took a deep breath. She had come this far and there was no turning back. Luke ushered her into the room, closing the door behind them.

'Well, this is a surprise. I thought you didn't want anything to do with me.'

'I don't, at least not in the way you mean.' Clara faced him with her hands clasped tightly in front of her. She must not show any signs of weakness or she would be lost. Luke had a way of making her forget everything other than the force of his personality.

'Won't you take a seat?' He assumed the air of a genial host, smiling benevolently although there was a wary look in his eyes. 'You must have a good reason for coming here today, Clara.'

She remained standing. 'Do you know where I can contact Bert Bragg?'

'No, I don't, and that's the truth. He doesn't come here very often.'

'But he must have an address in Paris. Could you ask his mother for me?'

'Why would I put you in touch with an evil person like Bert? You might have a poor opinion of me, Clara, but I still care about you.'

'And I like you, Luke – it's just your way of life I can't stand, and you chose that over me. I wouldn't want anything bad to happen to you.'

'That's a comforting thought. I'll remember that when I'm about to swing from the gallows.'

'Don't say things like that.'

'If I was the villain you think I am that is what would happen to me if I returned to London. I admit that I was aware that the Skinner brothers were in imminent danger, but there was nothing I could do about it. In any case, they were vicious men and they'd murdered scores of people – some of them innocent, I've no doubt.'

'Then why did you associate with them, Luke? Why didn't you try to get honest work?' Despite her misgivings, Clara wanted to believe the best of him. The old, familiar tug of attraction was still there, no matter how she fought against it.

'There you have me, my love. I like the things that money can buy, and I didn't see any other way of achieving my ends.'

'At least you admit your faults,' she said grudgingly, 'but that doesn't mean to say I agree with what you do or the way you live. Coming here today wasn't easy, but I need your help. I have to find Gertie and I want to go home. I must return to London because I've left the girls on their own. Heaven knows how they've been getting on in my absence.'

'So you've come to ask me for money.' It was more a statement of fact than a question. Luke went to stand by the window, staring down at the street below. 'How much do you need?'

A wave of relief washed over Clara, bringing her close to tears. 'Just enough to get me to London. I'll pay you back as soon as the store is making a profit.'

'Don't worry about that. You were fond of me once; maybe I can redeem myself in your eyes with another generous gesture.'

'I'd rather not be beholden to you, but I am very grateful, Luke.'

'When do you want to travel? I'll take you as far as Calais, but from there onward you're on your own.'

'After what I've been through travelling alone won't trouble me at all. I just wish I could find Gertie, or at least speak to Bert.'

'Forget him, Clara. Keep well away from Bragg.' Luke glanced at the clock on the mantelshelf. 'I don't want to seem inhospitable, but Patches will be back any moment now and it's probably best if she doesn't see you here.'

'Why? I haven't done her any wrong.'

'You're young and pretty and she knows that I'm fond of you. Patches may be past her prime but she's a jealous woman. She doesn't encourage followers, if you get my meaning.'

Clara stared at him in astonishment. 'You and she? No, surely not?'

'Not on my part, but Patches likes to think of herself as being desirable. I flatter her and entertain her, but not in the way you're thinking.'

'I didn't imagine so, not for a moment.'

Luke threw back his head and laughed. 'Then why are you blushing? I can assure you that there is nothing untoward between Patches and myself. She thinks she has a chance with me, but as far as I'm concerned there is only one woman for me, and you know who that is.'

'I have to go, Luke. I need to get back to the store and explain things to Paquet and to Sabine, who has been so kind to me.'

'If you're ready to leave tomorrow morning I'll come for you at seven.'

*

Clara had intended to return to the store, but she was close to the Conservatoire and she could not leave Paris without one last attempt to contact Nathaniel. If, on his return to London, he discovered that she had been in Paris and had not done her very best to see him, he would never forgive her, and she valued his friendship too much to allow that to happen. Nathaniel had allowed her to accept his aunt's bequest without contesting the will – but for his generosity she and her sisters would have been homeless. It was a debt she could never repay.

Catching him between engagements might be a vain hope, but when she reached the building she marched inside, assuming an air of confidence she was far from feeling. The man at the reception desk did not understand a word of what she said and her efforts at mime seemed to confuse him even more. She was just about to give up when an elderly gentleman whose silver-streaked hair, walrus moustache and impressive beard marked him out as someone to be reckoned with, came to her rescue. He spoke to the concierge and after a brief conversation he turned to Clara with a disarming smile.

'I know the young man you seek,' he said in perfect English with just a hint of a lilting accent. 'I believe he has just returned from a tour of the provinces.'

'I need to see him urgently, Monsieur. Do you know where I might find him?'

'Unless I am very much mistaken, there is a rehearsal in progress. It would be my pleasure to escort you to where I think you might find your friend.'

Clara could have kissed him, but that would be going too far. She seized his hand and shook it, thanking him over and over again.

'Come.' He led the way through the echoing corridors but as they reached the concert hall the door opened and the members of the orchestra filed out.

'I will leave you now.' Her new friend walked away and was swallowed up in the crowd as musicians flooded out of the concert hall, but at that moment Clara spotted Nathaniel and she edged her way towards him, waving and calling his name.

'Clara.' His astonished expression melted into a wide smile. 'How wonderful. I can't believe it's you. What are you doing here?'

She sidestepped a young man who was holding his violin over his head and waving the bow as if in a cavalry charge. 'Is there somewhere we can talk, Nat? I'm leaving for home in the morning.'

'Of course, but how did you come to know the great man?'

Clara stared at him blankly. 'Who?'

'Our esteemed conductor, Monsieur George-Hainl. You were talking to him just now.' Nathaniel guided her to a side room and opened the door, closing it behind her. 'That's better; now we can hear ourselves speak.' He laid his violin on the table as tenderly as if it were a new-born baby, placing the bow neatly at its side, before turning his attention to Clara.

'I was trying to make the concierge understand what I wanted when that old gentleman came to my aid. He was very charming and he said he knew you.'

Nathaniel's eyes widened and he let out a long breath. 'I'm astounded. I thought I was the lowest of the low. That's wonderful.' He pulled up a chair. 'Even more wonderful is seeing you. Sit down and tell me everything.'

Clara sank onto the hard wooden seat, but after a couple of false starts, due to Nathaniel interrupting with one question after another, she managed to give him an outline of the events that had taken place since he left London.

'I'm so sorry,' he said when she finished speaking. 'I wish I'd been here when you first arrived. I can't begin to imagine what you've suffered in such a short space of time.'

'I know,' Clara agreed, 'it's little more than a week, but it feels as if I've been in Paris for months, and now I've found you again it's just to say goodbye.'

'Do you have to leave tomorrow, Clara? Couldn't you stay just a while longer? You didn't get to hear me play at the Gaiety, and now you'll miss the opportunity to attend the concert tomorrow evening.'

He seemed oblivious to her problems, even though she had explained the situation in detail, and she stared at him in dismay. 'I've told you I can't leave my sisters to cope on their own for any longer than necessary. I have to go home, even though I can't find Gertie.'

He frowned. 'Of course. I see that it's important to you, but I still wish you could stay for one more day. I'd be so proud to have you in the audience.' He took her right hand in his. 'And you still wear my ring, although on a different finger.'

'You know we were never really engaged.'

'I know, but I hoped you might be waiting for me when I return to London. I've finished my concerto and I'm trying to find an opportunity to ask the maestro his opinion of my work. It would mean everything to have the approval of such a great man.'

Clara rose to her feet. Nathaniel seemed different from the person she had known in London. He even looked different, although it was hard to pinpoint the exact change in his appearance. What was becoming clear was his unswerving devotion to his music. He was pleased to see her, but it was obvious that his mind was on other things.

'I have to go now, Nat. I have things to do.'

'So soon? But we've hardly had time to talk.'

'I understand how music rules your life, and there is little room for anything or anyone else.' She reached up to brush his cheek with a kiss. 'I wish you every success. I'm sure you'll become very famous and I'll be proud to say I knew you when you were a struggling musician.' She slipped off the ring and laid it on the table next to his violin. 'You don't need a fiancée now, Nat. In a few months you'll have everything you ever wanted.'

He snatched up the ring. 'I'd like you to keep it to remind you of me. Please stay a little longer.'

'I'm sorry. I really do have to go.' She left the room, half expecting him to rush after her, but the door remained closed and as she walked away she could hear the sad strains of Mendelssohn's Violin Concerto echoing through the corridors.

That evening, as they were getting ready for bed, Clara broke the news to Sabine.

'Of course I understand that you have to leave us, but I'll miss you.' Sabine's large eyes brimmed with tears and she wrapped her arms around Clara. 'It will be like losing a dear sister.'

Clara returned the embrace, trying hard not to cry. 'I'll miss you, too. You've been a good friend to me, and I can't thank you enough. I might have ended up sleeping on the riverbank if it hadn't been for you.'

Sabine held her at arm's length. 'Are you sure that you can trust Luke? You might find yourself in the same position as Gertie.'

'He isn't a bad man at heart, and I don't believe he would do anything to harm me.'

'I hope you're right, Clara.' Sabine produced a crumpled hanky and blew her nose. 'You must let me know how you are getting on.' Her voice broke and she turned away, her shoulders heaving.

Clara slipped her arm around her friend. 'Don't be upset, Sabine. I promise to write to you and I'll return to Paris at the first possible opportunity. After all, this is the fashion capital of Europe, and Automne is the most famous department store in France.'

'That's right, and I hope you will remember me when you are rich and successful. Maybe I'll come and work for you.'

'That would be wonderful, but what about Paul? You will probably be married with half a dozen little ones by the time I make anything of my store, and it won't be as grand as Automne.'

'I love Paul, and he says he loves me, but sometimes I think he loves his work more than anything or anyone. I will always be second best.'

'I think you're wrong,' Clara said stoutly. 'It's obvious that he's devoted to you, but if he doesn't come up to scratch there will be a position waiting for you at The Button Box.'

'The Button Box,' Sabine repeated, smiling. 'Is that what you call your store?'

'I named it after my most precious possession, and I will have a stand devoted to buttons of all shapes and sizes. When you come to London I will show you my collection of memories, each one as important as the last.'

Sabine clapped her hands. 'It is a lovely idea.' She was suddenly alert, listening with her head cocked on one side. 'Someone is coming. It's probably Nina; she never stays out late, unlike Hortense, who is probably in a café drinking absinthe with Gaston and his friends.'

'Don't tell her that I'm leaving,' Clara whispered. 'I don't want to go through it all again. It was bad enough explaining to Monsieur Loussier, who was good enough to give me work when I was in desperate need. I asked him to explain to Paquet, and make my apologies for leaving so abruptly.'

Sabine nodded, saying nothing as the door opened to admit Nina, who flounced in and threw herself down on her bed, rattling off a string of sentences in rapid French.

Clara pulled back the covers and climbed into bed. Tomorrow night she would be at home with her family, and then the hard work would really begin. Despite her worries for Gertie's safety, her head was buzzing with ideas for improving her small dominion. The lessons she had learned here at Automne would help her to put her theories into practice. She closed her eyes and fell asleep to the sound of Nina's complaining tones.

Chapter Seventeen

Luke was waiting for Clara next morning when she left by the side door. She had crept out of the bedroom without disturbing the sleeping girls, and had managed to make her way along the narrow corridors and down the back stairs without being seen. It seemed strange, but in a way she was sad to leave.

The horse's breath steamed in the cool air as it pawed the ground and snorted, as if telling her to hurry up. Luke opened the door of the fiacre and tossed Clara's valise onto the seat before handing her into the vehicle. He climbed in after her, giving a curt instruction to the cabby.

'You are doing the right thing,' he said seriously. 'Nothing good could have come of it had you decided to remain in Paris.'

She settled into the seat, keeping as far away from him as possible. 'Why do you say that? What do you know?'

'Just that Patches is very protective of her reputation and that of her son. In London she doesn't care, but here in her native France she wishes to be known as a pillar of society.'

'But she's made her money from crime. If Paul Bonnet and his colleagues know about her why don't they publish the truth?'

'Patches still owns a fashionable club in Paris and has influential friends. She donates large sums to selected charities, and I suspect that she offers bribes to certain people in authority. I can't prove it because she's too clever to be caught, but one day she will slip up and the truth will out.'

Clara met his gaze with a questioning look. 'Why do you stay with her, Luke? You could do so much better for yourself.'

'I told you why, my love. I'm an idle fellow who likes to live in luxury without having to work too hard.'

'I don't believe you mean that,' Clara said slowly. 'I've seen a different side of you, and you're not the person you make yourself out to be.'

He leaned back against the squabs. 'Go on. I like the sound of myself as you see me.'

'You can joke about it, but I remember the time that Jane had mumps and couldn't eat for days.

You bought oranges from the market, because they are her favourite fruit, and she could sip the juice from a feeding cup, and you gave her a rag doll. You always remember her weakness for sugared almonds and Jane adores you. She cried when you went away.'

'Did you cry, Clara?'

She turned her head and gazed out of the window. 'No, Luke. You'll never make me cry.'

'I'd rather see you smile,' he said earnestly. 'No matter what you think of me, I still love you.'

'No,' she said slowly. 'You may think it's so, but if you truly loved me you wouldn't have come to Paris with Patches. Anyway, I don't want to talk about it, Luke. We'll only end up quarrelling.'

'Have it your own way, but you know where I am if you ever need my help.'

She let this pass without a response. Luke had a way of charming her into agreeing with everything he said, and she was not in the mood for small talk. For most of the onward journey they spoke only when necessary.

They parted on the quay at Calais. Clara was about to board the cross-channel steamer bound for Dover when Luke took her in his arms and planted a kiss on her lips. 'That's to remember me by, Clara. This isn't the end of you and me.'

'You're wrong, Luke. This is goodbye, but that doesn't mean I'm not grateful for everything.' She turned away and was about to step onto the gang-plank when he caught her by the hand.

'There's one thing that might help you find your friend. I don't know whether she's with Bert, but he has rooms in Clarges Street that Patches knows nothing about.'

'Why would you think he's taken Gertie there?'

'Bert Bragg can never keep out of trouble for long. If he's had a brush with the *gendarmerie* he might have decided to return to London.' He thrust a leather pouch into her hand. 'You'd best board the ship, Clara. This will pay for your railway ticket and a cab to Oxford Street, with a bit more to keep you going.' He laid his finger on her lips as she opened her mouth to protest. 'You'll repay me – I know. Now go or you'll be left standing here, and you'll have to stay with me. You wouldn't want that, would you?'

'Thank you, Luke.' Clara gave him a reluctant smile as she tucked the money into her reticule. 'I won't forget this.' She hurried aboard but when she turned to wave to Luke there was no sign of him. He had disappeared into the crowd, and a momentary feeling of loss was replaced by a sigh of relief. She was on her way home at last.

'Oh, so you do remember where you live, Clara Carter.' Betsy slammed the door with unnecessary force. 'We thought you were never coming home.'

'I've been travelling all day and I'm cold, tired and hungry. I'm not in the mood for your sulks, Betsy.' Clara put her valise down and peeled off her gloves as she glanced round at the depleted shelves. The shop floor was dusty and pieces of cotton thread were interlaced with balls of fluff, adding to the general atmosphere of disarray.

'We've been too busy to think about sweeping and dusting. Just finding enough money to buy food has taken all our time,' Betsy said defensively. 'You said you were going for a couple of days.'

'I know, and I tried to explain in my letter, but I'll tell you everything over supper.'

Betsy locked the shop door and pulled down the blind. 'You'll have to get used to bread and scrape again. I expect you've been living like a toff in Paris.'

'You have no idea what I've been through,' Clara said tiredly. 'Is Jane in the kitchen?'

'You'll probably find her crying her eyes out. We've run out of everything, including coal and candles, so we haven't been able to boil water and we've had to feel our way upstairs in the dark. Even worse, I had to share a bed with Jane to keep from freezing to death, and Lizzie isn't speaking to us because you went to Paris with her beau.'

Clara opened her reticule and took out the purse. Luke had been generous, as always – meanness was not one of his failings – and what remained after paying for her fare home would keep them for a week or more.

'Joss Comerford isn't her beau and never was, except in Lizzie's imagination, and she's better off that way. He abandoned me in Paris and after I'd paid our hotel bill I was left penniless with no way to get home, so don't mention his name to me again.'

Betsy stared at the coins as they glinted in the gaslight. 'Where did you get so much money? You can't have earned that in the shop you mentioned in your letter, which only arrived a couple of days ago.'

'I'll tell you over supper.' Clara slipped the coins back in the pouch. 'I'll just let Jane know that I'm home, and then we'll go out and get everything we need. Things are going to be better from now on. I promise you that.'

'Where's Gertie?' Betsy demanded. 'Did you leave her in Paris?'

'I don't know where she is, and that's the honest truth. I'd have come home sooner if I hadn't been trying to find her.'

Clara made her way to the kitchen where she found Jane attempting to scrape the last of the dripping onto a crust of stale bread.

'Clara!' Jane dropped the knife and, moving as quickly as her calipers would allow, she rounded the table and flung her arms around her sister's neck. 'You've come home. I've missed you so much. Why did you stay away for so long?'

'I'm here now and I won't go away again.' Clara hugged her and was alarmed to feel the thinness of Jane's small body, even allowing for the layers of clothes she was wearing. 'Explanations later. First we're going out to get essentials. Are you feeling strong enough to come with us?'

'I should say so,' Jane said stoutly. 'I'm not letting you out of my sight in case you disappear again, and I'm so hungry my stomach hurts.'

'We can't have that.' Clara patted Jane's cheek. 'Everything will be all right. I've come back from Paris with new ideas for the shop, and you'll never guess who I met there.' She took Jane's cape from the back of a chair and wrapped it around her sister's shoulders.

'I can't think.'

'It was Luke, and he sends you his love. He's given us money to tide us over, for a while at least.'

Jane clapped her hands and her eyes shone. 'I love him too. I wish you'd married him, Clara. He's a good man really.'

'Never mind that now. Food and warmth are the most important things at present. Betsy's locked up and we mustn't keep her waiting because she's not very pleased with me at present.'

'I don't care about anything as long as you're here, Clara.'

*

With the fire burning brightly in the range and the kettle bubbling on the hob, Clara and the girls sat round the table finishing their supper. The hot meat pies and baked potatoes, oozing with butter, had disappeared within minutes, and they had done justice to the chocolate cake that Clara had bought as a special treat. In between mouthfuls she had gone through the events that had led her to Automne, and her experience of living and working in the prestigious Parisian store. Betsy and Jane listened avidly, throwing in question after question, especially when it came to Clara's brush with Patches and her reunion with Luke. Betsy was more interested in the latest Paris fashions than in Clara's meeting with Nathaniel, but Jane wanted to hear every last detail of how he had looked and what he had said. Clara was beginning to think that her little sister was growing up fast, perhaps too fast, as her pale cheeks were flushed and her eyes brightened each time Nathaniel's name was mentioned.

'I would like to go to Paris to study the latest fashions.' Betsy fixed Clara with a steely gaze. 'It's not fair that you have all the fun.'

'I can't say it was entirely enjoyable,' Clara said with a wry smile. 'But, if we do well, I think it would be a good idea for you to spend some time in Paris.'

'Really?' Betsy was clearly stunned by this response. 'You'd trust me to do that?'

'Of course I would. I told you, we're all in this

together. We're a family firm and we have to rely on each other if we're to make a success of the business. Working together, we'll be unstoppable.'

'Well, I suppose I could start by making the tea,' Betsy said, rising to her feet. She went through the ritual. 'Real tea,' she said, closing her eyes as she inhaled the fragrant steam. 'We've used the old leaves so many times that we've been drinking hot water.' She filled three cups. 'And fresh milk – such luxury.'

Once again a wave of guilt washed over Clara. A few years ago they had taken such mundane things for granted, never thinking that their comfortable way of life would come to an end. Pa's addiction to gambling had left them on the verge of bankruptcy, but starting up in Oxford Street had been equally risky, and it was her ambition and determination to succeed that had left her sisters in a sorry state.

'This is just the beginning,' she said, trying to sound confident. 'We'll make a success of The Button Box. It will be the best store in Oxford Street, and if things go well I'll send you to Paris, Betsy. You will have Sabine to show you around.'

'You sound as though you enjoyed working at the fancy French store,' Betsy said suspiciously. 'I'm surprised that you came home.'

'It was an experience I wouldn't have missed, but it wasn't easy. I couldn't speak their language, and not everyone made me welcome, but I'm home now, and glad to be here.'

'What will you do about Gertie?' Betsy sat down to finish her slice of cake. 'Maybe she doesn't want to be found.'

'I want to be sure that she's safe,' Clara said slowly. 'I think I ought to pay her sister a visit. She knows Paris well and she might be able to offer some advice. Anyway, I'll think about that tomorrow. I'm tired and I'm ready for bed.'

Jane stood up and began to stack the plates in the stone sink. 'At least we have candles to light our way tonight.'

'The first thing I'll do when we make a profit will be to have gaslight on all floors,' Clara said, yawning. 'Just like . . .'

'Just like they had in Paris.' Betsy finished the sentence for her. 'I think we're going to be heartily sick of hearing about your wonderful French department store, Clara.'

'Well, I love the sound of it,' Jane said firmly. 'I don't suppose I'll ever see Paris, but I can dream, can't I?'

Clara stood up and moved swiftly to her side, giving her little sister a warm hug. 'Hold on to your dreams, poppet. Who knows what the future holds, but I promise you we'll never go back to being poor.'

As she pulled up the blinds next morning and light flooded into the shop, Clara was dismayed to find that things were worse than they had seemed last evening. The bolts of cotton, silk and satin looked plain and uninspiring, and the range of colours was limited and unexciting. The window display was dusty and, compared to the extravagance of the large Paris department stores, it appeared amateurish and clumsy. She began by clearing everything away, other than the button box as it rested on its black velvet cushion. The result was stark, but striking, and she folded the lengths of blue and green satin, adding them to fill the gaps on the shelves.

She swept the floor and tidied up, but she knew in her heart that it was not enough. If she wanted to attract customers she must have more merchandise, and there had to be something in her emporium that was not to be found in the established stores. With the shop closed Clara had plenty of time to think. Finding Gertie was important, of course, but if the shop failed they would lose their home yet again. She waited until Betsy put in an appearance, munching a slice of toast.

'Jane says you're to go and get your breakfast,' she said, licking her lips. 'I know we've been closed, but I think you owe me a day off.'

'Do you want to go somewhere special?'

'I was thinking of asking Miss Lavelle to take me on again. We can't make enough money to support three of us, let alone four, should Gertie decide to come back.'

Alarmed, Clara laid her hand on her sister's arm.

'Don't do that, Betsy. By all means take time off, but I need you here to help me build up the business. You worked long hours for that woman with very little in return.'

'But at least I was paid. I haven't a penny to my name, Clara. I can't afford to buy a pair of stockings and we barely have enough to eat. We can't go on like this.'

'You're right.' Clara took a deep breath. 'And I know what to do about it. Will you stay here with Jane for the rest of the morning? You can go out this afternoon and the whole of tomorrow, if you like, but there's something I must do, and I hope it will be to our advantage.'

'What are you up to now? You're not going to disappear again, are you?'

'I sincerely hope not. I'm going to Bedford Square and I'm going to make Joss Comerford face up to what he's done. He owes me money and he has a warehouse filled with exotic goods, including Indian silks, surah and chintz, which he can't sell, but I can.'

'He'll laugh in your face.'

'If he does I'll go straight to his father and tell him how his precious son treated me, or at least I'll threaten to do so. I think Joss is terrified of his pa and he'll do anything to get in his father's good books.'

'All right,' Betsy said, grudgingly. 'But only until

midday. If you get nowhere with Joss Comerford I'm going to see Miss Lavelle.'

'That should be long enough. I'll get my bonnet and shawl.'

Joss was about to leave the house when Clara alighted from the cab, and she was glad that she had opted for the luxury of a carriage ride instead of walking to Bedford Square. She was meeting him as an equal and not as an inferior, begging for a favour. He had seen her and was about to hurry past, but she barred his way.

'I'm in a hurry, Miss Carter. Get out of my way, if you please, and remember to use the tradesmen's entrance.'

Ignoring the insult, she faced him squarely. 'My business is with you, sir.'

'You won't get a penny out of me.'

'I don't want your money, but I have come to offer you a business deal.'

His bark of laughter scared the birds that had been peacefully pecking for food in the gardens and they took flight with a great flapping of wings. 'You want to do business with me? You haven't got two halfpennies to rub together.'

'Largely thanks to you. It was a caddish trick to leave me with the hotel bill, and you took our return travel tickets with you.'

'Oh, that! It was an oversight. Anyway, you

obviously got yourself home or you wouldn't be standing here now, wasting my time. Move out of the way, or do I have to make you?'

Clara stood her ground. 'I'll be to the point, sir. You owe me a considerable sum of money, as well as compensation for the inconvenience I suffered because of your behaviour.'

'Well, get to the nub of the matter, my dear. How much do you want?' His full lips were drawn back in a sneer that might easily develop into a lupine snarl if he were crossed further.

'You have a warehouse filled with goods you cannot shift. I'll take them off your hands and sell them, giving you a percentage of the profit.'

His expression changed subtly. 'What? I've never heard of such impertinence. Have you any idea what those goods are worth?'

'Not very much while they're locked up and probably deteriorating in a damp dockside warehouse.'

'Go away and leave business to your elders and betters. You have as much chance of succeeding in your little shop as I have of becoming King Emperor.'

'As to that, I think the odds are on my side, but if you refuse I will be forced to go to your father. I don't think Mr Comerford would be pleased to learn of your conduct towards me, or to hear that you've been flirting with my sister, a servant in his house.'

'He wouldn't believe you.' Joss ran his finger round

the inside of his starched collar and his face reddened. 'Don't try to blackmail me, miss. It won't work.'

Clara mounted the steps and raised the door knocker. 'We'll put it to the test, shall we?'

'Wait.' He held up his hand. 'Perhaps we can discuss this over dinner tonight?'

'We settle it here and now or I'll knock on the door and demand to see your father.'

He gave her a calculating look. 'Very well, but I want sixty per cent of the profits.'

'As I'll be doing all the work and accepting the risk that some of the contents might be damaged and therefore worthless, shall we say thirty per cent for you?'

'Fifty,' he countered.

'Forty.' She held out her hand. 'And I'll take off the money you owe me for your share of the hotel bill.'

Reluctantly, he shook hands. 'Agreed, but you pay for transporting the goods from the warehouse.'

'That's fair enough, but I want to see what I'm getting.'

He took a gold half-hunter watch from his waist-coat pocket. 'I'm late. All right, I agree, you witch. I'll meet you at Comerford's Warehouse, London Docks, the North Quay, tomorrow morning at ten o'clock. Don't be late.'

The warehouse was one of many, huddled together in the narrow streets close to the London Dock.

The putrid smell of the river and the stench of overflowing sewage mingled oddly with the scent of roasting coffee beans, tinged with a hint of spices imported from the East Indies, and the treacly scent of molasses and rum from the West Indies. The sound of barrels being rolled over cobblestones, cranes creaking and cartwheels rumbling, formed a background for the shouts of stevedores and the hoots of steamers as they negotiated the tide. Clara had never been this close to the throbbing heart of the city, grown rich from trade and commerce. She felt dwarfed by the tall buildings and suffocated by the miasma rising from the muddy foreshore. She was almost relieved to see Joss striding towards her, although his expression was hardly welcoming. Tagging along behind him was a shabbily dressed man wearing a battered bowler hat.

Joss stopped outside the double doors of Comerford's Warehouse and his companion produced a bunch of keys, trying each in turn until he found the right one.

'About time,' Joss said impatiently as the side door swung open. 'Come inside, Miss Carter. This shouldn't take long.'

Clara followed him into the dark cavern of the warehouse where the air was thick with dust and the smell of mildew and mould.

'Light the damned gas mantles, Stimson.' Joss gave

the unfortunate man a shove that sent him teetering into the gloomy interior.

Moments later the flare of a match was greeted by a loud pop and a hiss, and the contents of the warehouse shimmered in the gaslight. Clara's hand dropped to her side as she gazed at the bolts of richly coloured fabric. Some of them were plain and others heavily patterned with threads of gold and silver. She had imagined it to be an Aladdin's cave and she was not disappointed. Joss had failed to mention was that there was a selection of brass lanterns fitted with jewel-like glass, oriental jugs and vases, and small tables inlaid with mother-of-pearl.

'You are welcome to all this,' Joss said, encompassing the entire contents with a wave of his hand. 'It's the sort of thing sold in the bazaars of Bombay and the souks of North Africa. My father must have been out of his mind to purchase rubbish like this. Take the lot and sell it if you can, but I predict that you'll be bankrupt before the year is out, and I'll be lucky to see a penny profit.'

Clara was dazzled by the exotic splendour, but she was not going to say so in front of him. 'I might be able to shift some of it,' she said casually. 'Although I can see that I'll be doing you a favour by taking it off your hands.'

Stimson nodded. 'She's right, sir. We can fill this space ten times over. I've had dozens of enquiries from merchants wishing to use our facilities, and they're willing to pay handsomely for the privilege.'

Joss was silent for a moment, as if weighing up the situation. 'All right, you have a deal, Miss Carter. Fill out the necessary documents, Stimson, and I'll sign them. Miss Carter will be responsible for removal of the stock within two days.' Joss turned to Clara with a sardonic grin. 'Do you think you can manage that, miss?'

'Certainly,' Clara said firmly. 'I'll make the arrangements, but first I want a written agreement setting out the terms of our contract.'

'What's the matter, Miss Carter? Don't you trust me?'

'It's not personal, Mr Comerford. It's business.'

'Then I take it you have someone to handle such matters?'

Clara could see that Joss was beginning to enjoy himself, and it was obvious that he considered her to be too young and unused to the ways of the world to manage her own affairs. She faced him squarely. 'I'll instruct my agent, Mr Plumley, to draw up the papers. His office is in Bond Street. You might have heard of him – Ambrose Plumley?'

Joss stared at her, eyes wide and jaw slackened. 'You are acquainted with Plumley?'

'He handled the business side of things when I rented the store in Oxford Street. I don't know why you are so surprised, considering that Gertie is Lady Quinn's sister and an heiress in her own right. You'll be hearing from Plumley in due course.' Clara walked out of the warehouse with her head held high, but the North Quay was not the place where it was safe for a young woman to loiter and she quickened her pace, looking straight ahead and ignoring the lewd comments from labourers and stevedores. She hailed a passing cab in Nightingale Lane.

'Bond Street, please, cabby.' She climbed inside and made herself comfortable. This was the start of a great adventure, and having seen the contents of the warehouse she was confident that she had done the right thing.

Ambrose Plumley was not convinced. He sat back in his throne-like chair, folding his hands over his bulging belly. 'It's a huge risk, Miss Carter. I admire your courage, but if you haven't examined the stock thoroughly you might find it of poor quality, and a proportion is likely to have been damaged either in transit or in the warehouse.'

'It's a chance I had to take, Mr Plumley. After all, it's cost me nothing because Joss would never have repaid the money he owed me.'

'Ah, yes, that was in Paris, as you've just told me.'

'It was, and I regret that I had to leave without finding Gertrude.'

'Maybe she didn't want to be found. As I recall, Miss Batt has a mind of her own, and a very strong will. In that she resembles her sister, although in other respects they are completely different.'

'I don't suppose you know where she might be?' Clara asked hopefully.

Ambrose shook his head. 'I haven't heard from Gertie for many years, and I still find it hard to believe that she was living in one of the attic rooms above the shop. Extraordinary.'

'I've been wondering if I ought to tell Lady Quinn that her sister has disappeared.'

'That, of course, is entirely up to you, Clara. I may call you Clara, mayn't I?'

'Please do.' Clara hesitated, biting her lip. 'I'm not sure what course to take, but I would like to know what you think, Mr Plumley.'

'I can't speak for her ladyship. She is unpredictable at the best of times, and I'm not sure whether past grievances against her sister would overcome family feeling. I could mention it to her, if you wish.'

'It might be better coming from you,' Clara said tactfully. 'She doesn't have a very high opinion of me, and in a way it's my fault that Gertie is missing. It wouldn't have happened had she not accompanied me to Paris. I'd be grateful if you would speak to Lady Quinn. At least I'd know that I had done everything I could to help Gertie.'

'Yes, I see.' Ambrose eyed her thoughtfully. 'I have to speak to Lady Quinn on another matter and I'll bring up the subject at the first possible opportunity.'

'Thank you,' Clara said, smiling. 'And I would really like you to represent me.'

'I will be happy to do so, but – not to put too fine a point on it – my fees are not the cheapest.'

'I dare say that's true, but I'm certain you wouldn't allow Joss Comerford to swindle me. If you are willing to be patient as far as money is concerned, I'll endeavour to settle your bills as quickly as possible.'

'Fair enough.' He leaned forward, reaching for his pen. 'Let's get down to business. May I suggest that for the moment you forget about dear Gertie. She has a habit of disappearing and then reappearing at a time to suit herself. She might walk into your shop any day and, I've no doubt, would be surprised to learn of the trouble she has caused.'

'Yes,' Clara said slowly, 'but I have a feeling that it's different this time. If she is involved with Bert Bragg it's not likely to end happily.'

Plumley rose from his seat. 'I suggest that you concentrate on re-opening your shop, Miss Carter, and leave the legal side of things to me.' He went to open the door. 'I'll let you know if I have any news concerning Gertie.'

Chapter Eighteen

Clara put a sign in the shop window advertising a 'GRAND REOPENING on Wednesday 1 May'. They would lose even more money in the interim, but Clara needed time to turn the storeroom and the usable floor space into a shopping experience that would draw in the crowds. The entire contents of Comerford's Warehouse were delivered, and Clara, Betsy and Jane were in the process of unpacking the tea chests when Lizzie arrived, bristling with indignation.

'When were you going to tell me about all this?' she demanded angrily. 'I heard about it from Miss Jones, of all people. You didn't even have the decency to let me know what you were about, Clara.'

Betsy and Jane stopped what they were doing to stare at their sister. Jane's bottom lip trembled. 'Don't be cross, Lizzie. This is important.'

'I'm sorry,' Clara said quickly. 'I should have come to see you, but I've had so much to do that it slipped my mind.'

'It was humiliating to be told that you were going into business with Joss when I knew nothing about it.'

'I know I should have made a point of telling you, but everything has happened so fast, and there were things to be done. I'm afraid I didn't give you a thought, Lizzie.' Clara laid her hand on her sister's shoulder. 'And for that I am genuinely sorry.'

Lizzie smiled reluctantly. 'At least you have the decency to say so, but you should have told me what you were planning, just as you ought to have informed me that you were going to Paris with Joss.'

'It was purely business, and he walked out on me, leaving me to pay his hotel bill. Anyway, let's forget him – he's unimportant.' Clara held up a bolt of cloth interwoven with gold thread. 'Look how beautiful this is. I can't think why the Comerfords had difficulty finding buyers.'

'Joss is a spoiled only son,' Lizzie said bitterly. 'He thinks of no one but himself.'

'I thought you fancied him.' Betsy winked at Jane and they turned away, their shoulders shaking.

'You can laugh,' Lizzie snapped. 'But you wouldn't think it so funny if a philanderer had broken your heart.'

'Think yourself lucky that you didn't get too

involved with him,' Clara said calmly. 'He's a stupid, selfish fellow who's not fit to lick your boots, Lizzie.'

Lizzie's eyes reddened and she sniffed. 'I thought he fancied me. He was always making eyes at me and trying to corner me when I was working. The servants are all laughing at me behind my back, I know it.'

'Leave the Comerfords,' Clara said impulsively. 'Come and work with us to make this the finest store in Oxford Street.'

'What? Work in a shop?'

'Not any old shop, Lizzie. This is our department store, or it will be when we get going properly. It's a family-run business and we should be in it together.'

Lizzie sank down onto an unopened tea chest. 'What do I know about working in a shop?'

'As much as any of us,' Betsy said, pulling a face. 'We're learning as we go along, and we certainly need all the help we can get.'

'Yes, do come and live here,' Jane pleaded. 'It will be lovely to have all my sisters together again.'

Lizzie glanced round suspiciously. 'Where's Gertrude? I thought she'd taken my place.'

'Of course she hasn't.' Clara stared at her in dismay. 'I don't know what gave you that idea, Lizzie. We helped her when she was down and out, but in reality she owns the building.'

'And she's gone missing,' Jane added. 'She disappeared in Paris and Clara has been searching for her.'

'But Gertie isn't family,' Clara said firmly. 'She's a friend and I hope to find her, but you are my sister, Lizzie, and I would take it as a great favour if you decided to come and help us build The Button Box into a thriving business. After all, you know more about ladies' fashions and what's in vogue than any of us.'

'Hold on,' Betsy protested. 'I know more about millinery than Lizzie does. I'll be in charge of that department, when it opens.'

'And it will, in due course, and you will be in charge, but we have to start somewhere.'

Lizzie fingered the flimsy material. 'What will you do with this?'

'I want to make the shop look like an oriental bazaar. It must be something unique to bring in the customers, if only out of curiosity. It will be like stepping into Aladdin's cave, and we've got just ten days to transform a dingy workplace into something exotic and beautiful.'

Lizzie stood up, brushing dust from her black skirt. 'It will take a miracle to make all this match your dream, Clara. I think you must be mad, and perhaps I am a little crazy, too, but I will leave the Comerfords and throw my lot in with you three.'

Clara uttered a cry of delight. 'The Carter sisters will conquer the West End. There's nothing we cannot do if we put our minds to it.'

'I hope so,' Lizzie said glumly. 'I doubt if I'll ever get to be a proper lady's maid now.'

'Never mind that. I'll make you head of the fashion department, which is much more important. I remember how Mademoiselle Boucher ruled the roost in Automne. She was a person to be reckoned with, just as you will be, Lizzie. But for now, let's unpack everything, and then we can sort out what is saleable and discard anything that is not up to scratch.'

They worked on throughout the day, with Lizzie staying until late afternoon before setting off for Bedford Square to collect her belongings. She returned an hour later, having been sacked on the spot for telling Mrs Comerford a few home truths, which relieved her of the necessity of working out her notice. Needless to say, Mrs Comerford had refused to give her a character, but Lizzie was unrepentant.

'I told her exactly what I thought of her son,' she said as they sat round the table at suppertime. 'I repeated what you'd told me about him abandoning you in Paris and leaving you to pay the bill. I left her in no doubts as to his conduct with the maids, myself included, and I walked out of the house with my head held high. I'll never go into service again as long as I live.'

Clara clapped enthusiastically, with Jane and Betsy

joining in. 'Good for you, Lizzie. I'm afraid we haven't got your room ready but you can have Gertie's for tonight, and tomorrow we'll sort something out.'

'I don't mind,' Lizzie said, smothering a yawn. 'I'm up every morning at six thirty and I rarely get to bed before midnight, sometimes later if I have to wait up for the mistress.'

'I suggest we all turn in early.' Clara rose to her feet and began stacking the dishes. 'We'll be fresh in the morning and able to work better after a good night's sleep. I'll see to the washing up.'

'I'm very tired,' Jane admitted. 'Good night, Clara.'

Betsy picked up a chamber candlestick and headed for the stairs. 'I'll light the way. Come on Jane. We'll show Lizzie where to go.'

Clara could hear them laughing and talking as they ascended the stairs and she smiled. It was good to have all her sisters under one roof. She washed the dishes and settled down at the table to make a few quick sketches, putting her ideas for the various displays on paper, and when she had finished she took the button box from a shelf.

Sifting through the colourful contents, she found the button from Gertie's frock that had fallen under the bed in the *atelier*. She held it in the palm of her hand, closing her eyes as she tried to imagine the scene in the artist's studio. Had Gertie gone there willingly? Or was she being held captive and attempting to escape when the button was torn from the bodice? Clara set it apart as she scooped up a handful of her treasures and let them fall, one by one. The last of them was the ornate silver button from Luke's waistcoat. She gazed at it for a long moment. How typical of Luke to insist on silver instead of brass. The precious metal absorbed the warmth from her hand and she sighed as she laid the button carefully back in the box. Luke was lost to her, just as the button was lost to him. If he returned to London he would be arrested and sent for trial, the outcome of which was a foregone conclusion. However much it hurt her to admit it, there was no hope for Luke, but Gertie was another matter and something must be done to help her. Clara closed the box and replaced it on the shelf.

The days passed in a frenzy of activity, during which the shop and storeroom were transformed into something that Clara hoped would entice prospective customers into the store. She used everything she had learned in Paris, adding her own ideas to the theatrical backdrop she created out of shimmering silks, satins and filmy muslins. The brass lamps and trays were polished until they shone, and Clara arranged the smaller items on low tables purchased from a second-hand dealer in Seven Dials. Lizzie and Betsy entered into the spirit of things and they trawled the pawnbrokers and dolly shops in the East

End, returning home with baskets of glass beads, dyed ostrich feathers and plumage from peacocks' tails, all of which added to the romantic ambience. The aromatic scent from the carved cedar-wood boxes filled the air, and paper lanterns, created by Jane's nimble fingers, dangled from the ceiling. Clara risked life and limb, climbing on chairs and tables to hang them where they could best be seen.

Plumley arrived the day before they planned to open the doors to the public. He stepped inside, looking round with an appreciative smile. 'Well, well. What an amazing display.'

'I'm glad you approve,' Clara said, wiping her hands on her grimy apron. 'We've all worked hard.'

'I can see that, my dear Miss Carter. I feel as though I've stepped into a room filled with treasures from the Orient.'

Clara smiled proudly. 'That was what I intended, sir. I wanted to make shopping an exciting experience.'

'I think you've succeeded, and I'm very impressed.' Plumley handed her a folded document. 'This is the contract between yourself and Mr Comerford. Study it and add your signature, if you agree to the terms as set down. I'll arrange a meeting with the gentleman in question.'

'Thank you, Mr Plumley. I'm very grateful, and I hope you'll be here for the opening.'

'Have you asked anyone to perform the ceremony?'

Clara stared at him in surprise. 'I was just going to open the door at nine o'clock and invite people in.'

'Not good enough.' He shook his head. 'Too dull, if you want my opinion. You must make something more of it than that. Someone who is well known should be asked to officiate, and you ought to provide a glass of sherry wine or something similar for your first customers. Make it an occasion, Miss Carter.'

'But I don't know anyone like that. I'm afraid the people I've come across have been less than respectable.' Clara had a vision of Patches in her lurid crimson gown welcoming the customers, and she stifled a giggle.

'I'm serious, Miss Carter. As it happens I'm on my way to see Lady Quinn. She's well known, if not notorious.' Plumley smiled and patted Clara's hand. 'Scandal was the Batt sisters' constant companion years ago. Lady Quinn used to enjoy reading about her own exploits in the newspapers. She pretends to be shocked by her sister's escapades, but really there was nothing to choose between them.'

'I still find that hard to believe.' The vision of Patches was replaced by her memory of Lady Quinn, but it was hard to imagine that an arrogant, stiff-necked woman like Garland Quinn had ever been young and flighty.

'I can see what you're thinking, Clara – I may call you that, mayn't I?'

She nodded, eager to hear the rest of the story. 'Of course.'

'And you may call me Ambrose. Now where was I? Oh, yes. Dear Garland had a succession of lovers, some of them very well known indeed, and mentioning no names, at least two of them were politicians.' He tapped the side of his nose. 'But the public has a long memory and I believe women will flock here, if only to see the *femme fatale* of Berkeley Square in person.'

'Then you must ask her, Ambrose,' Clara said hastily. 'I'll provide some sort of refreshment, according to how much money we have left, although I doubt if I could run to wine or sherry.'

'Champagne would be better.' Plumley put his hand in his pocket and produced a handful of coins, which he pressed into Clara's hand. 'A couple of bottles of good champagne for her ladyship, and those in the know, will suffice. I suggest some cheap white wine for the ladies who will flock in to see her. Send one of your sisters to the wine merchants and they will hire glasses out to you as well. Make a splash, my dear Clara, and you will encourage the ladies to part with their husbands' hard-earned money.'

'I can't repay this much,' Clara said, aghast at such extravagance.

'Don't worry, my dear, it will go on your bill, but for now, do as I suggest.' He picked up a brass coffee pot. 'I might buy this for myself. Anyway, I must go now.' He put his hat on, pausing in the doorway. 'And music helps. If you know any itinerant musicians you should hire them for the morning. A couple of sandwich men advertising the opening would spread the word, and it should start as soon as possible in order to advertise the grand opening.'

Clara nodded, dazed by his enthusiasm. 'I'll see what I can do.'

'That's a good girl. I must leave you now, but I'll be here early on the great day, so make sure that everything is just right.'

'Yes, thank you, Ambrose.'

As the door closed on him Betsy hurried over to lock it before anyone else tried to come in. She turned to Clara with an excited giggle. 'Champagne and wine. I heard what he said. Whatever next?'

Clara sank down on the nearest chair. 'He's like a whirlwind. I suppose I should have argued against his wild ideas, but in a way they make sense.'

'You must do as he says, Clara. Lizzie and I will go and get the champagne, if you like. I've always wanted to taste it. They say the bubbles go up your nose and make you giggle.'

'I think it's the alcohol that makes you tipsy, but if Ambrose thinks it necessary we must take his advice.'

'So I'll go and tell Lizzie, shall I?'

'Yes, thank you, Betsy. You do that and I'll tidy up.' Clara replaced a bolt of beaded and embroidered silk on the shelf. It had been an exhausting couple of weeks, but she was satisfied with the setting she had created for her merchandise. It was striking and it was different, and more importantly, this was merely the beginning.

She had just finished putting things away when Lizzie and Betsy came bustling in from the kitchen, dressed for outdoors. Clara gave them the money that Ambrose had left, with strict instructions to spend it wisely. Two bottles of champagne and perhaps half a dozen bottles of white wine with a case or two of glasses to be delivered the next day. They left together, chattering excitedly, and Clara was about to lock the door when she spotted a familiar figure hurrying along the street. He clutched his hat in his hand and his tawny hair was whipped into tangles by the wind. She let him in and was enveloped in a bear hug that took her breath away.

'Nathaniel,' she gasped when he released her, 'what are you doing here?'

'That's not much of a welcome.' He placed his hat on the counter and took a step backwards, gazing round at the transformation open-mouthed. 'By all that's wonderful, this is amazing. If you weren't standing beside me I'd think I was in the wrong shop.'

'Do you like it, Nat? Or do you think I've gone too far?'

'Too far? No, indeed not. It's like being transported to another land. I've never been to the Orient, but this is like travelling on a magic carpet, and it seems that I'm just in time for the grand opening.'

'Yes, I can't believe it's almost here. We've worked so hard to bring it to fruition, and now I'm scared. I wouldn't admit it to my sisters, but what will I do if the customers hate it?'

He slipped his arm around her shoulders. 'They'll be bowled over backwards. It's like nothing I've ever seen.'

'Come through to the kitchen and see Jane – she's busy finishing off the paper lanterns. You've just missed Lizzie and Betsy. They've gone to order champagne and wine for the grand opening.'

'You really are doing it in style.' Nathaniel followed her as she threaded her way through the maze of displays.

'It was Ambrose's idea.'

'Who is he?'

'He's Lady Quinn's man of business and now he's mine as well. I've come such a long way, Nat. I've so much to tell you . . . But I thought you were settled in Paris, and that you'd stay there for ever.' Clara hesitated with her hand on the doorknob. 'Why have you come back?'

'If I'm honest I suppose I was homesick. I had a

wonderful time at the Conservatoire and I learned a lot from the maestro, but I never intended to make playing in an orchestra my life's work. Composing is my true love, and I'm certain of that now.'

'You seemed so wrapped up in your own affairs when I last saw you,' Clara said warily.

'You caught me off guard. I'm sorry if I gave you the impression that I didn't care, but I really did miss you.'

Clara allowed this to pass. She believed him, but the memory of their last meeting refused to go away. 'Are you going to stay in London?'

'I have to face up to my responsibilities. I can't allow my uncle to take over the estate. It's not what my father wanted.'

'I realise that.' Clara opened the kitchen door. 'Jane, look who's come to see us.'

Jane looked up and her expression of surprise melted into a smile. 'Nathaniel. You've come home.' She raised herself to her feet. 'How lovely.'

He gave her a hug. 'I'm afraid I don't deserve such a welcome, Jane. I've been so wrapped up in my work that I've neglected my friends.'

'No, never say that. You've been doing what you had to do, but now you're here with us again. I'm so pleased to see you.'

Nathaniel dropped a kiss on Jane's blonde curls. 'I have a lot to catch up on, Jane. You must tell me everything that's been happening in my absence.'

'That might take some time,' Clara said, smiling. 'And I have a lot to do.'

'Am I being asked to leave?'

'No, of course not, Nat. But Ambrose gave me some ideas for promoting the reopening and I ought to look into them.'

'Is there anything I can do to help?'

Clara eyed him thoughtfully. 'He did suggest that music would help things along.'

'Then I'm your man. You have only to ask and I'd be delighted to play all day, if you wish.'

'Would you, Nathaniel?' Jane sat down again, beaming at him. 'That would be so lovely.'

'Yes, it would be wonderful,' Clara added enthusiastically. 'If you could spare the time, although I can't afford to pay you very much.'

He held up his hand. 'I wouldn't think of accepting payment. I'll play such merry tunes that the customers will flock in.'

Jane clapped her hands. 'I wish I could dance to them, but I'm afraid I'll never go to a ball.'

'When I come into my inheritance I'll give a ball just for you, Jane,' Nathaniel said seriously. 'You will have a beautiful gown and I will claim the first dance.'

Colour flooded Jane's cheeks and her eyes shone. 'Will you really? But my calipers will clank and everyone will hear the noise.'

'No one will notice because they will be lost in admiration, and I will instruct the orchestra to play loudly.'

Clara shook her head. 'That sounds wonderful, but if we can return to the present, I have work to do. Where are you staying, Nat?'

'I booked into a hotel last night, but I can't afford their prices, so I'll have to find somewhere else soon. I gave up my room in the lodging house before I went to Paris, which was a bit stupid.'

'Then you must stay here,' Clara said firmly. 'That is, until you find suitable accommodation elsewhere. Lizzie has moved in with us but Gertie's room isn't being used at the moment.'

'Is there still no news of her?'

'None at all. I'm hoping that Lady Quinn might be able to help, even though she and Gertie don't get along. Ambrose is going to ask her to open the store, so I'll try to get her on her own, and hope she's in a good mood.'

'I'll do whatever I can to help, but in any event I'd be grateful for the use of her room, and I'll start looking for work and lodgings right away.'

'You must stay and have something to eat,' Jane said eagerly. 'I want to hear about your adventures in Paris, Nathaniel. Please don't go just yet.'

'Betsy and Lizzie will be back soon,' Clara added. 'Jane has made some vegetable soup and I'll go to the bakery and get some fresh rolls. It will be like old times.' She was about to leave the room but Nathaniel reached the door first.

'I'll go and get the bread. It's the least I can do, and I want to help you, Clara. You've worked wonders with this place, and you deserve to be a success.' He followed her through the shop. 'I've been selfish and I want to make amends.'

Clara came to a halt, turning to face him. 'You did what you had to do, Nat. You don't owe us anything. You could have challenged your aunt's will and taken the shop in Drury Lane from me, but you didn't. If it weren't for your generosity none of this would have been possible.'

He looked away. 'I don't deserve such praise. I had my heart set on my own goals and I wasn't thinking of you.'

'And there's no reason why you should. I'm happy to pretend to be your fiancée until you claim your inheritance. I owe you that at least.'

'It isn't that simple, Clara.' He took her hands in his, meeting her startled gaze with a beseeching look. 'The fact is that I have to be a married man before I come into what is rightfully mine.'

'That wasn't what we agreed, Nat.' Clara attempted to pull her hands free, but he tightened his grip.

'I know it's a lot to ask, but I have sincere feelings for you, Clara.'

'I don't think you should say any more, Nat. What you want is impossible.'

'No, it isn't. I know you like me and we're like-minded in many ways. It could work out well for both of us, Clara. I'd be happy for you to continue with your ambitions for the store, and I'd have the funds to help you.'

'Stop there, Nathaniel. This is all wrong.'

'No, I can't. I've gone too far to give up now. I left my job in Paris and I've returned to London for one purpose only and that is to ask you, very humbly, to be my wife. Will you marry me, Clara?'

Chapter Nineteen

Clara wrenched free from his grasp. 'No, I'm sorry, but what you're asking is impossible.'

'Why, Clara? You like me, don't you?'

'Of course I do. I'm very fond of you, but not in that way. A sham engagement is one thing, and anyway, I gave you back your ring. Marriage is another matter altogether.'

'I know I could have put it better, but time is running out and my uncle is no fool. I care about you, Clara, and I respect you for what you're trying to achieve. Help me and I'll look after you. You and your family will never want for anything again.'

She shook her head. 'I'm sorry, Nat. I've given you my answer.'

He took off his spectacles and polished them on a grubby hanky. 'Perhaps if I give you time to think it over you might have second thoughts?' His myopic blue eyes pleaded with her, and without his glasses he looked young and vulnerable. Clara was tempted to comfort him as she might a small child, but she knew that would be fatal and she kept her distance.

'My mind is made up, Nat. I'd do almost anything for you, but marriage is out of the question.'

'Is there someone else?' he asked suspiciously. 'Are you still in love with Luke?'

'Of course not. I don't know what gave you that idea.' She opened the shop door. 'One of us has to go to the bakery or we'll all go hungry.'

He bowed his head. 'I'll go. I'm sorry if I've upset you.'

'I'm all right, Nat. Let's not mention this again. You're still welcome here as long as you understand that I won't change my mind.'

He nodded wordlessly and stepped outside into the warm spring sunshine. Clara watched him walk away with his shoulders hunched as if he were carrying a heavy weight, and she felt a moment of regret. Nathaniel Silver was a gentleman in all senses of the word and she was certain that he would do his best to make her happy. They might live amicably but she knew now that would not be enough for her. Until recently her life had been spent caring for others, giving her little time to think about her own wants and needs, but she had come to realise that a life without love was only half lived, and that most basic of human emotions had a habit of catching a person unawares. She closed the door and locked it while she waited for Nat to return.

The rest of the day passed in a frenzy of activity with everyone working hard to complete the preparations for the grand opening. Jane and Betsy wrote advertisements for The Button Box on paste boards, and Nathaniel found two out-of-work musicians who were delighted to earn a day's pay as sandwich men, walking up and down Oxford Street to promote the new department store. One of them, Danny Williams, a tow-haired youth of seventeen, had often accompanied Nathaniel in his busking days, and after supper that evening he entertained them by playing lively tunes on his flute. Nat picked up his violin and joined in and the music was so toe-tappingly irresistible that Betsy and Lizzie jumped to their feet and began to dance. Clara was quick to note Jane's wistful expression and she crossed the floor, holding out her hands.

'Come on, Janie, let's show them how it's done.'

Jane shook her head. 'No, I can't. You know I can't.'

'Nonsense. You're among family and friends.' Clara pulled her gently to her feet and, holding her sister's hands, she guided her across the floor, swaying in time to the rhythm.

Jane moved slowly at first, casting anxious glances in Danny's direction, but he was intent on his music, and gradually she began to move faster and with growing confidence. Soon they were all cavorting around the kitchen with Betsy and staid Lizzie kicking up their heels, and Jane doing her best to emulate them. When the music stopped Jane was pink cheeked and laughing, and her blushes deepened when she realised that Danny was smiling at her. She was about to back away but Clara gave her a gentle push in his direction.

'Talk to him,' Clara whispered.

'I don't know what to say.'

'Just tell him you like his music. He won't bite.' Clara put her arm around her youngest sister's shoulders, giving her an encouraging squeeze. 'Jane loves your music, Danny,' Clara said firmly. 'You will play for us at the grand opening, won't you?'

'I will, if Nat agrees.' Danny turned to Nathaniel. 'We used to be popular when we entertained the crowds, didn't we?'

Nathaniel nodded, smiling. 'We did, and we can do it again, if Clara permits.'

'I most certainly do.' Clara pulled up a chair for Jane, who had paled suddenly and was swaying on her feet. 'Sit down and catch your breath, dear. Perhaps Nat and Danny will play something soothing.' She shot a warning glance at Betsy, who opened her mouth as if to protest.

Lizzie threw herself down on the nearest chair. 'I'm fagged and need to catch my breath. Play us something sweet and romantic, please.'

Nathaniel struck up again and Danny followed, picking up the tune with ease.

'Do you think he noticed my limp?' Jane whispered.

Clara shook her head. 'He just saw a pretty young girl dancing.'

'Pretty? I'm not pretty.'

'You will eclipse us all in a year or so. Now enjoy the music and if you feel like dancing again, I'll stand up with you.' Clara went to sit at the table next to Betsy, leaving Jane where she was in a position to talk to Danny.

'Are you matchmaking?' Betsy said in a low voice. 'She's just a child.'

'She's nearly fifteen, and she needs friends of her own age. He seems like a nice young fellow and he's very talented.'

Betsy cocked her head on one side, giving Clara a calculating look. 'Have you upset Nat? He seems different somehow.'

'We had a slight difference of opinion,' Clara said, trying to sound casual. 'But we're still friends.'

'Did you turn him down?'

'I don't know what you're talking about.' Clara was about to rise when Betsy caught her by the sleeve.

'Yes, you do. You told me about the fake engagement,' she insisted in a low voice. 'Did he propose?'

'Hush, he'll hear you. I'm going to make some tea, and then I'm going to bed. It's getting late and I'm tired.' Clara stood up but Lizzie barred her way.

'What were you two whispering about?' she demanded.

'It's just Betsy being nosy as usual,' Clara said casually. 'Would you like tea or cocoa?'

'Tea, please.' Lizzie took the seat that Clara had just vacated. 'I will find out. Betsy will tell me.'

Clara leaned towards her. 'Keep your voice down. I'll tell you both when we're on our own.' She straightened up as the music came to an end, and she clapped. 'Thank you, Nat and Danny, that was delightful. I'm going to put the kettle on, so who would like tea and who would like cocoa?'

Later, when Danny had left to return home and Nathaniel had gone to his room, Clara was about to follow Jane upstairs when Lizzie stepped in her way, standing arms akimbo.

'Now then, miss, tell us what's going on between you and Nat.'

'Yes,' Betsy agreed. 'You can't fool us, Clara. We know something is amiss.'

Clara could see that they were not going to be easily satisfied. 'All right, I'll tell you, but I don't want the whole world to know.'

Betsy drew her back into the kitchen. 'Why did you turn him down?'

'He's a good match,' Lizzie said, frowning. 'You're not pining for Joss, are you?'

'Certainly not.' Clara sank down on a chair at the table. 'If you'll both just sit down and be quiet I'll explain.'

She told them as briefly and succinctly as possible. Fatigue was making her feel light-headed, but she answered their questions as fully as she could.

Lizzie's eyes were alive with interest. 'And you say he's worth a fortune?'

'That's what she's been telling us,' Betsy said impatiently. 'Haven't you been listening?'

'I have, but I wanted to get it straight in my mind.' Lizzie leaned her elbows on the table, fixing Clara with an intense gaze. 'And he owns a town house and a country mansion?'

'That's right. I haven't seen the country house, but the one in London is very impressive.'

'And you rejected him?' Betsy rolled her eyes and leaned back in her chair. 'What were you thinking of, Clara? Are you insane?'

'Not at all. I like Nat and I'm fond of him, but I don't love him.'

'I could bring myself to love a man who could offer me a lifetime of luxury,' Lizzie said with feeling. 'Betsy's right. You're quite mad.'

Clara rose to her feet. 'Think what you like, but

I'm going to bed. If either of you wants to make a play for Nat, feel free to do so. I'll be happy for you.' She headed for the stairs. There was too much to think about with the opening of the store to worry what her sisters might or might not do. She would be genuinely pleased to think that Nathaniel would be part of their family, but he would have trouble on his hands if he took on ambitious Lizzie or flighty Betsy. She walked slowly up the stairs, her mind filled with niggling worries about opening day. If only Sabine were here to give her the advantage of her experience in retail management; she would even welcome Mademoiselle Boucher, who knew exactly where items should be placed to attract the eye of the customer. She went to bed but sleep evaded her. If the oriental theme of her store did not go down well with the public she would be facing ruin, and The Button Box would close. She drifted off to sleep and was plagued by nightmares in which a figure she knew to be Dagobert Duclos took on the persona of the evil Abanazar from the pantomime *Aladdin*, and Gertie was his unfortunate victim locked in the cave filled with treasure. Clara was helpless to save her friend and Lady Quinn refused to say the magic spell that would open the door and free her errant sister.

Clara awakened in a cold sweat with the bedclothes knotted and entwined around her body. It was not yet light but she rose from her bed and lit a candle.

Having washed in cold water she put on her newest gown, a plain grey merino with a white collar and cuffs. It was more suitable for a governess than the owner of a thriving emporium, but the rest of her clothes were patched and darned, and too shabby to wear for such an occasion. She remembered the bolt of cloth that Luke had chosen, insisting that she should have a new dress. Perhaps she ought to have listened to him and taken more pride in her appearance, but it was too late now. In a few hours Plumley would arrive, accompanied by the redoubtable Lady Quinn, who would be decked out like a peacock, and no one would notice the drab little sparrow standing in the shadow of her radiance. Clara put up her hair and went downstairs to the kitchen to stoke the fire. Today was the big day.

Everyone was waiting. Betsy and Lizzie were visibly nervous, but Jane was bubbling with excitement. Danny had arrived early and was standing by with Nathaniel, ready to strike up a tune when the doors opened, but Lady Quinn had not yet arrived. Clara could see a crowd gathering outside and she was beginning to worry. They had decided that ten o'clock was a good time to open up, and there were only seconds to go before she must allow the public into the shop.

Then, just as Clara was beginning to fear that her ladyship had decided not to officiate at the opening ceremony, a carriage drew to a halt at the kerb and a liveried footman leaped down to open the door. He put down the steps and assisted Lady Quinn to alight, closely followed by Plumley. As they processed across the pavement it was difficult to decide which of them was the most garishly dressed. Plumley, resplendent in a blue velvet frock coat, scarlet waistcoat trimmed with gold braid and black-and-white check trousers, tucked his top hat under his arm and fell into step with Lady Quinn. But she outshone him quite literally in a silver satin gown embellished with waterfalls of lace, bugle beads and sequins. Her hair was piled into a coronet, and she wore a diamond tiara with a matching necklace and earrings. The stones turned to white fire in the sunlight and there was an audible gasp from the onlookers. If Queen Victoria herself had come amongst them it could hardly have created a bigger stir.

Clara held the door open, bobbing a curtsey as her ladyship sailed into the shop with Plumley at her heels, panting like a pet pug.

'So this is it?' Lady Quinn came to a halt, raising her lorgnette to peer at the contents of the shelves and stands. 'It's certainly different.' She turned to Plumley. 'What am I supposed to do now?'

'A few words, my lady,' Plumley said silkily. 'I'm sure the public will be gratified by your presence.'

'There's no need to toady, my man. I am well aware that my presence gives an air of respectability to this venture.' She glanced round, shaking her head. 'But it looks like a souk. I can't think that all this clutter will sell.'

Clara bit back a sharp retort. 'Just a few words, please, my lady.'

'Very well. Let's get it over and done with. I'm only doing this to further my sister's interests, although considering the way she's behaved I think it's very magnanimous of me. Open the door, miss.'

Clara was about to unlock the door when a hansom cab drew to a halt behind Lady Quinn's equipage and a large woman enveloped in a black cloak clambered to the ground.

Clara's hand flew to cover her mouth. 'It can't be,' she gasped.

'Who is she?' Lizzie whispered.

'Whoever it is, she's coming this way.' Betsy took a step backwards as the woman marched towards the door, swinging her arms as she cut a swathe through the crowd.

Clara had a feeling that it would take more than a mere lock to keep Patches Bragg out and she opened the door. Patches barged past her without saying a word and came to a halt in front of Lady Quinn.

'All right, Garland Batt, what has your slut of a sister done to my Bertie?'

There was a moment of complete silence. Clara could neither move nor speak, and the crowd outside had advanced like a tidal wave and were hammering on the door, demanding admittance.

'Who is this person?' Lady Quinn demanded coolly. 'Take her away, Plumley. I don't speak to fat trolls who deck themselves out like scarecrows.'

Patches grunted and gave her a shove that sent Lady Quinn tumbling backwards. She attempted to right herself but her feet became entangled in the train of her gown, and she would have fallen had Nathaniel not stepped forward to save her.

Clara abandoned her place at the door and made a grab for Patches, who side-stepped with surprising agility, rounding on her with clenched fists.

'Leave me be,' Patches growled. 'I'll throttle the bitch unless she tells me where her sister is hiding.'

'Please don't make even more of a scene.' Clara stepped between them. 'I don't know why you're here, Patches, and we don't know where Gertie is.'

'She's beguiled my boy with her magic spells.' Patches made a move towards Lady Quinn but Plumley intervened.

'I say, madam, this isn't the way to behave.'

She turned on him, eyes narrowed like a snake about to strike. 'Who are you, you overdressed maggot?'

'This person is my man of business.' Lady Quinn adjusted her tiara. 'I'll have you arrested for assault on my person, Patches Bragg, or should I say Amelie Duclos?'

'Just try it, you boiling fowl.' Patches moved a step closer but was held back by the combined efforts of Clara and Plumley.

'Stop it,' Clara cried in desperation. 'You're ruining my opening ceremony.'

Patches spun round to face her, but her jaw dropped as she glanced over Clara's shoulder. 'What the hell are you doing here?' she demanded angrily. 'I told you to stay in Paris, you fool.'

Clara released Patches. She knew who had just walked into the shop without looking round, but she turned slowly, coming face to face with Luke.

'I'll go and fetch a constable.' Lizzie edged past Patches, eyeing her nervously. 'You'll end up in prison where you belong, madam.'

'I'll come with you.' Betsy hurried to join her sister, but Clara held up her hand.

'No. We don't need the police. Luke knows how to handle this woman.' She met his gaze with a defiant lift of her chin. 'Why did you let her come here to ruin my big day?'

'I knew she was out for trouble but I was too late to stop her. However, I'm here now.' He laid his hand on Patches' shoulder. 'Come away before this gets out of hand.'

'I do as I please.' Patches pushed him away. 'But you can't afford to be seen in London, Luke Foyle, unless you want to end up in Newgate.'

'Come with me now, Patches. We'll talk about

this on the way to Angel Court.' Luke proffered his arm but Patches was not looking.

'We aren't going anywhere.' She jerked her head in the direction of the door as the crowd swarmed into the shop.

At a signal from Clara, Nat and Danny struck up a tune and Lady Quinn elbowed Patches out of the way. She stepped onto a box that was meant to resemble a dais, and it creaked ominously beneath her weight, slight though she was.

'I declare this new department store in London's Oxford Street well and truly open.' She had barely drawn a breath when she was surrounded by people jostling and elbowing her out of the way. She collapsed in an undignified heap of lace and tulle, knocking over the table containing the wine glasses, which shattered and covered the floor in shards.

Patches slapped her thigh and roared with laughter. 'Serves you right, you overdressed dollymop.'

Plumley rushed over to help Lady Quinn to a chair, his booted feet crunching on the broken glass. He produced a scarlet silk hanky and mopped his brow. 'What a to-do,' he said, repeating himself several times until Lady Quinn snatched the hanky from him.

'Shut up, you silly man,' she cried in exasperation. 'You're no help. Get that person out of my sight.'

'I think you've done enough, Patches. I'll take you home.' Luke held out his hand but Patches slapped it away.

'I'll leave when I'm ready. Go back to Paris, Luke. I don't need you – I'm here to find my son and save him from the clutches of the Batt creature.'

'It's obvious that they know nothing of his whereabouts, Patches, and I'm going nowhere without you.'

'It's true,' Clara said earnestly. 'We don't know where Gertie is. If you have any idea where they might be, please tell me.'

'He's not in Clarges Street, if that's what you're thinking. I know all about his love nest and it was the first place I went.' Patches paused to reach out and grab the hand of a woman who was attempting to conceal a brass goblet beneath her shawl. 'You've got to be quicker than that, love, or you'll have your collar fingered by the law. Luckily for you I'm in a good mood, so scarper before I change my mind and call a copper.'

Despite everything, Clara could not help but be impressed. 'I didn't see what she was doing. How did you do that?'

'Takes one to know one, girl. I might have been born in France but I was raised in Seven Dials, and I learned how to dip pockets as soon as I could walk.'

Luke took her by the arm. 'Come on, Patches. We're not doing any good here. Let me see you home.'

'I'm not going back to Seven Dials. It's time Patches

Bragg took her rightful place in society.' Patches shot a withering look in Lady Quinn's direction. 'I'm as much of a lady as she is.'

Clara could see that this conversation was going nowhere and the shop was filled to bursting point with people who might be tempted to spend money. She turned to her sisters, who were standing as stiffly as mannequins. 'Lizzie, Betsy, remember what we planned. Go to your stations and look after the customers.'

'I'm at the till,' Jane said eagerly. 'I haven't forgotten what to do, Clara.'

'Good girl.' Clara caught Nathaniel's eye and nodded. 'Play something soothing, please.'

He struck up a waltz and Danny took up the tune, and this seemed to have a calming effect on the crowd. Luke escorted the would-be thief from the premises.

Lady Quinn rose from her seat, waving aside Plumley's attempts to mollify her. 'I am deeply offended,' she said, glaring at Patches. 'You are a common, vulgar woman.'

'Pot calling the kettle comes to mind, love.' Patches stood arms akimbo. 'You didn't get those diamonds by being an angel.'

'My late husband gave them to me,' Lady Quinn said stonily.

'That's not what I heard, you trollop. You wasn't above having a little fling every now and again, if the price was right,' Patches countered, grinning and exposing the gaps between her teeth. 'Anyway, your old man was a jumped-up shopkeeper, and he made his money by selling goods that came in through the back door.'

'Well, your father was probably the villain who smuggled them into the country, so you can't talk.'

Clara had had enough of this ill-tempered spat. 'Get out, both of you,' she said angrily. 'I don't want to listen to this spiteful chit-chat. You are grown women and you should be ashamed of yourselves.'

Patches and Lady Quinn stared at her open-mouthed and unusually silent.

Plumley cleared his throat. 'Might I escort you to your carriage, my lady?'

'I'll hail a cab.' Luke sent a warning look to Patches. 'I'll take you wherever you want to go, as long as it's far away from here.' He winked at Clara. 'You haven't seen the last of me.'

Clara watched them all leave but the feeling of relief was tinged with anxiety. Luke should not have returned to London. He was risking arrest and imprisonment, and all because of Patches Bragg. But for now there were more pressing things to worry about and she could see that Jane was struggling to cope with the demands of customers queuing up to pay for their purchases. At least they could get a refund on the champagne and wine, even if they had to pay for the broken glasses. She put everything out of her mind other than the business in hand and went to help Jane.

It was evening when Clara finally closed the shop door. The others were in the kitchen preparing supper and it was good to hear her sisters laughing, and the deeper tones of Nat and Danny, who had been invited to share their meal. It had been a long day and sales had been brisk, but she had yet to count the money in the till. She had just settled down to do so when a loud knocking on the door made her look up with a start. Her first thought was that Luke had returned, but when she lifted the blind she saw two police constables standing on the pavement. Her heart was thudding against her ribcage as she turned the key in the lock and opened the door.

'Good evening, Officers,' she said, forcing herself to sound calm. 'What can I do for you?'

'We have reason to believe that you are harbouring a felon.' The elder of the two stared at a point over the top of her head.

'I can assure you that's not the case.' Clara ushered them in. 'You may search the building if you wish, but you won't find any criminals.'

'Begging your pardon, miss, but we have it on good authority that a person named Patches Bragg was here earlier.'

Clara knew instantly who had made the report.

Lady Quinn was out for revenge. 'It's true, Officer. That person interrupted the opening ceremony and made quite a scene. She had to be escorted from the premises, but I don't know where she went.'

'We will need to make certain, miss.' The elder policeman gave her a sidelong look. 'It's routine procedure.'

'Of course, I understand. Come this way.' Clara led them through to the kitchen.

Silence greeted them as everyone turned to stare in surprise at the unexpected interruption.

'The Officers are looking for Patches Bragg,' Clara said calmly. 'They need to search the premises.'

Nathaniel rose from his seat at the table. 'Perhaps we ought to leave, Clara. Danny's invited me to stay at his lodgings and it's been a long day.'

'No, don't go.' Lizzie jumped to her feet. 'You must stay for supper. You've earned it after all your hard work.'

He sat down again. 'I must say that Jane's soup smells delicious, and I am hungry. I don't suppose I'll get food like that when I find more permanent lodgings.'

'Not only is she pretty but she's a good cook.' Danny winked at Jane, who blushed and turned away to stir the pan.

'We won't take up more of your time than necessary,' the Officer said gruffly. 'Potter, you take the back yard and I'll go upstairs.'

Clara waited until they had left the kitchen. 'Patches is the last person I'd shelter.'

'It's a good thing that Luke didn't stay,' Jane said, glancing over her shoulder as if expecting Constable Potter to be lurking in the doorway. 'But he said he'd come back. I heard him.'

'Serve the stew, Jane,' Clara said briskly. 'It's getting late. I dare say he's on his way to Paris by now.' She was about to pass round the bread when she heard a knock on the shop door. 'Don't get up,' she said as Betsy was about to stand. 'I'll go. It's probably more policemen. Patches' reputation must be common knowledge if they need a whole army of them to arrest her.'

Clara hurried through the dark shop, praying that the constable was out of earshot. She opened the door.

Chapter Twenty

'Luke!' Clara whispered. 'What are you doing here?'

'I came to see you, of course.'

She held up her hand as he attempted to enter the shop. 'You can't come in. There are two police constables searching the premises.'

'Already?' He stared at her, frowning. 'I'm sorry, Clara. I should have known what Patches had in mind and done something to prevent her from coming here and making a scene.'

'I don't understand why she chose to disrupt the opening ceremony, especially if it brought her to the attention of the police.'

'Who knows how her mind works?'

Clara glanced anxiously over her shoulder. 'Please go, Luke. Return to France where you're safe.'

'So you do care what happens to me?'

She met his quizzical gaze with a frown. 'Of course I do. I can't pretend to understand your reasons for being with Patches, but if you're caught they'll hang you. So please go now, and don't come back.'

His smile faded and he seized her in his arms, holding her to him in a grip that was brutal in its intensity. His mouth claimed hers in a kiss that made time stand still. A small voice in her head warned her that he was a dangerous man and she must resist, but instead she found herself returning his kiss shamelessly and with an abandon that she could never have imagined. It was over in seconds, and she leaned against the doorpost, stunned and breathless as they held each other's gaze in a duel of wills. The temptation to break down and admit her feelings for him was overwhelming and another breath, another second in time would have spelled her downfall, but the sound of heavy footsteps and male voices brought her back to reality.

'You must go now. Go as far away from here as you can.'

He blew her a kiss as he backed out into the street. 'This isn't the end, my love.'

She was close to tears as she shut the door, but she took a deep breath and turned to face the policemen with an attempt at a smile. 'Do you believe me now, Constable? We aren't hiding any felons.'

The older man nodded. 'There's nothing to report, miss. I'm sorry to have troubled you.'

'It's no bother, Constable. I'm always ready to support our gallant police officers in the call of duty.'

'Good evening, miss. Make sure you lock the door after us. There are dangerous people abroad at night.' The younger constable followed his superior out into the street.

Moving automatically, Clara locked the door. Her lips burned from the heat of Luke's kiss and she could still feel the strength of his embrace, as if his arms were still wrapped around her. She could hear Lizzie calling her name and, after a moment's hesitation, she walked slowly towards the kitchen. Nothing had changed, she told herself, but in her heart she knew that in a split second, her whole world had turned upside down. She was a prey to an emotion stronger than anything she had ever experienced, and, even though she had struggled against it, her heart had been taken prisoner.

'Coming,' she called. 'They've gone. There's no need to worry.'

The grand opening had been a success. The word had spread and customers flooded through the door, although not all were intent on purchasing the goods on display. Clara was aware that many came simply to view the exotic fabrics and artefacts from the Orient, but at the end of the week the figures were encouraging. Even after deducting the amount due to Joss, they had made a significant profit, enough to start restocking the shelves. Clara and Lizzie visited several warehouses in Wapping where they selected the items they needed, but with a subtle change in emphasis. The materials they chose were the more popular cottons, bombazine and silk taffeta. They added to their stock of fine lace, and spent hours picking out sets of buttons in all shapes, sizes and colours.

Lizzie was keen to open a fashion department selling ready-made ladies' garments, but Clara kept a tight rein on the amount they were to spend. 'It's a good idea,' she said as they watched their purchases being piled into a hackney carriage. 'But if you saw the ladies' fashion department in Automne you would know that we need a separate space, with changing rooms for the customers.'

'But, Clara, we have all those rooms on the first floor. It wouldn't take much effort to turn a couple of them into something of that nature.'

Clara tipped the porter before climbing into the cab after her sister. 'If you think you can make it work, I agree, but they should be furnished elegantly. It will take more money than we have at present.'

'That's where I can help,' Lizzie said eagerly. 'I spent many afternoons standing like a mute while Mrs Comerford entertained her friends to tea, and I listened to their conversations.'

Clara settled her skirts around her and tapped on the roof to let the cabby know they were ready to move on. 'What did they talk about, other than their children and servant problems?'

'There were plenty of moans and groans, all very ladylike, but sometimes they spoke about their husbands' businesses, and most of them were in trade. They relied on banks to provide funds when they wanted to expand, and that's what you could do, Clara. Go to the bank and tell them our plans. Show them we're making a profit and see what they say.'

'It's certainly an idea, and we won't make a fortune with just the one floor. It's worth a try.'

'And you won't have to bother with people like Joss Comerford, but you could use his name. After all, you do business with him.'

'Yes, but that's finished now.'

'That doesn't matter, it's the name that counts. Joss may be an idiot but his father is very successful and well respected.'

'Lizzie, you're a genius. You've been wasting your time being in service.'

'Not really,' Lizzie said, smiling. 'My eavesdropping seems to have paid off already.'

'We'll see.' Clara sat back, staring out of the window at the crowded streets and the chaotic mix of cabs, drays and costermongers' barrows. 'You must accompany me to the bank, Lizzie. It might be a man's world, but we'll have a go at conquering it together – we are the unstoppable Carter sisters.'

*

The bank manager received them with a patronising smile, but while he listened to Clara's carefully thought-out request for funds it was obvious that his mind was elsewhere. His attention kept wandering to the gold ring on his left hand as he tapped his fingers on the tooled leather of his immaculate desk, leaving Clara to wonder if he had left home that morning after an altercation with his wife. However, the mention of the Comerfords brought him back to the present, and she knew that she had the upper hand. The interview then took on a much more positive note and, after a lot of negotiating, Clara and Lizzie came away with the amount they had decided was necessary if they were to carry out their plan.

'I learned that, too,' Lizzie said triumphantly as they left the bank premises. 'Always ask for more than you need and then strike a bargain for something more realistic.'

Clara linked arms with her sister. 'Your time with the Comerfords was well spent. It's just a pity that Joss toyed with your affections.'

'Oh, I don't care about him now. I was flattered, I suppose, and his charming manner turned my head, but I know now that he's a philanderer and a cad. I have my sights set on someone far nicer and much wealthier, or at least he will be when he comes into his inheritance.'

Clara came to a sudden halt. 'You don't mean Nathaniel, do you?'

'Yes, what's wrong with that?' Lizzie shrugged. 'You turned him down, so he's fair game.'

'I didn't want to hurt him. Our engagement was simply to make Nat's uncle believe that he could fulfil all the conditions of his father's will. I never said I'd marry him.'

'Which is just as well, because I intend to rectify that error. When I'm the wealthy Mrs Nathaniel Silver I'll do all my shopping at The Button Box.' Lizzie tossed her head and walked on.

Clara followed more slowly. She was shocked by Lizzie's announcement, but not surprised when she thought it through. Maybe her down-to-earth sister would be good for someone like Nat, whose feet barely touched the ground when his head was filled with music.

She quickened her pace and took Lizzie by the hand. 'Just be kind to him; he's a good man.'

'I know that,' Lizzie said, smiling. 'Come on, Clara, let's get home and make plans for the first floor. We'll need yards and yards of carpet and lots of gilded chairs, and mirrors everywhere. Most important is to have gas mantles fitted so that we have good lighting. Maybe we can arrange that first.'

'I think you've spent the loan already,' Clara said, smiling. 'But it sounds very elegant and maybe we can make room for millinery as well. Betsy will see to that, with Jane's help.'

'I've had another idea, too,' Lizzie said eagerly.

'You know what a splendid cook our little sister is? Well, I thought we could use part of the old store-room to serve cups of tea and dainty cakes to our customers. The Aerated Bread Company have a few tearooms where ladies can go unescorted, which, I believe, are becoming popular. It's another way to attract customers. What do you think?'

'It's a good idea, but we must ask Jane first. She's very young to have such a responsibility thrust upon her, but we could start with a few tables, and if it's a success we could take on someone to help her.'

'Yes, you're right.'

'All this is very positive and exciting,' Clara said, frowning. 'But we're forgetting one important person, and that's Gertie. It's her building and I think Plumley might insist that we wait to get her permission before making alterations. Besides which, I'm worried and I have to find her. I must make sure that she's safe and well.'

'I think you ought to put us first, Clara. I'm sure Gertie can take care of herself.' Lizzie reached the shop door and went inside.

Clara hesitated, staring critically at their new window display. Lizzie was right, of course, the store had to come first, but it was not easy to put Gertie's plight out of her mind, and she had not forgotten Luke. The memory of his kiss and the look in his eyes when they parted had haunted her dreams and her waking hours. She could only hope that he had returned to France, where he was safe from arrest. There had been no sign of Patches, but Clara had a suspicion that Lady Quinn knew more about Gertie's disappearance than she would admit. It was just a notion, of course, with no substance behind it other than a feeling that Gertie's sister did not want her to return. Clara made up her mind to pay another call on her ladyship at the first possible opportunity.

Lady Quinn refused to see her, but Clara pushed past the startled butler and marched up the grand staircase despite his urgent pleas for her to stop.

He followed, begging her to wait until he had warned his mistress of her arrival. She came to a halt on the landing, spinning round to glare at him. 'You'll have to throw me out bodily,' she said angrily. 'Lady Quinn will see me now and I'd advise you to leave us alone, Baxter. What I have to say won't take long and then I'll leave of my own accord.'

'Yes, miss, but . . .'

She walked off without waiting to hear him out. The less-than-friendly reception had only served to make her more determined to get the truth from Garland Quinn. She burst into the drawing room without bothering to knock.

Lady Quinn rose slowly from her chair by the fire. 'How dare you barge in like this? Where is Baxter?'

Clara stood her ground. 'Don't blame him for my intrusion, Lady Quinn. I need to speak to you urgently.'

'I suppose it's about Gertie. She always managed to put herself forward and get everyone's attention, and nothing has changed.'

'Yes, of course it's about your sister,' Clara said, emphasising the last word. 'She's been missing for weeks and anything could have befallen her. Don't you care?'

'Why should I? We never got along and that's the truth.'

'Even so, I think you know more about her disappearance than you're saying.' Clara moved closer. 'Please, Lady Quinn, if you have any idea where I might find Gertie, I'm begging you to tell me.'

'Begging, are you?' Lady Quinn's hooded eyes gleamed with triumph. 'I like the sound of that. It puts you nicely in your place, shop girl.'

'I don't care what you call me, just tell me anything you know that could lead me to find Gertie.'

'I don't know why I should. Life has been so peaceful without her and her megrims.' Lady Quinn sank down onto her chair, holding her bony hands out to the fire even though it was a warm day and the heat in the room was stifling. She shot a sideways glance at Clara and bared her teeth in a smile. 'You must have gathered that there is a connection between Patches Bragg and myself?'

'It's obvious that you didn't get along,' Clara said warily.

'That's right. We don't see eye to eye on many things.'

'I really don't understand, and I'm not leaving until you tell me what you know.'

'You are a persistent little thing, aren't you?' Lady Quinn sighed, shaking her head. 'All right, I'll tell you everything. What I have to say will shock, but then that's how I've lived my life. I was beautiful once.' She leaned forward, fixing Clara with a piercing look. 'Can you believe that?'

'Yes, it goes without saying.'

'A good answer. Sit down, shop girl.'

Clara pulled up a stool. 'I'm listening.'

'I was fourteen when my mother died after a long illness. Papa remarried within weeks of Mama's funeral and his new wife was already with child.'

'Gertie?'

'Yes, of course. I was hurt and angry, and disliked my stepmother on sight. Papa decided that it would be best for everyone if I was sent to Paris to study art and music, but I knew it was just to get me out of the way. I stayed with a family who were only interested in the money that my father paid them to keep me, and I ran away. I ended up in Montmartre working as a waitress and it was there I met Laurent Duclos.'

'Duclos?' Clara was suddenly alert. 'Was he related to Patches' husband?'

'He *was* Patches' husband, although I didn't know that at the time. I was young and inexperienced and I thought he was in love with me. It was only when I told him that I was with child that I discovered he had a wife, and she also was *enceinte*, as the French say.'

'How awful,' Clara said sincerely. 'What did you do?'

'I couldn't go home. Papa would have disowned me, and I was penniless. I had to rely on Laurent to take care of me until my baby was born.'

'What happened to the child?' Clara hardly dared ask, but she had to know.

'It was a boy.' Lady Quinn's eyes filled with tears. 'I held him for a few moments only and then the midwife took him away. That was the last I saw of Dagobert.'

Stunned, Clara stared at her, struggling to come to terms with what she had just heard. 'Dagobert? But he is Patches' son.'

'Her child was stillborn only hours before mine. I didn't find out until days later, but Amelie, as she was known then, was ill for some time after the birth. Laurent told me that he put my baby in the cradle and the dead child was buried in an unmarked grave.'

'Why didn't you tell anyone?'

'Who would have believed me? I was little more than a child myself, and I was far away from home.'

'What happened then?'

'Laurent set me up in an apartment with a generous allowance, which would cease if I breathed a word of it to anyone or if I tried to see my son. I had no alternative but to accept. I had a maid to look after me, and Laurent introduced me to some of his wealthy friends.'

'So you became a courtesan?'

'If you wish to call it that, then yes, I did. I don't mind admitting it. I learned to use men as I had been used, and eventually I met Sir Frederick Quinn, who was on a business trip. He was much older than me, but he was kind and thoughtful. When he proposed marriage I decided that I'd had enough of Paris and I wanted to return to London. When I saw this house for the first time I knew I had made the right decision.'

Clara frowned thoughtfully. 'So Dagobert Duclos, also known as Bert Bragg, is your son.'

Lady Quinn nodded. 'He is.'

'Then Gertie is his aunt.'

'Funny, isn't it? Gertie knew nothing of my history, and my boy grew up under the influence of that evil woman. He is a lecher and a criminal, and Gertie was fool enough to imagine herself in love with him.'

'How did they meet?'

'Her mother died in childbirth when Gertie was two, and the baby lived only a few days. Our father passed away when Gertie was eight and, as her only living relation, I was honour-bound to take her in and raise her. I did my duty and put her in the charge of a series of nannies, followed by a strict governess. I had no sisterly feelings for the child and I have none now. She has always been a thorn in my flesh and now I'm quite certain she's taken my son from me.'

'But he was lost to you at birth. Terrible as that must have been, you parted with him long ago, Lady Quinn. Why haven't you told Gertie the truth?'

'I wasn't to know that she would meet him. She was a wayward child and became even more rebellious as time went by. When she was too old for the schoolroom I sent her to Paris and allowed her to live in the apartment that Laurent had bought for me. I'd kept it even after I married Freddie. It was a symbol of my freedom, as I thought, and it was somewhere I used to go when life in London became too much for me.'

'But Paris is a big city. It seems a huge coincidence that led to a meeting between Gertie and your son.'

'Patches is a vindictive woman. She came to see me one day at the apartment shortly after I married Freddie. She had suffered from smallpox and survived, but she was scarred for life. I think it had twisted her mind too and she was insanely jealous of any woman who had ever known Laurent. She knew that we had been lovers and she threatened to have me killed if I ever saw him again.'

'Did she know that Bert Bragg was your son?'

'No, but she knew I had a half-sister. Perhaps she thought she would hurt me by introducing her son to Gertie. She must have been aware of his reputation as a womaniser and a libertine, and I think she wanted him to break Gertie's heart. If I hadn't sent her to Paris none of this would have happened.'

'I don't understand,' Clara said, mystified. 'If Laurent Duclos was so wealthy, why would Patches come to England and set up a gaming house in Angel Court, of all places?'

'She has a weakness for the gaming tables. She inherited the exclusive gaming club in Paris when Laurent died, but I've been told that she upset so many of the members that she was banned from the premises, even though she was the owner. So she came to London and with Bert's help she set up her own club. Like water, they found their own level and fell in with the criminal fraternity. My baby boy has grown up to be someone I am ashamed to call my son. He has broken my heart, but she will never have the satisfaction of knowing that.'

For the first time, Clara felt sorry for Garland Quinn. The harrowing tale had touched her more than she could have thought possible and she could see that the retelling had taken its toll on Lady Quinn.

'That is a terrible story.'

'I might never have known about their relationship, but Gertie returned from Paris a year ago demanding equal shares of the money that our father had left, even though it was willed to me, and she wanted control of the trust fund that she had inherited from her mother. Bert had finished with her and she was desperate to win him back.'

'Did you tell her that he is your son?'

'No. I couldn't bring myself to admit the truth, even to my sister. I don't know if it was shame or pride that prevented me from saying anything, but I wish now that I had had the courage to speak out.'

'No wonder Gertie was in such a state when I found her.'

'I don't want the shop or the money that was left to her. There is no love lost between us, but I was genuinely trying to protect her interests.' Lady Quinn met Clara's gaze with an apologetic smile. 'I didn't know anything about you when we first met, and it seemed to me that you were a poor girl, out to take advantage of my sister. Perhaps I was mistaken.'

'Yes, you were. I will make a success of the store, but Gertie will always be the owner and she will share in the profits. And, it may seem odd to you, but I care about her as a friend. Maybe if you got to know her better you would like her too.'

'I don't know about that, but when all is said and done, she is my half-sister.'

'Do you have any idea where she might be now?'

'If she's still with Dagobert they might be in my Paris apartment.' Lady Quinn rose from her chair and walked over to a rosewood escritoire. She sat down and began writing something on a sheet of paper. 'I'll give you the address, should you decide to go to the rescue. I, alas, am too old for such heroics.'

'Do you think he's holding her against her will?'

'I think it would amuse him to treat her badly.' Lady Quinn turned her head to give Clara a long look.

'He's still your son, Lady Quinn.'

She shook her head. 'My son was lost to me the moment Patches held him in her arms. She twisted the child's mind. From the cradle he was taught to think only of himself and to worship money and possessions. He's inherited a cruel streak from his father and I know I'll never see him again, but Gertie can be saved.' She dipped her pen in the inkwell. 'I'm writing a cheque for an amount that will help you in your search for my sister. If this isn't enough you must come to me again and I'll give you more.'

Clara stood up and crossed the floor to take it from her. 'This is far too much.'

'Nonsense. Call it a salve to my conscience. If you find Gertie you can tell her that I'm sorry for what she's suffered and I would like to make amends. Life is too short to bear grudges, and I have no other family.' She folded the piece of paper and handed it to Clara. 'This is the address. The concierge has been there ever since I can remember, and his sharp eyes miss nothing.'

'Do you think that Patches will be there, too?'

'I doubt it. She lives in rue de Rivoli.'

'Yes, I've been there.'

'You know that you don't have to do this, shop girl,' Lady Quinn said with wry smile. 'It's a lot to ask when you're just getting your business going. I could hire a private detective to find Gertie.'

'I wouldn't hear of it. Gertie is my business partner and I won't rest until I find her and bring her home. My sisters can manage the shop for a while. They're perfectly capable of taking care of things for a few days or even a week or two. I'll leave for France as soon as possible.'

'What?' Lizzie demanded angrily. 'You're going away again?'

'I think it's the right thing to do,' Jane volunteered.

'Be quiet, Jane. You don't know what you're talking about.' Lizzie gave her a withering look. 'We're just beginning to do well, Clara. You can't leave us.'

'You are all more than capable of looking after the shop in my absence, and I'll only be gone for a few days.' Clara turned to Betsy, who had remained silent. 'You can manage, can't you?'

Betsy nodded. 'Just as long as it is only a few

days, Clara. If it turns out to be longer we might find it hard to cope.'

'Anyway, you can't journey to France on your own,' Lizzie said firmly. 'Look at the trouble you got yourself into last time.'

'That was not my fault. You know what Joss Comerford did.'

Lizzie's jaw set in a stubborn line. 'You still need a chaperone. You're a young, unmarried woman. It's just not done.'

Clara looked to Nathaniel, who had been sitting quietly at the kitchen table. 'Paris isn't the end of the world, is it, Nat? You know it better than I do.'

He stood up, brushing crumbs from his jacket. 'That was delicious cake, Jane. Your customers will love it.'

'Never mind that,' Clara said impatiently. 'Please tell my sisters that I will be quite safe in Paris.'

'There's no need to worry, ladies,' Nathaniel said, smiling. 'Clara won't be travelling on her own. I intend to accompany her.'

Chapter Twenty-One

Leaving the shop in the care of her sisters was not as straightforward as Clara had anticipated. She had made arrangements with the bank for Lizzie to handle the financial side of things in her absence, and had given her permission for the alterations to the upper floor to go ahead. It had been a difficult decision, but Clara had to admit that Lizzie was perfectly capable of overseeing the work, and they sat up late one evening going over the plans in detail.

'There's just one thing,' Lizzie said as they were about to retire for the night. 'I want you to promise me that you won't give Nat any encouragement. We're getting on very well, and I think he likes me, so I don't want you giving him the wrong impression and spoiling things.'

Clara laughed and patted her on the shoulder. 'I

promise I won't do anything of the sort, but I think you overestimate my powers of seduction.'

'Clara Carter, wash your mouth out with soap. What would Pa say if he heard you talking like that?' Lizzie's stern tone belied the twinkle in her eyes. She leaned over and kissed her sister on the cheek. 'I trust you to bring him home with his heart intact.'

'I believe you care more for Nat than you're letting on,' Clara said slowly.

Lizzie shrugged. 'Maybe, but I don't get sentimental. Just keep you dainty hands off him, sister dear.'

Clara smiled as she made her way up the stairs to her room. Lizzie might pretend to be immune to tender feelings, but she knew better.

Three days later, Clara and Nathaniel arrived in Paris. They took a fiacre to a small hotel in rue Lepic, and after they had registered and left their luggage in their respective rooms, they set off to find the address that Lady Quinn had given Clara. It was late afternoon and the street was thronged with people going about their business, and the usual chaotic mix of horse-drawn vehicles jostling for position with pedestrians risking life and limb as they attempted to cross from one side to the other. The sun was low in the sky, creating deep shadows, and gas lights were beginning to twinkle in shop windows. The sound of music played on an accordion wafted from a nearby café, and the pungent odour of French tobacco mingled with the scent of wine and garlic. At any other time, Clara would have found the ambience magical, but she was too worried about Gertie to fully appreciate her surroundings.

She slipped her hand through the crook of Nathaniel's arm. 'I suppose it's too much to hope that we'll find Gertrude there.'

He squeezed her fingers. 'It's a start. This seems to be a friendly neighbourhood where everyone knows everyone.'

They found the apartment easily enough but, as Clara had feared, there was no answer when she rapped on the door. They went downstairs to question the concierge, who shrugged and shook his head, despite Nathaniel's attempts to converse in French.

'I think he knows something,' Clara said when they were outside in the street. 'But whatever it is he's not prepared to share it with us.'

'My French is far from perfect, but I'm sure he understood my question. He was either being difficult because it pleased him to be so, or someone had paid him to keep quiet. What do we do now?'

'I suggest we take a cab to boulevard Haussmann. Sabine will help us, and so will Paul. Anyway, I'd like to see them again. They were good to me when I was last here.'

'That sounds like good sense.' Nathaniel looked up and down the busy thoroughfare. 'There's a fiacre dropping off passengers at the end of the street. Maybe we can flag it down if we hurry.'

With a cry of delight, Sabine dropped the pair of gloves she was wrapping. 'Clara. You've returned to us.'

'I'd give you a hug,' Clara said, smiling, 'but Mademoiselle Boucher is glaring at us.'

'What are you doing here?' Sabine shot a sideways glance at Nathaniel. 'This must be your musician friend.'

He reached over the counter to take her hand and raised it to his lips. 'Nathaniel Silver, and I know that you are Sabine. Clara has told me all about you.'

'Excuse me for a moment.' Sabine picked up the gloves, apologising to the irate customer who was tapping her foot on the floorboards and tut-tutting impatiently. She barely waited for the item to be wrapped before stalking off in the direction of Mademoiselle Boucher. 'Oh dear,' Sabine said, sighing. 'I'm going to suffer another telling-off. It becomes tedious after a while.'

'I'm sorry. We didn't mean to interrupt, but I need your help. What time do you finish?' Clara asked in a low voice.

'Eight o'clock, as usual.' Sabine shot a wary glance in Mademoiselle Boucher's direction. 'I could see you then. I can't wait to hear all your news.'

'Perhaps you could dine with us this evening – Paul, too, of course.'

'Paul is working, but, as you will remember, I am always hungry. I would love to have dinner with you, and I know just the place to eat. Meet me outside at eight o'clock.'

'We'll be there,' Clara said, nodding. 'We'd best move on, Nat. Mademoiselle Boucher is heading this way.'

Sabine took them to a café not far from rue Lepic, and while they waited for their food Clara explained the purpose of their visit. Sabine listened in silence.

'Maybe I can help,' she said eagerly. 'Let me speak to the concierge. I'll make up some story about being one of Dagobert's lady friends and appeal to his romantic side, if he has one.'

'Maybe we should leave it until morning,' Nathaniel suggested. 'It will be a bit late by the time we finish our meal.'

Sabine gurgled with laughter. 'This is Paris, my friend. I thought you had lived here long enough to learn that we Parisians need little sleep.'

'You're right, of course.' Nathaniel raised his glass of wine in a toast. 'I was being very English.'

'Here is our food,' Sabine said, smiling. 'You will not get a better onion soup anywhere, I promise you that.'

Clara sniffed appreciatively. 'It smells so good. I can't wait to taste it.'

Later, replete after an excellent meal and several glasses of red wine, they made their way to rue Lepic. Clara and Nathaniel waited while Sabine went to speak to the concierge. She was gone for several minutes and Clara was becoming restive when Sabine strolled out of the building. Clara would have run to meet her, but Nathaniel held her back.

'Keep in the shadows. Someone might be watching.'

'Surely there's no real danger?'

'You know more about these people than I do. Your friend Luke must have warned you to keep away from Patches and her gang.'

'I haven't seen or heard from Luke since he left London after his last visit.' Clara tried hard to sound casual, but if she were to admit the truth, she was hurt and angry. Luke was full of promises he would never keep, and his protestations of love were nothing more than empty words.

Sabine hurried towards them. 'I don't trust that man,' she said breathlessly. 'He is hiding something.'

'But did he know anything about Gertie?' Clara asked anxiously.

'I allowed him to think that I was one of Dagobert's conquests,' Sabine said with a wry smile. 'I pretended that I was in a jealous rage because I'd heard he was involved with another woman – an Englishwoman.'

'And what did he say to that?'

'He laughed and took great pleasure in telling me that Monsieur Duclos had left for the country, and he wasn't on his own.'

'Did he say where he'd gone?' Nathaniel asked. 'He could be anywhere in France by now.'

'All I could get out of him was that Monsieur and his companion had gone to "the château by the sea".'

Clara grasped her hand. 'Did he mention the woman by name?'

'No, but he gave me a lecherous look and said he was surprised that Monsieur had chosen an older woman over someone like me. I didn't take it as a compliment.' Sabine shuddered and wrapped her shawl more closely around her body.

'You've done well, Sabine,' Clara said earnestly. 'Thank you.'

'I can't say it was a pleasure, but at least we know where he's taken Gertie.' Sabine glanced over her shoulder. 'Let's get away from here. I can still feel that man giving me looks that stripped me down to my chemise.' She hurried on and Clara quickened her pace in order to keep up with her.

'You said he'd taken her to "the château by the sea",' Clara said breathlessly. 'Do you know where that is?'

'I could be wrong, but I think he meant the old house where Patches was born.' Sabine's teeth were chattering so loudly that she could hardly speak.

Nathaniel linked arms with both of them. 'Let's go to the hotel and talk about it over a cup of coffee. It's getting cold and you're both shivering.'

Conversation ceased until they were seated round a small table in the hotel dining room. The aroma of garlic and wine was overlain with cigar smoke and the scent of the pine logs crackling and spitting as the fire blazed up the chimney, adding to the fuggy atmosphere. The last of the diners were seated around a large table, drinking brandy and chatting amicably.

Clara held her hands out, warming them in the heat from the fire. It might be spring but the nights were still cold and she was chilled to the bone.

'Obviously it wasn't a pleasant experience talking to the concierge,' Nathaniel said gently. 'I'm sorry we put you through it, Sabine.'

She took a sip of coffee. 'It's not something I would wish to repeat.'

'Tell us what you know about Patches' family home,' Clara said eagerly. 'Is it far from here?'

'I know that she was born in a small village on the coast, because Paul wrote an article about the smuggling gangs who operated from our coasts. For some reason it never went to press, but I think he got too near the truth as far as some high-up people were concerned. Fortunes made that way are not something that rich people like to boast about.'

'Where is this place?' Clara asked.

'Paul could tell you that. All I know is that the village is not far from Dieppe and the château itself is almost derelict. It sounds like a good place to hide someone you want to be rid of.'

Clara gasped in horror. 'You don't think he means to murder her, do you?'

'Surely not?' Nathaniel said hastily. 'Why would he want to harm Gertie? I thought they were lovers. He can't know that they are related by blood. Garland Quinn kept her secret well all these years.'

'Maybe Gertie knows too much about his criminal activities.' Sabine stirred her coffee, a frown puckering her brow. 'If he released her she could go to the authorities and put an end to the Duclos gang. They've evaded the law here for years.'

'I want to go there as soon as possible,' Clara said eagerly. 'Can you arrange it, Sabine? I know it's a lot to ask, but perhaps Paul would take us there. It might make a good story for his newspaper.'

'I'll see him this evening when he finishes work, and when I tell him what you're doing I'm sure he'll want to help, especially if there's a good story at the end of it.' Sabine rose to her feet. 'I must leave you now, but if you come to the shop in the morning I hope I'll have some news for you.'

Nathaniel pushed back his chair and stood up.

'You must allow me to see you safely to Paul's apartment.'

'No, really. I'll be all right.'

'At least allow me to find you a cab.'

'You're very gallant. Thank you.' Sabine turned to Clara. '*Au revoir, Clara.*'

Clara half rose in her seat. '*Au revoir.*' She sat down again. It had been an eventful day, but each time she thought they were close to finding Gertie, it seemed that they were doomed to disappointment. The ruined château by the sea sounded romantic and just the sort of place she had read about in Mrs Radcliffe's Gothic novels, but the idea of Gertie being held prisoner by her former lover seemed highly improbable. This was not the Dark Ages and Dagobert Duclos – or Bert Bragg, whichever name he chose to go by – was not a monster created by an author drugged on opium and chloral hydrate. Perhaps the truth was stranger than fiction after all, and probably even more shocking. Neither of them was aware of the fact that they were related, and that would come as a shock when the truth was told. Clara finished her coffee and made her way into the vestibule. Through the open door she could see Nathaniel handing Sabine into a fiacre and she waited for him to come inside.

'I'm going to my room, Nat. I'm tired and I intend to get up early.'

He nodded. 'You must be exhausted, but I think I'll have a drink in the bar before I turn in.'

She held out her hand. 'I haven't thanked you for coming to Paris with me.'

'I could hardly allow you to travel all this way on your own. We might not be engaged, but I am still very fond of you, Clara.'

'And I you, but in the same way as a sister might feel for her brother.'

He held her hand in a firm grasp. 'There is something I want to say, and perhaps this is the best time to bring up the subject.'

'Perhaps a brandy would help me sleep,' Clara said, closing her fingers around his. 'You know you can tell me anything.'

'Let's see if we can find a table and enjoy a nightcap together.'

Hand in hand they entered the crowded bar. Couples sat huddled together, drinking and gazing into each other's eyes, while noisy groups of young men crowded around the bar, sipping a milky-looking mixture of absinthe and water.

'What was it you wanted to tell me?' Clara asked when Nathaniel brought their drinks to the table. She was unused to drinking spirits, but, judging by Nat's serious expression, she had a feeling she might need something stronger than lemonade.

He sat down, staring at the amber liquid in his glass. 'You are well aware of my position, Clara. My uncle expects me to fulfil my father's wishes to the letter before he will give up his claim to the estate.'

She took a sip of brandy, coughing as the strong spirit burned her throat. 'I am.'

'You did the right thing by turning me down. I am very fond of you, but I realise now that we are not well suited.' He shot her a sideways glance. 'I don't want you to take this the wrong way, but I would like your permission to pay court to your sister, Lizzie.'

Clara choked on a mouthful of brandy. 'You would?'

'I've only known her for a short time, but she's a beautiful and intelligent woman, and I think she likes me.'

Recovering quickly, Clara nodded. 'Yes, she does like you, Nat. But this is very sudden – are you sure you are doing this for the right reasons? Lizzie deserves to be happy and if you marry in haste, only to discover later that you aren't suited, it would be a disaster for both of you.'

'I know that, and that's why I'm asking your permission to pay court to her. I've told Lizzie about the will and its conditions, and she fully understands.'

'Aren't you afraid that, under such circumstances, she might be willing to marry you for the material things you can provide?'

'I think we are both old enough to be aware of the dangers, but I need a wife and I think we have just as much chance of making a success of marriage as those who fall hopelessly in love at the outset.'

'And is Lizzie of the same opinion?' Clara knew the answer already, but she needed to hear it from Nathaniel's lips.

'I believe so.'

'This conversation should have been between you and my father.'

'I know, but he's miles away in Dorset and I can't afford to wait for his return. What do you say, Clara?'

'I'm only a year older than Lizzie, but in my opinion you are both quite capable of managing your own affairs. I won't stand in your way.'

Nathaniel reached across the table to cover Clara's hand with his. 'Thank you.'

She raised her glass. 'Good luck, Nat. I wish you well and for my part I think Lizzie would make you an admirable wife, whereas I would not. And now I'm going to my room. Tomorrow will be a busy day, and I hope a successful one.'

Sabine and Paul arrived at the hotel next morning before Clara and Nathaniel had finished breakfast. Sabine had persuaded one of her friends to tell Mademoiselle Boucher that she was suffering from a migraine and confined to bed, and Paul had obtained permission from his editor to investigate the rumours concerning Dagobert Duclos. His English alias was unknown in Paris and this alone would make a good story.

They left the hotel, taking a cab to Saint-Lazare railway station, where they boarded a train for Dieppe. From there they travelled on a farmer's cart to the tiny village where Patches had been born. The steep cliffs fell away sharply to a sheltered cove and overlooking it was the remains of what must once have been an elegant château, but, as Sabine had said, it was now little more than a ruin. Clara's hopes were dashed when they drew nearer. She could not imagine anything other than bats and foxes inhabiting a near-derelict house which, for the most part, was open to the sky. A fire many years ago had ravaged the building and the roof had fallen in. When they entered through the gap where a front door had once welcomed guests, Clara found herself in a hollow shell. Fireplaces that had once warmed elegant rooms now gazed blindly into space, and the walls were pockmarked with gaping holes where rafters would have supported the upper floors. Ferns sprouted from the blackened brickwork and small trees struggled for survival with their roots reaching out like fingers clutching desperately at anything that would support them. Birds flew overhead, disturbed from their nests by the intruders, their warning cries echoing eerily around the fire-ravaged building.

'They can't be here,' Nathaniel said, shaking his head.

'It's where the concierge thought they had come.'

Sabine leaned on Paul's arm. 'I'm afraid we've had a wasted journey.'

Clara shielded her eyes against the intense sunlight. 'I smell wood smoke, but I didn't see any other houses on the way here. Maybe there's something still standing on the far side.'

Nathaniel took her by the hand. 'Let's go and look. We can't give up now.' They made their way around the crumbling ruin, stepping over piles of moss-covered stones until they came to a thicket of brambles. They were now in the shadow of the west wall and as Clara looked up she saw a plume of smoke rising from the side of the building facing the sea. It took some time to find a way through the undergrowth, but as they emerged into the sunlight a relatively undamaged part of the château came into view. Overlooking the Channel, it appeared to be a later addition to the eighteenth-century dwelling. Hens wandered freely on the cliff top, pecking at the ground and ignoring the newcomers, but a pair of geese set up such a noise of honking and flapping wings that it brought a plump woman from the house. Small and swathed in an overlarge pinafore, she might have been anyone's much-loved granny, until the moment she raised an ancient blunderbuss, pointing it at each of them in turn, and her shrill cries were obviously meant as a warning. Clara choked back a cry of fright and clutched Nathaniel's arm.

Paul held up his hands, advancing slowly and speaking in a conciliatory tone. Clara could only guess at what he was saying, but the woman did not look convinced.

Sabine, seemingly recovered, took a step towards her, holding out her hand. Her gentle voice appeared to have the desired effect and the woman lowered her weapon. She answered Sabine in gruff monosyllables.

'What is she saying?' Clara asked anxiously. 'Is Gertie here or not?'

'She doesn't understand English so we can speak freely. I haven't asked about your friend, but I've told her that we've lost our way. I asked if we might have some refreshment before we leave. She's very wary of us, but I said we could pay and that seemed to work.'

Paul continued the conversation in rapid French and his charming smile seemed to have an effect on the woman. Her weathered cheeks reddened and she giggled girlishly as she motioned them to follow her into the house.

Clara exchanged relieved glances with Nathaniel. 'We'd best keep our mouths shut,' she whispered. 'We don't want to make her even more suspicious.'

Nathaniel nodded. 'We'll leave the talking to Paul. He seems to have got her measure.'

They followed Paul and Sabine into what turned out to be a spacious kitchen. A pan of something savoury bubbled away on the range and a large pine table was strewn with vegetable peelings and flour.

'Just do as we do,' Sabine said in a low voice. 'She's going to give us something to eat and drink. Offering her money seems to have worked to our advantage.'

'Can you find a way to ask if Gertie is here without getting us thrown out?'

'I'll try, but it won't be easy.' Sabine eyed the old woman warily. 'She keeps that old gun within reach, and I don't think she'd hesitate to use it.'

'I think it might blow up in her hands,' Nathaniel said in a low voice. 'Best keep on the right side of her.'

Sabine moved away to join Paul, who was smiling and nodding in agreement with everything the woman said. She bustled over to the range and ladled some of the contents of the soot-blackened saucepan into one large bowl, which she placed on the table, adding a chunk of freshly baked bread and one spoon.

Paul said something that made her blush and hide her face beneath her apron. She snatched up a pitcher and went outside.

'Madame Fabre has gone to fetch water from the well,' Paul said, pulling up a chair. 'Sit down and eat. She's only given us one spoon so we'll have to share, but she says she wants us to leave quickly as the master will return soon.'

Clara sat on a stool and made a space by brushing

a heap of potato peelings onto the floor where they fell amongst cabbage leaves and turnip tops. She broke off a piece of bread. 'Is there any way we can distract her so that I can look for Gertie?'

Sabine spooned some of the soup into her mouth. She swallowed and pulled a face. 'I can tell you something, Madame Fabre is not a good cook. I pity your friend if she has had to put up with food like this.'

'We can't afford to offend her.' Clara dipped her bread into the bowl. 'I'll eat it even if it poisons me.'

Nathaniel was about to comment when Madame bustled back into the room, slopping water on the muddy tiles. She slapped the pitcher down on the table and moisture dribbled down the sides to make milky pools in the flour. Paul thanked her effusively and she slapped him on the back, causing him to choke on a mouthful of bread. She stood behind him watching them until they had consumed every last drop of broth and the bowl was empty. Clara had difficulty chewing a particularly tough lump of meat, but the moment Madame Fabre turned her back she fed the stringy piece of gristle to a large wolfhound that had wandered into the kitchen. The shadow of a tall man spread out on the floor like an ink stain.

'*Maître*.' Madame Fabre dropped a curtsey as the intruder crossed the threshold.

Clara's hand flew to her mouth as she stifled a gasp of surprise.

Chapter Twenty-Two

It was all she could do to keep from calling out his name, but Luke's grim expression was enough to silence her. He turned his back on them and spoke to Madame in fluent French. Flustered and mumbling something beneath her breath, she curtseyed again and hurried from the room.

'What are you doing here?' Luke demanded angrily. 'Why have you come here, Clara?'

She rose to her feet. 'I might have guessed you'd be mixed up in this,' she said bitterly. 'You can't keep away from the Braggs, can you?'

'Come outside. I want to talk to you in private.'

'You can't speak to Clara like that, Foyle.' Nathaniel pushed his chair back and stood up.

Luke looked him up and down. 'I didn't ask for your opinion.' He turned to Clara, frowning. 'You could have chosen someone who would take better care of you. Do you realise the danger you are all in by coming here?'

'Nathaniel has been a good friend to me, which is more than I can say for you,' Clara said angrily. 'I thought you'd finished with Patches and her gang, but I can see that you are still her lackey.'

'I'm at a loss here,' Paul said hastily. 'Will someone please explain what is happening?'

'This is a private matter, not headline news for your gossip column.' Luke pointed to the door. 'Get out before I throw you out.'

'Luke, you don't know what you're saying.' Clara grasped him by the arm. 'Paul and Sabine have helped me and they deserve to be treated with civility, even by you.'

'I'm warning you, Clara,' Luke said icily. 'This is no place for you. Bert and his mother are on the way, and I can't protect you if they find you here.'

'I'm not leaving without Gertie,' Clara cried passionately. 'I've come all this way to find her and take her home where she belongs.'

'Has it occurred to you that she might not want to be found? Or that your ill-judged interference might create danger for her where there was none before?'

Clara met his angry gaze with a defiant stare. 'I'll believe that if I hear it from her own lips, and I'm not leaving until I've spoken to her.'

His grey eyes darkened to the colour of a stormy sea and his generous lips set in a hard line. 'You are a stubborn woman, and will be the downfall of everything I've worked for.'

'What do you mean by that, sir?' Nathaniel demanded angrily. 'Let Clara see Gertie and decide for herself.'

Sabine jumped to her feet. 'Clara wants to see her friend. You can't stop her.'

'You don't know who or what you're dealing with, Clara,' Luke said urgently. 'Leave now, or do I have to pick you up and carry you?'

Nathaniel moved closer to Clara, but she shook her head. 'Don't worry, Luke won't harm me. We've known each other for a long time and he's never raised a hand to me in anger.'

'I should think not,' Nathaniel said, thrusting out his chin. 'Only a coward would strike a woman.'

'Enough of this.' Luke beckoned to Clara. 'I'll take you to Gertie, but only if you promise to leave as soon as you've satisfied yourself that she wants to be here.'

She nodded wordlessly. Her heart was beating wildly and her pulse was racing as she followed him from the room. A narrow staircase led to the first floor where three doors opened off a small landing. Madame Fabre emerged from one of them. She muttered something in French and Luke nodded.

'What did she say?' Clara asked anxiously. 'What's

going on, Luke? Why are you here? Surely you can tell me now that we are alone?'

'It doesn't concern you. Just do what you have to do and then go.' He caught her by the arm, drawing her so close that she could feel his breath warm on her cheek. 'Patches would be happy to stand by and watch her mad son slit your throat, and she'd enjoy seeing him put paid to the lives of all your friends. You don't know what you're dealing with, Clara. Go home.'

She wrenched free from his grasp. 'You don't frighten me. You're just trying to cover up your own misdeeds by making Patches out to be worse than she is.' Clara pushed past him and stepped into a large room, sparsely furnished with a small table and two chairs beneath a dormer window, a washstand and a chest of drawers, and a single bed placed against the wall. For a moment Clara thought that the room was empty, but a slight movement from the bed made her take a closer look. She thought at first that the tumbled mass was simply an unmade bed, but when she pulled back the coverlet she saw Gertie lying in a ball, with her knees drawn up to her chest. She was shivering and her eyes were open but vacant as if she were sleepwalking.

Clara perched on the edge of the bed, stroking Gertie's matted hair back from her brow. 'It's me, Gertie. It's Clara. I've come to take you home.'

The inert figure remained unresponsive, and Clara

was suddenly afraid. She looked up to find Luke standing in the doorway, watching her. 'What have you done to Gertie?' Clara demanded. 'She's been drugged, that's obvious.'

'I have nothing to do with the woman,' Luke said carefully. 'Madame Fabre looks after her.'

'By keeping her under the influence of laudanum or something similar.' Clara jumped to her feet. 'Why is she being kept prisoner?'

Luke crossed the floor to take hold of her hand, holding it close to his chest. His stormy eyes were even more troubled than before. 'I believe a ransom note has been sent to her sister. I can't tell you more than that. Please, Clara, go home. I'm begging you to leave now.'

She snatched her hand free. 'What? Do you really expect me to return to England knowing what a state she's in? And what happens if Lady Quinn refuses to pay up? Which might easily happen as the sisters have been estranged for years. Will Patches slit her throat or throw her off the cliff into the sea?'

'Not if I can prevent it. You have to trust me, Clara.'

'Trust you?' A hysterical bubble of laughter escaped from Clara's lips. 'You are the last person on earth I would trust with anything, let alone a helpless woman who's been drugged until she's half dead already.' She hurried to the top of the stairs. 'Nat, Paul, come up here, I need you now.'

Luke seized her by the shoulders as she tried to reach the bed. 'No. Listen to me, Clara. Patches and her deranged son will be here at any moment. I'm deadly serious now. Do as I say and I'll do my best to help you.'

Clara glanced over his shoulder as Nathaniel burst into the room followed by Paul.

'Are you all right, Clara?' Paul took a step towards them, but she held up her hand.

'Give me a moment. I want to hear what Luke has to say.'

'Get away from here while you can,' Luke said in a low voice. 'There's an inn on the outskirts of the village. I'll meet you there after dark tonight.'

'But what about her?' Clara looked down at Gertie and her eyes misted with tears. 'She deserves better than this.'

Luke propelled her towards Nathaniel, thrusting her into his arms. 'If you care about her at all, take her to safety now.'

Nathaniel met Luke's stern gaze with a curt nod. 'We'll stay at the inn tonight.' He put his arm around Clara's shoulders.

Clara was reluctant to leave the château without Gertie, but they reached the hired wagon just as the farmer was preparing to drive off, and it took Paul some time to persuade him to transport them to the inn.

'He says he'll take us there, but we'll have to pay

double,' Paul said, shrugging. 'He has animals to tend to, so I suppose you can't blame him.'

Clara nodded. 'All right, tell him I agree. It's too far to walk and if what Luke said is true, Patches and her son will be heading this way. I wouldn't want to meet them on the road.'

Nathaniel helped Clara onto the cart where the odour of the farmyard still clung to the boards. Sabine was next and she sat beside Clara. 'I thought the countryside was supposed to smell sweet,' she said, wrinkling her nose.

'It's no worse than the streets of Seven Dials or the Thames foreshore.' Clara sighed as a wave of homesickness threatened to overcome her. France was beautiful and Paris was romantic, but London was calling to her. She missed home and even the bickering of her sisters would sound like sweet music. Clara moved up to make room for Paul and Nathaniel. The driver flicked his whip and his horse lunged forward, as if eager to get back to his stable.

A fresh breeze fanned Clara's cheeks and the fruity aroma of damp earth mingled with the heady scent of bluebells as they passed through the wooded countryside. The sun was setting in a fireball, leaving streaks of orange and purple slashed across an azure sky, and soon dusk would creep up like a thief to steal the land and sea.

'Sabine and I have to return to Paris this evening,' Paul said, clutching the side of the wagon as it lurched over the rutted track. 'I need to write up my report and Sabine has to get back to the store.'

'Of course,' Clara said, smiling. 'You've both been wonderful. We couldn't have managed without you.'

'What will you write?' Nathaniel asked. 'It might put Gertie's life in danger if you put what we've learned today in print.'

'I think the gendarmerie would be interested to learn about the château.' Paul brushed a stray lock of hair back from his forehead. 'An anonymous tip-off will set them on the right trail. But your friend Luke will be implicated in their crimes and arrested, Clara.'

'He isn't my friend. He might be helping us now, but after I return to London I'll never see him again.'

Sabine squeezed her hand. 'Sometimes the heart refuses to obey the head.'

'It was over long ago,' Clara said firmly. 'I was very young and impressionable when I met Luke. There's nothing between us now.'

'If you say so.' Sabine kissed her on the cheek.

They parted outside the inn. Clara paid the farmer to take her friends to the railway station in Dieppe, but it was an emotional parting and both Sabine and Clara were close to tears.

'We will meet again,' Clara said, kissing Sabine on the cheek. 'And there will always be a place for you in my store, should you wish to leave Paris.'

'*Au revoir, Clara.*' Sabine managed a tremulous

smile as Paul helped her onto the wagon. He shook hands with Nathaniel and kissed Clara's hand. 'Maybe we'll have our honeymoon in London.'

'Is that your way of proposing, Paul?' Sabine demanded. 'If it is, it leaves much to be desired.'

He climbed up to sit beside her, taking her hand in his and raising it to his lips. 'I will do better, I promise.'

Sabine's reply was lost as the wagon was driven off, leaving Clara and Nathaniel to wave until it was out of sight.

'I've booked two rooms,' Nathaniel said softly. 'We can do nothing now but wait and hope that Luke keeps his word.'

'He will, if it's at all possible. Luke might be a criminal, but he's always been a man of his word. If he said he'll meet us here tonight, he will, of that I'm certain.'

'I see.' Nathaniel proffered his arm. 'So you have no tender feelings for him at all?'

'Absolutely none.' Clara walked up the path to the inn. 'I'm starving. I hope their cook is better than Madame Fabre.'

They were just finishing their meal in the bar when Luke walked in, bringing with him a gust of cold night air. He came to their table. 'You must come now, Clara.'

'Where are you taking me?'

Nathaniel reached across the table to grasp her hand. 'You're going nowhere with him.' He met Luke's stony gaze with a hard stare. 'Explain yourself, sir.'

'I don't have to tell you anything. This is between Clara and me.'

'I'm not letting her out of my sight. You're a wanted man, Luke Foyle.'

Clara glanced nervously at the landlord, but he was fully occupied serving a customer. 'Keep your voice down, Nat,' she whispered. 'This must be important or Luke wouldn't be here now.' She rose from the table. 'Have you brought Gertie with you?'

'She's not in a fit state to travel far. I've taken her to a safe place, but she needs you to take care of her. Will you come?'

'Of course.' Clara turned to Nathaniel. 'I must go. You do see that, don't you?'

He was already on his feet. 'I'm coming with you.'

'All right, if you're sure.'

'I wouldn't think of allowing you to go without me. Wait here and I'll settle the bill.' Nathaniel walked to the bar and waited his turn.

'Where is this place, Luke? Is it far from here?' Clara asked anxiously. 'Are you sure we'll be safe there?'

'It's a mile or so from here. An isolated cottage.'

'Why can't we take Gertie back to England? I can look after her.'

'Patches will have her men watching the ports. You wouldn't get as far as Calais. Gertie is a valuable hostage, but you and your musician friend are worth nothing to her. She wouldn't hesitate to have you put out of the way for good. Do you understand?'

Clara swallowed hard. She had known that Patches was a hard woman, but to murder innocent people in cold blood made her little better than a monster. 'Yes. I understand.'

Luke plucked her mantle from the back of her chair and thrust it into her hands. 'Put it on. It's chilly outside.'

'But I left my bonnet in my room.'

'We must hurry. It's only a matter of time before they discover that Gertie is missing. Patches can summon up an army of underlings, if need be, and they'll scour the countryside.'

'Why are you with them?' Clara demanded. 'I thought better of you.'

'This isn't the place for such a discussion.' Luke beckoned to Nathaniel. 'I've got a pony and trap outside. It's the only transport I could find at short notice.'

Nathaniel joined them as they headed out of the inn. 'Where are we going?'

'You'll find out,' Luke said tersely.

*

The sure-footed pony negotiated the rough farm tracks in almost complete darkness, but the cart jolted and bumped over the ruts, making the journey uncomfortable, and at times it seemed that they were in danger of overturning. Eventually, at the end of a narrow lane, Luke drew the animal to a halt outside a small cottage surrounded by dark woods. The clouds parted momentarily, allowing a shaft of moonlight to reveal a thatched roof with a dormer window gazing down at them like a sleepy eye. A ghostly white owl skimmed the trees, silent and deadly as it swooped on its prey, and the only sound was that of waves lapping the shore. There were no lights to be seen and the only sign of habitation was a thin plume of smoke rising from the chimney.

'It feels like the middle of nowhere,' Clara whispered as Luke leaped down from the driver's seat.

He lifted her to the ground. 'You'll be safe here for a couple of days.'

Nathaniel climbed stiffly from the vehicle. 'I'm not sure about this, Foyle. I think it would be better if we made for Calais and took our chances.'

'Trust me,' Luke said over his shoulder. 'I know what I'm talking about and this is the only way.'

'Let's go inside,' Clara said, shivering. 'It's cold out here.'

'We'll stay for one night,' Nathaniel conceded grudgingly as he followed them indoors.

A fire burned dully in the rusty range and Luke

used a spill to light an oil lamp, which he placed on a table in the centre of the room.

'Where is Gertie?' Clara glanced round the sparsely furnished room.

Luke lit a candle and tossed the spill into the fire. 'She's upstairs, asleep.'

Clara headed for the wooden ladder that led to the first floor. 'Are you sure she's here? Or is this a trick?'

'She's in bed, heavily sedated with laudanum. It was the only way I could get her away from Madame Fabre. I spent an hour plying that wretched woman with apple brandy, and when she dozed off I managed to get Gertrude away before Patches arrived.' Luke handed her the candle. 'Here, take this. I didn't leave one upstairs in case Gertie knocked it over and burned the place down.'

There was only one room at the top of the stairs, and Gertie lay comatose on the bed. A quick examination put Clara's mind at rest: Gertie might be heavily drugged, but her breathing was regular and her forehead cool to the touch.

'You're safe now, Gertie,' Clara whispered. 'I'll sleep in the chair and I'll be here when you wake up.' She tucked the covers around Gertie, but raised voices from below made her hurry downstairs.

'What's going on?' she demanded. 'Can't I leave you for two minutes without you falling out?'

'We're never likely to be friends,' Luke said angrily.

Nathaniel glared at him. 'I don't trust you, Foyle. I want to know the real reason why you've brought us to this place?'

'I'm not going through it again simply to please you,' Luke said impatiently.

'Why should we believe anything you say? You're as much a criminal as the Braggs.'

'Believe what you like, but everything I've told you is the truth. You must remain here for a day or two. When it's safe to leave for Calais I'll arrange transport to Rouen. It's likely that Patches will have someone watching the railway station at Dieppe. After that it's up to you.'

'Just tell me one thing,' Clara said hastily. 'How are we to survive in this out-of-the-way place?'

'I've left food and there's plenty of wood for the fire. You have no need to go further than the stream for water.'

'It's as if this was all planned.' Nathaniel's eyes narrowed. 'You couldn't have known that Clara would come looking for Gertie.'

'No, of course not. This cottage has been my hideaway. I can tell you nothing more, but do as I say and you should get home safely.'

'Thank you,' Clara said earnestly. 'I don't know why you're doing this, but I am grateful.'

Luke hesitated in the doorway and his expression softened with a hint of a smile that faded as he turned to give Nathaniel a warning glance. 'I hope you appreciate what you've got. In my opinion you're not the man for Clara, but she has a mind of her own.'

Nathaniel shook his head. 'You're making a mistake. It's not like that—'

Luke grabbed him by the lapels and shook him. 'Play her false and you'll have me to deal with.' He stormed out of the room before either Clara or Nathaniel had a chance to speak.

Clara hurried after him, but he leaped onto the cart and was driving off into the night before she could stop him. She went inside and closed the door.

'He thinks we're together,' she said dully.

'What does it matter?' Nathaniel took off his overcoat and threw it over the back of a chair. 'You're unlikely to see him again after we return home, so why should it bother you?' He gave her a searching look. 'You don't care for him, do you?'

'Of course not.' Clara unbuttoned her mantle, avoiding meeting his gaze. 'That was over a long time ago.'

Nathaniel leaned back in the chair. 'I can't stay here much longer, Clara. I know what Foyle said about Patches and her ruffians, but I have to return to London. There are things I have to do that can't wait.'

'Does my sister come into that category?'

He looked up, startled. 'I don't think of Lizzie in such a cold-hearted way. I admire her greatly and I want to get to know her properly, and for her to know me better. I don't want her to marry me for money and position, although I can offer her both.'

Clara smiled. 'I know you well enough to believe you, Nat. You're a kind, generous man, even if you are obsessed with music.'

'Is that going to go against me? I would try to be a good husband, but music will always be a major part of me. I won't be able to settle down to the life of a country squire.'

'I think that Lizzie would be most accommodating. She has an independent streak – in fact all four of us have, even Jane, who is still very young. I think Lizzie would be happy to see you follow your career and she would do all she could to help you.'

'So you think I have a chance with her?'

'I most certainly do, and you have my blessing. Not that you need it.'

'Thank you, Clara. That means a lot to me, and I'll always love you, but as my sister.'

A groan from upstairs brought the conversation to an abrupt halt and Clara said goodnight to Nathaniel before negotiating the steep stairs to the bedroom.

Clara slept fitfully, waking up every now and again to check on Gertie. Sleeping in an upright wooden chair was not the most comfortable way to spend a night, and when she finally awakened at dawn, she was cold and stiff. She stood up and went over to the bed to find Gertie staring at her.

'Clara?'

'You remember me.' Clara could have wept with relief, but she did not want to upset Gertie. She forced a smile. 'How do you feel?'

'Terrible.' Gertie held her hand to her head. 'I have demons with picks stabbing my brain and my mouth is dry.'

'I'll fetch you a drink.' Clara plumped up the pillows. 'Lie there until I come back and don't try to move. You've been drugged for goodness knows how long, and it will take a while for you to feel your old self.'

'I can't remember anything,' Gertie said dazedly. 'My mind is in a fog like a peasouper.'

'Give it time.' Clara patted Gertie's hand as it rested on the coverlet. 'I can't tell you how relieved I am to have found you.'

'I'd love a cup of tea,' Gertie whispered.

'And you shall have one as soon as the kettle boils.' Clara went down to the kitchen, hoping that Luke had had the forethought to provide tea. She found Nathaniel slumped in the chair, still sound asleep. He seemed to have kept the fire stoked with logs, and although it had burned down to glowing embers it took only a little effort to rake them into flames, and the water in the kettle was soon bubbling and sending out clouds of steam.

Clara went through the only cupboard in the room and found a tin filled with tealeaves and a sugar loaf. She remembered that Luke had a sweet tooth, and for that she was grateful. Gertie loved sugar in her tea and although there was no milk, a brew sweetened with cane sugar would be infinitely more acceptable than a simple glass of water. Clara found a pair of nips and set about breaking lumps off the glistening cone.

Nathaniel awakened as she was filling two cups with tea. He stretched and yawned. 'Is that for me, Clara?'

'I'm taking one to Gertie. This one was for me, but there's more in the pot, and sugar too, but no milk.'

He reached out to take the cup she had intended for herself. 'Maybe there's a farm nearby. I could take a walk and get a jug of milk, and maybe a loaf of bread.'

'There's a loaf in the crock, but I think we ought to lie low. If what Luke said is true, Patches has spies everywhere.'

'I don't believe that, but I'll try to be patient, although I'm eager to be away from this hovel. He might have found us somewhere better to stay.'

'Stop grumbling and drink your tea. It's only for a short while. I'm sure we can manage until Luke tells us it's safe to leave.'

'I'm still not convinced, but I'll go along with it

for today. If we don't hear from him by tomorrow afternoon I'm going to walk to the nearest village and hire a cart to take us to the railway station.'

Clara nodded. She could see that Nathaniel had made up his mind and it was useless to argue. 'I'll see to Gertie. You'll be glad to know that she's awake and she recognised me. Hopefully she'll be well enough to travel in a day or so.'

Gertie revived quickly, although there were huge gaps in her memory. She knew that she had been kept against her will, but when questioned about her relationship with Bert Bragg she became distressed and Clara quickly changed the subject. She concentrated instead on making sure that Gertie had enough to eat and drink, and by evening she was steady enough on her feet to negotiate the steep steps and sit downstairs by the fire.

Nathaniel was restless, and had spent most of the day collecting firewood. He went out again after dark, protesting that he needed the exercise, although Clara suspected that he was on a mission to find the nearest village. She trusted him not to do anything that might lead to their discovery, but even so, she was worried and would not relax until he returned.

Gertie had just gone upstairs and Clara was washing their supper plates in the stone sink when the door opened and Nathaniel walked into the room. 'I was wondering where you'd got to,' she said, making an effort to sound casual.

'I was careful not to be seen.' He sat down and took off his muddy boots. 'It's about three miles to the village, and there are only a handful of houses, a church and the inn where we were supposed to stay. Do you think that Gertie could make it that far?'

Clara stared at him in horror. 'You're not thinking of leaving here tonight?'

He shook his head. 'No, that would be stupid and would certainly draw attention to us. But if we left early tomorrow morning, even allowing for going slowly, we could get there in about an hour. I'm not waiting here on the off chance that Foyle will come to the rescue.'

'But he promised, Nat. He said as soon as it was safe for us to leave he would come for us.'

'What do you think would have happened when Patches discovered that Gertie was missing?'

'I – I don't know. I hadn't given it any thought.'

'She'll know who was to blame, and your friend Foyle will be in serious trouble. He might not be in a position to help us, so we have to look out for ourselves. We're leaving tomorrow whether you agree or not, Clara.'

Chapter Twenty-Three

Despite Clara's reservations, she knew that what Nathaniel had said made sense. She had put her trust in Luke, but she had overlooked the fact that by helping Gertie escape he had placed himself in a difficult situation. Patches was unlikely to forgive such treachery and, having lost the chance to cheat Lady Quinn out of a considerable ransom, would only make matters worse.

They set out soon after dawn. Gertie was still a little unsteady on her feet, but she was as determined as she was stubborn, and she kept walking even though at times each step seemed to cause her pain. Clara and Nathaniel supported her towards the end, but when the village came in sight Gertie let go of their arms and marched on with her head held high.

'Never let it be said that Gertie Batt was beaten by a Bragg.'

Clara exchanged worried glances with Nathaniel. She had not had it in her heart to tell Gertie that the man who had been her lover and then her captor, was related to her by blood. That shocking news could wait until Gertie was fit enough to learn the truth, and the best person to tell her was her sister.

'How much money have we?' Nathaniel asked in a low voice. 'I need to get to a bank in order to withdraw funds.'

'I have enough to pay someone to take us to Dieppe, and the fare to Calais.'

'Remember what Foyle said about Patches having the station watched. Perhaps we should head for Rouen, even though it would cost more.'

'Never mind the expense. We have to get Gertie home as soon as possible, even if we have to walk to Calais.'

A grim smile twisted Nathaniel's lips. 'That doesn't appeal to me in the least. I'll see what I can do to arrange suitable transport. I'm sure the landlord at the inn will be able to help.'

Unfortunately there seemed to be only one vehicle available, and that was the wagon in which they had travelled previously. Rouen, the farmer said, was out of the question, but he was bound for Dieppe anyway. He sucked on his clay pipe, waiting for them to come to a decision, but as the alternative was to go on foot, it was not a hard choice to make.

The farmer dropped them off not too far from the railway station and, having purchased tickets, they mingled with the crowd on the platform. Clara glanced around nervously, but their fellow travellers did not seem to pose a threat. Nathaniel bought them coffee and croissants from a stall near the ticket office, and they found a bench where they could sit and wait for the train. It was a nerve-racking time for Clara. Luke's words of warning came back to her each time someone approached them, but at last the train roared into the station and there was a scramble for seats.

Gertie slept for most of the journey, despite the fact that a large woman came to sit next to her with a couple of fat hens in a wicker basket, both of which kept trying to escape with much clucking and ruffling of feathers. The woman left the train at Rouen, but her seat was taken by an elderly man who smelled strongly of garlic, and an indescribable odour that was all his own. Clara moved closer to the window and hoped that he was not travelling all the way to Calais. He alighted at the next station but the smell lingered like a bad dream.

It was late when they arrived in Calais and they found an inn close to the docks where they took two rooms for the night. Gertie fell asleep almost as soon as she lay down on the lumpy mattress, but

Clara could not forget Luke's warning. She drifted off to sleep eventually but was disturbed by dreams where Patches and Madame Fabre were waiting on the quay, armed with guns and with knives clutched in their teeth, like pirates of old. She awakened in a cold sweat to find a trickle of daylight seeping in through moth holes in the curtains. It crossed her mind that she could do a good trade selling curtains made to order, and the landlord of the inn would be her first customer in France. She stretched and smiled at the thought. It was foolish to worry about what might never happen; she was on her way home and no one, not even Patches Bragg, was going to stop her. From now on she would concentrate on making The Button Box the best and biggest store in Oxford Street. Lady Quinn's money would go a long way to help, and Gertie was safe. For now that was all that mattered.

She rose from the uncomfortable bed. 'Wake up, sleepyhead,' she said cheerfully. 'We're going home, Gertie.'

The paddle steamer ploughed its way across the Channel. The sea was relatively calm with only a slight swell, but Gertie opted to stay in their cabin. Nathaniel and Clara went to the saloon, but it was crowded and the atmosphere was smoky. Clara drank a cup of coffee, but outside the sun was shining and she was suddenly desperate for fresh air.

'I'll come with you,' Nathaniel said, half rising from his seat. 'Although I'm sure it's safe enough as long as you don't fall overboard. I haven't seen any suspicious characters wandering around the vessel.'

'It's quite all right, Nat. You stay here and enjoy your coffee. I'm happy to go outside on my own, and I'll check on Gertie. She wasn't looking too well earlier.'

Nathaniel sank back on the seat. 'If you're sure . . .'

'I am,' Clara said, smiling. 'Don't worry about me.' She had to edge past groups of people, mainly men, as she left the fug of the saloon for the fresh saltiness of the breeze on deck. Nathaniel had been right: the looks she received had been speculative, some of them bordering on lecherous, but none had been threatening. Perhaps Luke had exaggerated the danger from Patches and her gang after all.

She took deep breaths of the sharp, clean air and leaned against the ship's rail, gazing at the ever-changing colours of the water from deep indigo at the horizon to iridescent viridian and translucent aquamarine. The paddles rumbled and splashed as they churned up the waves, and plumes of smoke feathered into the azure sky. The sun was warm on her cheeks and she closed her eyes, savouring the moment of peace when a sudden shriek was followed by shouts and the sound of pattering feet.

Clara turned with a start just in time to make a

grab for a small child and prevent him from hurtling into the dangers of a roped-off area. The frantic mother rushed up to her and took the howling boy in her arms.

'Thank you, miss. He's a little monkey, always up to mischief.' She cuddled the child to her bosom and hurried back to join a group of chattering women.

'That was well done indeed.'

Clara spun round to see a tall, handsome gentleman, nattily dressed in a grey frock coat and striped trousers, with a glimpse of a shot-silk waistcoat in shades of brown and gold.

'He is very little,' she said lamely.

'And you saved him from sudden death.' He spoke perfect English, with a hint of a French accent, and his eyes were a startling shade of blue set beneath straight black eyebrows.

'I don't think so.' Clara smiled, unable to resist his innate charm. 'But I might have saved him from a nasty bump on the head.' She shivered, as the breeze sharpened.

He proffered his arm. 'You are cold, Mademoiselle. Shall we promenade around the deck? We might persuade ourselves that we are on a steamship crossing the Atlantic to New York.'

His pleasant expression and caressing tone of voice made it impossible to refuse and Clara took his arm without giving it a second thought. 'It is getting a little bit chilly,' she agreed.

They walked slowly and his witty conversation and gentle banter made the minutes fly past. It was only when Nathaniel stepped out of the saloon and almost cannoned into them on their second or third lap of the deck that Clara realised how it must look.

'Who are you, sir?' Nathaniel demanded suspiciously. 'I don't think we've met.'

'It's quite all right, Nat. This gentleman and I have been taking the air. It's very bracing.' She knew she was blushing like a naughty schoolgirl, caught out in the act of playing truant, but she hoped that her escort would put her rosy cheeks down to the bracing wind. 'I'm afraid I don't know your name, sir?'

He doffed his top hat with a flourish. 'I, on the other hand, am well aware of your identity. You are Miss Clara Carter and I assume this gentleman must be your musician friend.'

'How the devil do you know that, sir?' Nathaniel faced him with a pugnacious set to his jaw.

'Yes,' Clara added, staring at him curiously. 'Who are you?'

'My name is Dagobert Duclos, or you might know me better as Bert Bragg.'

'Is this some kind of joke?' Clara demanded angrily. 'If so it's in very poor taste.'

'You didn't seem to think so just now, my dear. I thought we were getting along very well until your

442

friend popped out of the saloon like a jack-in-the-box.'

'You're a wanted man, Bragg, or whatever name you are using at present.' Nathaniel slipped a protective arm around Clara's shoulders. 'I have only to alert the captain and you will be held until we dock in Dover.'

'On what charge?' Bragg's lip curled and his eyes narrowed. 'Go away and play your fiddle. Don't interfere in matters that don't concern you.' He fixed Clara with a piercing gaze. 'Where is Gertie? I know she boarded the ship with you, and I will have her the moment you disembark.'

'You will not,' Clara said angrily. 'If I'd known who you were I wouldn't have passed the time of day with you.'

'But you did, my dear, and I believe that you enjoyed our time together. Don't try to deny it.'

'You tricked me. You should have made yourself known.'

'I might say that you were a ripe peach ready for plucking. Given the right time and place, I think your seduction would have been complete.'

Nathaniel uttered an enraged roar and took a swing at Bragg, who dodged with the nimbleness of a ballet dancer.

'I should call you out for insulting a lady.' Nathaniel squared up to him, raising his fists.

'My dear fellow, surely you don't want to risk

breaking the bones in your hand by striking me?' Bragg said, smirking. 'I am an expert in the art of fisticuffs, an excellent marksman and an accomplished swordsman. If duelling were legal I would gladly take you on, but I am a law-abiding citizen.'

Clara grabbed Nathaniel by the arm. 'Don't let him provoke you, Nat. Can't you see what he's doing? He wants to put you in the wrong so that you will end up in custody, not he.'

A glimmer of respect flickered in Bragg's eyes. 'You are a clever lady, and as such I suggest you take your musical friend back to your cabin. But be aware, I will await Gertie on the dock and I will have her. She belongs to me.'

'It's time someone told you the truth,' Clara said furiously. 'I was going to leave it to your mother to put you straight, but you've left me no choice.'

He replaced his hat at a jaunty angle. 'I am shaking in my shoes, my dear. I doubt that Madame Duclos will listen to a shop girl like you.'

'Patches Bragg is not your mother.' Clara paused, meeting his cynical glance with an unblinking gaze. 'It's true that she raised you, but your real mother is Lady Quinn.'

His bark of laughter startled a seagull that had landed on the ship's rail. It flew off to circle overhead, mewing and shrieking. 'Don't be ridiculous.'

'You were swapped at birth. Patches' baby was stillborn and your father, Laurent Duclos, placed the infant that his young mistress had given birth to hours earlier in the cradle. Patches doesn't know that you are a cuckoo in the nest.'

His shocked expression would have been comical in any other circumstances. A succession of emotions flitted across his face. 'You're lying.'

'I am telling you the truth. Your father took advantage of a fourteen-year-old girl who had run away from home and was working as a waitress in Montmartre.'

'And you believed the word of a common prostitute?'

'No, although I wouldn't have disbelieved a woman just because she had fallen on hard times. Your mother is Lady Quinn, or Garland Batt, as she was before she married Sir Freddie. Gertie is her younger sister and that makes her your aunt.'

Bragg's pallor was tinged with green. 'It's a pack of lies.'

'Clara is telling you the truth,' Nathaniel said triumphantly.

'Even so, it doesn't change my plan. Lady Quinn will pay a considerable ransom for the return of her sister, and I intend to collect it.' Recovering his aplomb, he doffed his hat and walked off with a swagger in his step.

'So that is the infamous Bert Bragg,' Clara said slowly. 'He seemed to be such a gentleman.'

'Appearances can be deceptive. He's a dangerous

man.' Nathaniel guided her towards the companionway. 'We'd better make sure that Gertie is all right.'

Clara nodded. 'Of course. But I think I should warn her that Bragg is on board.'

'Are you going to tell her who he really is?'

'No, I don't think she's strong enough to learn the truth, not yet anyway. That will have to come later.'

Nathaniel patted her on the shoulder. 'I'll be in the saloon, but I'll come back before we dock at Dover.'

Clara entered the cabin to find Gertie wide awake and reclining on the bunk. 'I'm feeling much better now, Clara. I thought I might take a turn on deck.'

'That's not a good idea.' Clara gave her a searching look. The colour had returned to Gertie's cheeks and she seemed much more like her old self. 'There's something I must tell you.'

'Sit down, please. Looking up at you is making my neck ache.' Gertie made room for her, and Clara obeyed, reaching out to take Gertie's hand in hers.

'I don't want you to be alarmed, but I've just met Bert Bragg.'

Gertie sat upright, withdrawing her hand. 'Does he know where I am?'

'He must have had us followed, but we won't let him get his hands on you again, Gertie.'

'I was a fool to get involved with him in the first

place, but if you've met him you must have seen why I was so attracted to him.'

Clara nodded. 'How did you meet? I know you lived in Paris once, but that's all.'

'I always knew that Garland resented me. She was fifteen when I was born and as soon as I was old enough she sent me to a convent school in Paris. She was about to marry Freddie Quinn and I was a nuisance.'

'She did mention something of the sort.'

'I wasn't convent material,' Gertie said, chuckling. 'A couple of us used to sneak out at night and we used to visit a café in Montmartre, hoping that someone would buy us drinks. We were young and pretty and there were plenty of offers, none of them honourable.'

'I suppose you were caught.'

'Yes, and I was expelled. The nuns were more forgiving in Marie-Claude's case because her papa was a prominent member of the Government and very rich. They didn't want to lose his patronage, whereas I was just an unwanted girl from England whose sister paid the basic fees and nothing more.'

'I'm sorry,' Clara said sincerely. 'It must have been very hard for you.'

'Not at all. I was free and I intended to enjoy every minute. I went to the café and sat drinking coffee all day until I spotted the man I had in mind. He was many years my senior but he was charming and he was rich. He set me up in rooms close by and I became his mistress. I was, even if I say it myself, a courtesan of some note. I moved in the best Parisian circles and I lived a life of luxury.'

'Did your sister know about this?'

'Of course she did. Garland pretended to be shocked, but I had heard rumours about my dear sister. She is not as pure as she likes people to think.'

'So why did you return to London? And why were you hiding in the attic? You were in a terrible state when we found you.'

Gertie turned her head, avoiding Clara's inquisitive gaze. 'I never allowed myself to care too deeply for any of my lovers. It was purely business as far as I was concerned, and then I met Bert who was the love of my life, but he betrayed me. He was only interested in the fortune that I had inherited but had never claimed, and that's all he wants now.'

'I am so sorry,' Clara said sincerely. 'That must have been a hard blow.'

'The hardest, but I am recovered now.' Gertie sniffed and dashed her hand across her eyes. 'He is nothing to me, but I had to see him one last time, which is why I agreed to accompany you to Paris. I wanted to make sure that any feeling I had for him had died.'

'And is it so?'

'Most definitely.'

Clara turned her head at the sound of someone at the door. She was about to leap to her feet but she subsided with a sigh of relief when Nathaniel walked into the cabin.

'The white cliffs have come into sight. We're almost home.'

When the ship docked in Dover there was a rush for the gangway. Clara glanced round anxiously but there was no sign of Bert Bragg. Even so, she clutched Gertie's hand and Nathaniel kept as close to them as was possible in the midst of the pushing and shoving as passengers, eager to get ashore, surged forward in a solid mass. They had to join the queue of people waiting to hire cabs, and Clara glanced nervously over her shoulder, half expecting to see Bragg striding towards them.

'Maybe he's learned his lesson,' Nathaniel suggested in a whisper. 'Perhaps he's too ashamed to show his face.'

'There's no need to treat me like a child,' Gertie said angrily. 'I'm not afraid of him.'

Clara was about to answer when a cab drew to a halt in front of them and the door flew open. Luke leaped to the ground.

'Get in, quickly.' He picked Gertie up and tossed her into the vehicle. 'Now you, Clara. Don't argue.'

She was about to resist when he lifted her off her feet and dumped her on the seat beside Gertie.

'What's going on?' Clara caught him by the sleeve. 'Did Bragg put you up to this?'

'I came to Dover to meet Bragg, and then I saw you attempting to hail a cab. You've got to get away before he sees you,' Luke said urgently.

'But he knows we were on the ship,' Clara protested. 'Why are you still with them, Luke? I simply don't understand.'

'You will one day.' He turned to Nathaniel. 'See them safely home.'

Nathaniel hesitated, but Luke had already directed the cabby to take them to the station and Nathaniel only just managed to climb inside as the vehicle pulled away from the kerb. He collapsed onto the seat.

'I don't know what's going on, but I'll be very glad when we get back to London.'

'Bert might be a villain,' Gertie said solemnly, 'but he's not stupid enough to try to kidnap me on English soil. He's too crafty for that.'

'I hope you're right,' Clara said, sighing. 'I don't know why Luke has risked his freedom to be here, but it must be something serious.' She leaned back against the scuffed leather squabs. The relief of being back in England was tempered by fear. From what she knew of Bert Bragg, he was not going to give up without a fight. The fact that he knew the truth about his birth might fuel his hatred of Lady Quinn, although that in itself seemed odd. Clara could only think that such a strong emotion must have been fostered by Patches, for reasons best known to herself. Gertie was still unaware of the truth, and Clara was afraid that the shock of such a revelation might be too much for her to bear, coming so soon after her experience in France.

'There'll be plenty of time for discussion when we get home,' Clara said firmly. 'I don't know why Luke helped us, but we must be glad that he did. Perhaps he was plagued by a guilty conscience, I simply don't know.'

Nathaniel glanced out of the window. 'I can see the railway station. We'll be home soon and I can't wait to be back in London.'

Walking into The Button Box brought tears of happiness to Clara's eyes. The shop was busy by any standards, and the ringing of the till was the sweetest music of all. Jane was the first to see them and she hurried from behind the counter to throw her arms around Clara's neck.

'You've come home. Why were you away for such a long time?'

'I'll tell you everything later, but we've brought Gertie with us, and it was quite an adventure.'

'Miss.' The shrill voice of a middle-aged matron brought them back to the present. 'Miss, are you serving or are you not?'

'I'm sorry, madam.' Jane returned to her post.

Clara walked to the linen counter where Betsy was measuring out a length of calico. 'Don't stop,' Clara said when Betsy looked up and saw her. 'Where's Lizzie?'

'Upstairs with the painter. He's almost finished and it looks wonderful.' Betsy turned back to the customer with a bright smile. 'I'm sorry, madam. Four yards, was it?'

Clara led the way through to the kitchen and was met with a scene of total chaos. Her sisters had obviously put all their efforts into the shop, but their culinary efforts looked like a disaster. Pots and pans were piled high in the sink, and the table was littered with the remains of at least two meals. The floor was covered in dust and ash from the fire and the smell of sour milk and rancid butter made her stomach churn.

Gertie had followed her into the room and she came to a halt, gazing round with a look of horror. 'It looks as if we could do with a scullery maid.'

'And a cook, too.' Clara took off her bonnet and draped her mantle over the back of a chair. 'Where is Nathaniel?'

'He asked me to tell you that he's gone to his lodgings to change his clothes.' Gertie gazed down at her crumpled and soiled skirt. 'I think I could do with a wash, or a bath would be nice.'

Clara rolled up her sleeves. 'I'll stoke the fire if you'll fetch some water from the pump. Do you feel well enough to help?'

'I'm ready for anything now that I'm free from those people. I'd happily watch Patches swing from the gallows for everything she's put me through – and Bert, too. I can't believe that I once thought I was in love with him. He looks and sounds like a gentleman, but he's a monster.'

'Forget him for now, Gertie. Let's get this place straight before we do anything.'

Gertie went outside to fill buckets and Clara riddled the ashes, adding more coal to the glowing embers. When she was satisfied that the fire was burning well she went to find Lizzie, and to her delight she saw that the stair carpet had been fitted and the banister rail cleaned and polished until it gleamed. She ascended the stairs, feeling quite grand, even though it was her own shop. The smell of paint lingered, but the effect was startling. No longer was it a grey uninviting space; it was now light, bright and welcoming. The gilded second-hand chairs were arranged against one wall, and Lizzie was balancing precariously on a box as she pinned a pelmet above the changing-room door. She stepped down and came to meet Clara, smiling broadly.

'So you've come home. I hope you had a lovely time in Paris.'

Clara kissed her sister on the cheek. 'I've so much to tell you, but it will have to wait until we're all together.'

'What's wrong?' Lizzie held her at arm's length.

'I know you too well, Clara. You never could keep anything from me.'

'We found Gertie in terrible conditions. She was being kept prisoner by Patches' men.'

'But you must have rescued her or you wouldn't have come home.'

'We did, but she's still in danger. Bert Bragg isn't what you might think, and he's dangerous.'

'You met him?'

'Yes, on board the paddle steamer, although I didn't know who he was at first. I can see why Gertie fell for him, but there's more to it.'

Lizzie turned to the painter who had just finished putting the last touches to his work. 'Thank you. That's splendid. Go downstairs and my sister Jane will pay you.'

He tipped his cap and headed for the stairs, giving Clara a curious look as he left the room.

'Now then,' Lizzie said eagerly. 'You can't leave me in suspense. Come and sit down. You must tell me everything.'

Clara had to unburden herself. She had kept the truth from Gertie, thinking that it was best for Lady Quinn to explain how and why the situation had come about, but it was a relief to tell Lizzie the whole sad story.

'Well, I never did,' Lizzie said when Clara finished speaking. 'Who would have thought it? And more to the point, what are you going to do about it?'

'I'm not going to tell the others everything, not yet, anyway. I need to go and see Lady Quinn as soon as possible and then it's up to her to speak to Gertie. I can't do much about Patches and her wretched son, but we must keep a close eye on Gertie.'

'There's something else. What is it?'

'If you see Luke, ignore him. He's on their side.'

'But you said he helped you get away from the port.'

'I don't know why he did that, but he's still part of Patches' gang and not to be trusted. I hope he returns to France where he's safe. If he stays here he'll be caught and arrested.'

'I thought you didn't care for him.'

'I don't, but I was fond of him once, when I was a girl.'

'And you're a woman of the world now?' Lizzie raised a delicate eyebrow and her lips twitched.

'Don't tease me. I'm tired and my nerves are fraught. I don't want to disgrace myself by bursting into tears.'

'Maybe you should let go occasionally, Clara. You've tried to be mother and father to us all these years and you're not yet twenty-one.'

Clara sniffed and wiped her eyes on the back of her hand. Lizzie put her hand in her pocket and produced a clean hanky. 'Why do you never have a hanky? Ladies should always carry one in their pocket – and a phial of *sal volatile*, in case of faintness.'

'Stop lecturing me and look to yourself. You have a smudge on the tip of your nose. By the way,' Clara added mischievously, 'Nathaniel will be joining us later.'

Lizzie leaped to her feet and rushed over to one of the mirrors. 'Oh dear, and my hair is a mess. I can't see him looking like this.'

'I'm sure he won't care,' Clara said, laughing. 'I think he's on the brink of falling in love with you, Lizzie, and you with him. It will only take a small push and you will be hopelessly infatuated, and I couldn't be happier. He's a fine man and a wonderful musician.'

'Thank you.' Lizzie turned her head to give her sister a bright smile. 'You could have had him for yourself.'

'We're not suited. We would have made each other miserable, but you and he are an ideal couple. I'll be delighted to be your bridesmaid, rather than the bride.'

Chapter Twenty-Four

Despite her bravado, Gertie kept close to home for the next couple of weeks, and although Clara was busy with business matters she was always on the alert for signs of danger. She had warned her sisters to be on the lookout for anyone meeting Bragg's description, or any suspicious-looking characters who entered the store. Betsy had made friends with the local bobby, a handsome young constable who called in every evening at closing time to make sure that all was well. Clara suspected that Betsy was the real reason for this extra-special treatment, and not the cup of tea that was always offered and gratefully accepted, but it was good to know that Constable Smith and his colleagues were patrolling the streets, keeping a watch on the shop, especially during the hours of darkness.

She might have felt differently if Luke or her father were still involved with the illegal gambling clubs, but Pa was safe in Dorset and she could only hope that Luke had returned to the relative safety of France. Even so, he was never far from her thoughts, and, no matter how hard she tried, she could not forget how he had come to their aid in Dover, but none of his actions recently made sense, and she would probably never know the answer.

Her days were filled with business matters, but at night, alone in her bed, she found herself going over their last few meetings in a state of confused emotions. She had sent him away for the best of reasons, but he was as much a part of her as the air she breathed, and sometimes, when sleep evaded her, she would open her precious button box and take out the silver button that had once adorned his waistcoat and clutch it to her heart. If only he had found it possible to give up a life of crime she might have felt differently, but he had made his choice and was lost to her for ever.

'What's the matter with you, Clara?' Lizzie demanded at breakfast one morning. 'You've been home for three weeks but you still look exhausted. I'm the one doing all the work to make the ladies' fashion department ready for the grand opening tomorrow.'

'I know, and I'm very grateful, Lizzie. You've

done wonders, and I'm sure it will be a huge success.'

'You do look tired, Clara,' Jane said with a worried frown. 'Are you ill?'

Clara shook her head, forcing a smile. 'No, I'm perfectly all right. I didn't sleep well, but I expect it's a case of agitated nerves. Opening another department is a huge step for us.'

'We'll soon be as big as the other stores,' Gertie said proudly. 'You girls are all wonderful.'

'Are we going to have a ceremony like last time?' Jane asked innocently.

'You mean when Patches attacked Lady Quinn?' Lizzie winked at Clara. 'That was a spectacle in itself.'

'I think Patches is far away in Paris,' Clara said hastily. 'We can do without that sort of excitement, but perhaps we ought to ask Lady Quinn to officiate again? She is still a leader of fashion. What do you think, Gertie?'

Gertie pulled a face. 'If you like. I suppose I ought to make an effort to be nice to Garland. After all, she did help with a generous donation when you came to find me, Clara. I should thank her for that at least. Anyway, I'm tired of being cooped up like a hen hiding from the fox. Bert has probably realised that I'm as safely guarded as the Crown Jewels and has returned to Paris.'

'There's been no sign of him,' Clara agreed. 'But he's not the sort to give up easily.'

Gertie smiled. 'No, I'll say that for him. Once he's made up his mind he's unstoppable.'

'Oh, do be careful,' Jane cried anxiously. 'I don't want anything to happen to either of you.'

Lizzie stood up, brushing crumbs from her black bombazine skirt. 'I have some finishing touches to do, and Nat is coming round later to discuss what music would be most appropriate.' She was about to leave the room but Clara drew her aside.

'I know he likes you a lot, but sometimes I worry. You are genuinely fond of him, aren't you, Lizzie?'

'Of course,' Lizzie said sharply. 'I admit that I quite fancy myself as the wife of a wealthy man, but that isn't why I'm going to accept Nat when he proposes marriage.'

'You seem very certain that he will.'

Lizzie tossed her head. 'We've discussed it at length. Some people are romantic and like to be swept off their feet, but I prefer a more practical approach. Besides which, someone has to keep Nat in the real world. He's a dreamer and he needs me to take care of him and organise his life.'

'You'll do that all right,' Clara said with a wry smile. 'I wish you both well. He's a good man, and he does need a strong woman to look after him.'

Gertie abandoned the toasting fork and came to stand beside them. 'Shall we go to Berkeley Square this morning, Clara? I'm perfectly well now and I really ought to make my peace with Garland.'

Clara was about to agree when the sound of someone hammering on the shop door made them all jump. 'Whoever can that be at this early hour? I'll go and see who it is.' She left the kitchen before anyone could stop her and hurried through the shop to open the door.

'Pa!' She stared at her father, open-mouthed.

'Yes, it's me, daughter. Aren't you going to let me in? Or are you going to stand there gaping like a codfish that my cousin has just landed.'

'Of course, Pa. I'm just surprised to see you. Come in.'

He entered the shop and dropped his pack on the floor, looking round in amazement. 'Well, I never. Is this all yours, girl?'

'Not exactly, Pa. I rent the premises from the owner, and all of us are working hard to make it a success.'

'My girls,' he said, grinning. 'How well you've done in my absence. I'm proud of you, Clara.'

'Why are you here, Pa? What brings you back to London?' Clara could not prevent a note of alarm from creeping into her voice.

'I haven't come to shame you by reverting to my old ways.' He slipped his arm around her waist. 'As a matter of fact it was Luke who persuaded me to return to London. He came to see me in Dorset and we had a long chat. He said you needed me.'

'Luke?' Clara stared at him in amazement. 'Why

would he travel all the way to Dorset to see you, Pa? And why did he think you ought to return to London?'

'A cup of tea and something to eat would be nice, love. I've been travelling for hours and I haven't had a bite of food since last night. Besides which, I want to see your shop. Where are my girls?'

'You'd better come through, Pa. We'll talk later.' Clara led him to the kitchen where he was greeted with shrieks from Jane and Betsy and a cool welcome from Lizzie, who moved to Clara's side.

'What's he doing here?' she demanded angrily. 'He'll wreck everything we've worked so hard to achieve.'

'Give him a chance,' Clara whispered. 'At least allow him to explain.'

'He'd better have a good excuse.' Lizzie folded her arms across her chest. 'If he tries to interfere between me and Nat I won't be responsible for my actions.'

'I'm sure he'll do no such thing.' Clara edged her way towards her father. 'Pa, you haven't met our good friend, Gertie Batt. She owns the building.'

Alfred bowed over Gertie's hand. 'Did you have a sister by the name of Garland?'

'Yes, she's my half-sister. How did you know that?'

'You have the look of her. Is she well?'

'Tolerably so, but we don't see much of each other.'

'Why are you here, Pa?' Clara asked. 'I hope you aren't going back to your old ways.'

Alfred held up his hands. 'I was addicted to gaming, I admit it freely, but living a simple life by the sea has made me come to my senses. I'll never gamble again as long as I live.'

'You must have something to eat, Pa,' Jane said eagerly. 'Sit down and I can make you something.'

'I'll get a room ready for you.' Betsy kissed him on the cheek. 'You will stay with us, won't you?'

'I'd like to, if that's all right with everyone.' Alfred took a seat at the table. 'It's good to see my lovely daughters again, but I'm only here for a few days. I've settled down in Dorset and there's a comely widow who craves my attention. I might even make an honest woman of her, if my daughters have no objections.'

Clara patted him on the shoulder. 'Pa, you can do as you wish. All we want is for you to be happy and free from Patches Bragg and people like Luke.'

'Thank you, daughter, but Luke might surprise you yet.'

'I don't understand,' Clara said, frowning. 'Why did he come to see you?'

'He wanted me to warn you all that Patches is back in London and she's dangerous. She's bankrupted the club in Paris with her extravagant ways, and the police there are on the lookout for her. Luke says that she's opened up her club in Angel Court and she's in desperate need of money.' He turned to Gertie. 'You must be careful, miss. You escaped them once but Patches is not the sort of woman to cross, and she has her eye on your fortune.'

'Let her try.' Gertie tossed her head. 'Neither she nor that son of hers will get a penny piece out of me.'

'Bert Bragg isn't her son.' Alfred's casual remark was followed by a shocked silence.

Clara cleared her throat nervously. 'Shall we go into that later, Pa? Gertie and I have to visit Lady Quinn and the shop will open in half an hour.'

'What do you mean, Mr Carter?' Gertie demanded. 'Why do you say that Bert isn't Patches' son?'

'I've known Patches for a long time and, before I met your mother, I worked for Monsieur Laurent Duclos when he had a gaming club in London as well as the one in Paris.'

'You never mentioned his name before,' Lizzie said slowly. 'What else have you kept from us?'

'It wasn't important.' Alfred shook his head. 'It was nothing that would affect my family, but as for you, Miss Batt, I can tell you, hand on heart, that Bert is not Patches' son.'

'No, Pa,' Clara said quickly. 'Please don't go on with this.'

'Don't stop there, Mr Carter.' Gertie moved closer to him. 'Tell us what you know.'

'I was an ambitious young man, employed as a

clerk in one of Monsieur Duclos' London clubs. For some reason he took a liking to me and he offered me the chance to work for him in Paris. I was the trusted employee who was sent to collect the infant that Monsieur put in place of his wife's stillborn baby.'

A gasp rippled round the room and Clara held her breath. She closed her eyes, swaying on her feet as if caught in a howling gale. Gertie was about to learn the truth and there was nothing she could do about it.

'Monsieur Duclos had a liking for young women and he was wealthy enough to buy their silence,' Alfred continued with obvious relish. 'A girl he had taken a fancy to had given birth just hours before Patches went into labour. When his own son was born dead he sent me to the lodging house where his young mistress was living, and the poor creature had little choice other than to give up her baby.'

Jane began to cry and was comforted by Betsy, and by this time Lizzie was bristling with anger. Clara was shocked to learn that her father knew Lady Quinn's dark secret, but there was no stopping him now.

Gertie cleared her throat. 'What was the poor girl's name, Mr Carter?'

'Christine Boucher. She was an orphan who had been working for the Duclos family as a scullery maid, but I'll say this for Monsieur Duclos, he paid her handsomely, and secured her a position in a drapery. He was not a cruel man.'

'Well, I never did,' Gertie said dazedly. 'Who would have thought it? That piece of information will take him down a peg or two. I wish I'd known the truth when he kept me captive.'

'It's hard to believe.' Clara sank down on the nearest chair. This latest revelation was even more astonishing. Lady Quinn was convinced that Bert was her child, when in fact he was the son of a servant girl, but she might never know what had happened to her infant, and that would be even harder to bear. And was Christine Boucher the same woman who ruled the female staff at Automne with such efficiency? Or was it simply a coincidence? It was not a piece of gossip that Clara was prepared to share, even with Sabine.

'You've gone very pale,' Gertie said, peering down at her with a worried frown. 'Are you all right, Clara?'

'Yes, quite all right. Just a dizzy spell. I'm fine now.' Clara managed a weak smile. At least Gertie had been spared the humiliation of thinking that she was related to the man who had almost ruined her life. She took a deep breath and rose to her feet. 'We still have to visit your sister if we're to persuade her to officiate tomorrow. I just hope that Patches won't turn up and ruin the occasion for a second time.'

'I seem to have missed a lot,' Alfred said eagerly. 'I could do with something to eat and drink, Jane my love, and you can sit down and tell me everything while your sisters get on with their work.'

'I'll make your breakfast, Pa.' Jane began cutting slices from what remained of the loaf. 'But I have a job in the shop, too. I am the cashier.'

'Well, I never did,' Alfred exclaimed, smiling. 'My little girl really has grown up.'

'And she has an admirer, Pa,' Betsy said slyly. 'A musician called Danny, and he's very nice.'

Jane's pale cheeks flamed with colour. 'He's just a friend, Betsy.'

'Of course he is. Don't tease her.' Clara took her mantle from the back of her chair and plucked her bonnet from the row of hooks behind the door. 'We'll be as quick as we can, Lizzie. The gowns we ordered from Comerford's Warehouse should arrive this morning.'

'I think there'll be a great deal of interest in ready-made clothes,' Lizzie said eagerly. 'I've had enquiries already.'

Gertie wrapped her shawl around her shoulders. 'I am in desperate need of a new wardrobe. I will be your best customer, Lizzie.'

Clara and Gertie left the shop and took a cab to Berkeley Square. Gertie could talk of nothing but Bert, and seemed thrilled to think that he was in no way related to Patches. The fact that he had treated her so badly seemed to have been forgotten, and had she been a much younger woman Clara would have suspected that she was still head over heels in love with him. Clara tried to look interested but her mind was occupied with thoughts of Lady Quinn's child. What could have happened to her ladyship's illegitimate baby? Perhaps it too had died soon after it was born? Maybe the question would never be answered.

They alighted in Berkeley Square and the door was opened by Baxter. His lined faced creased into deep furrows when he smiled at Gertie.

'You've come home, Miss Gertrude.'

'For a visit only, Baxter. How are you keeping?'

He ushered them into the entrance hall. 'Can't complain, Miss Gertrude. Shall I inform her ladyship that you're here?'

'We'll surprise her, Baxter.' Gertie sailed past him. 'Don't worry. She'll know it was my fault.'

Clara smiled apologetically and hurried after Gertie, who was already halfway up the grand staircase.

Without bothering to knock Gertie entered the drawing room, leaving Clara little option but to follow her. A fire burned brightly in the grate and the windows were shut tight, even though the sun was shining and it was a warm day.

Dressed, as always, in the height of fashion, Lady

Quinn rose majestically to her feet, but her austere expression was replaced by one of surprise. 'Gertrude?'

'Yes, sister, it is I, returned from the perils of being abducted and kept against my will in France. Did you think I was dead?'

Lady Quinn's thin hand flew to her throat. 'Don't say things like that, Gertie. I know I haven't been the best of sisters, but I realise now that I've been unfair in my treatment of you.'

Gertie pulled up a chair and sat down. 'Well, that's a change indeed. I accept your apology.'

'I didn't say I was sorry, although I do regret some of my past actions.'

'Perhaps old age is catching up with you,' Gertie suggested, smiling broadly. 'Come now, I'm just teasing you, Garland. You always were a prime target because you have no sense of humour.'

'I am only forty-five. That doesn't put me in my dotage. My hair might be tinged with silver, but I was as dark as you are not so long ago.'

'You are still a handsome woman, Lady Quinn,' Clara said tactfully. 'A leader of fashion, so I'm told.'

'Don't hover.' Lady Quinn waved a bejewelled hand. 'Sit down, do.'

Clara perched on the edge of the damask-upholstered sofa, digging her toes into the Aubusson carpet to prevent herself from sliding off its slippery surface. 'We've come to ask your help, my lady.'

'What's the matter, Gertie?' Lady Quinn turned to her sister. 'Has the cat got your tongue? You used to have a lot to say for yourself. Do you need a shop girl to speak for you now?'

Gertie leaped to her feet. 'Garland, if you insult Clara again I'll be forced to slap your silly face.'

'Ladies, this is getting us nowhere,' Clara said angrily. 'You may be wealthy women, brought up in society, but you sound like my own sisters.'

Gertie sat down again. 'You're right, Clara. It's a habit of a lifetime, I'm afraid. I apologise for my uncouth behaviour, Garland.'

'I was a little hasty,' Lady Quinn said reluctantly. 'But I've just had a tedious visit from Plumley, and talking business matters always puts me in a bad mood.' She subsided on to her chair. 'I'm glad you found my errant sister, Miss Carter. Now, what can I do for you?'

'You were kind enough to officiate at the opening of my store, The Button Box.' Clara shot a sideways glance at Gertie. 'I mean, our store. Anyway, tomorrow is the grand opening of our ladies' fashion department, and we would be most grateful if you would cut the ribbon.'

'Why me?' Lady Quinn demanded. 'Especially after the disaster last time when that dreadful woman Patches Bragg caused such a vulgar disturbance. Who's to say that she won't do it again?'

'I will make sure that she's kept away,' Clara said

hastily. 'But you really are an arbiter of fashion. Everyone copies the outfits you wear. Who better to convince the public that we are offering both quality and style?'

'Yes, come on, Garland. Don't be stuffy.' Gertie rose to her feet. 'You know you love being the centre of attention.'

For a moment Clara thought that Gertie had gone too far and her sister was about to explode with anger, but Lady Quinn's stern expression melted into a smile and she threw back her head and laughed. The sound reverberated around the ornate cornices and bounced off the walls as Gertie joined in, and soon all three of them were giggling like schoolgirls.

'All right,' Lady Quinn said, wiping her eyes on a scrap of lace that served as a hanky. 'I'll do it. What time do you want me to arrive?'

'Thank you so much, Lady Quinn.' Clara exchanged triumphant glances with Gertie. 'Come early and we can show you round the new department.'

Everything was ready. The store was busy downstairs but the red ribbon tied across the bottom of the staircase acted as a barrier until the official opening. Betsy's beau, Constable Philip Smith, had promised to patrol the street outside as a warning to Patches, who had so far managed to evade the police even though her club in Angel Street was known to be up and running again. Attempts to close it down had so far failed. Prior knowledge of impending raids had the gaming tables stripped of evidence, and each time the police stormed into the basement it was to find a prayer meeting in progress. Clara could only hope that Luke had cut all ties with the gang and had returned to France, where he was safe from arrest. But for now all she wanted was for the day to go well, and for Gertie and her sister to become friends.

There was a festive atmosphere in the shop. Clara had been up early to make certain that the floors were swept and the counters dusted. Jane had come downstairs soon after and was busy baking small cakes to serve with cups of tea. Tables and chairs had been purchased from various second-hand shops, using the last of Lady Quinn's generous contribution to their funds. Gingham cloths had been laid in readiness, and the smell of baking wafted from the kitchen, filling the shop with the tempting aroma.

Breakfast was a hurried meal and they were all at their posts on the dot of nine when Clara opened the doors to the public. Constable Smith was the first person to step over the threshold. He took off his helmet and tucked it under his arm.

'Just to let you know that I'll be close at hand should you need me, miss.'

Clara smiled and nodded. 'Thank you, Constable.'

His glance slid to the linen counter where Betsy was standing to attention, her cheeks flushed prettily and a smile on her lips. 'A pleasure to be of service, miss.'

'You must come for supper one evening, Constable.'

'Thank you, miss. That would be very nice, and the name is Pip, by the way – when I'm off duty, of course.'

'I'll remember that.' Clara stood aside. 'You might like to have a few words with Betsy. I'm sure no one would mind.'

'Thank you, miss.' He strode across the floor and Betsy greeted him with a wide smile.

'There's a budding romance,' Lizzie whispered. 'And here's the first customer. You'd better get Jane to handle the till, Clara. It looks as if we're going to be very busy. Perhaps Gertie would give a hand.'

'I'll ask her, and I'll take care of the till until Jane has finished baking. I thought Gertie might serve the tea when we offer refreshments.'

'Nat is coming soon.' Lizzie patted her hair in place although it was immaculate as always. 'He's bringing his young friend Danny to accompany him on the flute as before. I dare say Jane will be pleased. They seemed to get on very well last time he was here.'

'I still say that she's too young to have a beau.'

'She's fifteen next week, almost a woman. You'll have to mother someone else, Clara. Maybe it's time you had a gentleman friend of your own.'

'Not I. I've had enough of men.' Clara tossed her head and walked off to greet Lady Quinn, who had taken her at her word by arriving an hour early.

'How kind of you to come, Lady Quinn.' Clara held the door open, but she had to wait while her ladyship struck a pose and waved a gloved hand to the crowd of onlookers.

There was a further delay when a reporter asked her ladyship for a comment for his readers. She obliged at length and eventually Clara managed to get her into the shop and hurried her through to the kitchen, away from prying eyes.

Alfred was seated at the table finishing off one of the cakes that Jane had made, and Jane herself was at the sink washing a pile of dishes. She almost dropped the one she was holding when she turned and saw Lady Quinn, dressed in a magnificent gown of green and gold shot silk with a matching hat trimmed with dyed ostrich feathers, and a velvet shawl draped casually over her thin shoulders.

Alfred leaped to his feet, wiping his fingers on his waistcoat. 'By God, it is you, isn't it?'

Lady Quinn paled to the colour of wood ash. 'After all these years – it can't be . . .'

Chapter Twenty-Five

'Garland Batt – I almost didn't recognise you done up in all that finery.'

Lady Quinn's thin cheeks were stained with a blush and she fluttered her eyelids. 'Alfie Carter. You haven't changed a bit.'

'What's going on?' Gertie demanded as she walked into the kitchen. 'What have you said to him, Garland? The poor man looks as though he's about to have an apoplectic fit.'

'I told you I knew this lady, but I wasn't aware she married a title.' Alfred seized Lady Quinn's hand and raised it to his lips. 'We're old friends, aren't we, Garland. We've known each other for thirty years, although it's been almost that long since we last met, but I couldn't forget little Garland. Such a sweet girl, and so badly done to.'

'Hush, Alfie, you're making me blush.' Lady Quinn sank down on the chair that Alfred had vacated. 'I feel quite faint. A tot of brandy wouldn't go amiss.'

Jane hurried to the cupboard and brought out a bottle.

'Make that two glasses,' Alfred said cheerfully. 'This is a celebration. Tell me about yourself, my dear. I've read about you in the papers, but that was just gossip. Have you found happiness after what happened all those years ago?'

'I don't think this is the right time to rake up the past,' Clara said hurriedly.

'Your daughter is aware of what happened, Alfie?'

'Yes, but she only knows half the story, Garland.' Alfred gave her a sympathetic smile. 'I told Monsieur Duclos at the time that it wasn't fair to keep you in ignorance, but of course he paid no attention to me, a mere underling.'

'We all know that my sister has an unsavoury past,' Gertie said casually. 'As have I. We are only half-sisters, but we have that in common.'

Clara frowned at her father, willing him to think before he spoke, but Lady Quinn was giving him her full attention.

'Come on, Alfie. You can't leave remarks like that hanging in mid-air. If you have something to say, then for heaven's sake, say it.'

'For once I agree with my sister,' Gertie said impatiently. 'You can't leave it there, Mr Carter.'

'Alfred,' he said grinning. 'But my friends call me Alfie.'

Jane poured two generous measures of brandy. She passed them along the table. 'I'd love to stay and hear what you have to say, Pa, but I'd better go and help Betsy.'

'Thank you, Jane,' Clara said hurriedly. 'I'll tell you everything later.'

'I'll keep you to that.' Jane left the kitchen, lingering for a moment in the doorway with a wistful look on her pretty young face.

'I know what you're going to say, Alfred.' Lady Quinn swigged her drink back in one and coughed delicately. 'It shames me to admit that Dagobert Duclos, or Bert Bragg, as I believe he's also known, is my flesh and blood.'

'It's high time you learned the truth, Garland. I was sworn to secrecy, but given the choice I would have told you at the outset.' Alfred put his glass down and cleared his throat. 'It was a long time ago, but I remember it as if it were yesterday.'

'Do get on with it, Pa,' Lizzie said impatiently. 'We've got the opening ceremony in less than half an hour.'

He held up his hand for silence. 'This takes some telling, but the gentleman in question, Laurent Duclos, is long dead – killed in a duel by a jealous husband. Young Garland had no one to protect her when Duclos took her in.'

'He seduced her,' Gertrude said with a cynical smile. 'Don't be afraid to tell the truth, Alfie.'

'Yes, that's the nub of it,' Alfred agreed, nodding. 'And when she gave birth to his child, Monsieur Duclos sent me to collect the infant.'

Lady Quinn dabbed her eyes with a lace hanky. 'It broke my heart to part with my baby boy, but I knew it was for the best for him to be raised by his father.'

'That was what Monsieur wanted you to believe,' Alfred said softly.

'But, Pa,' Clara protested, 'you told us that Bert Bragg is the son of a shop girl called Christine Boucher.'

'Is this true, Alfie?' Lady Quinn clutched his hand, her knuckles whitening visibly. 'If so, what happened to my baby? Tell me, for God's sake.'

'Your son is alive and well, Garland. Bert was born a couple of months before your boy, and, to be fair to her, Patches was a devoted mother, but she was growing weary of her husband's infidelities. Monsieur didn't want her to find out about you, so he ordered me to find a foster mother for your infant.'

'So he gave my baby away. How could he be so cruel? I trusted him to do the right thing, Alfie.'

'I know you did, girl, and I was an unwilling partner in the deception.'

Lady Quinn held her empty glass up for a refill

and Jane obliged. 'If Madame Duclos didn't take my son, who did?'

Alfred puffed out his chest, glancing round at his audience with a smug smile. Clara could see that her father was enjoying himself, but she had a feeling that he was going to announce something momentous. 'Go on, Pa,' she said urgently. 'Don't keep us in suspense.'

'I'm coming to it, Clara. Don't rush me.' Alfred downed the last of his drink. 'I gave the child into the care of a young woman called Kitty. She had been a servant in the Duclos household but had left to marry one of the grooms, a young Irishman who was good-hearted but had a weakness for drink.'

'You gave my baby to a drunken Irishman and a housemaid?' Lady Quinn's voice rose an octave. 'How could you, Alfie? Knowing that he was with Laurent's wife was bad enough, but a maid and a groom – even worse.'

'They were returning to London, and I knew that the boy would be loved and cared for. Kitty Foyle, as she became when she married, was a good woman.'

'Foyle?' Clara stared dazedly at her father.

'Yes, daughter. The baby was christened Luke and raised by his adoptive mother in Spitalfields, but I kept an eye on him while he was growing up. I owed you that, Garland.'

Clara pulled up a chair and sat down. Her legs

had given way beneath her as she struggled to come to terms with her father's casual pronouncement. If what he said was true, Luke was Lady Quinn's long-lost son.

'I don't know whether to be angry with you, or grateful,' Lady Quinn said slowly. 'Where is he now, or did he turn out to be a villain like Bert?'

Alfred reached for the brandy bottle and refilled his glass. 'Kitty came to me for help when her husband was trampled to death by a runaway horse. I suspect that Paddy Foyle was the worse for drink when it happened, but Kitty was left widowed with a young son to raise on her own.'

'I feel quite faint.' Lady Quinn fanned herself with her hand.

'Don't fret, Garland,' Alfred said gently. 'Monsieur Duclos saw to it that neither Kitty nor the boy went without. Luke was sent to a good school and received a sound education.'

'Then why did he turn to crime?' Clara cried passionately. 'What possessed him to get mixed up in the gangs?'

Alfred laid his hand on her arm. 'I don't know, love. I can't tell you any more than I have already.'

'So he is a criminal,' Lady Quinn said angrily. 'I'm shocked, but then what would one expect of a boy brought up in Spitalfields? Why couldn't you have told me all this sooner, Alfie?'

'Luke isn't a bad person at heart. I don't know

how he became mixed up with Patches, but she's the one to blame for involving him in crime.' Clara turned to her father. 'Does he know that Lady Quinn is his mother?'

Alfred shook his head. 'I was sworn to secrecy so I never told him. I can't speak for poor Kitty.'

'Can we discuss this later?' Lizzie stood up and moved to the door. 'It's time for the opening ceremony, Lady Quinn. I need to give Nathaniel his cue to start playing.'

Clara jumped to her feet. Her father's pronouncement had come as a total shock, but there had always been a slight air of mystery surrounding Luke and, however hard he tried to fit in, he was different from the people with whom he associated. He had risked everything by helping them to escape from France, and that was not the action of a ruthless criminal, but now she was even more confused.

'Clara, stop daydreaming. This is our big moment.' Lizzie's voice broke into her thoughts and Clara snapped to attention. Luke was not her concern, she had made that clear to him, and now she had more important things to do.

'Come this way, my lady,' she said, ushering Lady Quinn into the store. 'Pa, will you be a dear, and boil plenty of water so that we can make tea when it's needed? Gertie, you'd better come with me, just in case things go wrong.'

They made their way to the foot of the stairs

where the ceremony was to take place. Nathaniel and Danny had already struck up a medley of popular music, but they stopped playing at a signal from Clara and she stepped forward to introduce Lady Quinn to the expectant customers.

Holding herself erect, Lady Quinn kept up the appearance of ice-cold calm as she cut the ribbon and declared the ladies' fashion department open. She stepped aside to avoid the genteel stampede of well-dressed ladies, their feathered hats bobbing as they took the stairs like an invading army. Lizzie had had the presence of mind to be at the front and had reached the top in time to show them around. Clara could hear her sister's authoritative tones and she knew that the customers were in good hands. Lizzie could be very persuasive when she chose.

Clara left Gertie to deal with Lady Quinn, who immediately took a seat at the top table and was joined by Alfred, who plied her with tea and cake. Clara suspected that he had laced their cups with brandy, but if it kept her ladyship happy and smiling for her audience, that was all to the good. The tables filled, and the clatter of teacups and high-pitched chatter, accompanied by lively music, created a relaxed and festive atmosphere. Clara went to relieve Jane at the till, but it was becoming obvious that, if trade continued to grow, they would need to take on more staff. Clara was delighted with the way things were going, but her thoughts kept straying to her father's latest revelation, and the fact that Luke was Lady Quinn's son made the gap between them even greater. A sudden flurry of activity near the door made her turn with a start.

Jane was handing change to a woman who had bought an entire bolt of silk when someone screamed and two masked men burst into the shop, brandishing shotguns.

'Get out.' Clara was too angry to feel fear and she placed herself between her sister and the intruders. 'Go away.'

One of them advanced, pointing the weapon at her. 'Give us the money and no one will get hurt.' Even through the mask she recognised his voice.

'I know who you are. We've met before, Bones. You're one of Patches' men.'

'That's right, dearie.' Patches strutted into the shop. 'I'll take the money, but it's the painted whore I really want.'

'I don't know what you're talking about,' Clara said angrily.

'Yes, you do. I want the harlot who tried to steal my husband.'

'I've heard that he had many such conquests. Maybe you should blame him and not the innocent girls he seduced.'

Jane tugged at Clara's sleeve. 'Give them the money. It's not worth dying for.'

'That's right.' Bones tossed a leather pouch at Clara. 'Fill that up and we'll be gone.'

'I want that woman first,' Patches insisted. 'I'm going to duck her in the Serpentine and then we'll see her for what she is. I've punished all the others in one way or another and she's the last on my list.'

'You're insane,' Clara said angrily. 'The police will be here soon.'

'I'm not stupid.' Patches took a step closer. 'D'you imagine I haven't thought of that? They're too busy dealing with a bank robbery close by to worry about a shop. If you don't get Garland Batt I'll fetch her myself.'

At that moment Lady Quinn broke through the crowd of terrified women. She marched up to Patches. 'You evil woman. You were responsible for stealing my baby.'

'I dunno what you're talking about.' Patches flexed her fingers as if getting ready for a fight. 'You took advantage of the fact that I fell ill with smallpox and lost my looks. You lured my husband into your bed, and from that moment onward my marriage was a sham. I've been waiting for a chance to scratch your eyes out ever since, and now is as good a time as any.'

'I'm not afraid of you,' Lady Quinn countered. 'Just look at yourself in the mirror, you fat freak. Who would choose you over someone like me?'

'I was beautiful once. I had a perfect complexion

until I fell ill and nearly died.' Patches balled her hands into fists. 'If it's a fight you want, I'm ready for it.'

'That's not a good idea, Patches.' A male voice rang out, drowning a string of epithets that tumbled from Patches' lips, causing gasps of horror to ripple round the frightened customers who had huddled together at the foot of the stairs.

Patches spun round to face Luke, who had followed her into the store.

'Luke, go away,' Clara cried, wringing her hands. 'She'll drag you into this and the police will be here soon. Don't let them catch you.'

'Don't worry about me, Clara. I'm on the right side of the law this time.' Luke grabbed Patches' wrists and snapped handcuffs on them. 'This is long overdue, but Patches Bragg, alias Amelie Duclos, you're under arrest.'

Bones and his accomplice made a run for the door but were waylaid by Constable Smith and one of his colleagues.

'What's going on, Luke?' Patches demanded furiously. 'You're one of us.'

'No, I'm not. In fact, I was never part of any gang. I'm an officer in the Metropolitan Police and I've been working to bring about the end of the street gangs.'

Clara stared at him in amazement. 'You're a policeman?'

'I'm a detective. I'm sorry if you're disappointed.'

'Disappointed!' Clara could hardly speak. All these years she had thought of him as misguided, but this was not the man she had thought she loved.

'You bastard,' Patches cried, seizing the nearest thing to hand, which happened to be a brass coffee pot, but she was hampered by the cuffs and it fell harmlessly to the floor.

'I'm afraid you're finished, Patches,' Luke said calmly. 'This is the end as far as your criminal career is concerned.'

'I thought you were my friend and I treated you like my own son,' Patches said bitterly, 'and this is all the thanks I get.'

'You have no son.' Lady Quinn moved a step closer. 'Your child was stillborn.'

Patches glared at her. 'You're a damned liar, you trollop.'

Lady Quinn drew herself up to her full height. Her eyes narrowed and she drew back her head like a spitting cobra. 'Your husband switched your stillborn son for the love child of a scullery maid. I'm sure Bert will be delighted to learn the true facts of his birth. We've both been misled by your cheating swine of a husband.'

'You evil bitch. You've made this up to hide the fact that you're a high-class dollymop.' Patches attempted to lunge at Lady Quinn, but Luke restrained her.

'Now, now,' he said lightly. 'There are ladies present, Patches. There's no need to use such language.'

'Let me get at her,' Patches insisted. 'Give me this once chance to right a wrong.'

'You'll have a chance to tell your story in court,' Luke said firmly. He guided her to the door but she dug her heels in, refusing to budge an inch.

'What happened to your little bastard then, Lady High and Mighty?' Patches demanded, curling her lip. 'I heard that you'd given birth to another of Laurent's bastards. Where did he end up?'

Clara's breath caught in her throat. She could not bear to see Luke humiliated publicly. 'This isn't the right time to speak of it,' she said firmly. 'It's for his mother to tell him in her own good time.'

Luke hesitated. 'What are you talking about, Clara?'

'She's trying to tell you that I'm your mother.' Lady Quinn threw up her hands in a dramatic gesture. 'You are my son. That woman's husband stole you from me to cover up his infidelity. He gave you to a servant to raise, when by rights you should have had the best of everything.'

'Best of everything.' Patches spat the words as if they were a bad taste in her mouth. 'You were a wanton, a runaway and an adulterer. You might have married a rich man, but you're still a harlot.'

Clara could see that Patches' harsh words had hit

their target. Lady Quinn was rigid with suppressed rage, and Luke's expression was taut. She sensed his inward struggle to deal with the information that had been tossed at him in such a public manner, but her desire to comfort him was tempered by anger. He had professed his love for her, but he had not trusted her enough to tell her that he was on the right side of the law.

His expression was inscrutable as he gazed at his mother. 'And you've kept it secret all these years. How could you treat your own flesh and blood in such a manner?' He thrust Patches into the arms of the sergeant, who threw her over his shoulder as if she were a featherweight, which she most certainly was not, and carried her outside to the waiting Black Maria.

Clara stood, mute with shock. Her heart ached with sympathy for mother and son, and yet she could not bring herself to forgive Luke for his deception.

'I knew nothing of this until today, Luke.' Lady Quinn's eyes brimmed and her lips trembled. 'I was little more than a child when you were born and I couldn't stop them taking you from me. I thought your father was going to bring you up as his son, which of course you were.' She clasped her hands to her bosom and tears rolled slowly down her cheeks. 'I will never forgive him for what he's done to us.'

'My mother tried to tell me something of the sort

on her death bed,' Luke said slowly, 'but she couldn't find the words.'

'I'm truly sorry. If you could find it in your heart to give me a second chance, maybe we could get to know each other?' Lady Quinn raised her hand and then let it drop to her side with a heavy sigh. 'I don't expect you to pardon me for what happened in the past, but perhaps . . .'

Gertie pushed her way to the front of the stunned onlookers. 'Ladies, we apologise for the unfortunate circumstances in which we find ourselves, but I'm sure that a nice cup of tea and a fancy cake will do much to calm shattered nerves.' She beckoned to Betsy. 'We could do with some help in the kitchen, love.' Gertie herded the fascinated onlookers away from the front of the shop with Betsy bringing up the rear like a well-trained sheepdog.

'You should talk this over in private,' Clara said hastily.

'I can't pretend that it's not a huge shock.' Luke made a move towards the door. 'I think we both need time to get used to the situation, and I really must leave now.'

'Clara knows my address,' Lady Quinn said meekly. 'I would very much like it if you would come and see me, Luke. I know I can never replace the woman who raised you, but blood ties are important. I realise that now.' She walked away, heading for the kitchen.

Luke paused in the doorway. 'I'm sorry, Clara.'

'I'm still reeling from the fact that you're a different person from the man I thought I knew.'

'I'm exactly the same and still very much in love with you. I'm sorry I deceived you, Clara, but I couldn't tell anyone.'

'You should have trusted me, Luke.'

'I have to go now, but we'll talk later.' He hurried from the building, and through the window she saw him climb onto the box of the police wagon. The driver urged the horses to a walk and then a trot, but Patches was not going quietly. The sound of her protests gradually died away.

'Come and help us, Clara,' Betsy called excitedly. 'They all want refreshments and Lizzie is fully occupied upstairs. We're rushed off our feet. Nat and Danny are helping in the kitchen and Pa is serving the ladies. They think he's wonderful.'

Lady Quinn went home early, having invited everyone to dine at her house the following evening.

When the shop shut, after a most eventful day, the family gathered in the kitchen.

Alfred assumed his position at the head of the table. 'I've decided to remain in London and help my girls build up this business.'

'But, Pa, what about your lady friend in Dorset?' Betsy said with a mischievous smile. 'I thought you were eager to see her again.'

'I'll have to return to Dorset to collect the rest of my belongings, and I'll let her down gently. I've other things on my mind now.'

'Are you going to work in the shop?' Jane asked.

'Well, my little pearl, I'm pretty good with figures, even if I say so myself. I'm just not lucky when it comes to gambling. I was a bookkeeper in the City for years and I might not know anything about fashion, but I do know how businesses are run.'

Clara glanced round the table and her sisters' smiles said it all. 'That would be wonderful, Pa,' she said eagerly. 'But only if you promise never to go near a gaming table or a racecourse again.'

'I might have an occasional flutter at the races, but I've learned my lesson and I'll keep well away from gambling clubs, especially those run by criminals.'

'Talking about criminals – what are you going to do about Luke?' Always direct, Lizzie gave Clara a disapproving look. 'He's deceived us all. Surely you aren't going to forgive him?'

'I don't want to talk about it,' Clara said dully. 'He didn't trust me, and I'm not sure if I can forgive him for that.'

'Sometimes the heart speaks for you.' Gertie wrapped her arm around Clara's shoulders. 'I've forgiven Bert no end of times. We were good together once, before that woman turned him against me.'

'Gertie, you're not thinking of seeing him again, are you?' Clara demanded. 'Surely not, after the way he treated you in Paris? You were his prisoner.'

'That was Patches' doing,' Gertie said lightly. 'Sometimes there is only one man for a woman, despite his failings.'

'He had you drugged and treated you abominably.' Nathaniel shook his head. 'I don't understand women.'

'I agree with Nat,' Lizzie said firmly. 'We see eye to eye on so many things.'

Danny cleared his throat and made a move towards the door. 'This is family business. I think I'd better go back to my lodgings.'

'You're right, Danny,' Nathaniel said hastily. 'We should go anyway. I need to be up early tomorrow to attend a rehearsal. My music is to be performed at the Theatre Royal, Drury Lane.'

'Oh, how wonderful, Nat.' Lizzie jumped to her feet and threw her arms around his neck.

Clara stared at her in astonishment. Such a display of emotion was normally quite alien to Lizzie's staid demeanour. Clara smiled and clapped her hands. 'Well done, Nat. I knew you could do it.'

He held Lizzie at arm's length. 'I've achieved one ambition, but there's another much dearer to my heart.'

'Are you going to propose to Lizzie in front of us

all?' Jane demanded breathlessly. 'Oh do, please, Nat. It would be so romantic.'

'No, Jane, it would be very embarrassing.' Nathaniel turned to Clara. 'It seems my family has come full circle. What started out in Drury Lane has returned there, and I owe much of my success to you, Clara.'

She shook her head. 'I did nothing, Nat.'

'You encouraged me when I was at my lowest point, and you put up with a sham engagement so that I might face my uncle and tell him I'd fulfilled the terms of my father's will.'

'That was nothing,' Clara said hastily. 'Really, Lizzie, there was never anything between us.'

Lizzie smiled. 'I know, Nat has explained everything, and now he has something to ask me, and it most certainly won't be in public, Jane.' Lizzie ushered Nathaniel into the shop, closing the door firmly behind them.

Jane tugged at her father's sleeve. 'Shouldn't he ask your permission to marry Lizzie, Pa?'

'He did, poppet, and I said I would be proud to have such a fine young man as a son-in-law.' Alfred wagged his finger at Clara. 'You're next my girl, or you'll be on the shelf.'

'Really, Pa, I'm only twenty.'

'I always favoured Luke, even when he was part of the Skinner gang. There was something about him even then, and now we know that he's Gertie's nephew and heir to his mother's fortune, I like him even better.' Alfred guffawed with laughter, and Betsy and Jane giggled behind their hands.

Clara refused to be drawn on the subject. 'I'll bear that in mind, Pa. However, what's more important now is what are we going to have for supper?'

'I suggest we go to The Green Man and Still tavern.' Gertie looked from one to the other. 'I've heard they do excellent steaks and chops, and I'm starving.'

'I'm afraid I can't join you,' Betsy said with a smug smile. 'Pip – I mean Constable Smith – has asked me out.'

'You sly minx.' Alfred threw back his head and laughed. 'You kept that quiet, miss. But invite him along. I want my whole family round me.'

Jane moved closer to Danny. 'You could come too. I'm sure Pa won't mind.'

'The more the merrier,' Alfred said cheerily. 'I'm sure we'll be celebrating, but they're taking their time about it. Go and see what they're doing, Clara.'

'I don't want to interrupt a tender scene.'

'Nonsense, girl. We're all hungry. Go and see what's keeping them.'

Clara let herself into the shop. She could hear voices but they were coming from upstairs in the fashion department and she had no intention of interrupting them. She stood for a moment, knowing that if she went back too soon her father would only send her out again. She walked about the shop, automatically tidying the stands as she went, but as she reached the front counter she heard someone knocking and she opened the door.

'I had a feeling it was you, Luke.'

He stepped inside, taking off his hat. 'I said I'd come back.'

'Yes, you did, but I'm not sure I'm ready to talk.'

'I need to tell you why I was forced to deceive you, Clara.'

'It was all a lie,' Clara said, avoiding his gaze. 'You pretended to be someone you're not, and I don't know who you are now.'

'Come out with me and we'll talk over dinner. There's a restaurant in Regent Street I know of. It's not too far, although we'll get a cab if you're too tired to walk.'

Clara was weakening. There was nothing she wanted more than to spend time alone with Luke and hear what he had to say, but just as she was about to agree, Lizzie appeared and came hurrying towards them. She was waving her left hand and a diamond sparkled in the reflected light of a street-lamp.

'Look at my beautiful ring. Nat has proposed and I've said yes.'

'Luke was just leaving,' Clara said hastily.

'Nonsense. He must come with us. It's not every

night that a girl gets engaged, unless of course it's Clara, and she does it for a pastime.'

'That's not fair,' Clara protested, but she could see that Luke had taken Lizzie's thoughtless remark to heart.

'I won't take no for an answer,' Lizzie said firmly. 'You will come, won't you, Luke? I want to get to know you all over again.'

Clara knew then that it was going to be a difficult evening.

During the meal Luke answered the questions put to him, but there was a reserve in his manner and he avoided meeting Clara's eyes. It was not until they were walking home that Clara had a chance to speak to him privately.

'What's the matter? Surely I'm the one who's been deceived, so why are you being like this?'

He glanced down at her, his expression unreadable. 'You were engaged to Nathaniel? You didn't tell me that.'

'You pretended to be a villain for years and all the time you were working for the police. You didn't think to mention that either.'

'Clara, I've said I'm sorry, but I was under cover. I couldn't tell anyone, not even you.' He grasped her hand. 'I've just discovered that the mother I loved was not related to me, and I'm the son of someone who is a complete stranger.'

'I know, and that must be really hard, but you're not the only one to have been deceived. You should understand how it feels.'

'You haven't answered my question. You were with him in Paris. Were you in love with the musician?'

The tension she had been under all day, and even more so this evening, erupted in anger. 'You've no right to cross-examine me. You've been living a double life for so long that you've forgotten how to treat a friend.'

'A friend? I thought we were more than that, Clara.'

Clara was about to give him a sharp response when she realised that everyone had stopped and her father was unlocking the shop door. A wave of exhaustion swept over her mixed with a bitter feeling of disappointment. Luke had jumped to the wrong conclusion and had not bothered to discover the truth. It had been a long and emotionally trying day, all she wanted now was the peace of her own room and the comfort of her own bed.

'I can't talk about it now. Good night, Luke. I expect I'll see you at Lady Quinn's tomorrow night.'

'Clara, wait.'

She ignored his plea to stop. Lizzie and Nathaniel were saying good night with a fond embrace while Danny and Jane hovered in the background, together with Betsy and Pip, who had eyes for each other only. Clara followed her father and Gertie into the shop.

'What's the matter?' Gertie demanded as they ascended the stairs. 'It was a very successful day. You've got your father back and Luke is running round after you. What more do you want?'

'A bit of trust would be nice.' Clara's voice broke on a sob.

'Come into my room and tell me all about it.' Gertie propelled her up the remaining stairs to the room at the top. 'Now sit down and start from the beginning. Tell me what he did to upset you.'

Gertie listened without saying anything until Clara came to a tearful conclusion.

'It's jealousy,' Gertie said simply. 'He can't bear the thought of you being in love with someone else.' She held up her hand. 'That's men for you. They live by one set of rules but they expect us to behave quite differently.'

'You were prepared to forgive Bert Bragg anything. Would he treat you the same?'

Gertie patted Clara's cheek, laughing. 'Of course not, and I've thought it over. I would be insane to give him another chance. My place is here, in London, and I'm going to give you a half-share in the building. We will make The Button Box great together.'

'Really?' Tears forgotten, Clara gave her a hug. 'I've had my eye on the premises next door, but I thought I could never afford to buy it.'

'We'll look it over together. Now go to your room and get a good night's sleep. Things will be clearer in the morning. I can't advise you, but I think you will know what to do.'

Clara dressed with care next evening. She picked a gown from their collection that was almost the same colour as the material that Luke had chosen for her when she first moved into Miss Silver's shop. Silk flowers cascaded over one shoulder, emphasising the *décolleté* neckline, and in the centre of a full-blown rose she had sewn the silver button from Luke's waistcoat. The result was stunning and she did a twirl in front of the tall mirror in the dressing room, admiring the way the draped skirt flattered her tiny waist and the frilled bustle swished as she walked. Betsy had attended to her coiffure and Lizzie had loaned her a pair of pearl-drop earrings. Clara knew she looked well and she was determined to make an entrance. What was not visible was her special button, the one she had found in the snow all those years ago. It had started the collection that had changed her life, and was now sewn onto a blue garter and hidden beneath a froth of taffeta and tulle petticoats.

Candlelight flooded the magnificent entrance hall in Berkeley Square and Baxter escorted them to the drawing room. Luke was there already, talking to his mother in a relaxed and friendly fashion that made Clara's heart miss a beat. He looked handsome in a black tailcoat with silk lapels, a black waistcoat over a spotless white shirt and smartly tailored trousers. He was every inch a gentleman, and Clara wondered what Patches would have made of his attire, but she was languishing in prison, awaiting trial and, according to Pip, was likely to spend many years incarcerated in one of the grim women's prisons. Bones and several others had also been caught. It was the end of the Bragg gang and the club in Angel Court was closed for ever.

Clara stood aside as Lady Quinn greeted everyone in turn, but Clara knew that she had Luke's full attention and she could not help congratulating herself. She wanted to make him see what he was in danger of losing if he did not change his ways, but when he came towards her she knew she was already lost. The look in his eyes was an embrace without touching, and when he raised her hand to his lips she felt a tremor run through her. Was it her imagination or did the cut-crystal drops on the chandelier tremble and chime like wind bells?

'Clara, forgive my boorish behaviour last evening,' Luke said humbly. 'I should be shot for making you unhappy.'

'I wasn't unhappy,' she lied.

'Well, I was. I could have kicked myself for my stupidity.'

She met his earnest gaze with a straight look. She

was not going to let him down too easily. 'I admit I was angry,' she said lightly. 'You shouldn't jump to conclusions. I did pretend to be Nat's fiancée for a while, but it was a sham.'

'I know that now. Nathaniel is a good chap. We walked part of the way together last night and he told me what you'd done for him, and how you supported him and helped him to make the right decisions regarding his career. I have to apologise profusely. Am I forgiven for that, and for my deception in the past?'

She eyed him curiously. 'Will you stay with the police, or are you going to be a gentleman of leisure?'

'I haven't changed in anything but my name, Clara.' He fingered the button she had sewn into the centre of a silk flower. 'I recognise this. It's mine.'

'I found it in my button box,' she said carelessly.

'And you kept it with your treasures. That must mean you care for me just a little.'

She met his earnest gaze with a smile. 'Of course I do. In spite of everything, I think I've always loved you, Luke.'

All around them people were talking. The scent of roses and hot candlewax would always remind her of the moment in Berkeley Square when Luke seized her in his arms and kissed her in front of her whole family.

'I'm not letting you go again,' Luke said, going down on one knee. He produced a small box from his breast pocket and flicked it open. A solitaire diamond shone like molten ice. 'My dearest Clara, I can't risk losing you again, and I can't wait another moment to ask you to do me the honour of becoming my wife.'

The room was suddenly silent. No one moved.

Clara looked into Luke's eyes. A future without him was unthinkable. Her heart was full and her eyes moist. 'Yes, I will.' She held out her hand and he slipped the ring on her finger, rising swiftly to his feet to wrap her in a passionate embrace.

Look out for news online about Dilly's brand new novel

THE TOP TEN SUNDAY TIMES BESTSELLER

DILLY COURT

The Mistletoe Seller

Coming 2nd November 2017

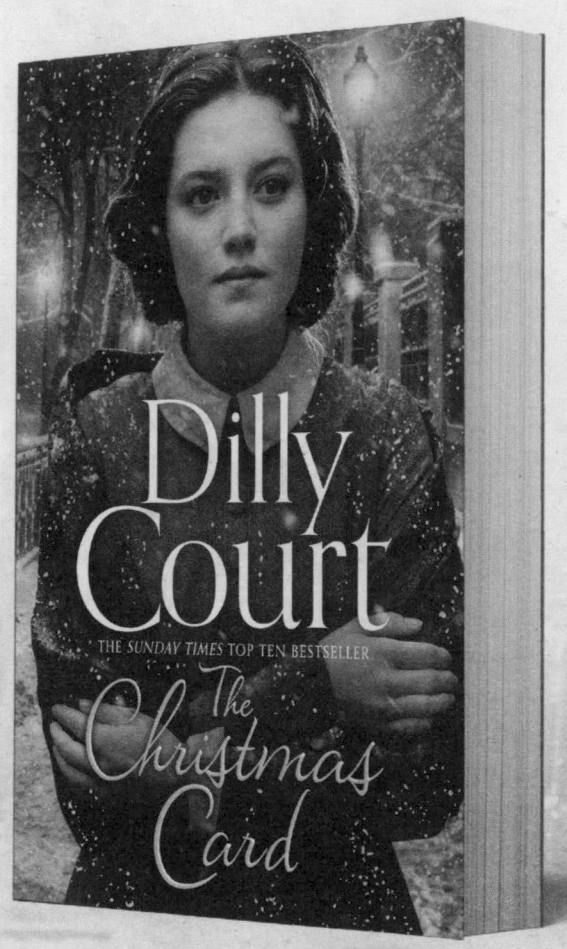